Solomon's Exile

James Maxstadt

Solomon's Exile

First Printing, 2019

ISBN-13: 9781790470051

James Maxstadt

Visit at jamesmaxstadt.com

Cover art: SelfPubBookCovers.com/Saphira

To my family, who have always supported my weirdness and sometimes participated in it. And, as always, to Barb.

Titles by James Maxstadt

Tales of a Nuisance Man
      The Duke Grandfather Saga, Part 1

Duke Grandfather Saves the World*
      *or at least a small part of it
      The Duke Grandfather Saga, Part 2

Duke Grandfather Hears Voices
      The Duke Grandfather Saga, Part 3

Duke Grandfather Unleashes Hell

Duke Grandfather: The Whole Story

Death Lessons
      Lilly the Necromancer, Book 1

Work-Death Balance
      Lilly the Necromancer, Book 2

Solomon's Exile
      The Travels of Solomon, Book 1

Solomon's Journey
      The Travels of Solomon, Book 2

Solomon's Odyssey
      The Travels of Solomon, Book 3

Rejected Worlds: A Short-story Anthology

CHAPTER 1

Solomon hit the ground face first, his chin bouncing off something hard. Above him, the air crackled with discharged energy and a light flared brilliantly before quickly dying away. With a groan, he rolled onto his back.

"Wait," he croaked, but it was too late. The light was gone and he was alone.

He struggled to sit up, holding his head in his hands. All right, he was here now. But where, exactly, was "here?"

He seemed to be in an alley, a narrow pass-through between tall buildings on either side. At the far end, he could see cars crawling by and hear the sound of horns angrily blaring. Even from here the cacophony made him wince.

The noise was far different from—

With a start, Solomon realized he didn't know *what* the noise was different from. From where he'd been before this, but where was he had no idea.

That made no sense, he thought to himself. He was just there a minute ago.

But, try as he might, he couldn't summon up a single image of before. He couldn't remember the sights, the sounds, or the smells. All he had left was an almost overwhelming feeling of loss, like something precious had been ripped away from him.

Was it the place... or someone? Someone who was dear to him, maybe?

He struggled to his feet, but after the fall he took and not knowing where he was or where he'd come from, the disorientation almost overcame him. He stumbled backward, having a hard time keeping on his feet, until his back came up against the hard, brick wall of the alley.

The more he tried to remember, the worse his head hurt.

"I am Solomon," he said, more to reassure himself that it was true than for any other reason. If nothing else, he remembered that. His name was Solomon. Whatever else there'd been was hidden from him as surely as if it had never been.

"Focus," he whispered to himself. But the effort only sent bolts of pain stabbing into his head.

With another groan, he sank down to sit on the damp concrete. It was only then that he noticed the smell that made his nose wrinkle in disgust.

There were a few garbage cans, lids askew or laying on the ground nearby, but they were closer to the other end of the alley. A dumpster, with a runnel of fetid water oozing from beneath it, was closer, but Solomon didn't think any of those were the cause of the stench.

No, it was him.

He looked down at his long legs, now encased in filthy blue jeans, with holes in the knees and ragged hems at the bottom. He was shoeless, and his feet were filthy, as if he had walked into the alley on his own rather than being unceremoniously dumped there. The shirt he wore matched the jeans. It might have been a white tee shirt at some point, but was now a dingy gray, with large stains marking the front.

Solomon ran his hands over his long face, feeling the scruffy beard and tangled mass of hair.

He was pretty sure, although he still couldn't remember, that this wasn't how he normally looked and dressed. If so, he wouldn't have been so appalled by his appearance now.

"Who am I?" he muttered, hoping the mere question would jar something loose. It didn't.

He looked around again, feeling a tightness in his chest that was making it hard to breathe. Stone, concrete, and brick. All hard, unyielding, dead materials that pressed in on him. He felt like he was in an open-air tomb, waiting to be covered over.

Wherever he was from, it wasn't a city like this.

Hot tears stung his eyes as he put his head back against the wall and squeezed them shut. One, lone large drop escaped and ran down his cheek. Solomon brushed at it and could feel grime on his face smear.

"I can't stay here," he said.

He didn't know where he belonged, but it wasn't there. That much was certain.

The end of the alley closest to him led to an even busier street, where the traffic seemed to move more rapidly and smoothly. Beyond the cars flashing by was the green of growing things. The leaves of trees rustled in a slight breeze, and he caught glimpses of what looked like grass as well.

A park, he assumed.

The trees seemed to call to him, so he rubbed his face once more and blinked his unshed tears away. Time enough for them later. He needed to calm down and reassess his situation.

Whatever was taken from him— and he was sure something was— it was gone now. *This* was where he was, so he needed to make the best of it.

The thought brought him a slight bit of comfort.

He was Solomon. He could beat anything. That much, he knew. He didn't need to remember it; it was simply part of who he was.

"Stop pouting, get moving," he told himself.

He pushed himself to his feet and shuffled down the alley, until he reached the end and peered out. He paused before leaving, already noting the carefully avoided eyes of passersby. He wished he could tell them that he wasn't going to ask them for money or assault them with end of the world prophecies. He only wanted to reach the park.

He waited at the traffic light, along with other, cleaner people, and crossed with them, his eyes focused on his destination. He ignored the others, as they ignored him. He wound his way along the park paths until he reached the trees and breathed in, a calmness settling over him.

The day was warming and he sat with his back against one of the trees, feeling the rough bark through his thin shirt, but enjoying the sensation. For a long time, he simply sat, watching people make their way through the park, some with an obvious goal in mind, others simply enjoying the day.

Solomon had no plans for what to do or where to go. He had no idea what he would do for food, or where he would spend the night. At the moment, he was content enough where he was. If he had to be lost, and in this city, rather than home— wherever that was— then he could at least be among the trees.

He settled back and looked up. The leaves fluttered and moved in the breeze, and squirrels ran through the branches, chasing one another and the birds that landed briefly, before flying off again on mysterious errands. As long as he could do this, he thought, he could be content.

Maybe he was just crazy. Maybe he *had* always lived there. But it didn't feel right.

He wasn't sure how long he sat there before he heard the scream.

Solomon wasn't even aware of jumping up, but he was running in the direction that the scream had come from. It was an automatic reaction to the sound of someone in peril.

He came around a curve in the path, to a large lawn where people were sitting out, enjoying the sunshine or playing games. On the path was a young woman, who had come with her small children, a boy and girl, and it was she that was screaming.

In front of them was a huge dog, emitting a palpable sense of menace, snarling and slowly moving closer. Others were up and yelling, but no one had approached the massive beast. It had mangy, dark gray fur, and a long snout. Its lips were curled back to reveal huge, bared, teeth, and saliva dripped from its jaws.

Solomon didn't hesitate but ran in front of the woman and her children, putting himself between them and the dog. The dog snarled louder, but stopped approaching and began pacing back and forth, its eyes fixed on Solomon.

"Go on!" Solomon yelled at it. "Get!"

The dog didn't, and its pacing brought it closer to him. He felt the woman behind him start to move away.

"Don't," he hissed at her. "If you run, it will chase you. Give me a minute."

He turned his full attention back to the snarling beast in front of him. It still showed no signs of running away and ignored everyone else, its attention entirely fixed on Solomon. He could see the muscles bunching, and knew, as surely as he knew anything, that it was going to attack.

"Come on then," he said, his voice quiet and calm. "You won't be the first Hunting Hound that I've faced."

As he said it, Solomon knew it was true. The sudden memory almost made him falter, but he held on by force of will, knowing that losing focus would spell certain doom.

The Hunting Hounds were sent out after certain prey, he remembered. He didn't know by whom or why this one was here, especially in a public place in broad daylight, but it *had* been sent. Which meant it must either be after the young woman behind him or one of her children.

The dog leapt forward and Solomon threw up his arm. Jaws clamped down and teeth punctured his skin. He ignored the pain and stepped forward, stopping the dog's momentum. He reached down with his other hand, grabbed the front leg of the hound and twisted. He felt a pop, and the teeth released his arm as the dog howled in pain and fell to the ground. It tried to rise, but its one leg didn't work right anymore, and it stumbled off to the side and fell to the ground.

Solomon stepped near intending to launch a vicious kick to the thing's ribs. It lay there, panting, not even trying to rise, and watching Solomon's approach from the corner of its eye.

"Go," Solomon said, feeling that killing the thing would be a dishonorable act. It was merely a puppet, a slave sent by its master.

The dog dragged itself to its feet, looking at Solomon as if it understood what was occurring. It gingerly put its weight on its injured leg, before running unsteadily away. People watched it go, not trying to interfere, as it disappeared though the trees. Solomon could have sworn that it vanished as it stumbled away, becoming less substantial, almost ghost like, but chalked it up to a trick of the light.

Solomon turned to the woman and her children. "Are you okay?"

"Yes, we're fine," she said to him, watching him warily. "Thank you. It came out of nowhere…"

"It's gone now," he said. He smiled at the children, but they sank back behind their mother.

"Let me give you something," the woman said, reaching for her purse.

"No, really. But thank you."

He turned and began walking away, aware that several people were staring at him, pointing, and talking in whispers. Now that he knew the woman and her children were safe, all he wanted was to return to his private spot under the trees.

A few people trailed after him, calling him a hero. He smiled quickly but kept walking with his head down. Others asked why he had let the dog go, or why hadn't he killed it, didn't he know that it would attack someone else? Those, he ignored.

He returned to the tree and sat back down, refusing to answer any questions and shutting his eyes to block out the sight of people staring at him. After a bit, they became bored and went away, and he was left in peace again.

Until the mother and her children approached.

"Please," she said, placing a sandwich and a can of Coca-Cola on the ground beside him. "At least take this. I don't know what else to do."

Solomon looked down at the sandwich and then at the woman. It was a kind gesture and shouldn't be rebuked.

"Thank you," he said.

She nodded and smiled sadly at him, before taking her children's hands and walking away. The small boy looked back at him and shyly lifted a hand. Solomon waved back.

He spent the rest of the day under the tree, eating the sandwich and drinking the Coke when he felt hungry and thirsty. His arm hurt where he had been bit, but that faded as the day went on. When night fell, he expected police to come through the park and chase him away, but none did. He'd been surprised when no-one had come to question him about the dog, but they hadn't done that either.

Finally, he lay down and fell into a deep sleep.

The trees towered around him, soaring into the clear night sky. The fountain bubbled and splashed, throwing up a mist with rainbows sparkling in the light of the lamps. There was music everywhere, shapes gliding along in time with it. There was a warm hand in his, and he was gliding along as well.

The hand slipped from his, and the trees swayed in a breeze that grew into a wind, and then into a tempest. Cold rain fell from the sky and the music hit a discordant note and stopped. When he turned, the fountain was frozen, the water still.

It was black, and cold. He ran, looking for the dancers, but they were gone. The trees, the fountain, the music, the shapes, and especially the warm hand that had been in his. All of it was lost.

Solomon woke with a gasp, his cheeks wet with tears that he'd shed in his sleep. He lay on the ground, not daring to move as the effects of the dream slipped away.

He knew that it was true dreaming. He had been in that place of trees and music. And there had been someone who had held his hand and danced with him. The sense of loss was as keen as it had been in the alley, and it tore at him.

Gazing through the darkness at the tree above him, he knew that he couldn't stay there either. The park was pleasant, and the trees were nice, but they weren't home. They couldn't replace what he had lost— whatever it was— and he needed to move on.

There would be no more sleep tonight. He still felt fatigued, as if he had worked hard all day, rather than having sat under a tree. It was from the dream, and he hoped that walking would bring him release. With nothing to gather, he set out across the park, hoping to be well out of the city by daybreak.

As he walked, he listened to the sounds of the night. There was little noise from the city beyond the park. Vehicles still moved, and occasionally there was a cough or a snippet of laughter as late-nighters went about their business. Here in the park, it was silent. No one stirred, and there was no hint of animals moving around.

Other homeless people shared the park with him, but they were all sleeping, wrapped in rags, or papers, or sprawled out on a bench. Solomon passed, but felt no kinship with any of them. Whatever he had been, wherever he had come from, it wasn't there. He hadn't been there long enough to make friends or enemies with any of the other unfortunates he passed.

He noticed a shadow moving, following him at a distance, off to the side. Stopping, he peered through the darkness and saw the figure stop, sit on its haunches and wait. When he moved again, the figure rose and kept pace. Finally, he stopped again, turned and approached it.

The Hound sat and waited for him. It showed no sign of aggression or of the injury that Solomon had inflicted on it during the day. Its tongue lolled out of its mouth as it watched him approach.

"Are you hunting me now?" Solomon asked it.

The dog didn't answer. Solomon would have been surprised if it did.

"Well, come on then," he said, and started away again.

The dog fell in at his heels and padded along behind him.

CHAPTER 2

Florian, of the Whispering Pines, strode to his estate, seemingly serene to all who saw him, but fuming on the inside. Despite his best attempts, and against all reason, Jamshir of the Glittering Birches, the current monarch of the Greenweald, had decreed that Solomon be merely exiled, rather than executed. It was inconceivable, and done, Florian was certain, only to spite him. A fact that made him sad considering their one-time friendship.

But, it would not, could not, stand. He would take matters into his own hands, and Solomon would pay for what he had done. His failure of duty was unforgiveable, but Jamshir didn't seem to mind the agony that had been dealt to Florian.

His mood contrasted sharply with the environment through which he walked. As he neared the grounds of his home, the pines that his House revered grew dominant over all other trees. The air was thick with their scent, which usually calmed Florian, but today had no such effect. Walking on the soft carpet of their fallen needles muffled what would otherwise be heavy footsteps, uncharacteristic for one of the Folk. Of a race who valued grace as a way of life, Florian was out of sync with the world around him today.

He was tall and slim, as were all the Folk, and dressed in a long flowing robe of dark green, to match the needles on the evergreens around him. The color was unique to House Whispering Pines, and no others could wear it, as he could never don the silver hue of the Glittering Birches, or the somber gray of the Towering Oaks. To do so would bring dishonor to his house.

Nothing seemed to calm Florian's ire on this day. He wondered if anything ever would. He stalked through the shaped gates that marked the entrance to his estate, and continued on the path that led to the doors of his house. The fountain that sparkled and splashed, providing a refreshing mist to cool one on a hot summer's day, drew no interest from him, nor did the fish that swam in the pool beneath. Walking through his extensive gardens was a joy that Florian indulged in regularly, but today, as with all else, it didn't even register in his mind.

Servants, also clad in dark green, but less fine, clothing, opened the door to him as he approached. The entire house was shaped from the living pines. They had offered themselves in his House's service, and were revered for it. No tree was ever cut in the Greenweald. Instead, they were shaped to the desire of the Folk, but only with their own permission. Fallen branches or entire trees were gathered and given places of honor, used only with permission of the still living trees.

No one was sure why the trees would agree to serve the Folk as they did. Some thought it was because the Folk provided care, or kept them from being harvested by others outside of the Greenweald. Some thought it was because the trees could sense what had happened to their kind in other places, such as the wretched earth to which Solomon was exiled, and were fearful of the same things happening here. And yet others said that as long-lived as the Folk were, they were here and gone quickly in the life of the trees, so they served at their own whim, and with amusement.

Whatever the reason, the relationship between the Folk and the trees had been honored for centuries, and it worked well. Even the most radical among the Folk had no desire to see that facet of their society changed.

Once inside his house, Florian dropped the carefully maintained façade that he had worn since leaving Jamshir's palace. His face grew dark, his fists clenched and tears started from his eyes. The servants glanced at each other and quickly walked from the room, knowing that to stay and see their master in such a state would be embarrassing to him, and possibly dangerous to them.

Florian stormed across the floor of the entry hall and entered his refuge. This was his library, his sanctuary. He valued the natural world as much as any of the Folk, but he also had a great love for poetry, tales, and folklore. He read science, and the history of how they had come to be in the Greenweald, and the first of them to commune with the trees. If he was not found in his gardens, then chances were Florian would be found here, amongst his precious books.

He closed the doors behind him, slumped back against them and allowed his rage and frustration to come out. The howl that he unleashed was heard throughout his house, and those in attendance looked at one another in shock, and then continued on with their affairs, pretending not to have heard it.

After his shameful scream of despair, Florian stumbled to his favorite chair and fell into it. It was of pine, of course, and shaped from a single large piece of trunk from a fallen tree ages ago. Soft cushions covered the seat and the back, and he sank into them, allowing the tears to fall from his eyes unchecked. It was all that he knew how to do to honor Celia, his precious daughter.

Sometime later there was a knock at the doors, and they were opened before Florian could reply. Thaddeus entered, glanced over at him, and moved to a side board, where he poured a pale, yellow liquid from a crystal decanter into two glasses. He brought one to Florian, handed it to him, and then sat in a chair across from him.

"I don't want any," Florian said, holding the glass out to Thaddeus.

"Don't be ridiculous. Of course, you do. Drink up, it will help."

Florian looked down at the glass in his hand, but made no move to drink from it.

"It won't. Nothing will. She is gone forever, Thaddeus. And he walks free."

"Mmm. I don't know that I would say that he walks free exactly. Can you imagine being banished from the Greenweald? I think I'd *rather* be executed. I don't know that Jamshir did him any favors."

"I want him dead. I don't care where he walks, he walks, and she no longer does. How is that just in any world?"

"Perhaps it's not, but it is the reality of it. Jamshir has made his ruling and at this point, it's done. Solomon is gone."

Florian threw back his drink in one swig, causing Thaddeus to raise his eyebrows, but he stood and refilled their glasses without comment.

"There is one option," he said, handing one of the glasses back to Florian.

"And what's that?"

"The Hounds. You could dispatch a Hunting Hound after him."

Florian sipped his drink and considered. "Yes, I could, couldn't I? But…if Jamshir was to hear of it…"

"He wouldn't. The Master of the Hounds holds no great love for the Glittering Birches, or any other House for that matter."

"Then why would he give us a Hound?"

"Because," Thaddeus replied, "there is one thing that he does have great love for. Money. We pay him well, and no one will ever be the wiser."

Florian considered, leaning back in his chair and regarding the other.

"Yes," he said again. "You're right. You will arrange it, Thaddeus. First thing in the morning."

Thaddeus was taken aback. Dealing with the Master of the Hounds was distasteful, and he had assumed the task would be assigned to some lesser noble.

"Oh, come now Florian," he began, "surely there's someone else who…"

"You, Thaddeus," Florian interrupted. "Cousin or not, you still answer to me as Head of House. You will do this, as commanded."

Thaddeus could only sigh. "Yes, cousin. Of course."

The next morning, Thaddeus walked through less cultured forest, one of the areas in the Greenweald that was claimed by no House. It was safe, as far as things went, with only the occasional wild animal encounter, which held no fear for him. Despite being a member of House Whispering Pines, and not one of the more martial houses like Towering Oaks, he was a competent swordsman, an even more accomplished mage, and at this point would almost relish a foe to fight. Anything to take his mind off the task ahead of him.

But his trip was uneventful, and before noon he arrived at the Master of the Hound's compound. He could smell it before it was even in sight, and wrinkled his nose in disgust. Why the place wasn't kept cleaner was beyond him, but then again, this was a person who chose to live isolated from all others, with no company save that of his numerous dogs.

The compound came into sight as Thaddeus came around a curve in the path, and into a large clearing in the trees. There was a stone hut in the middle of the clearing, itself an oddity in the Greenweald. Spaced haphazardly around the clearing were several kennels, some with dogs leashed to them, some with fences of old tree branches woven together. Thaddeus didn't know if the Master had been granted those branches by the trees, or if he had taken them, in defiance of established mores.

Large, gray or black mutts, with mangy fur and long jaws were everywhere, lying in the dusty, brown, dirt that covered the clearing, or roaming where they would. Several of them watched him approach and began barking and howling, while three others silently raced forward.

Thaddeus considered drawing his sword, but realized that no matter how good he thought he was, it wasn't going to be good enough to make a difference here. Instead, as the lead dog neared, he stopped walking and held his hands up to shoulder height, palms out.

"Master of the Hounds!" he called out, directing his voice toward the stone hut. "Come out and call off your dogs! We have business to discuss!"

There was no movement from inside the structure, but the dogs didn't attack. They didn't move off and let him advance any further either, but stood in front of him, growling menacingly if he tried to step forward. The others scattered around the clearing stopped barking, but most stood at attention, ears and eyes pointed in his direction.

He had almost given up when a curtain that was hung in the doorway to the hut moved aside, and the Master of the Hounds came out. Thaddeus thought of the Master as a he, but in truth, he didn't really know. The figure was tall and slim, as was expected of one of the Folk, but wore a robe with a deep hood that hid its face. Its voice, when it spoke, was a husky whisper that could have been that of a man, or an old woman, or even someone trying to conceal their gender. There was no telling. The robe that they wore matched the rest of the clearing. It was filthy, with poorly patched areas, and abundant snags and worn areas. Thaddeus couldn't even tell what color it had once been.

The Master of the Hounds approached, slowly shuffling along. Two of the dogs guarding Thaddeus ran to him, settling into a sedate walk beside him at a motion of his hand. The largest dog stayed in front of Thaddeus, showing no sign of moving off.

"Master of the Hounds," Thaddeus began again. "I come on behalf of my master, Florian of House Whispering Pines. He instructs me to purchase a Hunting Hound, to be sent in pursuit of an enemy of our House."

The Master stopped a few feet away from Thaddeus. "Why would I send one of my beauties to that wretched earth after a disgraced soldier?"

"So you are aware of the punishment meted out by Jamshir yesterday. Then surely you know the anguish that this ruling has caused Florian."

"I care not for the *anguish* of anyone, lest of all that fool you call master. I ask you again, and for the final time…why should I send one of my precious beauties to a place from which they may not return."

"Because of this," he said, and reaching into his tunic, he removed a leather bag, tied with a cord. It clinked softly as he tossed it at the Master's feet. "There. There's enough silver in that pouch to buy all of your mongrels. It should more than suffice to purchase one."

The Master made no move to pick up the pouch. There was a sniffing noise from inside the hood, and he turned and whistled.

Far off, at the edge of the clearing, a dog lifted its head, looked in their direction, and came running. When it reached the Master, it stood before him. Thaddeus could see that it was slimmer and shorter than most of the other dogs gathered. It had the look of a runt of the litter, who had been dominated by the others in the pack. The dog in front of Thaddeus growled, and the newly arrived one shrank back.

"This is the one that I will spare," the Master said. "Worthless for most purposes, like your master Florian. Take it. Do with it what you would."

The Master made a hand signal to the dog, who cowered, and slunk to Thaddeus with its ears back and its tail tucked between its legs. Then he turned without another word and shuffled back to the stone hut, the other dogs following. Finally, when he was inside and the curtain drawn back over the opening, the dog in front of Thaddeus turned and walked away as well.

Thaddeus looked down at the hound at his side, and grimaced.

"The runt of the litter. I hope you're tougher than you look, cur."

He brought the Hound back to Whispering Pines, where it didn't look so scrawny without the rest of the dogs to be compared to. He said nothing to Florian about the cost, the fact that it was a runt, or the Master's disparaging comments.

"So?" Florian said. "Now what? How do we get it to go kill Solomon?"

Thaddeus realized that he hadn't asked about that. But how hard could it really be? This was a Hunting Hound, it was born and bred to do the job.

"I believe we simply have it smell something that belonged to Solomon and it will go find him. It's what they do, isn't it?"

"How should I know? This was your idea. Now make it work." Florian glanced once more at the dog, and walked off.

After some thought, Thaddeus left the dog in the care of a servant, and returned to his chambers. Little did Florian, or anyone, know, but Thaddeus had collected an assortment of items that he thought he might find useful at some point. These included relics or writings from the other houses, samples of hair, or clothing that had been discarded, or misplaced. Anything that may give him more knowledge, or could be used in a spell, he kept.

He found a small item from one of the Towering Oaks soldiers. It was a broken arrow head that was left near an archery butt. It spoke to his skill at subterfuge that Thaddeus had been able to even come near a Towering Oaks training center.

After that, he opened a locked chest and rummaged through the contents. A moment later, he pulled out a piece of paper. It was brightly colored and slick to the touch. The writing on it was indecipherable to him, but showed horrible, square, buildings, soaring into the sky with no sense of harmony with the world around them. Humans were everywhere, swarming like insects feasting on a fallen log. He shuddered when he looked at this artifact of earth, glad that he never had to return there again.

He took the arrow head and the paper, and returned to the Hound, relieving the quaking servant. He called the dog to him.

"This is the House of your quarry. He is called Solomon."

The Hound looked at Thaddeus as if it could understand what was being said. It sniffed at the arrow head, but showed no indication of starting the hunt there and then.

"Good," Thaddeus said. "Now…this is where he is…"

The Hound sniffed at the paper too, and moved as if it had the scent already.

"Go!" Thaddeus commanded, and the dog took off like a shot from a bow.

Its barks rang out through the forest, but started to fade too quickly to simply be from distance. Thaddeus smiled. The Hunting Hound was doing its job, and Solomon would be caught completely unaware, and unprepared for it.

CHAPTER 3

The upside of living way out in the country was the privacy, and Lacy loved that aspect of it. She could walk from her house, across the yard to the above ground pool, buck naked if she chose, and no one would ever be the wiser. Not that she did so, but she could if she wanted to, and that was the point. She relished that, and loved to be alone with her thoughts, and watching the deer that walked through her yard, or the hawks circling overhead.

Of course, there was a downside too, and that was also all the privacy. It was a hassle if she found out that she had forgotten some vital ingredient for dinner, and a night out meant maybe going to the two-screen theater in town for a second run movie. Never mind the possibility of meeting someone nice to spend time with.

It was a double-edged sword for sure, but overall, Lacy preferred living out here to living in the city, which she had done as well. She would take star gazing and nature walks over people-watching and neon lights any day of the week. Even if it did get a little lonely at times.

Living here hadn't started out as lonely, of course. She didn't think she ever would have bought the place if it hadn't been for Luke. Luke and Lacy, it even sounded cute, which everyone had said they were. For a while, it was true too. Then…well, things had changed, and not for the better. Now, here she was living out in the middle of nowhere, and who knew where he was.

She straightened up from weeding the tomato plants and pulled up her shirtfront to wipe the sweat off her face. Not very lady like, but who cared? It wasn't like anyone was around. She sighed as she looked at everything that needed to be done. The garden was only half way weeded, if that. The pool needed some attention, or she'd find herself battling the bright, green algae that always seemed one sunny day away from blooming. The house needed a new paint job, but that wasn't going to happen any time soon, and the steps down from the back deck were starting to rot at the bottom. She wasn't even sure what to do about that.

Still, it would all get done, eventually.

"One thing at a time," she said aloud, which was a habit that she had fallen into over the last few weeks. Ever since Luke had done what felt like would be his final disappearing act.

She bent back to her task, knowing that if she didn't keep up on it, the weeds would take over the whole garden. While that may not be the most urgent thing that needed to be done, she enjoyed it, no matter how hot and sweaty it made her. There was something satisfying in finishing the job. After, she would get a tall glass of iced tea, sit in a chair on the deck and look out at her freshly weeded garden and the slightly green pool. Maybe later, she'd shock the pool so that tomorrow she could jump in. Since it was the weekend, an early morning swim might be the perfect thing to start the day.

Later, she sat on her deck, hating the feel of the bug spray that she put on after her shower, but if she hadn't, she'd be eaten alive by the mosquitoes. It was another dichotomy of living where she did. She looked out over her yard, with the woods beyond, already deep in shadow as evening came on. The fireflies glowed on and off as she watched, and when she looked up, the occasional bat flitted through the air. She smiled, wishing more of those were around. They didn't creep her out, like they did a lot people, and she'd rather have them than the mosquitoes any day.

She raised her glass of iced tea to her lips, and froze, staring into the gloom under the trees. Not for the first time, she swore she saw something there. It wasn't large, maybe a little smaller than her, but hunched, as if whatever it was walked bent over on two legs. She wasn't even sure it was there, or if her eyes were playing tricks on her. It was just a shape, slightly darker than the rest of the forest around it.

She slowly rose to her feet, setting the iced tea down carefully on the arm of the Adirondack chair she had been lounging in. Moving as silently as she could, she crept to the edge of the stairs and down them, then across the lawn. This was the first time she had approached the figure. The other times she had merely stared until her eyes watered, listening to the sound of her rapidly beating heart, until the night had grown darker and the shape melted in with the other shadows. It had scared the life out of her then, and did now, too.

Her breath came a little quicker than she liked as she moved forward, and she could feel her palms becoming moist.

"Relax," she told herself, "it's a stump or something. You're being stupid."

But it wasn't. She knew her yard well enough to know that there were no stumps, or fallen logs, or anything else like that right there. That area was a makeshift compost pile that she threw spoiled vegetables from the garden on. Supposedly, if you did that, the deer and the rabbits would find it and go there, rather than nibbling on the good stuff still growing. At least, that was the theory; in reality, she didn't see much difference.

As she got closer, she could see that the shape was moving. Not much, but a little bit. It was right behind her compost pile and swayed back and forth slightly. Maybe it was a branch or sapling, stirring in the breeze. Not that there was a breeze tonight, but still.

She stepped on the rock when she was still a few yards away, feeling the sharp point punch up between her toes. An involuntary yelp escaped her as she danced up onto one foot. There was a sudden noise of crashing undergrowth, and her head whipped around, but whatever had been behind the compost pile was gone. Now, instead of a dark shape, she could see deeper into the woods, and there was nothing there.

That would teach her to try to sneak up on something barefoot. Next time, tomorrow night maybe, she'd be ready. With shoes on and flashlight in hand, she'd scare whatever this was away for good. Or at least she hoped she would.

Halfway back to the deck it occurred to her what the shape was. It must have been a bear cub. They weren't common in the area, but they weren't unheard of either. Although, if there was a cub around, then momma must be nearby too. Maybe she'd have to rethink trying to sneak up on it after all.

The morning swim cleared away the lingering remnants of the night's scare. She was even able to smile about it as she floated in the water. Now that the sun was out and she could see everything clearly, she was certain that it had been a young bear at the compost pile. The deer may be ignoring the spare vegetables, but at least something was enjoying them.

She looked over that way again, and noticed something that she had missed earlier when she looked out the window. There was a scrap of something hanging from a branch. From here, she couldn't tell what it was, but it fluttered in the slight breeze. It almost looked like a piece of cloth.

She slipped off her float and climbed the ladder to get out of the pool. Wrapping her towel around herself, and slipping on her flip-flops, (no rocks in the bottom of her feet this time, thank you very much!), she walked to the compost pile.

It *was* a scrap of cloth, caught on a sharp point that was the result of a branch breaking off. Lacy had no idea how it could have come to be there, but she reached out and plucked it off the branch to examine it more closely. It was a pale blue color, and made of cotton, like a t-shirt. One side of it was hemmed, the others torn, as if it had been ripped from a finished piece of clothing. She hadn't seen it yesterday, but it was possible that she had overlooked it. Only…

She looked back at her garden. Yesterday, she had done all the weeding and had found several tomatoes, peppers and cucumbers that were no good. They had all gone directly into a bucket she kept by her when working, and dumped in the compost pile when it was full. As a matter of fact, she had done that twice…and hadn't noticed this good-sized piece of bright cloth either time.

Her mind flashed back to the figure in the shadows the night before, and the sudden flight when she had made noise. It had to have been a bear, right? Except that bears don't wear clothes.

The thought that someone, not s*omething*, but *someone*, had been crouched here in the shadows, possibly watching her, made goosebumps break out on her skin, and she tugged the towel more tightly around her. She turned and hurried back to her house, shutting the door and locking it behind her. From the windows, she examined the woods, eyes searching for any sign of anything out of the ordinary.

But there were only trees and undergrowth, squirrels and birds, the leaves and the wind, and nothing more.

It was times like this that she missed Luke the most. Despite the drinking, and the delusions, she wished he were here right now.

CHAPTER 4

The city ended eventually and at last Solomon walked along country roads, surrounded by trees, fields and the occasional farm. His way wound up into the hills, deeper into forested land, the trees growing larger and more closely packed, and the undergrowth more dense. The Hound walked beside him, and every now and then, he would put his hand down and scratch it between the ears. The first time he had done that, the dog had flinched away, but now it pressed its head up into his hand, urging him to scratch harder and to keep going.

There were lots of stares and suspicious looks from the occasional car that passed, but Solomon understood why that would be. He was still filthy, still wearing the old clothes that he had found himself in when he awoke, and was walking with a positively massive dog by his side. So he ignored the looks, and kept walking into a more and more rural area.

Eventually, he came to a fork in the road and stopped.

"Well, what do you think?" he said to the dog. "Should we take the turn, or keep going the direction we were?"

The dog sniffed at the blacktop, took a step forward, and trotted to the road cutting off to the right. It lifted its head, sniffed the air, turned back to Solomon, and barked.

"Well, I guess that answers that. To the right we go. Good boy," he said, scratching the dogs head again as he passed.

The road led into deeper woods, and the air cooled under the leaves. Solomon relished the smell of the trees and the way the light danced on the pavement. This was better. He had yearned to be among nature again, and was becoming more relaxed as he walked along.

Suddenly, the dog gave a soft woof, and bounded off the side of the road, disappearing into the undergrowth.

"Hey," Solomon called, "where are you going?"

There was more rustling in the weeds, and the dog popped back out onto the road. It looked at Solomon, barked at him, and ran back into the woods.

"I guess I'm supposed to follow."

He smiled as he stepped off the road, pushing his way through the mass of weeds and bushes that lined the side of it. He had never heard of anyone becoming friends with one of the Hunting Hounds, he realized, certainly not when they were the prey. As he had been walking over the last day and a half, it had occurred to him that *he* must have been the Hounds target, not the young woman or her children. If that had been the case, the Hound wouldn't have stopped when it was healed and had come back from...

From where? Where had it come from in the first place? The same place that he had lost, he suspected. Having the dog around him made the ever-present feeling of loss slightly more tolerable. It was as if he had a little piece of his home here with him. A strange piece to be sure, but nevertheless, it was something.

He followed the crashing of the dog through the woods, until it started to be drowned out by a different noise. Pausing, it took him a moment to recognize the sound of rushing water.

Solomon picked up the pace, hurrying along, until he finally saw it.

In front of him was a large stream, with clear, rapidly running water. It flowed over and among several large rocks, where it collected in pools with sandy bottoms. The dog was already in one, splashing around and sniffing at the water, the rocks and the bank.

"Good boy!" Solomon cried.

Within seconds, his few clothes were shed and he had waded into one of the pools. The water was crystal clear and icy cold, but to Solomon it felt like heaven. He sank under, his hands scrubbing at his hair. He sluiced water over his arms, his shoulders and his face, wishing that he had soap, but glad for the water at least. The current whisked away the grime as he scrubbed it off, using sand from the bottom to help scour the worst of it.

When he was done, he pulled his clothes into the water and scrubbed at them, then laid them out on rocks to let them dry. He splashed around a bit more in the cold water, climbed out, and stood shivering in the mottled sunlight coming through the trees. He looked around to make sure no one else was near, and climbed onto some rocks, near the middle of the stream where the sun was stronger, to dry.

The sun beat down on him as he stretched out, and he luxuriated in its rays. He closed his eyes and let himself doze, lulled by the sound of the rushing water. Before he was even aware that it was happening, he slipped into sleep.

There was water rushing by him, the current tugging against his body, trying to push him further downstream. It wasn't strong enough to do so though, and he laughed as someone splashed water into the back of his head. He turned and splashed the person back, the water obscuring her face, but he could hear her laughter. Like the tinkling of bells, it was light and airy, and it made his heart soar to hear it.

The water tasted sweet and pure, and he knew that he would never thirst while he was near it. He looked up at the trees arching overhead, and felt that everything was perfect with the world. On the bank of the stream where he and the other person swam was a pile of clothes, folded carefully, with a sword belt on top of them, the sword still firmly encased in its sheath.

He looked back at his companion, but she was gone. He smiled as he dove under the water, expecting to catch her trying to sneak up on him from below, but she wasn't there either. When he surfaced, it had grown darker, the clouds covering the sun. A wind was kicking up, and the water started to chop into small waves.

He stroked toward the side, intent on getting to his sword, feeling that he needed it. Although what good a sword would do against wind or water, he didn't know. The current grew stronger, and no matter how hard he swam, the bank stayed out of reach.

There was a noise like thunder, and he looked upstream to see a wall of water descending toward him. There was a scream, he couldn't tell from where, and then the water hit him. It tumbled him under, and pushed him along, dragging him deeper. Too deep, the stream couldn't possibly reach this far down…but he couldn't get out…

He woke with a start and a giant gasp. He was panting and his chest hurt as if he had been holding his breath for too long. He lay there, staring up at the sky, still hearing the laughter, and that scream, and knowing, again, that it was a real memory. He *had* swum with someone in a stream, or a pool, in some other land, in some other time.

The sun had moved across the sky, and Solomon realized that he had been sleeping for a couple of hours now. The stream was apparently remote enough that no one came to it, at least not in the middle of a weekday, a fact he was profoundly grateful for, considering his state of undress. Now that he was cleaner, he was more conscious of how it would look should someone discover him. He gathered his clothes, the shirt, pants and

21

underwear dry for the most part, and pulled them on. He had soaked the sneakers too, and they were still wet, but he stuffed his feet into them anyway.

When he was dressed again, he looked around for the dog. It was lying on a rock near the one he had fallen asleep on, its head on its paws, snoring gently.

"Come on," Solomon called to it. "Time to head out."

The dogs head came up, and with a bound it was off its rock and at his side.

Solomon looked down at the shaggy, gray head looking expectedly up at him.

"You need a name. How about Fido?"

If it was possible for a dog to look skeptical, this one did. Solomon laughed. No, a Hunting Hound needed a better name than Fido for sure. Plus…a thought occurred to him and he bent down and looked.

"Guess I should have done that before, huh?" he said, smiling. "Okay, then, how about Princess Buttercup?"

The Hound didn't even bother to acknowledge that one, but turned her back on him. Solomon laughed.

"Well, whatever your name is, you certainly are a smart one. Come on, we'll keep thinking while we walk."

They moved off through the woods together, side by side.

As far as towns go, it was small, and quaint. Solomon had seen it from above as they skirted a small cliff a short time ago. The road looped around and down the hillside, the forest thinned, and the houses became closer together. Soon, they were walking through pleasant suburban areas, and heading toward the middle of the village.

There was a small park in the center of town, more just a grassy, open area, with a few benches, a few trees, and a fenced in area for people's dogs to run. It was a quiet evening and there weren't many people around, and he noticed that the town had that half run-down look that some get when there weren't many people living in the area and businesses had dried up from big box competition.

He made his way to a bench and sat down on it, intending to rest there for a few moments, and then find a place where they could sleep for the night. Neither he nor the Hound had eaten at all and his stomach was starting to feel it. He imagined that hers was too. Tomorrow, he would have to make a plan to find some food, and maybe some new clothes. He couldn't continue to wear the same thing day in and day out.

All day, as he had walked along, he had been trying to remember more of his past life, but nothing had come to him, other than the dream earlier. It seemed as if he needed a specific stimulus to remember anything, like encountering the dog. That had spurred memories of the Hounds, and knowing that he had encountered them before, but nothing else. Not when, or why.

He left the bench, walked to one of the trees, and settled down with his back against it. He really wasn't sure if he'd be left alone or if someone would confront him and ask about his presence here, but until that happened, he wasn't going to be too concerned.

A few people did pass him by, and there were curious glances at both him and the Hound. No one stopped or said anything however, so after a while, Solomon closed his eyes, and prepared to focus again, to see if he could force any other memories to the surface.

He had barely started when he heard the noise.

"Ahem."

Solomon opened his eyes and saw the policeman that stood a few feet away. He was a middle-aged man, who looked to be in his forties, with a small paunch, and dark salt-and-pepper hair.

"Oh. Hello officer."

"Hello yourself," the man said, not unkindly. "Can I help you?"

"No, but thank you. We're fine. Just looking for a place to bed down for the night."

"Not here you're not."

"Ah. Well, the thing is, sir, that we really don't have anywhere else to go."

The officer considered this.

"You don't have any money? No one around to take you in for the night?"

"No, sir. We were passing through."

"To where?"

"I have no idea," Solomon said. "At the moment, we're kind of wandering."

"So you're a vagrant. Where did you come from?"

"That's the thing. I don't know."

"Mm-hm. You don't know."

"No, sir. I have no idea. I woke up yesterday morning, in an alley, near a dumpster. I don't know how I got there, or anything about what happened to me before, or who I was. Who I am, for that matter."

The officer squatted down, and absently reached out to rub the Hound, who suffered it tensely for a moment, but then relaxed under his hand.

"Really?" he said. "Well, what about a name? Got one of those?"

"Solomon. It's one of the only things I do know."

"Well, here's the problem, Solomon. We don't have a vagrant problem here in Martinsburg, and we don't want one. Plus, your dog here needs to be on a leash. Vicious thing that she is."

He smiled as he said this last and rubbed the dog a little more vigorously.

"We didn't mean any harm," Solomon said. "We can move on, no problem."

"Now, hold on a minute. I said we don't have a vagrant problem, and I don't think we have a problem now. I haven't always been a small-town cop. I've done a little work in bigger cities too, and have some experience with homeless folks. Most of them have been decent people, but a lot of times, there's been some problem as well. I don't think there is with you, other than the memory thing…if you're telling the truth about that. Something tells me you are though."

He pursed his lips and looked down at the Hound, then at Solomon.

"How about her? What's her name?"

"Matilda?" Solomon said.

The dog glanced at him, then laid her head back down to receive more attention from the officer.

"Seems not," Solomon said. "I actually don't know her name. We just met the other day."

The cop nodded. "Okay, that's weird, but whatever. How about if you come with me? You can bring her with."

He stood up and extended his hand to Solomon, who grabbed it and let the officer pull him to his feet. Automatically, he gauged his strength against the cops, and knew that he was significantly stronger, and that there were several ways to turn the friendly gesture into a combat move if he so wished.

"Whoa. You're a tall one, aren't you?"

Solomon stood at least a head taller than the cop, who measured a little over six feet himself.

"Yeah," Solomon said. "I think I always have been."

The absurdity of the comment made him laugh, and after a second, the officer joined in.

"I would imagine you have been," he said. "Tall and thin. I bet you're hell on the basketball court."

Solomon shrugged. He had no idea if he was or not.

"Alright, let's head on over this way."

They walked across the park to a large stone building across the street. A broad flight of stairs led up to glass doors, which the officer unlocked.

"Oh, by the way," he said, as he led the way into the building. "You can call me Ed. I'm the local sheriff, which means I spend a lot of my time catching idiots who didn't realize they had too much to drink before getting behind the wheel. Or busting the kids who want to experiment with pot. That sort of thing. Not much real crime around here, which is fine with me."

Ed opened the doors and motioned for Solomon to go in.

"I can't let you sleep out in the park. But, I can put you up in here. It's against all sorts of rules, I'm sure, but screw it."

He led the way down some stairs and along a corridor until they came to a door with a clouded glass panel set into it. It read "Sheriff's Office" in black, block letters across it. Ed unlocked this door as well, and opened it for Solomon.

Inside was a small office with a couple of desks and chairs, some filing cabinets and a sofa. There was a coffee pot on a counter along one wall, with a narrow window set above it, looking out onto a street level view.

"Be it ever so humble," Ed said. "This is where I work. Steve is my deputy, but he's off duty now, and won't be in until tomorrow morning. I'll let him know you're here in the unlikely event that he comes in early. Probably won't happen. He's got a new baby at home and isn't getting much sleep these days."

Solomon looked around.

"You want me to stay here? Am I under arrest?"

"Nope, not at all. As a matter of fact, I'm not even going to lock the door, so that you can go use the bathroom when you need to. But I thought that old sofa might be a little more comfortable than the ground."

"Oh. Thank you. I appreciate the hospitality."

"Not a problem," Ed said. "I don't know what it is...there's something about you though. Something that makes me comfortable doing this. I'm not going to have cause to regret it, am I?"

He looked at Solomon with a raised eyebrow.

"No, you definitely aren't. We'll bed down here tonight, and be out of your hair bright and early tomorrow. No problems from us."

"Good...now, one other thing. When's the last time you ate? Either one of you?"

"I guess that would be two days ago. A kind woman gave me a sandwich and a can of soda. Other than that, we've been moving along. When I woke up in that alley, I didn't have anything on me that you don't see. No money at all, so I haven't been real sure what to do. It's one of the reasons we've kept walking, I guess."

Ed nodded as he spoke.

"Kind of thought that might be the case. A guy, even one as skinny as you, needs to eat. Let's do this. We'll go grab something at Minnie's. Local dinner. Good food, good people. After that, we'll get something for Lucy?...no, not Lucy, I guess...and then get you settled."

Solomon shuffled his feet and looked at the ground. "Well, that sounds great...but I can't pay for..."

"Doesn't matter," Ed interrupted. "My wife is always telling me that I should be a better neighbor. Guess this counts, huh? Come on, we'll let Betty?....Nope...stay here, and we'll be back soon."

"You okay with that, girl?" Solomon asked the dog, who promptly jumped up on the sofa, turned about three times and tucked herself into the corner. She took up a cushion and a half out of the three.

Ed laughed. "Looks like you're going to have to argue with her about who gets the couch and who has to sleep in a chair."

The food at Minnie's was as Ed had advertised. It was good, filling and there was plenty of it. Solomon ate a burger and fries, and at Ed's insistence, wolfed down a second plate full, followed by two slices of apple pie and several cups of coffee. Ed laughed as he watched him eat.

"I guess it has been a while for you. You sure you've had enough? It's no problem if you want something else."

"No, thank you. This is more than enough. I'm not quite sure how to say thanks…"

"Don't worry about it. I'm glad to do it, and I think it did Minnie's heart good to see someone enjoying her food that much. What do you say we get something to bring back for your dog?"

"That's very generous of you. Thanks."

Ed called out to Minnie and asked her to come to the table.

She was a short, round woman, with a big pile of reddish, brown hair on the top of her head. When she spoke, it was with a soft, sweet voice, that would suddenly rise into a yell when she called an order in to the kitchen.

"What do you need, honey?" she said to Ed when she approached.

"Minnie, this is Solomon. He's passing through, but I'm kind of hoping maybe we can find a reason for him to stick around. In the meantime, he's got a beautiful dog with him who's about as hungry as he was. Since the nearest open store is a good half hour away, I thought I'd see if you had anything laying around that we could take to get her through the night."

"Are you calling my food fit for a dog, Ed?"

"What? No! Of course not! I was…"

Minnie started laughing. "I know what you're doing Ed, and yes, I'm sure we can find something. Give me a minute. Nice to meet you Mr. Solomon."

"Just Solomon, please," he said. "And thank you."

She smiled at them both and moved away.

"Minnie is good people," Ed said. "She's got a heart of gold, so she'll fix something up."

"This is really wonderful," Solomon replied. "But…what did you mean you hoped I'd find a reason to stick around?"

"Ah, hell, I don't know." Ed seemed slightly embarrassed. "I'm not sure where that came from. But, you know, if you wanted to settle down in one place for a while, see if you can start to remember things…well, there are worse places to do it than Martinsburg. That's all."

Solomon nodded, looking out the window at the small town.

"Maybe I can."

CHAPTER 5

Being awake a large part of the night had made Lacy's day go by slowly. Not that being a book-keeper for a construction company was ever very exciting, but it paid the bills and usually she was able to muster up at least a semblance of enthusiasm.

She had returned to the back windows the rest of the night, turning off the kitchen light so there was no reflection in the glass, and peering out into the darkness, trying vainly to see if someone was sneaking across her back-yard. Of course, she never did, and when she would turn on the rear floodlight, she'd see nothing then either. She kept telling herself that nothing was there, to go read a book, or watch television, but that scrap of cloth kept preying on her mind, and she'd find herself back at the kitchen window.

Finally, at around midnight, she turned off the television that she wasn't really watching, made sure all the doors and windows were locked and went to bed. In the darkness, every sound, every creak of the house, became ominous and the sound of stealthy footfalls in the hallway. She would doze off, sleep lightly, and then wake up, eyes wide and staring into the dark, listening for the noise that had awakened her. It was a long, stressful night, and it took a toll on her today.

The guys at the job were always joking around and teasing her, which was to be expected at a place like that. That was fine. Lacy was tough and able to give as good as she got. They knew it, and knew what they could get away with and what crossed the line. Today though, she snapped at unwanted comments or jokes, and knew that the "that time of the month" remarks were making the rounds. Honestly, she couldn't have cared less.

The problem was that as tired as she was, and as much as she didn't really feel in the mood to be in the office, she was scared to go home. And that thought pissed her off. It was her home, dammit! No shadowy figure and stupid scrap of cloth was going to keep her from it. She was trying hard to make it her own, and establish her own routines, now that Luke was gone. She was starting to enjoy her life again, and refused to be scared off.

She had thought about calling Ed and telling him about the shadowy figure, but decided against it. What was she going to tell him? "Gee Ed, I don't know what it was, but it couldn't have been a bear because there was this piece of cloth, which means it was wearing clothes." He'd laugh her out of the office.

And that was saying something. She had actually gotten to know Ed quite well over the last few years. Unfortunately, it wasn't under the best of circumstances. As Luke had gotten worse, the delusions had become more frequent and the drinking increased, to the point that people in town had called on Ed to corral him on more than one occasion. Lacy had had to come and pick him up on several of those. Ed was a good man, and hadn't wanted to arrest Luke, recognizing that something was wrong, and that he wasn't just another drunk.

She knew that he caught some flak for that, too. There were plenty of people that thought he was being too soft, too lenient on the town maniac. But Ed had ignored them, and tried his best to help, right up until Luke had run off and stayed away. Since then, he had checked in on Lacy now and again, to make sure that she was doing okay and holding up.

Yeah, Ed was good people all right. So there was no way she was going to him with this. It would make her look as crazy as Luke was.

The day dragged on, and Lacy's thoughts kept turning to her home, and what she could do. When it was finally over, she said goodnight to her boss and walked slowly to her car. Part of her was thrilled to be going home, where she could relax, another part was terrified, and yet another part, which was growing, was angry. By the time she pulled up the steep driveway that led to her house, the angry part had taken over.

She changed into old, grubby, work clothes, which she often wore when working in the garden, or outside, or if she was fumbling her way through some home repair. Luke used to laugh at her, and tell her that no matter what she wore, she was always sexy to him. Often enough, he set about trying to prove it to her. She made a wry face at the memory of better days, and went out to her shed.

When they had bought the place several years ago, it came with a good sized shed off to the side of the property. The previous owners had left all sorts of stuff piled in there. Luke had always said that a lot of it was good, and he'd find uses for it. He had shoved it all to one side and made room for their lawn mower and yard tools, and there the pile had stayed. He had never gotten around to going through it, and Lacy had gotten used to seeing it there and never even thought about it.

Now though, she was pretty sure she had seen something in the pile of junk that she wanted. She started rooting through it, pushing aside scraps of wood, broken hand tools, hunks of wire and pieces of metal. An occasional spider scrambled to get out of the way, and she had to stop to sneeze a few times from the dust she raised. Finally, she found it. A length of stout metal pipe, thick walled, and about three feet long and an inch or so in diameter. It fit nicely in her hand, and had a good heft to it.

She wasn't entirely sure why she thought this piece of pipe would be what she needed, but she remembered seeing it once when Luke had first started moving all the junk to the pile he made, and thinking to herself that it was the perfect size to brain someone with. The thought had startled her, since she was normally a very non-violent person. Now though, she was glad that she had remembered it.

She pulled it out of the shed, wiping off the cobwebs as she did, and carried it with her back to the house. Inside, she dug through the junk drawer in the kitchen and found the flashlight. Of course, the batteries were dead, so that was the next hunt, which proved a little more difficult. She finally found them in a box filled with batteries and extension cords at the back of a closet. How they ended up there was beyond her, but things like that happened. The flashlight worked perfectly after she installed them, and she was ready for night to come.

The rest of the afternoon and evening she occupied herself as she always did. She worked in her garden, although her eyes kept going to the compost pile. She made sure that she added to it, including a couple of tomatoes that were perfectly fine. After dinner, she watched the news, went upstairs to her bedroom and changed her clothes again. There were some brambles near the compost pile and she didn't want anything to slow her down, so she donned heavy jeans and a long-sleeved shirt, knowing that she would be sweating in the warm summer air, but willing to put up with it. She laced her feet into her sturdy work boots.

Going outside again, she settled down next to the pool, sitting on the ground in its shadow. The sun was heading down, and already the woods beyond the house were starting to darken. If whatever it was came back tonight, she'd be ready for it.

Quicker than she would have thought, the sun dropped down behind the hills and the yard sank into deep evening colors. The woods behind the compost pile were quite dark now, and Lacy stared into them, peering at anything that she thought she could see move and listening as hard as she could.

Her vigilance paid off. A dark shape detached from the deeper shadows of the woods and slowly made its way to the compost pile. She could see it well enough to know that it did move on two legs, but walked with a hunched over, shambling motion. For having such an awkward looking gait, it moved through the forest silently, regardless of the sticks and dead leaves it must have walked over.

Lacy felt a tingle down her spine as it approached, and knew that the sweat running down her face wasn't only because of the heat. Her heart was hammering against her chest and she felt a strange sort of disconnected feeling, like what she was seeing couldn't be real.

But it was, and she steeled herself, determined that she wasn't going to live in fear in her own house. When the figure reached the compost pile, Lacy carefully rose to her feet and started forward, the flashlight in her left hand, and the pipe clutched tightly in her right. She had made it close to the thing last night, and tonight, no misplaced rock in the yard was going to interfere.

She snuck forward, going to the edge of the yard far to the right of where the compost pile lay, and worked her way back, trying to stay out of the figure's sight. It seemed to be working. Whatever it was, it was eating the tomatoes that she had put there, as well as the spoiled stuff.

When she was a few yards away, she turned on the flashlight and aimed it at the figure. The beam of light hit it, and it raised its arms against the brightness. It was a human after all, with dirty, emaciated arms and legs. Tatters of clothes hung from its gaunt frame and its hair was filthy and matted. From beneath its raised arms she could see a scruffy beard, the remnants of compost pile scraps hanging from it.

It lowered its arm enough to look toward Lacy and she reeled back, dropping the pipe. She knew that face, despite the grime and the dirt, the wild hair and beard. Eyes of bright blue peered at her, and then he turned and ran, crashing back into the forest.

"Luke?"

Lacy couldn't believe it, and stood stunned for a moment, but snapped out of it and took off into the woods, following the sounds of his retreat.

It was Luke! She was sure of it. But why? How? Was he that far gone that he was living in the woods like an animal? How would he have even survived for the last few weeks?

She ran after him, calling his name, but he was outpacing her. She could hear the noise of his passage through the woods fading. Stopping, she stood sobbing, her breath hitching in her throat.

"Luke! Luke! Come back! Please! It's Lacy, Luke! Let me help you!"

No sound came to her but the faint echo of her own voice, loud in the still night air.

The *very* still night air, she suddenly realized. There were no other sounds in the forest. Not of bugs, birds, or night creatures. No rustling in the leaves of small nocturnal animals trying to escape her intrusion into their world. Nothing.

And why was it so cold? She could see her breath as easily as if were deep winter.

It was eerie, and in spite of her anguish over seeing Luke, Lacy began to get frightened again. As it usually did, being scared also made her angry.

"Fine!" she yelled in the direction that she had last heard him. "Stay in the woods! See if I care!"

She turned to start back to the house when something grabbed her wrist. It was a hand, extending from a ragged black sleeve, bone white and skeletal thin, the skin stretched over it like parchment. The touch was freezing cold, as if the hand were made out of ice. She screamed and looked up at what had a hold of her.

A shapeless black form stood beside her. Maybe it had on a hood of some sort, but if so, it was deep. So deep that she couldn't see a face, only blackness inside of it, with two tiny pinpricks of bright green, glowing where its eyes would be.

It hissed at her and the cold from its hand spread into her arm, the agony of it spreading down to her fingers and up to her shoulder. She tried to scream again, but the pain and the cold moved fast, into her neck, and to her head. It was the worst headache Lacy had ever felt, and her jaw worked soundlessly as she tried to pull away.

The last thing she remembered as she fell to the ground was the hooded shape bending over her and hearing another hiss.

CHAPTER 6

The sound of the door opening, and the Hound jumping down from where she had been curled up on his legs, woke Solomon. He groaned at his stiffness from sleeping on the sofa with a huge dog, and climbed to his feet, expecting to see Ed entering the room.

Instead, it was a short, pretty woman, with long dark hair, slim, and probably in her forties. She carried an arm load of clothes and smiled at him as she set them down.

"Hi," she said, "you must be Solomon. At least I hope you are since you're the only one that should be sleeping in her with a giant dog."

She stuck out her hand, and Solomon took it.

"I'm Maggie. Maggie Caufield. Ed's wife."

Ah, that would explain it, Solomon thought to himself. Then, out loud, "Pleased to meet you, Mrs. Caufield."

"Please, call me Maggie. Everyone else does. Around here, we're Ed and Maggie."

"Maggie then."

The Hound pushed its way past Solomon's legs and stood looking up at Maggie, who bent down in front of her.

"And you must be the un-named dog, huh?" she said, rubbing the Hound on each side of its head. "We're going to have to do something about that, aren't we?"

The dog seemed to agree, as long as Maggie kept on petting her and showering her with attention.

Solomon shook his head. He remembered a little bit more about the Hounds, that they were typically relentless hunters and vicious killers. For one to have abandoned its quarry, even after Solomon had defeated it, was very unusual. For one to allow such close contact from others was unheard of.

Maggie roughed up the dog for another few seconds and stood.

33

"So here's the plan. Ed told me you were here and what was going on. First thing we're going to do is see if some of these things fit you well enough. It's a bunch of Ed's old clothes. You're quite a bit taller and thinner than him, but maybe we can find a few things that aren't too bad. At least for now. Then, you're going to come on home with me. You can take a shower, have some breakfast and talk to Ed. We'll figure out everything else after that. Sound good?"

It did sound good, but... "I can't do that, Maggie. I've put your husband out enough already."

"Nonsense. We already talked about it and it's settled. You need a hand right now, and we're happy to give it. You seem like the type that would do the same for someone else. So, take the clothes, go on down the hall to the men's room, and see if you can find something that fits well enough for now. If you can, we'll get rid of those rags you're wearing and head on out."

Maggie was a force of nature, and Solomon knew that he had no way of declining the offer of help. Actually, he didn't want to. For the first time, since waking in that alley, he felt a sense of well-being. The mystery of who he was still ate at him, of course, but at least he was among good people.

A few minutes later, he was dressed in pants that came up to his shins and a shirt that hung loosely on him around the shoulders and middle, but rode up over his stomach, and with sleeves that came up well above his wrists.

Maggie took one look at him and tried unsuccessfully to suppress a smile.

"Well, it will work for now. At least they're clean. Let's head back to our place, where we can work on getting you a couple of things that might fit better."

It was still early morning when they left the Sheriff's office and got in Maggie's car. She drove through town, pointing out things like Minnie's Diner, which Solomon was already familiar with, the dual screen old movie theater, the drug store and the local bar.

"Not too many problems around here, as I'm sure Ed mentioned to you. Everyone is pretty decent. For the most part. You'll like it here."

Solomon smiled at the assumption that he would stay around, but admitted to himself that maybe he would. Martinsburg was a nice small town, and it was rural enough that he would be able to get to the woods

34

when he wanted to, unlike when he woke in the city. Just knowing that was a comfort to him.

They drove for twenty minutes or so, with the Hound panting out the window in the back seat, until Maggie turned into a driveway that led between wooded copses on each side. There was a neat, brick ranch set back on a carefully tended lawn, which surrounded the house on all sides. Ed was standing on the front porch, a steaming cup of coffee in his hand, and waved as they pulled in.

Like Maggie, he tried to hide the smile when he saw Solomon.

"I'm sorry," he said, when he saw by Solomon's expression that he hadn't done a good job of it. "I'm not trying to laugh at you. But we'll definitely have to get you something else to wear. You're too tall to fit into my old cast-offs."

Ed showed him where the bathroom was, gave him a towel and left him to it. Solomon took a hot shower, enjoying the feeling of truly being clean again. He scrubbed his hair and beard, watching the suds disappear down the drain. When he was finished, he looked at himself in the mirror.

A long, slim face looked back at him. One with blue eyes, a slender nose, and pale skin. His hair was almost black, with strands of gray peppered through it. His beard was the same and he wondered how old he really was. He certainly didn't feel old, but he didn't feel particularly young either. Figure middle-aged maybe? In his thirties or forties? He didn't know.

After he finished in the bathroom, Maggie made breakfast, and Solomon ate as hungrily as he had the night before. Ed had stopped at the store on his way home after leaving Solomon in his office and picked up dog food, which they poured in a bowl for the Hound. She wolfed it down greedily, lapped up a bowl of water, and lay down with a sigh of contentment.

"Looks like Daisy is satisfied," Maggie said.

They all watched her expectedly, but the dog didn't stir, or look up at the sound of the name.

"Really?" Solomon said. "Is that it? Is your name Daisy?"

The Hound stayed where she was, although one ear perked up slightly.

"Looks like Daisy it is. How did you know?" he asked Maggie.

She shrugged. "I don't know. It just came to me."

This is the strangest Hunting Hound, Solomon thought. But he was glad that she had taken to him.

Solomon spent the day with Ed, riding in his patrol car with Daisy in the back. They got Solomon clothes that fit him better, although it was a challenge due to his height and build. Ed had radioed in to the station to let Steve know that he was around if needed, but wouldn't be in to the office until later in the day.

He showed Solomon around the town, repeating some of the same sights that Maggie had shown him earlier, but Solomon didn't mind. He was enjoying the company, and was finding that he did indeed like Martinsburg, particularly the visit to the barber shop, where he got his beard taken off, and his hair cut.

"If I stay for a while," he said to Ed at one point, "I'd have to do something to earn my way."

"True. What can you do? Any idea what you used to do for a living?"

"I think I was a soldier. I'm not sure why I think that, though. It feels very far off, or long ago."

"Hmm, not much call for soldering around here. I'd hire you on, but we honestly don't even have enough work for two of us as it is, so I can't imagine the town board approving it. Let me think about it some. We'll come up with something."

The day passed as they drove around, occasionally stopping to talk with people that Ed knew.

"I think I was right about you," Ed said as the afternoon went on.

"What do you mean?"

"You probably don't notice this, but everyone's reaction to you. They respond to you like they've known you forever, and are happy to see you again. Hell, even I had that reaction, and I'm paid to be suspicious. What is it, do you think?"

Solomon shrugged. "I really don't know. I like people, I think I always have. Maybe most can kind of feel that? Like I give off good vibes or something?"

Ed laughed. "Yeah, good vibes. Maybe that's it. Whoops, hold on."

The radio squawked and Ed picked it up and mashed the button. "Go ahead, Steve."

"Chief, we've got an accident. Out on the edge of town, but you're closest. Sounds like it could be pretty bad."

"On it."

Steve gave him the address and Ed flipped on the lights and accelerated. Minutes later, he was braking hard near a sharp bend in the road, where a car was overturned, laying on its roof in the ditch. There was a strong smell of gasoline, and the ticking noise of a hot engine, slowly cooling off.

Solomon and Ed jumped out of the car and ran to it, Daisy watching them from the window. The car must have been going too fast as it came around the bend, lost control and hit the shoulder and rolled. Torn up grass, dirt, and weeds started several yards back, indicating how far it had tumbled.

Ed ran to the driver's side door and pulled on it, but it was stuck fast, being held by the partially collapsed roof. Solomon could see a young man inside, hanging upside down by the seat belt, with blood dripping from his head. He weakly stirred as they approached.

"We've got to get him out of there," Ed said. "I don't know how long we've got."

Solomon moved past him, grabbed hold of the car door and pulled, the muscles in his thin arms standing out. The door moved, grudgingly, but then hung up again. He put more into it, drawing a deep breath, bracing himself, and giving a sudden yank. This time, the door popped open, sending Solomon stumbling back. He recovered, reached inside, and pushed the young man up into the seat with his shoulder, so that he could relieve the tension on the belt and unlatch it.

The man tumbled down, and Solomon scooped him up and carried him away from the car as if he was a child. Laying him down on the side of the road, he turned around to see Ed's stunned face.

"Wow," Ed said. "That was…well, that was something…"

He tilted his hat back and scratched his head. "You sure are a strong one there, Solomon. I thought that door was stuck solid."

"Leverage, I guess."

"Maybe. Anyway, I hear the ambulance coming. Head on back and take care of Daisy, I'll deal with them."

An hour later, after the ambulance had taken the young man away and the wrecker had come for the car, Ed came back to the cruiser where Solomon and Daisy waited. They got back in and Ed turned to Solomon.

"Not sure how you did all that," he said, "but I told you it was a good thing you stuck around. Saved that young man a lot of pain, I believe."

"Glad I could help. It wasn't a big deal though, really."

Ed was about to respond when the radio squawked again.

"Yeah, Steve."

"Sorry about this, Chief," Steve's voice came back. "I know you're finishing up out there, but we just got another report."

"*Another* accident? Geesh. Where is it this time?"

"Not an accident. Lacy Roberts is in the hospital. In and out of it, from what I understand."

"What happened?"

"Not sure. She says she was attacked though, out at her place."

"What? By who?"

"No idea. She's not making any sense."

"Alright. I'm on my way."

He glanced over at Solomon. "Sorry to do this to you, but I think I need to get there right away."

"No problem," Solomon replied. "Daisy and I are fine."

Ed went into the hospital while Solomon stayed outside with Daisy. They walked along the grounds, looking at the few sites, and then sat on a bench to wait. After a while, Ed came out and found them, and took a seat next to Solomon.

"Weirdest thing," he said. "When she's awake, Lacy swears she was attacked in the woods by something, but she doesn't know what. She says it grabbed her arm, she got cold and passed out. Sounds ridiculous, only her arm really is messed up, and the doc's not sure what's wrong with it."

Solomon felt a spark of recognition at the description. It was on the edge of his mind, like the name of a movie or show that he couldn't quite remember. There was something there though...

"And get this," Ed continued. "She also swears that she saw her husband. He's been gone for the last few weeks now, but she says he must be living in the woods near their place."

He suddenly stopped and looked at Solomon. "Why am I telling you this? It's not like me to share an investigation with a civilian. I don't even tell Maggie a lot of things."

Solomon shrugged. "I don't know. Maybe I'm a good listener? But Ed, don't tell me anything you don't want..."

He trailed off, his memory jogged by what Ed had told him. The icy touch and the damage to the woman's arm...some sort of legend that he

38

had once heard…only…it wasn't a legend. He knew it was true, some scary monster of childhood come to life.

He realized that Ed was staring at him. "You okay? You kind of phased out there for a second."

"Yeah. Yeah, I'm fine, just remembering something, I thought, but it's gone again. I don't think it was important."

But he knew that it was. He was pretty sure that if he could talk to Lacy Roberts, he'd find out more about himself, and where he came from.

CHAPTER 7

The figure on the bed next to her didn't stir as Shireen slipped away and walked to the window opening. The night breezes cooled her pale skin and stirred the silver hair that hung down her back as she looked out over the garden, the flowers and shrubs carefully encouraged to grow just so, to be pleasing to the eye, but still maintain order. Beyond, the woods stood silent, the shadows between the trees undisturbed, unlike her mind.

"Come back to bed, Shireen," the other mumbled. "Why are you up?"

"You know why," she said, not turning from the window. "How could they have done that?"

The figure in the bed sighed and pushed himself upright, his back against the headboard as he rubbed his eyes.

"We've been over this. It's horrible, and was undeserved, we both know that. But there's nothing we can do about it. He's gone."

She didn't turn from the window, but continued to gaze out, not really seeing what she was looking at.

"How could Jediah have allowed it to happen, though?"

The man in the bed snorted.

"Do you think he had a choice? What if he had refused to turn him over? What then? Jamshir would have sent the full might of Glittering Birch against us, and been supported by the other houses as well. As tough as we are, even we couldn't stand against that. Not for long."

He sighed.

"Look," he said, "I'm upset too. Solomon was my best friend, but I can't bring him home. Please come back to bed. We have patrol tomorrow, and you know how tiring that is."

Shireen ignored him, staying by the window, her slim body framed against the opening.

There was a rustling noise behind her, and then Orlando's arms were about her, his body melding against hers. He placed his chin on her shoulder.

"I know," he said softly. "He was your friend, too."

With that, she turned in his arms and kissed him quickly.

"I know all that," she said, gently moving from his embrace. "It seems so unfair, though."

"It does. Although…"

"Although what?"

"He did fail, Shireen. As hard as that is to believe, he did. They could have executed him."

"That's completely wrong, Orlando! And you know it!"

"Okay, okay," he said, returning to the bed. "Come on though. We need to get some sleep. And if you're not tired anymore, come on back to bed anyway. If I have to be up in the middle of the night, it may as well be for a good reason."

He smiled at her, adding in a lascivious wink at the end. It looked so ridiculous that Shireen laughed in spite of herself.

"You're an ass, you know that?" she said as she slipped into bed next to him and snuggled against his body.

"I know. But I'm your ass, and you love me anyway."

"Not that I can figure out why."

They fell silent, both gazing into the darkness. Despite his words, Orlando didn't try to entice her into lovemaking. He simply lay with his arm around her, letting her pillow her head on his chest.

"Do you think he's okay," he finally said, quietly.

"I hope so," she responded. "But I can't imagine being exiled from the Greenweald. How would you survive without going mad?"

"I don't know. I'd rather have been killed, but I think Jediah pushed for exile, hoping that at some point he could get him back."

"Maybe. But that doesn't seem likely."

"No," he agreed. "It doesn't. But who knows? Let's try to get back to sleep. Or we'll both be falling off our horses tomorrow."

When the dawn finally came, Shireen had been awake for the rest of the night, and was pretty sure that Orlando had been too.

Solomon's exile was still the talk of the barracks at the Towering Oaks compound. All around the massive complex, rumor and speculation

41

swirled. Everyone had an opinion, from the archers practicing at the butts, to the swordsmen sparring in the yard. Even the officers that Shireen and Orlando passed in the command building were talking quietly about it, growing silent as the two walked by.

As scouts, they were often in the command building, walking through its live-grown hallways to report their findings to their superiors, or to get new orders. At times, their scouting missions involved coming close to the other Houses, so they were always given their orders deep in the building, away from any prying eyes of Glitter Birch, or Whispering Pines. The other minor Houses were of no real consequence, but those two had extensive networks of spies and infiltrators, who could even be here.

Today's orders weren't so clandestine, however. There was nothing that involved the other Houses. Instead, they were to ride to edge of the Greenweald, far to the north, to the border they shared with the realm of the Hairy Men. It was a long assignment, and one that they would need to take a couple of hours to prepare for. They would have to take weapons, of course, but also gear to live in the wild for a few days. That long a journey would take them out of the shaped lands of the Greenweald and into virgin territory.

Shireen looked forward to the trip, and knew that despite his grumbling, so did Orlando. They had been partners as scouts before they ever became lovers, and the chance to get away from the constant rumors and reminders of Solomon was welcome.

Solomon had been their commander for several years, as he was to a lot of the scouts. He had served Towering Oaks in a variety of roles over the years, and had excelled at them all. He was one of the most adept swordsmen the House had ever produced, was an expert archer and was able to read signs in the wilderness with an ease that no other scout had ever possessed. She had also heard that he was an insightful tactician, and that Jediah had deferred to him in forming battle plans whenever they were needed.

Because of that, some said that Jediah was envious of Solomon's abilities and fearful of his intentions. But Shireen didn't believe that for a moment. She was present when Jamshir had passed his judgment, and had seen the look that crossed Jediah's face. No, she was sure that like everyone else, the head of House Towering Oaks felt nothing but love and respect for Solomon.

42

She also knew that Orlando felt the same way, even more so. He had grown up with Solomon, the two of them inseparable from the time they were children. During their times on patrols, Orlando had told her of the games they would play, always invented by Solomon, and how exciting and fun they had been. About how Solomon had always stood by him, through their childhood and their adolescence, and into adulthood. Orlando knew that he could never measure up to Solomon's achievements, but never showed any jealousy. He said he was simply happy for his friend, as Solomon had been when he had found out that she and Orlando were now together.

Yes, being out in the open, with only Orlando around would be good for her. She was in a hurry to begin.

Later, they rode through the woods, their horses picking their way with ease. They were in no hurry, knowing that in spite of the orders to check on the Hairy Men, there was no real danger. The brutes wouldn't dare to attack the Folk, not after what had happened the last time they had tried. Shireen was sure they must still be recovering even now, years later.

"Glorious!" Orlando said, his voice ringing out through the forest.

Shireen smiled as she looked at him. "What is?"

"This!" he said, sweeping an arm out to indicate the world around them. "Being back on patrol, out in the wild, with no one else around. I've missed it."

"Me too. It's good to get away for it all."

Orlando glanced at her with a smile, then looked more closely. His smile faded.

"Still thinking about it, huh?"

"I guess so. I just feel so badly. And…" she trailed off, looking away.

"Yes?"

"Nothing. It's foolish."

"Huh, if I kept all my foolish thoughts to myself, we'd live in silence. Come on, out with it."

"I think we should try to get him back."

Now there was silence. She glanced over, but Orlando wasn't looking at her. Instead, he was staring down at the ground, his gaze vacant and unfocused.

"Orlando? Did you hear me?"

He stirred and looked up at her, a sad smile on his face.

"Yes, I heard you."

"I'm insane, right?"

"No. You're not. I have to admit, I've had the same thoughts."

"Really? You haven't said anything."

"I love Solomon, Shireen. He's the best friend I've ever had, and the best of us all, Towering Oaks or any other House. But to go against Jamshir is suicide. If we're caught, it won't be exile, and certainly not together if it was. And as much as I love him, I love you more. I won't risk that."

Shireen was touched, and felt the love that she had for Orlando wash over her, and fill her to near bursting.

"I know," she said. "I don't want that either. I love my life with you, and don't want to jeopardize it. But can we really do nothing?"

"No, I don't think we can. We'll have to think about it though. It's not easy to get to where he is. Only a couple of things are made to cross back and forth, like the Hunting Hounds. For us, we'd need help, and who would we go to?"

"That's one of the problems. I can't think of anyone. But let's at least keep it in our minds and we'll see what we come up with. In the meantime, I'll try to be better company."

Orlando grinned. "You're fine, but if you feel that way, you can make it up to me later, like tonight. But for now, it's a gorgeous day, and we have a long way to go."

Two days later they neared the border of the Greenweald. For the last day, they had ridden through the wilds, the areas where the Folk had no influence, or partnerships, with the trees. Nature grew as it would, untended and primal. The different types of trees grew together, competing for space, and spreading their seeds wherever they could. While it was messier, and not as easy to ride though, Shireen found it beautiful too. She enjoyed being away from the intrigues of the Houses and their constant bickering and jockeying for power.

Shireen had never understood that, the need to raise your House above those of your neighbors. She loved Towering Oaks, and was proud to be a part of it. Proud to be part of the House that shouldered the burden of keeping the Greenweald safe from outside threats, or protecting those from other Houses who weren't as strong, or chasing down rogue beasts threatening outlying farms or vineyards. That was what she loved, not the sneaking around to check the defenses of another House. Let the crawlers in Whispering Pines do that.

She knew Orlando felt the same way, which was one of the things that initially drew her to him. They had been assigned to patrol together, and you learned a lot about someone, alone in the wilderness with them. Before long, they were sharing both what they hated and loved about being scouts, and not too long after that, a bedroll for the first time.

She was lost in her thoughts, lulled by the sound of the wind rustling in the leaves overhead, when she was brought back to the present by Orlando's sudden indrawn breath.

"Shireen," he said, stopping his horse. "Look."

She stopped hers as well and looked at where Orlando was pointing.

Under a tree a short distance ahead, a Hairy Man was slumped against the trunk. She couldn't tell if he was alive or dead from there, but the fact remained that one of them had crossed the border, and it needed to be dealt with.

They started their horses forward again, and dismounted near the Hairy Man, drawing their swords as they did. But there was no movement from under the tree, and Shireen was fairly certain that he was already dead.

Shireen had always found the Hairy Men to be revolting, and a little frightening as well. Almost as tall as the Folk, they were much broader, and they were stronger. This one was a perfect example why. Huge muscles bulged in his arms and legs, and across a massive chest that was no longer rising and falling. There was no movement in those black eyes that stared out in death from beneath an overhanging brow. The long, matted hair and beard hung down, and it was that, as well as the hair growing thickly on the rest of his body that gave them their name. At least, that was what the Folk called them. Shireen wasn't sure what they called themselves.

"We need to back-track," she said. "Find out where it crossed and if it's part of a raiding party."

"Hold on," Orlando replied. "Let's take a look fist. Why is he dead?"

"Who knows? Maybe he was sick, or old, or something."

"I don't think so…"

Sometimes, Orlando's meticulousness could drive Shireen crazy. She wanted to be back on the horses, tracking the Hairy Man's movements and finding out where it had come from. Destroy the threat before it could be one. But Orlando wanted his answers first, forcing her to slow down. She knew he was right. At times of action, she would end up in front, knowing that he was right behind her, protecting her back. But at times like this, he often took the lead, setting the pace.

Orlando looked over the body, crouched down and pulled it forward with a grunt.

"Heavy one…"

He looked at the back of the Hairy Man's head, but didn't seem to see anything, and finally sat back on his haunches.

"I don't get it," he said. "There aren't any wounds that I can see. He's not old, and certainly doesn't look sick. So why is he dead? And look at his weapons. He's only got a knife and that old bow. I don't think he was coming for war. I think he was hunting."

"Then why is here, rather than on his own side of the border?"

"Don't know. But you're right about one thing. We do need to back-track and see where he came from."

It turned out that tracking the Hairy Man's progress back to the border a mile or so distant was easier than either of them had thought it would be. And yet harder at the same time.

Beyond the first body they found, there was another. This one was also a strong looking male, only he lay face down on the forest floor, as if he had been cut down while running, yet there were no marks on him either. Then a female, and another, and children. Mothers with young still in their arms, and in one place, a whole family, the male with his arms protectively around the female and the two young, all dead.

"What is going on here?" Shireen said, her heart heavy at the sight of what they had found, Hairy Men or not.

Orlando shook his head.

"I don't know," he said. "But they weren't attacking. They were fleeing."

"From what?"

Orlando shrugged. There were no signs of struggles or battles. Towering Oaks trained its soldiers and scouts well in the mannerisms and tactics of their enemies, so they both knew that the Hairy Men, while not very intelligent, were fierce fighters, and not easily prone to be driven off. During the last war, all those years ago, they had been defeated almost to the point of being wiped out, before they took to their heels.

To find so many dead, apparently in the act of fleeing was disturbing.

"We need to get back," Shireen said. "We need to report this."

"We do," Orlando agreed. "It's getting late though. Let's move off some and find a place to spend the night. Tomorrow, we'll head back as quick as we can."

Shireen agreed and the two moved away from the trail of bodies and further from the border.

That night, they built their fire large and kept their weapons close to hand. Every noise of wind or animal seemed a threat, and they kept their backs to the fire, looking out into the darkness. The day had cooled off as they had ridden further north, but it was still a warm summer's evening.

Until the temperature began to drop, until even close to the fire the two could see their breath. The forest fell silent, and there was a feeling of dread around them. They climbed to their feet, swords in hand, and stood close to each other, peering out into the woods.

But nothing came, and a few minutes later, the suffocating feeling of fear passed on, becoming less and finally disappearing. The night noises returned, and the temperature rose back to a normal level.

"Shireen?" Orlando said. "What was that?"

"I don't know. But I have a feeling it has something to do with all those bodies."

"What, like their ghosts or something?"

"No, more like what killed them in the first place. We really need to get back."

CHAPTER 8

Lacy woke in the hospital, answered Ed's questions, and slipped in and out of consciousness for the next several hours. She didn't know how she had gotten there, or what had happened after that *thing* had grabbed her in the woods. All she remembered was seeing Luke, running after him, and then a coldness that had spread from her arm up through her head. A coldness that had frozen her thoughts and seemed to be there still, making everything fuzzy and hard to concentrate on.

And her arm hurt. It was a slow, throbbing ache that started at her wrist and radiated up, past her elbow and into her bicep. It didn't matter if she kept it straight, or bent, or twisted to the side, the ache was still there. They had taken x-rays to see if there was a fracture or break, but nothing had shown. The doctor said it was probably a deep tissue bruise, most likely caused when she fell, and should clear itself up over the next several days. He was far more worried about her head.

In truth, so was Lacy. Her arm she could deal with, that was what they made Tylenol for. But her brain…the thought that she might have something wrong there sent chills through the rest of her. Although she guessed that if she was coherent enough to worry about it, then the damage couldn't be too bad. Could it?

Lacy could tell that Ed didn't believe her story, which didn't surprise her. She had known that was going to happen, which is why she didn't go to him in the first place. Oh, he believed she had seen something, but not that it was Luke, or that she had been attacked by some shapeless, black thing in the woods. Most likely it was a bear, he had told her, and in the dim light she had seen what she wanted to see. Never mind that she had hit Luke full on with a flashlight beam, or that there were no claw or bite marks on her.

She couldn't blame Ed though. Not really. She would be skeptical of someone saying they had seen their run-away ex living in the woods also, to say nothing of the ghost story.

But, she was more concerned with Luke, and what had happened to him, than she was about being believed, or about her attacker. For one, she couldn't really remember the figure very well, and thinking about it made that icy feeling in her brain worse, as if her thoughts shied away from it. And secondly, she still really cared about Luke, in spite of all his crazy and his drinking. Hell, she might as well admit it; she still loved him.

They told her that she must have made it out of the woods and to the road herself, before collapsing where a passing driver had found her. She didn't remember any of that. One moment, she was in the woods, the next she was here.

Her thoughts kept circling back, over and over, through the same events. The shadow near the compost pile, Luke, the attack, waking here. A never-ending spiral that occupied the times she was awake. And the pain pills they gave her for her arm weren't helping. They made her feel slightly disconnected, and her arm still hurt.

She wanted to go home, but hadn't done well enough on a couple of cognitive tests that they gave her, so they wanted to keep her overnight, to make sure she wasn't going to lapse into a coma or anything, she guessed. She was on the verge of telling them no, and that she was going home, when Ed had come in and convinced her otherwise.

Fine, she'd stay the night, but she was leaving early tomorrow. When she fell asleep later that evening, it was like a switch had been thrown, and she didn't even remember dreaming.

The next day her head felt a little clearer. She wasn't sure about the arm. The throbbing may have subsided somewhat, or it could be that she was getting used to it. Either way, the doctor had come in early and cleared her, as long as she promised to call if she started feeling strange again. They told her it would be a couple of hours until the discharge paperwork went through, which was annoying, but at least she would be out of there.

Since an ambulance had brought her in, she had no way of getting back out to her place, so her plan was to walk the short distance to Minnie's, get something to eat, and see if anyone she knew came in that she could bum a ride from. If not, she'd call Ed and see if she could get him to do it. She hated to bother him, but it was way too far for her to walk.

She was considering getting up and getting dressed, when a man gently knocked on the door to her room, before entering.

The first thing she noticed about him was his height. He was very tall, well over six and a half feet, probably closer to seven. Thin, with dark hair that was worn a little long, and pleasant features. He had arresting blue eyes and Lacy found herself instantly drawn to him.

"Hi," he said, almost shyly. "I know this is weird, but my name is Solomon, and I'd like to talk to you about what happened."

Lacy was surprised. Martinsburg was a small town, and she knew perfectly well that Ed and Steve were the only two cops. But maybe this one was from out of town, and maybe this wasn't the first time that someone had been attacked like this.

"Oh, sure," she said, sitting up a little straighter and running a hand through her hair quickly. "Glad to help."

Solomon smiled at that, and Lacy liked his smile. It put her at ease even more. He indicated a chair, and she nodded. He pulled it closer to her bedside before sitting down.

"Can you tell me anything more about what attacked you?" he asked.

"Not really. I mean, not if you've talked to Ed already, which I assume you have. All I remember is that it was this black...shape. I know that sounds weird, and Ed certainly doesn't believe me, but that's what it was. A shape."

Solomon was nodding, his gaze focused on the floor in front of his chair.

"Almost like it wasn't really there, right?" he said. "Like it was made out of smoke...or shadows...or, darkness itself."

Lacy shuddered a little at his words, the memory of the thing in the woods becoming clearer.

"Yes," she breathed, "exactly. Like it was made out of darkness...until it grabbed me. I saw it then, or at least a part of it. Its hand...it was bone white, and so thin. It looked like it was coming out of an old sleeve, like black burlap or something..."

"And it was cold," Solomon finished up for her.

"You've seen it," she said. "What was it?"

Solomon shook his head.

"No, I can't say I've seen it. I may have heard about it once, I'm not sure..."

"I'm just glad that someone believes me! Are you going to talk to Ed?"

"I'm sure I will. Thank you though. It's been a big help talking to you."

"No, thank you," Lacy said. "I hope you guys can catch it, whatever it was."

Solomon stood up to take his leave.

"Feel better Mrs. Roberts," he said.

Lacy watched him leave, glad that someone else was on the case and wistfully wishing that Solomon would come back and talk to her some more. Then it wouldn't be so bad waiting around to be discharged.

She walked into Minnie's right after lunch. Minnie lit up when she came through the door.

"Lacy! Lord's sake, what are you doing? Didn't I hear you were in the hospital?"

"Hi Minnie. Yeah, I was. But they cleared me to go home. I thought I'd grab a quick bite and see if someone was around that could drive me."

"Well, you just sit on down. We'll get you fixed up and one of us will get you back to your place, no problem."

Lacy smiled at that, once again struck by the good parts of living remotely. Martinsburg may not have a ton to offer, but it did have a strong sense of community, and she was grateful for it. Minnie, true to her word, drove her to her place after she had eaten, and stuck around long enough to make sure she was inside and safe. She smiled and waved from the door as Minnie backed the car around, and disappeared down the driveway.

But when she was alone, she wasn't sure that she felt safe after all. Whatever had attacked her was still out there, and so was Luke. It was okay right now, still broad day light, but soon enough, it would be night again, and the dark shape with the cold, white hands could come out of the woods. It could walk, or float, or whatever it did, right up the steps, onto her deck. She'd have the sliders shut tight and locked, yes, but couldn't extreme cold crack glass? If that thing put its hands on the glass and…

"Stop it," she said to herself, saying the words out loud.

But as the day went on, she was getting more and more nervous. Before it was even dusk, she had made sure that all the doors and windows were closed and locked. She kept going to the kitchen and looking out over the backyard, toward the compost pile and the woods beyond, but seeing nothing.

When she heard the sound of an engine, she went to the living room to look. Ed's police cruiser was pulling up, his solid frame behind the wheel, and a tall silhouette beside him. She felt a stirring of relief, and was surprised that as much as she admired and respected Ed, it was Solomon's presence that she was reacting to.

The two men climbed out of the car and came to the door. Lacy didn't make them wait, and had it open as they came up.

"Hey Ed," she said. "Come on in. Nice to see you again, Solomon."

She noticed Ed give Solomon a funny look when she said that, but glossed over it as something between them.

"Lacy," Ed said. "Glad you're feeling better. I wanted to check in on you, see how you were doing."

"I'm good. You know, the arm still feels weird, but otherwise, I'm good. Thanks though."

Ed nodded. "Glad to hear that, too. Keep an eye on that arm. It should clear up soon, sprains usually do. But, well, I don't quite know how to say it, but I'm more concerned with…"

"My mental state, right?" she interrupted. "I'm not going to lie to you. I'm pretty nervous. I know you don't believe me, but whatever that was, it's still out there."

Ed nodded again. "Yep. Here's the thing, it doesn't really matter if I believe you or not. Not tonight, anyway. For tonight, we'll stay around. My friend Solomon here and I will be out in the car. When morning comes and everything is good, we'll head out, but for tonight, you sleep."

"Don't be ridiculous, Ed," she protested, hating the idea of needing anyone to make her feel safe or protected. "You've got your own family. Maggie will want you home."

"Whose idea do you think this was? She told me to get out here, make sure you were okay and don't be home until it's light out again. I'm not going to argue with her. Or you, for that matter."

Lacy shook her head. "Thank you, Ed. And thank Maggie for me too. Do you guys want something to eat?"

"Nah, we've got stuff in the car. I want to get back out there, keep an eye on things as the sun goes down. You go ahead about your business and don't give two thoughts to us. We've got it."

He smiled and touched his hat brim, turned, and left. Solomon, who had remained silent through the whole exchange, glanced at her, and followed.

52

She had to admit that having them around did make her feel better. She kept an eye on them as they walked around her backyard, followed by a huge, shaggy gray dog that Solomon would reach down and pet every now and then. The dog sniffed around the compost pile, looked into the woods and sniffed around there as well, then returned to Solomon's side. That, more than anything else, made Lacy feel a little safer. Eventually, when nothing out of the ordinary happened, she went to bed.

CHAPTER 9

The trip back to Towering Oaks was harrowing. The coldness and feeling of dread had returned two more times during the course of the night, as if whatever was causing it was roaming the woods, seeking out prey. Shireen was positive that if not for their fire they would have become targets. They made sure it was well fed and took turns trying to sleep, but when the feeling returned it was so strong and pervasive that it penetrated into their dreams, forcing them awake.

When the dawn finally broke, they were both exhausted and dreading the long ride ahead, but eager to be on their way at the same time. For the first time in her life as a scout, Shireen was eager to get back to the civilized lands, and to the safety of the Towering Oaks compound. Just looking at Orlando getting ready as quickly as he could was enough to confirm that he felt the same way.

The journey throughout the day was uneventful, and they rode until the sun was starting to drop beneath the horizon and the shadows in the woods were growing long. They discussed carrying on, regardless of the darkness, but Orlando cautioned against it.

"It's too risky. We can't see the ground well enough and neither can the horses. What happens if one breaks a leg? Plus, I really think we need a fire again. Maybe we left whatever that was behind, but I'd rather not chance it."

Shireen had to agree, and they stopped near a stream to make camp. While Orlando gathered up wood for a large fire and started to prepare their evening meal, she tended the horses. After brushing them down, letting them drink their fill from the stream and giving them bags of oats, she brought them into the circle of firelight and hobbled them for the night.

After dinner, they sat near the fire talking about what they had found the day before, and coming to no new conclusions. Whatever had killed the Hairy Men had been terrible and indiscriminate, and almost certainly what had been around them the night before. Remembering that dread, they could understand why the Hairy Men had been running from it.

"But they were fleeing this way," Shireen said.

"So? Whatever it is caught a band of them in the open and they panicked. They probably didn't even think about what direction they were going in."

"But there are no settlements near the border. We know that. *You and I* know that. How many times have we slipped over to check, and came back before they even knew we were there? What was it, ten miles or more to the nearest settlement?"

Orlando tilted his head as he regarded her. "You're right, of course. I hadn't thought of that. Why would they have been down near the border, with nothing to indicate that they were trying to settle there, or were a raiding party, or anything?"

"Because they were already fleeing when whatever it was caught up to them."

"Then what happened up in their lands? Are they all dead?"

Shireen shrugged. "I don't know. But the Hairy Men aren't cowards. If they're running, it's from something pretty bad."

"Should we go back? Try to see what happened?"

"No," Shireen said, a little too quickly for her own comfort. "We need to tell Jediah what we saw. He can make the decision to send us, or someone else, back. But he needs to know."

She tried to make herself believe that that was the only reason she was saying they shouldn't go back, but truth was she was terrified. Whatever that was around their camp the night before had unnerved her badly, to say nothing of the sight of all the dead bodies they had found. If Jediah wanted to send them back, fine, she'd go without complaint, but she wanted to be better armed and prepared.

When darkness fully fell, they sat huddled together staring at the fire. They had ridden quickly during the day and were close to the shaped parts of the Greenweald. Barely into the wilderness, they hoped that whatever the menace was, it wouldn't come this close to civilization.

An hour later, their hopes were dashed. Again, the woods fell silent, an unnatural condition that rang out to the experienced scouts like the loudest alarm bells. The temperature plummeted again, and they sprang to their feet, back to back, swords in their hands.

But whatever it was wouldn't approach the circle of light and heat that their fire cast, although it did linger nearby longer than it had the previous night. The oppressive feeling stayed with them, the air heavy in their lungs until Shireen thought she would scream. The horses stirred against their hobbles and looked around with wild eyes and tosses of their heads. What felt like hours later, it finally passed on, the horses quieted and they sank to the ground, breathing heavily.

"It's going to be a long night," Orlando said quietly.

Shireen could only nod.

The menace returned more often this night than it had the one before. Enough that neither one of them slept, and by the time morning dawned they were both utterly exhausted. They packed up their supplies and groggily climbed on to their horses, eager to be gone from this spot.

Late in the day they rode into the Towering Oaks compound. Giving over their horses to a groom, they staggered to the main building and went inside. Other scouts and officers looked at their condition in surprise.

"What in all the gods' names happened to you?" Lawrence, their commander, asked when they entered his chambers. He was seated behind a large desk that rose in one piece from the floor.

"We need to see Jediah," Shireen said, sinking into an ornately shaped chair, while Orlando collapsed into another.

"You need to give me your report, first," Lawrence said, but rose and poured two cups of cool wine from a bottle on a sideboard for them.

"Come with us, then," Orlando suggested. "Trust us, Lawrence. We need to tell Jediah what we found right away."

"Chain of command…" Lawrence began, but Shireen interrupted him.

"Oh, come on! When have we, either of us, ever been so much as slightly unreliable? You know us. If we're saying we need to report directly to the Head of House, then we need to."

Lawrence pursed his lips as he sat back behind his desk. Finally, he nodded.

"I'll see what I can do. In the meantime, go get some food, rest until I call for you. It shouldn't be long."

Shireen was shaken awake by Lawrence a short time later. She and Orlando had left his chambers and collapsed in chairs in the common area, where she had promptly fallen asleep. From the looks of it, so had Orlando.

56

"Come on," Lawrence was saying. "Jediah will see us."

He led the way out of the command building and to the large central tree of the Towering Oaks compound, which was shaped from a massive oak that soared hundreds of feet into the sky. Like all the Folks' compounds, the central tree was so big that chambers had been formed inside of it, leaving the overall shape intact. The many balconies and platforms made from the living wood gave it a whimsical air, in direct counter-point to the iron-willed Head of House who dwelled there.

Lawrence led them into the tree and up the stairs within, until they came to a conference room. A long table had been shaped from the wood, with chairs pulled up around it. At the moment, the room was empty but for one man, who turned from the window as they entered.

Jediah, Head of House Towering Oaks, could have been shaped from wood himself. He was tall, even for one of the Folk and stood ram-rod straight. His skin was burned the color of old leather from the amount of time spent outside, in contrast to most of his people, who stayed fair-skinned regardless of their exposure to the sun. His long hair was an auburn color and was pulled back from his face and held in place by a golden circlet across his brow. Even here, in the heart of the Towering Oaks compound, he wore his armor. Burnished plate metal that gleamed from being polished, but that showed signs of wear and use. This was no ceremonial armor, but protection that was meant to be worn and put to hard use, and it had been.

Jediah was not known for his sense of humor, or patience. He was no-nonsense, liked to get to the point and expected loyalty and obedience from his troops. It was freely given, as every person under him knew that when trouble was afoot, Jediah was first in line to meet it.

Shireen had met with Jediah several times in the past, and every time had been uncomfortable. The only person that she had ever known that acted as if meeting the Head of House wasn't a big deal was Solomon.

"Shireen, Orlando," Jediah said when they entered. "Sit, both of you. You look like you're about to collapse. Lawrence tells me that you came back from patrol of the northern border with news that you believe should be brought directly to me."

As Shireen had remembered, direct and to the point.

"Yes," she said, sitting down gratefully, Orlando doing the same next to her.

They told Jediah and Lawrence what they had seen to the north, and also of the encounters during the nights. She wasn't sure that she had relayed the feeling of dread that had assaulted them accurately, but Jediah began nodding as they spoke.

When they were done, he asked one question. "There were no marks on any of the bodies?"

"None," Orlando said.

Jediah exchanged a look with Lawrence, who was visibly upset.

"You don't know what it was, do you?" Jediah asked them, his voice low and quiet.

Shireen shook her head, but noticed Orlando start to speak but then stop. Jediah noticed also. "Go ahead," he said.

Orlando looked uncomfortable. "My mother told me stories, but I was sure it was only that. Yet...what I saw, and more, what I *felt*, was an awful lot like what she had told me about." He hesitated, and then lifted his eyes to Jediah. "I think it was a Soul Gaunt."

Shireen started to laugh. Not at Orlando, never that. But at the audacity that he had to jest about this in front of the Head of their House. But then she noticed that neither Orlando nor Jediah were laughing. They were staring at each other and Jediah slowly nodded. The laughter died in her throat.

"Wait a minute," she said. "That's ridiculous. Soul Gaunts aren't real. They're made up stories to frighten children, like Orlando's mother did to him."

"Solomon fought one," Jediah said, turning his gaze to her. "He beat it, too. The only single Folk I had ever heard of doing such a thing."

Shireen felt as if her head was spinning. Part of it was being exhausted, she was sure, but the other part was very much because she was hearing children's stories being discussed by those she respected, as if they were true. But they couldn't be. Soul Gaunts weren't real...they were...weren't they?

Jediah must have seen the confusion and distress on her face.

"Calmly, Shireen," he said. "There are strange things in the world, you know this. Is it so unbelievable that the stories you once heard are based on some truth? It's often the way of things."

"But, no," she protested. "Solomon would have told us if that were true. He wouldn't have been able to keep that secret."

"He kept it secret because I asked him to," Jediah said. "Otherwise, there would have been panic."

"Where did this happen?" Orlando asked, his brows drawn down on his forehead.

"It's not important," Jediah said. "But you should know this. Yours isn't the only report we've had like this. There have been others, reports of strange deaths stumbled across by scouts. But yours is the first time that a Gaunt has come close to one of us. It was getting bolder, and what's more, I fear it may not be alone."

"That's impossible!" Orlando said, but Shireen knew that he believed it fully, but wanted it to not be so.

Jediah grimaced at the outburst.

"I apologize," Orlando said quickly. "I just mean that…how will we defeat them if that's true? One is bad enough, but more?"

"There is only one way that I know of," Jediah said. "We need to convince Jamshir to bring Solomon back."

"He'll never do it," Lawrence put in. "The pressure on him was too great."

"Yes," Jediah said, "I agree. Unless Florian can be made to see reason."

Shireen scoffed, "Good luck with that. He'll never forgive Solomon."

Jediah sighed. "I will try. And if I fail, then may the gods help us all."

CHAPTER 10

Solomon followed Ed as he looked over Lacy's yard. He noted the carefully tended garden, with its neat rows of vegetables all growing tall and strong, and felt a kinship with her. Here was someone who cared about growing things, and that spoke to him. He didn't think he had been a farmer of any sort, knew that he hadn't been as a matter of fact, but there was something inherent in him that responded to it nonetheless.

"What did she mean by that?" Ed asked as they strolled around.

"By what?"

"By saying that it was nice seeing you again." A slight hint of suspicion had entered Ed's voice.

"Oh, that. I went to visit her earlier, before she got out of the hospital."

Ed stopped walking and put his hand on Solomon's arm, bringing him to a halt as well.

"Two questions. Why? And why didn't you tell me?"

Solomon sighed. "I thought that maybe I could help. I had a feeling that I'd run into whatever had attacked her before. I still think that, but I have to admit, I'm not really sure. I didn't say anything, because I don't have any answers. I should have though. Regardless of what I found out, or didn't, I should have let you know. Sorry."

Ed nodded and let go of Solomon's arm.

"Look, you're a free man and Lacy is an adult. If she didn't want you to visit, she could have said so, and if she didn't want you here now, she could have said that too. I've known Lacy for a while, and trust me, she wouldn't have any problem doing that. But let me know if you do anything like that again. That way no one can claim you're interfering with an investigation or anything."

"You got it," Solomon said. "Didn't mean to step on your toes, Ed. Won't happen again."

60

"Good enough. Now come on. Let's check the trunk and see about a couple of flashlights. It's starting to get dark."

The sun was dipping below the tree line and casting long shadows in the yard and into the woods behind the house. Solomon walked back to the police cruiser with Ed and watched as he opened the trunk and rummaged around, coming out with a large, black, metal cylinder.

"Thought I had an extra one back here," he said, handing it to Solomon.

"What are those?" Solomon asked, pointing to a bundle of red, paper wrapped tubes.

"Road flares. You know, for emergencies at night. You light em up, then set them on the ground so that oncoming traffic can see that there's an emergency."

Solomon reached in and picked one up. "Are they very bright?"

"Oh yeah. Don't look directly at it when you light it, or else you'll be seeing spots for an hour."

"How does it work?"

"Simple. Pull the cap off the end, and strike the end of the flare against the rough end. Like lighting a match."

Solomon nodded, took one of the flares and stuck in in the back of his waistband before Ed shut the trunk.

"What do you need that for?" Ed asked. "We've got the flashlights."

"I don't know, really, but I feel more comfortable having a quick source of fire."

They walked back to the edge of the woods where Daisy sniffed around the compost pile. She stopped and raised her head, sniffing the air as well and looking into the forest, but didn't show any signs of alarm. After she had examined the whole thing, she came back to Solomon's side.

"Well, that says there's nothing here tonight more than anything I can think of," Ed said as she returned. "Still, I think we'll hang out here for a while."

"Fine with me," Solomon said. "If it makes Lacy sleep better, I'm all for it. Besides, even if Daisy isn't spooked, I have the feeling that whatever attacked her *is* still around."

They settled down in the front seat of the police car, while Daisy stretched out in the back, eating the sandwiches that Maggie had packed for them and watching night settle in over the yard. When it was fully dark, Daisy rose from where she had been sleeping and sniffed the air coming in from the open front windows. When she did, she got agitated and began to whine and paw at the door.

Solomon and Ed looked at each other, and climbed out of the car. As soon as Solomon opened the rear door, Daisy bolted to the edge of the yard, silently running. Once there, she lifted her nose, sniffed again, and plunged into the forest.

"So much for nothing being around," Ed muttered, as he and Solomon ran after her.

The woods were dark, and the flashlight beams only lit up narrow strips at one time. It was enough to stop them from stumbling over downed branches or undergrowth, as long as they went slow enough. The noise of Daisy crashing through the woods ahead of them continued, and they followed as quickly as they could.

Suddenly, there was barking and growling, followed by a yelp, and then silence fell over the whole area.

"What the hell..." Ed said.

Solomon called for Daisy and walked forward quickly, the flashlight beam picking out the trees and undergrowth in the darkness. He could see his breath from the suddenly freezing air steaming in the feeble glow. Hunting Hounds could take care of themselves, but that yelp worried him. Daisy had been a good friend, and he felt sick thinking that she had been hurt.

There was a crackling noise in front of them and they froze as something moved toward them. The air felt close, despite the chill, and Solomon saw Ed give a huge shiver that ran down his body, but then collect himself and call out, "Whoever that is, stop right there and identify yourself!"

The noise stopped for a second, then started up again, coming closer to the light.

Ed reached for his gun, unclipped the strap and put his hand on it.

"I don't want to shoot," he called out, "but I will if I have to. Now tell me who's there!"

Solomon stood still, trying to peer deeper into the darkness and listening as hard as he could. While he could feel the dread all around them, and knew that Ed was holding it back by force of will, he didn't feel any actual fear himself. He wasn't scared of whatever was coming, but cautious; wanting to know what it was so that he could make a plan for how to deal with it.

A figure entered the light, and Solomon saw a thin, ragged man, with matted hair and a scraggly beard stumble forward.

"Please," he said, his voice husky and raw. "Run…run…please…"

"Luke?" Ed's voice was barely above a whisper. Then stronger. "Luke! What the hell? What are you doing?"

Solomon stared at the new arrival, knowing that something was wrong here. There was something that he was missing.

He was starting to feel that he should be able to remember more, when he felt a horrible, cold presence behind them, and turned in time to see a black, indistinct figure flow up from behind Ed, and two, bone-white, thin hands grab him on each side of his head.

Ed's mouth opened in a silent scream, and his eyes rolled back so that only the whites showed. His hands curled into fists, the one clamped tightly on the flashlight, and his arms started to flail. In the wildly moving light, it was hard for Solomon to keep track of what was happening, but he moved quickly, throwing a punch over his friend's shoulder, aiming at the shape behind him.

His fist met no resistance, but he stumbled forward, knocking into Ed and sending him reeling, breaking the grip of those skeletal like hands. The figure flowed to the side, trying to avoid the light that Solomon was keeping trained on it. Ed lay on the ground, gasping and mewling, but he couldn't turn his attention from the thing in front of him.

It was tall, almost as tall as he himself was, and dressed in a long, flowing black robe, with a deep hood. There was a black mist coming off of the cloak itself, which made the figure indistinct and hard to focus on. The white hands disappeared into black sleeves, and the mist was too heavy near the ground to tell if the thing was actually walking, or if it was truly floating as it appeared to be.

Inside the hood, two eyes glowed a sickly green color, pulsing bright and then dimming. It hissed at him and moved forward again. Solomon attempted to dodge, but it was quick, and a hand shot forward and clamped down on his wrist.

It was as if someone had suddenly plunged his hand into an ice bath. It went numb and he couldn't feel his fingers, the cold beginning to spread up past his wrist. If he didn't break away, the numbness would spread up his arm, and then to his head, and he'd be on the forest floor next to Ed, helpless as the thing finished them off.

And it would. At the pain of the icy touch memories came flooding back. He had faced one of these things before, in a forest much larger and older than this one. It was a Soul Gaunt, and most of his people, the Folk, he now knew, considered them to be legends. But he had fought one. With a flaming sword, he had defeated it and watched as the fire and the steel had consumed it, and it writhed and burned and turned to ash. That day had almost been his last, he knew. The Gaunt had fought fiercely, and it was only luck that had enabled him to turn the tables on it.

But he had no such sword now, no way to kill it, or even to drive it away. For the first time, a small trickle of fear wormed its way up his spine, but that only gave him strength, and he jerked his arm free of the Gaunt's grasp with a sudden wrench. It hissed again and flowed forward, but now he was ready for it.

Reaching behind his back, he pulled out the flare he had taken from Ed's trunk, pulled the cap and struck the end across it, the red light glaring in the night. The Gaunt hissed louder and pulled back, but Solomon was on it. Turning his eyes from the flame, he thrust the flare into the things hood, hoping to blind it.

The Gaunt screamed, a thin keening sound that split the night air, turned and fled, moving like a black cloud over the ground. The flare fell to the forest floor where it continued to sputter and burn, but the Gaunt was gone.

Solomon stood rubbing his numb hand as the feeling slowly started to return. He bent and picked up the flare before it could set the dead leaves alight and watched carefully for any sign of the Soul Gaunt returning. A moment later, the sounds of night life began to return to the woods and the temperature rose to be that of a warm summer's night once more.

The only noise that was out of place was Ed's cries, quiet and plaintive. Solomon ran to him and knelt by his friend, cradling his head in his lap.

"Ed?" he said, speaking softly. "Ed? Can you hear me? It's going to be okay. We'll get you help."

But he wasn't sure if it was going to be okay. A Soul Gaunt could easily hurt one of the Folk with the way it had attacked Ed. Solomon didn't know what that would do to a human.

While its touch had harmed Ed greatly, it had had almost the opposite effect on Solomon. He remembered his past life, and more memories were returning every second. He knew what he was now, and it wasn't human.

He also remembered two very dear friends, Shireen and Orlando, who had backed him up in many a tight spot.

He was not of this world, but belonged to the Greenweald, a huge, ancient forest. He served House Towering Oaks, where he was a soldier, a scout, a platoon leader and anything else that Jediah, the Head of his House, needed him to be. He remembered being exiled, for failing to protect Celia, and letting the daughter of the Head of House Whispering Pines die.

That thought brought a sudden anguish to him, and he bent with the force of it. Not because of his exile, he deserved the punishment. But because he had loved her. And she had loved him. Florian may not have ever given his blessing for her to marry a mere soldier, but the emotions remained.

He was still bent over, fighting his grief, knowing that Ed still needed him, when a noise announced the return of Daisy. He lifted his head and saw her coming closer, limping and cut across her muzzle. She had fought the Gaunt before Solomon had and paid the price, and his heart broke for her loyalty.

Looking around, he saw that Luke had disappeared along with the Gaunt. Solomon had never heard of a Soul Gaunt using a mortal as an ally, or bait, but then again, he had never heard of a Gaunt crossing over between the worlds either. Solomon didn't know what any of it meant, but he did know that he needed to get Ed out of the woods, and back to Lacy's where they could get him help.

He lifted the man in his arms and called Daisy to his side, when he heard yet another noise in the woods. Bracing himself, he prepared to flee from the Gaunt if need be, to carry Ed to safety, when a beam of light appeared through the dark trunks. A moment later, he heard a voice calling out. Lacy had come to find them, and Solomon marveled at the courage of the woman, then strode ahead, the unconscious Ed held in his arms, to meet her.

CHAPTER 11

Now that she knew that Ed and Solomon were outside, Lacy felt a little safer and, to her surprise, found that she would be able to sleep after all. She was yawning as she made her way to her bedroom, and was asleep almost before her head hit the pillow. It was a deep sleep, dark and undisturbed by dreams or noises in the night.

At least until she heard the dog yelp. It was faint, as if it came from far away. Maybe she had imagined it, or dreamed it. She lay there in the dark, staring blindly up at the ceiling, listening for the sound to come again. But even though it didn't, she knew that she had heard it, and that it was from the huge dog that had walked along so calmly at Solomon's side.

Which meant she had to go. The thought sent ice through her veins, even as sweat broke out on her forehead from thinking about it. But if the dog was hurt, then it was possible that Solomon and Ed were as well. If not her, then who would go get them and make sure Ed made it home to Maggie?

She climbed out of bed and hurriedly dressed much as she had two nights before. The flashlight she had used that night was lost in the woods somewhere, but fairly frequent power outages had taught her to be prepared, so she had others. She grabbed one, laced on her boots, and steeling herself, opened the back door to the night air.

Pausing on the deck, she leaned over the rail and looked at Ed's car. It was empty, as she had thought it would be. She peered into the woods, hoping to see the two men returning, but not really expecting it. When they didn't appear, she sighed heavily, and ignoring the pounding in her chest, took the steps down to the lawn, and into the woods.

Immediately, she felt it. That same sense of tightness in the world, of something wrong, and yes, she had to say it, of something evil. It was here again. Whatever had attacked her was still around, which also meant that Luke could be too. She didn't want to believe that he was somehow involved with these strange matters, but she had seen him. Then he had run, and left her to be attacked.

Only…did he? There was no reason for her to still be alive. Whatever had attacked her, had had every opportunity to kill her. So why hadn't it? Did Luke somehow stop it, or convince it not to? That thought brought her little comfort, but at the moment, walking through these dark and forbidding woods, she would take what she could get.

Walking as quietly as she could, she strained her ears, listening for anything that would tell her where Ed was. But the woods were still, and again she was struck by how silent they were, until she heard Ed's voice, calling Luke's name. While she was glad to be vindicated, an even deeper chill came over her. What if that thing followed Luke? So that when Ed saw Luke, it saw Ed?

She began running toward where she thought the voice had come from, although it was hard to be certain at night. After she had taken a few strides, she no longer had to guess. There was the noise of a commotion, and then a sudden bright red light, flaring between the dark tree trunks. A horrible, high-pitched keening wail split the silence of the night and Lacy had to stop and put her hands to her ears, bending over, trying to block it out.

When it stopped, she straightened up, her breathing heavy and labored. She willed herself to go on, to keep putting one foot in front of the other, but it was too hard. Try as she might, she couldn't bring herself to move toward that light and that horrible noise. Her heart felt like it was going to burst from her chest, and all she could hear was the sound of her own panting.

But that old familiar anger surfaced. She thought of Ed, or Solomon, lying on the ground, hurt as she had been, but maybe worse. She thought of that beautiful dog lying somewhere dead, and her fury broke through her fear. There were people who needed help, and she was the one able to give it!

"Come on, Lacy," she growled out loud. "They need you. Move, dammit!"

She forced herself into a slow, cautious run. She'd be no good to anyone if she fell and broke an ankle. As she began to move, the heaviness in the air lessened, until it was finally gone and the normal noises of night in the woods had returned.

Moments later, she could hear a noise in front of her. It was Ed's voice, but it sounded strange; soft and strangled, as if he were struggling to speak.

"Ed?" she heard Solomon's voice. "Ed? Can you hear me? It's going to be okay. We'll get you help."

Lacy slowed down, not wanting to see what was coming. But she pushed herself forward, calling out. "Solomon! It's me, Lacy! Where are you?"

She came through the trees to find Solomon, holding Ed in his arms like a baby.

"Ed's hurt," he said, when he saw her, "Daisy and I are okay, but Ed needs help, right away. We need to get him to the hospital."

"Oh my God," Lacy said. "Come on. Follow me."

She turned and set off through the woods, back toward her house. Solomon followed behind, carrying Ed with no apparent effort, and Daisy came behind him, stopping every few seconds to sniff the air before moving on.

Minutes later they came out of the woods, and Lacy ran for her house.

"Put him in the car," she called over her shoulder. "I'll get my keys."

By the time she came back out, Solomon had Ed laid across the back seat of her car. She climbed into the driver's seat, while Solomon got in the other side, telling Daisy to stay put.

As she pulled out of the driveway, her headlights washed over the woods. There, standing slightly inside the tree line, she saw Luke watching as she drove away. She started to hit the brakes, but remembered Ed lying unconscious in the backseat, and kept moving instead.

It wasn't until she was on the road that she realized how badly her arm was bothering her.

CHAPTER 12

Luke watched Lacy's car pull away, with Ed in the back seat and that tall stranger in the front with her. He felt a quick flash of jealousy at that. The stranger had driven off the dark thing that controlled him now, but only for the moment. It would be back. But still, that was far more than Luke had ever been able to do.

Ever since it had come for him, had touched him and turned him into this…this…whatever he was now, Luke had been in thrall to it. If it demanded that he show himself to Lacy, to get her attention, he had no choice but to do it. He didn't know why he was being used, why he wasn't being killed, or what his master intended, but he did know that he was never going to get away from it.

Even standing there, watching the lights of Lacy's car dim as she drove away, was only allowed because the dark thing had run off. Otherwise, he wasn't quite sure what would have happened.

Luke was turning to go back deeper into the woods when the air temperature started to plummet and he shivered. He took a few steps and then froze, watching as a deeper darkness formed in front of him.

A thin, cadaverous finger touched Luke, right above his sternum, and it was as if cold, white fire spread through his limbs, locking them up and freezing him in place. A couple of tears made it part way down his cheeks before they too froze.

"You have defied me…" a voice hissed from the dark figure in front of him.

"No. No, master," Luke managed to get out.

"Yessss…and after I granted you a favor, too. Bad human."

"No, please, I didn't…"

"You did. You tried to warn them. The human male and one of the Folk. What was that one doing here? Hmmm? Why was I not told about him? He and his miserable hound?"

The finger pressed harder and Luke screamed as the agony shooting through his joints spiked. He would have fallen to the forest floor if he had been able to.

"Please! Master, I didn't know about them! I still don't! I thought that Ed would come alone! He's strong, and you said you needed someone strong…"

Luke felt like dying as he said this. He didn't know what plans the dark thing that ruled over him now had, but it had told him that he needed someone strong to take, not a weak-willed coward like Luke. It had been Luke's idea to get Lacy to lure Ed out here to the woods, where his master could take him, and then maybe he could be free.

But then he had heard Lacy scream, and he couldn't take that. He had begged his master to stop hurting her, to let her go, that it was enough. The thing had laughed at him, but let her go anyway. It had settled with hurting Luke again, but at least Lacy was going to be okay. When it was done with him, Luke had dragged her to the road, where a car was bound to see her. The thing had let him do that, at least.

The dark figure removed his finger from Luke's chest, and he dropped to the ground like a puppet whose strings had been cut.

"I will let you live…for now. You will bring the Folk back to me. You can kill the hound, and the human male. And the female, as well."

"Lacy?" Luke whimpered. "But you said that she'd be…"

"That was before you betrayed me!" It bent down over him. "Now, let it be part of your punishment."

"Part?"

It extended one thin finger, ending in a sharp talon-like nail. Luke watched, frozen, as it inched closer to his left eye. "Part," it whispered.

CHAPTER 13

Shireen was impressed in spite of herself. She loved the Towering Oaks compound, with its massive trees and well-planned layout. She was comfortable with its organization and ease of movement.

But Whispering Pines was different. It was much more…organic, she thought the word would be. While Towering Oaks was laid-out with a martial mindset, Whispering Pines gave itself over more to the aesthetic, and allowed plants to grow where they would, and had more areas dedicated to nothing more than being beautiful. It was pleasant to ride through, even if the reason they were here wasn't.

Orlando and she had accompanied Jediah. Even though the soldiers of Towering Oaks were more than a match for those of Whispering Pines, she still wouldn't allow the Head of her House to ride into the lion's den by himself. And Orlando went where she did.

They were watched as they rode, of course, but more with curiosity than with any open malice. Men and women, dressed in the dark green robes of House Whispering Pines, watched them pass, commenting to each other in quiet tones. Shireen was sure they were wondering what three armed and armored warriors of Towering Oaks were doing here, even if they didn't recognize Jediah himself.

As they approached the large tree that made up the main house of Whispering Pines, a man stepped out of the doors and waited patiently for them to arrive. Shireen recognized Thaddeus, Florian's cousin and chief advisor. Florian was dangerous enough, in an underhanded way, but Shireen had always suspected that Thaddeus was the real snake that needed watching.

"Jediah, Head of House Towering Oaks!" Thaddeus bowed deeply. "To what do we owe this unexpected honor?"

"I must speak with your master. Bring me to Florian."

"Ah, that might be difficult, I'm afraid. Florian is indisposed at the moment, and has asked me to see if I might be able to help you."

Jediah looked down at Thaddeus, then dismounted from his horse. He stepped near to the other man.

"I have no time for your foolish games, Thaddeus. You will bring me to Florian now, or I will leave and return with the full might of House Towering Oaks."

Shireen was surprised to hear Jediah speak like this. Openly threatening to attack another house was cause for war. But Thaddeus was smart, and she hoped that he would take the threat as the dramatic gesture that she was sure Jediah meant it as.

"Jediah," Thaddeus began, an unctuous smile on his face. "Let us not make unwarranted threats. We both know that Jamshir would bring Glittering Birch to bear on..."

"Damn, Jamshir! And damn his House!"

Shireen gasped, and glanced at Orlando, who looked on with wide eyes. Thaddeus stopped talking, obviously taken aback. He regarded Jediah for a moment, his brows furrowed.

"Lord Jediah," he said quietly. "Surely you don't mean..."

"I will speak with Florian," Jediah growled. "If I don't, it won't matter what Jamshir thinks anyway."

Thaddeus bowed again. "Allow me one moment, please. I will speak with Lord Florian and try to impress on him the...urgency...of your request."

He turned and reentered the house, while Shireen and Orlando dismounted also.

"That was risky," Orlando said quietly. "And I don't trust that Thaddeus. I'm sure that Jamshir will have word of this before the day is out."

"Let him," Jediah said. "If he wants, he can appoint another to rule over Towering Oaks in my stead. This is too important."

Shireen stood nearby, the butterflies fluttering in her stomach. To insult Jamshir was one thing, but to be openly defiant of his rule was another. Glittering Birch was powerful, their military prowess almost equal to Jediah's house, but they had an ability that Towering Oaks did not. If Jamshir called for it, all other houses would band together to remove a rogue house. If he made the demand, Towering Oaks would have the choice between accepting a new Head of House, selected by Jamshir, or being totally destroyed. Plus, it was rumored that Jamshir controlled powerful magic, either through his own house, or another tied closely to him.

And Jamshir would destroy them, of that Shireen had no doubt. While he could be noble, and magnanimous at times, he could also be petty and capricious. If he heard of Jediah's words, there was a good chance that he would take the opportunity to order his removal.

She stewed and watched those around them, feeling that they were in the middle of an enemy encampment, while Orlando talked quietly with Jediah. After several minutes had passed, the door to the massive tree in front of them opened, and Thaddeus returned.

"This way, please," the man said. "And please forgive my earlier impudence. I spoke out of turn."

He held the door wide and stepped aside so that they could enter. Again, Shireen found herself impressed, while not wanting to be. The interior was much as the grounds had been. Beautifully laid out, letting the organic nature of the tree influence how the space was used. Yet, still functional and practical.

Thaddeus led them to another set of doors that opened to an interior room lined with shelves full of books. Florian, the head of House Whispering Pines, was at his ease in a chair that flowed out of the floor, shaped from the living wood, and covered with a soft cushion. He looked up as they entered.

"Jediah," he said, rising to his feet and extending a hand. "It's been too long."

"Yes," Jediah answered, ignoring Florian's gesture. "Ever since you insisted on exiling the best of us. I want him back, Florian. More than that, we need him back. All of us."

"The best of us?" Florian frowned. "We've been through this, Jediah, and Jamshir himself agreed. Solomon failed in his duty. A duty that I never wanted him to have, mind you. For that, he deserved death, and you know it. The only reason I even consented to banishment was out of respect for you. But, as I say, we've been through this already. If that's the only reason you're here, then you can leave. Bring the might of your house against us, if you wish. I will not bow to you."

Shireen could see the muscles bunch in Jediah's jaw, and knew that he was holding his anger in check. For her part, seeing the man that was responsible for the exile of her dearest friend was a bitter pill to swallow. She ached to pull her sword from her sheath and bury it in the fool's ribs.

But that would accomplish nothing to help Solomon, or the Folk themselves. And with the threat of the Soul Gaunts being real, every able-bodied soldier would be needed.

With a visible effort, Jediah spoke. "Things have changed, Florian. There is a threat to the Greenweald. To all of us. I believe it is beyond all of us, as well. We need Solomon here."

Florian returned to his seat and gestured for Jediah to take the other. "Thaddeus, refreshments for our guests, please."

Thaddeus went to a side board and poured five crystal glasses of a yellow liquid. He served the Head of his House, then Jediah, Shireen, Orlando, and finally himself. Shireen sipped at the liquor, enjoying the slow burn of it in her throat.

"Now," Florian said. "Tell me, Jediah, what exactly is this threat that has you so worked up?"

"Soul Gaunts," Jediah said.

Shireen heard a gasp and the crack of a crystal glass hitting the wood floor. Thaddeus had dropped his drink. "Surely not," he said, ignoring the spill. "They are nothing more than stories to frighten children with."

"Yet you look frightened enough, Thaddeus," Florian said, a small smile on his lips. "And you're no child. But, why," and here he turned to Jediah, "would this be any concern of mine? Soul Gaunts, even if they have returned, have never been known to attack the Greenweald proper. And if they did, one man, even such a man as Solomon, would make no difference."

"You're wrong on both counts. One did attack the Greenweald, years back. It was defeated, killed even, by the only one of us that I have ever heard of doing so."

"You're going to tell me that Solomon killed a Soul Gaunt by himself? I find that hard to believe on many levels."

"Nevertheless," Jediah said, "it's the truth. One attacked a child walking in the forest. In the Greenweald proper, where she should have been safe. Solomon was riding nearby, hunting. He heard the screams, but by the time he got there, it was too late. The child was drained, but the Gaunt was still there, hiding. It attacked Solomon next, but that was its mistake. Solomon defeated it, with the help of a sword that he had at the time. It was a close call though, and he told me later on that if it wasn't for the magic of the sword, he didn't think he would have made it out."

"Hmm. Sounds unlikely at best. What was this sword that he supposedly used?"

"Solomon called it Justice, because that's what he believed in the most. It's had other names in the past. Flamebringer, Firebrand."

"Ah. So, now you expect me to not only believe in a child's boogey-man, but also in the existence of a legendary sword of fire? One that no one has seen in centuries? I know you're angry about losing Solomon, Jediah, but this is beneath you."

Jediah nodded, and took a sip of his drink. "Shireen, Orlando. Tell Florian what you told me. About what you encountered up north."

Shireen and Orlando took turns telling Florian of their patrol to the northern border, the dead Hairy Men that they had found, and the encounters they had suffered through at night on the way back to their House.

"I'm supposed to believe in this, am I?" Florian said when they had finished.

A flare of anger raged through Shireen. "I do not lie! And neither does Orlando! Believe it as you wish!"

Florian gave her a long, slow look, glanced at Orlando, and then turned back again to Jediah. "Let's say, for the sake of argument that I believe you. What would you have of me?"

"We need Solomon back, of course."

Florian frowned at this. "I know you have a great deal of esteem for the man. And, up until he proved unworthy, and cost my daughter her life, I did too. But I don't believe he's the only one who is capable of defeating a Soul Gaunt. What about this sword of his? He didn't have it when he was sent away. Where is it? Another could wield it as easily, couldn't they? You could do it yourself."

"No one knows," Jediah replied. "He hid it after that fight, saying that it would be kept safe until it was truly needed again. The impression I got was that the only thing he knew of that would cause him to retrieve it, would be another Gaunt."

"I see." Florian took a sip of his liquor and gazed around him. "I still don't see that I need to agree to bringing Solomon back here, though. But I will make one concession. You will send someone, and I will pick someone to accompany them. They can go to that other Earth and ask Solomon where the sword is. I will even consent to them bringing some articles from the Greenweald to make his exile more comfortable. Surely, that's reasonable."

Shireen saw the disappointment in her leader's eyes, but they were unlikely to get a better deal from Florian. At least at this point. Jediah opened his mouth to reply but was cut off.

"Umm," the voice of Thaddeus cut in. "That might not be quite as easy as it sounds."

Florian turned and looked at him. "What are you talking about? Why not?"

Thaddeus cleared his throat and looked uncomfortable. "Understand that, at the time, I was very angry over the loss of Celia."

"Get on with it, Thaddeus," Jediah growled.

Shireen could see the uneasiness in the man. It was in the way he refused to meet any of their gazes, in the way he turned his empty glass around and around in his hands.

"I made an…arrangement…with one of the mages who sent him away. For a price, I asked that one other thing be done. In hindsight, perhaps it was a kindness. Although, I have to admit, at the time, I couldn't imagine a worse punishment."

"What did you do?" Florian asked, his voice gone deadly quiet.

"I…well, I asked that his memory be removed. Totally."

"What?!" The exclamation burst from Shireen before she could control herself. She started toward Thaddeus, her hands aching to get around his throat, but Orlando got in front of her and held her back. "You worm!" she spat. "Wasn't it enough? To deprive of him of the Greenweald? You had to take away the memory of those that loved him? Of us?"

Jediah put his hand on her shoulder. She hadn't even realized that he had risen from his chair.

"Peace, Shireen," he said. She felt a slight sense of calm come over her. Jediah wasn't using any sort of magic on her, such things were beyond him. It was simply his presence, his own calmness which influenced her.

She stopped trying to get past Orlando and slumped against him, not caring about the break in military discipline at the moment. Then, she straightened, glared for a moment at Thaddeus, and returned to her place. Orlando let her go, but she knew he was keeping a careful eye on her.

"Well, Florian," Jediah said, returning to his chair. "It seems that one of your own has made it so that we can't simply ask Solomon to help us out of the goodness of his heart. And knowing him, he might have done exactly that. Now, we need to bring him back. Surely you can see that."

"No," Florian said, his eyes studying the floor in front of him. "No, Jediah. I cannot, will not, do this."

"Come on…" Jediah began, but Florian surged to his feet.

"She was my daughter! My daughter, Jediah! Do you understand that? Do you know how that feels? Of course, you don't! And now you ask me to pardon the man responsible for…"

But this time, it was Florian who was interrupted. A servant rushed in, dressed in the deep green of House Whispering Pines. "My lord…" he began, but stopped when he saw Jediah and the others in the room.

"Speak, man," Florian spat.

"But, my lord, what I have to say is…"

"I said to speak."

"Yes, lord. There's been an attack. A minor house, Rustling Elms."

"An attack?" Jediah said, turning to the man. "What kind of attack?"

"We don't know yet, lord. The bodies were seen, but no one has gone near the place."

"Bodies? More than one? And what do you mean no one has gone near?"

"More than one, yes, lord. And no one has dared to enter the compound. There's something there, something dreadful." He shivered as he said this, and Shireen could easily see the anguish in his face.

"Alright," Florian said. "Enough. We'll get to the bottom of it. Go and collect yourself."

Jediah turned to Shireen and Orlando. "Go. Find out what happened and report back here. Quickly."

"You too, Thaddeus," Florian said.

"Me?" his cousin objected. "Why would I…?"

"Because, I want my own pair of eyes there as well, and I trust yours. Is that enough of a reason?"

"Of course, cousin," Thaddeus sighed.

CHAPTER 14

For only the second time in his life, Solomon visited a hospital. This time however, it was to save the life of his friend, one of the only ones that he had. He had carried Ed inside, and passed him off to an orderly who knew who Ed was. Then he had returned to the waiting room and sat with Lacy.

They didn't speak, only sat, side by side and waited. After what seemed like a very long time, Maggie entered, and ran to them.

"What happened?" she asked, her voice full of the tears that she was holding back. "Is Ed alright?"

"We don't know," Lacy said. "He was at my place, and he and Solomon here went into the woods. Going after something they heard, I guess. I heard Daisy yelp and went looking, but by the time I found them, all I found was Solomon carrying Ed."

Maggie turned to Solomon. "What was it? What happened to him?"

Solomon looked at the distraught woman and knew that he couldn't tell her the truth. His memories were still spotty, but he remembered some of what he had once known about Soul Gaunts. He knew that there was little to no chance that Ed would return. The Gaunt had sucked out a part of his very soul, and with it, a lot of what had made Ed who he was.

"I don't know," he finally said, not able to meet Maggie's stare. "I didn't see it. Daisy ran after something. We heard her yelp, and I took off. I guess I was faster than him. Then, I heard him scream, from behind me…"

Maggie's fingers found his chin, and turned his head so that he looked down at her.

"Tell me," she said again.

"He was lying there, in the leaves, staring into the dark. I didn't know what to do, so I picked him up. I thought maybe if I could get him back to Lacy's."

"You picked up Ed?" Maggie said.

"Yeah, I guess it was the adrenaline, or whatever they say."

"I guess so. I'm going to go see him now."

Maggie turned away and went to the nurse's station. Solomon watched her go, his thoughts in turmoil. Should he have told her what really happened? There was a part of him that wanted to, but he also didn't want to dash any hope that she had. Over the next several days, Ed would get worse before he got better. He would slip away to the very edge of death before he stabilized. And Maggie would need her hope to be able to survive the ordeal. As much as it pained him to lie to someone who had been so good to him, he believed that it was a kindness.

"You're full of it, you know," Lacy said, quietly.

"I know. I had no choice."

He returned to his seat.

"Now what?" Lacy asked. "Are you just going to sit here?"

"What else can I do?"

"You can start by answering some questions. Come on."

She grabbed Solomon's hand and pulled him to his feet. He didn't protest as she led him to the cafeteria, got two cups of horrible coffee and found a table in the corner. The place was fairly deserted at that time of night, so they were able to talk quietly without being overheard.

"Now," Lacy said when they were settled, "you can tell me exactly what's going on. What was that thing? I only know that it was the same thing that got me. And who, or what, are you?"

"Me? I'm a…"

"Spare me. There's something you should know about me, Solomon. I'm a very practical person. I don't know what it is, but there's something about you, and that dog of yours. Something that's unreal. So spill. What is it? Are you an alien?"

Solomon smiled in spite of himself, remembering having had the same thought when he first awoke in that alley. "No," he said. "I'm not an alien. But I don't think the truth is going to sound any less strange."

"No surprise there. Keep going."

"My name really is Solomon, and Daisy really is named Daisy, apparently. But I didn't know her until a few days ago, and she's not really my dog. She's more like a friend."

"Sure, you and every other person with a Lassie fixation think your dog is your friend. That's still not telling me anything."

Solomon took a deep breath, and looked Lacy in the eyes. "I'm not from here. Not from this earth at all, I mean. I'm from a place called the Greenweald, but I was exiled from there several days ago. Until last night, I didn't have any memory of the place, but when the Soul Gaunt touched me, it brought some of my memories back."

"Uh huh. And I'm supposed to believe that, more than thinking the…what did you call it? A Soul Gaunt? Whatever that means. That that thing scrambled your brain the way it did Eds?"

"That would make more sense, I have to admit. But no. Look at me Lacy, you know I'm not making this up."

Solomon watched her watch him. Her eyes searched his, moving back and forth between them. Her brow was furrowed, and he could see the conflict within her. Not wanting to believe what she found that she was.

"Ridiculous," she finally muttered, dropping her eyes and taking a sip of her coffee. Solomon stayed quiet, letting her process what she was feeling.

"Fine," she finally said. "Let's say I believe you. Why did you get exiled from this other place? Are you like a criminal?"

"I guess you could say that. I failed in my duty. That was enough."

"Failed in your duty to do what?"

Now it was Solomon's turn to fall quiet. He took a sip of his own coffee, grimacing at the bitter taste. "I failed to protect someone important. And because of me, she died." His voice hitched on the last word, and he sipped at his coffee again to hide his embarrassment.

"Who was she?" Lacy asked, but her voice had softened. Solomon couldn't answer, not at the moment. His throat felt thick and closed up. "Never mind," Lacy said, "we can come back to that later. Right now, maybe we should talk more about Ed?"

Solomon nodded, and Lacy reached across the table to pat his hand. "So then tell me. You said that thing was called a Soul…what was it?"

"Gaunt."

"Right. A Soul Gaunt. So, what is that exactly? Not like we have them around here…or at least we didn't."

"They're a story to frighten children who won't go to bed when they're supposed to. Most of the Folk in the Greenweald don't even think they're real, but they are. There are few of us who have actually seen one, let alone lived to tell the tale."

"Like a bogeyman for you guys. But they're obviously real. So what are they?"

"No one knows for sure what they really are, spirit or flesh. They can suck the soul from a body, simply by grabbing hold. The damage is usually…irreversible. Your arm still hurts, right? I hate to say it, but it probably always will. It killed something within you when it grabbed you. If it had kept going…"

"Wait," Lacy said. "Are you telling me that Ed isn't going to get any better?"

Solomon had feared that Lacy would pick up on that right away. She was obviously too smart for the comment to have passed her by. He sighed. "No. I don't think he will. But I didn't have the heart to say that to Maggie."

Lacy sank back, her hands wrapped tightly around her coffee mug. She stared at Solomon, then let her gaze wander around the room. Her eyes glistened for a moment, before the tears slowly poured over and ran down her cheeks. She didn't sob, or wail, she just sat quietly and let the tears flow.

"Then why am I alive?" she asked after a few minutes had passed.

"It let you go. I don't know why. For some reason, it got interrupted and wasn't able to finish with you."

"Luke," Lacy said. "It had to have been. No one else was around."

"It could have been. There's a connection between Luke and the Gaunt that I can't figure out. It's not like anything I've heard of before."

"Then how do we kill this thing?" Lacy's voice had taken on an edge of anger. "I'm not a violent person usually, but this thing hurt me, hurt Ed, and has Luke. Unless you're going to tell me it has some other use, then I want it dead."

"Well, that takes some doing. Only one has ever been killed that I know of."

"Who killed it, then? How do we talk to them?"

"You are. I killed one, long ago."

"Then let's go! Let's get rid of this thing!"

Solomon smiled slightly. He had no doubt that Lacy would rise from the table, drive to her home and take off into the dark woods after it. Despite her obvious fear and hurt arm, she was ready to do battle.

"It's not that easy, Lacy. I only managed to do it because I had something to use against it. I know this will sound absurd to you, but I had a sword. A special one. Even with that, I barely made it. The battle almost killed me, too."

"But it didn't get your soul?"

"No, but that's not their only weapons. They have sharp claws, and they're strong and fast. And they can use actual weapons as well. They're smart, Lacy. They're not like animals."

"Then we need your magic sword, or whatever it is." A hitching laugh escaped from her. "I can't believe I just said that. This can't all be real."

"I know it's a lot," Solomon said. "I'm surprised you're taking it this well, to be honest."

"I don't know that I am. I think I'm so angry, and worried about Ed, that I haven't let it sink in yet. Give me time. But while I'm still in this weird place, let's go get your sword and finish this thing off."

"Well, that's a problem. See, I don't remember where it is."

"What? How do you forget where you put a magic sword?" She actually laughed this time. "This is insane."

"I guess taking my memories was part of my punishment. For whatever reason, the Gaunt's touch brought some of them back to me, but not all of them. There's all sorts of things I don't remember…" He fell quiet, trying to rack his brain for things that he didn't know.

"What if I get a gun and shoot the damn thing?" Lacy said suddenly.

"I don't think it will work. Most weapons pass right through them somehow. I would imagine that a bullet would too."

"Then we have no choice. We need to get your sword, which I'm guessing isn't around here."

"No," Solomon said. "Until my exile, I had never been to this earth. It's somewhere in the Greenweald. That much, I'm sure of."

"So we go to the Greenweald. How do we get there?"

Solomon spread his hands and shrugged. "I have no idea. It's why they could exile me here."

They fell silent, Lacy looking down at the table in front of her, her coffee cup still held between her hands. Solomon took a sip of his, and set the rapidly cooling drink on the table.

"Let me go think for a while," he said. "Maybe more will come to me. Besides, I need to go get Daisy."

"Oh my God! Daisy! I forgot about her!"

"It's okay," Solomon reached over to pat her hand. "She's fine. She's a Hunting Hound, and even a Soul Gaunt would have a hard time catching her if she didn't want it to. But still, I need to head back."

"I'll drive you. But let's stop in and say goodbye to Maggie first."

"Wait. What about the police? Won't they want to talk to us?"

"Oh, I'm sure they will. But if they're not here yet, they can find us out at my place. I'm not hiding from them."

"Fair enough. But, I'm not sure what to tell them."

"Come on," Lacy said, rising to her feet. "We can work that out on the way."

CHAPTER 15

As Lacy drove through the early morning hours, she kept studying the overly tall, thin man in the passenger seat, and going over the things he had said. It was insane. This guy had shown up in town, and was suddenly a "friend" of Ed's, and everyone accepted it. How did they know that he wasn't some sort of scam artist, or worse, that he didn't have something to do with the attack on both her and Ed?

But she did trust him. She didn't know why, but there was an almost palpable aura about him that made you think he was on the level. That every word he said was true. And it wasn't a slimy, used-car salesman type of feeling, like he was convincing you of something. It was a genuine, this-is-the-truth, kind of feeling.

Which only made the whole thing more odd. Of course, considering that she actually had been attacked by this Soul Gaunt thing, it might be easier for her to believe than for others. But that same instant trust that Solomon generated seemed to affect everyone. She glanced at him again, saw that he was watching the dark world outside the window pass by, and hoped that he was truly as good as he appeared to be.

"Hey," she said, breaking the silence, "so, not to bring up a sore subject, but if we're going to be in this together, then I should know some more, right? Like, what's this about failing in your duty stuff? And about you killing one of these things before?"

Solomon looked over at her, his expression unreadable. "We shouldn't be in this together, Lacy. A Soul Gaunt is…. horrible. By any definition of the word. I'll go after it."

"You really think I'm going to let that happen? It's got Luke. He may have been a pretty messed-up guy at times, but he was my messed-up guy. I'm going too. End of story."

"Okay," Solomon said, but she could hear the amusement in his voice. Was he laughing at her?

"It's not funny!" she said.

84

"I'm not laughing at you, Lacy, I promise. The exact opposite. You impress the hell out of me, to tell you the truth. It's not everyone, be they Folk or human, who would willingly go back into the forest knowing that a Soul Gaunt was around, and what it was capable of."

"Oh. Well. Thanks then, I guess."

She felt a flush of pride when Solomon praised her. She glanced over at him again, unsure of her feelings. There was an attraction there, of course. Solomon was tall, strong, and very good-looking. But the attraction wasn't sexual, or even romantic. There was no thought in her mind of trying to bed him, or of settling down with him. Instead, it was more that you wanted to be near him, in his circle, and part of his life. You wanted him to think well of you, and be the type of person that he would want around him. To be a better person, in short. It was a weird, disturbing feeling, and Lacy wasn't entirely sure that she liked it.

But there was also no fighting it. Unless she was actively thinking about it, striving against it almost, it just was.

"Anyway," she said, shoving those thoughts to the side. "I still need to know more. So which will it be? Fight with the Soul Gaunt, or failure of duty, whatever that means."

She heard him sigh. "Neither are pleasant memories, and both are somewhat incomplete. Which one would you like to hear about first?"

Lacy considered for a moment. "Tell me about this failure of duty thing. The Soul Gaunt can wait for now. I know you need the sword for that anyway."

Solomon stayed quiet, gazing out into the pre-dawn darkness. Lacy was about to prod him, when he started to talk.

"I loved her. Loved her more than I thought it was possible to ever love anything. But I shouldn't have. She was above me. My station, I mean. She was the daughter of a Head of House. Whispering Pines to be exact. And I was a soldier, or a scout, or whatever my House needed me to be at the time. I lived to serve, always had.

"But Florian, the Head of House Whispering Pines, decided that his daughter Celia needed a protector. She was head-strong, and didn't want to listen to her father, anymore that I imagine young people here want to listen to their parents. So she went where Florian told her not to go, and associated with people that he forbid her to talk to, things like that. Finally, he realized that he couldn't control her, so he thought to keep her safe instead."

85

He stopped talking, and Lacy saw him look down at his hands. The expression on his face was almost one of accusation, as if he were blaming his own appendages for their failure.

"Safe. Ha. She would have been better with a soldier from her own house. But my House, Towering Oaks, is known to be the best. We have the best soldiers, the craftiest scouts, the most cunning strategists. So why would Florian not request someone from there to guard his most precious thing in the world?

"Jediah, the Head of my House, loved Florian like a brother. He said that he wanted Celia guarded by the best, and so he chose me. I'm not a very humble person at times, I guess, or at least I wasn't then. I agreed with Jediah, I was the best. I would keep her safe, and at the same time, maybe be able to tone down some of her adventures.

"That didn't happen. Celia was indeed head-strong. And reckless. I don't think she was willfully so. She was one of those people that don't believe anything bad could ever happen to her. Maybe it came from being raised in luxury as the only daughter of the Head of a House. Or maybe she was born that way. I don't know. But she was right about one thing, she really was safe most of the time.

"That 'element' that Florian was worried about? Typical kids, who maybe got into a little too much wine, or laughed when their elders thought they should be solemn. Like I say, typical kids. And here I was, much older, and with a reputation. I tried to stay out of the way, blend in to the background. I wanted to give her space."

He paused and stared out the window again.

"But that's not what she wanted, was it?" Lacy said, her voice low and gentle.

"No. As it turned out, it wasn't. Celia was beautiful, a fact that I tried very hard to ignore. She was a kid. Or at least that's what I kept telling myself. For you, she would have been older than anyone alive here on this earth. Much older. But for us, she was still young.

"She was also smart, and funny, and full of life. We grew closer, which I guess is no surprise. How many stories have been told about that? She begged me to teach her how to fight, to use a sword, and to track a foe through the Greenweald. I didn't want to at first. She was the daughter of a Head of House, and her lot in life would be to take on that role herself one day. She more needed to be taught how to dance, and finances, and…well, all the things that it takes to run a House. Don't ask me about that stuff."

"None of that for you, huh?" Lacy said.

"No, that wasn't my role. I was there to support Jediah and Towering Oaks, but never to run it. It wasn't my place."

"Your world seems almost feudal."

"I guess in some ways, it is. We've lived like that for so long that I wouldn't know any other way. But, one can work their way up. You can start as a simple field worker and through hard work, become almost anything else."

"But not a Head of House," Lacy said.

"No, probably not. It's not unheard of, but very rare. That position has pretty much become hereditary."

"Got it. So, back to Celia. She got her hooks into you pretty good, huh?"

"She did," Solomon laughed. "She did, indeed. I taught her to fight and anything else she asked of me. The day came when she stumbled as we sparred, fell into my arms, and then, well…"

"I get it," Lacy interrupted. "I don't need details, thanks. But I'm also willing to bet that 'stumble' was no accident."

"No, probably not. As I said, Celia was both smart and headstrong. We tried to hide this new facet of our relationship, of course, but that never works, and it wasn't long before Florian found out. He was furious, as I would have expected him to be. He demanded that Celia and I refrain from seeing each other, and that Jediah assign someone else to watch over her, which he did.

"It didn't matter. We found ways to be with each other. Her new bodyguard was good, but, I was me. I knew how to slip away from him, avoid being seen, and steal moments with Celia. It was exciting, and dangerous, and we loved every minute of it."

He stopped again, his face turned toward the window. They were getting close to Lacy's home.

"Solomon," she said. "It's okay if you don't want to say anymore. I'm sorry, I shouldn't have pried."

"No, it's fine. It feels good to talk about it somehow. It's just that now that I remember, I realize that this all happened such a short time ago.

"We went swimming. Such a simple, innocent activity, right? I had gotten us away from Whispering Pines, and took us deep into the

Greenweald, to a place that I knew. I used every trick that I had to keep her bodyguard from following, and I expected that we would be alone for hours. The pool we came to was deep and clear, and looked so cool and inviting. We stripped off our clothes, and dove in.

"It was an ideal moment, like one of those that poets write about. Did you ever have one of those? We swam, and laughed, splashed, and made love. I had never been so happy in my life."

He stopped again. Lacy glanced over and saw him swallow hard, but this time, she stayed quiet.

"Then, I felt it. Something grabbed my ankle, like a cold hand, and yanked me under. I yelped, swallowed water, and came up sputtering. Whatever it was, it had let me go. Celia looked at me, a laugh beginning, and then she was gone. One moment, I was looking at her, and the next, she was pulled under the water.

"I dove, deep. Deeper than that pool had any business being. I saw her, struggling against something that was pulling her down. I reached her, grabbed her arms and pulled as hard as I could. Whatever it was, it pulled against me, and I was afraid that I'd pull her arms right off, but I held on. The thing dragged her down anyway, and me with her."

He stopped, sighed and continued with a hitch in his voice.

"I saw it. When her air ran out. The bubbles came out of her mouth, rising through the dark water. Her eyes closed, it looked like she tried to scream. But I still held on, being dragged down too. I was going with her, wherever it was. Then, I couldn't hold on any longer. My chest ached and against my will, I opened my mouth to draw a breath. The water rushed in, and it hurt, so badly. I'm sure I tried to scream too.

"The next thing I knew, I was lying at the side of the pool. My throat hurt like it was on fire, and I could hardly catch my breath. But I dove back into that pool, determined to be with her. I found the bottom only a couple of feet below where I could stand. Muck and mud, the occasional fish swimming past. I dove over and over, searching every inch for some deeper section, some passage that led further down. But there was nothing. Whatever it was, whatever water spirit had taken Celia, it had closed the door behind it."

"Why did it let you go?" Lacy asked.

"I have no idea. Maybe it was cruel. Maybe I didn't taste good. Who knows?"

"And for that, they banished you? But it wasn't your fault!"

"It was. I failed her, when she needed me the most. And, had I obeyed orders, she never would have been at that pool in the first place."

Lacy fell silent. She didn't want to admit it, but Solomon had a point. She turned into her driveway, the lights picking out the trees as she drove up the hill toward her house.

Daisy was sitting in the driveway, tongue lolling out of her mouth, waiting patiently for them. She stood and barked once, as they pulled in.

"Hey," Solomon said, all trace of sadness gone from his voice. "There she is! Told you she'd be okay."

"Yeah, you did," Lacy said, as Solomon climbed out of the car. She watched as he and Daisy ran to each other. The dog jumped up, tackling him, and they fell to the ground, roughhousing, and Solomon laughing.

CHAPTER 16

Thaddeus rode silently behind Shireen and Orlando. He knew what they thought of him, but that was fine. Let them think that he was a sneak and a serpent. He served his house, and Florian, with honor, and did the things that were asked of him. Just because he wasn't a soldier, didn't make him any less.

Still, he had to admit to a certain degree of envy when he regarded the two of them. They held themselves straight and alert in the saddle, ready for action at a moment's notice, even here in the heart of the Greenweald, where they should be perfectly safe. Considering where they were headed and why, Thaddeus was glad of that. It wasn't that he was any slouch himself, and had a fair amount of magical aptitude, but he preferred to know what he was up against first. Better to be able to prepare. If that somehow made him a snake, then so be it, but he saw no difference between what he did, and what the scouts of Towering Oaks did. Information was information, no matter how it was collected.

"What do you think we'll find?" he asked, more to see what the two would say than out of any expectation that they would know.

"Death," Shireen answered immediately. She didn't so much as glance back at Thaddeus.

"What? The whole House? Come now. Rustling Elms is a minor house, but still, they're not helpless."

He saw Shireen glance at Orlando, who sighed, and slowed his horse's pace so that he dropped back next to Thaddeus.

"Were you listening to us at all? Back at Florian's? We told you both what we had encountered. Did you think we were making it up?"

"No, I'm sure you weren't. But a few dead Hairy Men doesn't equal a whole House of the Folk being wiped out."

"It wasn't only the Hairy Men. It was what *we* felt on the way back, also."

"Yes, but don't you think…"

"What?" Orlando's voice had grown cold.

"I mean no offense. Seeing what you did, I mean, it would have upset me too. But isn't it possible that what you felt was somewhat…magnified, maybe…by what you had seen?"

Orlando turned his attention back to the path that led through the trees. "Possibly," he said after a moment. "Don't think that I hadn't considered the possibility. You haven't fought them, so you wouldn't know, but the Hairy Men aren't push overs. They're fierce fighters, and they seem to have no fear. The ones we saw? They were terrified before they died. So yes, it was possible that seeing that played into how we felt those nights."

"No," Shireen said from in front of them. She still hadn't turned to look at him, but Thaddeus knew that she had been listening. "It didn't. It was disturbing seeing those Hairy Men like that, sure. But what we felt those nights was real. Don't downplay it, Orlando."

"I'm not," Orlando replied. "You didn't let me finish. The thing is, Thaddeus, that I have thought about that, quite a bit. That dread that we felt was real, and finding out that it was probably a Soul Gaunt confirms it, doesn't it?"

"Well, finding out that it was a Soul Gaunt is still up in the air if you ask me. I know you feel that it was, and I'm not disparaging that, but I have a hard time believing that a child's tale has come to life."

"I can understand that. It never even occurred to either of us that that's what we were facing. But there is one thing to consider."

"And what's that?" Thaddeus asked.

"Florian's reaction. He didn't seem overly surprised to hear that one was real, only that it had come into the Greenweald."

Thaddeus had to pause. Orlando was right. Florian hadn't seemed at all surprised, and had even mocked Thaddeus's own reaction to the news. He knew that Florian was privy to information, as Head of House, that he himself wasn't, but still, he would have thought that his cousin would have told him of something like that.

"Yeah," Orlando said. "It's something to think about. Steel yourself, Thaddeus. We'll be there shortly."

He clucked at his horse and moved ahead to ride next to Shireen again, leaving Thaddeus alone with his thoughts. Suddenly, the Greenweald seemed a little darker and less safe than it had only a few moments before.

An hour later, they came to House Rustling Elms. It was more closely laid out to Thaddeus's own House, then to Towering Oaks. Rustling Elms wasn't known for anything in particular. Merchants, who made smart trades and had more contact with those outside of the Greenweald than most, they were also one of the younger Houses. Or at least they had been.

The first body they found lay outside of the compound. A young man, who had obviously been fleeing, and been cut down from behind. Orlando and Shireen dismounted, leading their horses slowly over to the dead man. Thaddeus told himself to climb down from his horse also, but found that his body didn't want to obey.

Shamed by his own lack of nerve, he called out. "What do you think? Sword or knife?" It was an inane question, and his voice came out much louder than he had intended.

"Quiet, you fool," hissed Shireen. "If you want to see, climb down here and look for yourself. Otherwise, keep your mouth shut and let us work."

Thaddeus saw Orlando gently place a hand on Shireen's arm and shake his head. He stood and walked over to Thaddeus. "There's no shame if you want to stay out here. This isn't going to be pretty. Shireen and I, we've seen things before. Not like this, maybe, but enough. But that's not your role."

He knew that Orlando meant it kindly, but his words stirred up resentment in Thaddeus. He wasn't some coward to be molly-coddled and pacified. His cousin, the Head of his House, had ordered him to accompany them so that he would have an account of what had happened that he could trust. Thaddeus wouldn't let that trust be in vain.

He swung out of the saddle, not replying to Orlando, and walked over to look at the body. He swallowed hard as he felt his gorge rise. The young man had been split open, and the bone of his spine showed clearly. Organs trailed out of the cavity, as if something had sliced him open, then reached in and pulled as the man tried to run. The sweat broke out on Thaddeus's brow, but he forced himself to look, then turned his gaze to the compound.

There were more bodies. Lots of them, scattered around. The ground inside the compound was soaked with blood, and everywhere that he looked he saw nothing but death. Shireen's prediction of what they would find had come true with a vengeance.

92

He wiped the sweat from his brow and followed the two scouts as they slowly walked deeper into the compound, leaving their horses tethered outside, away from the young man's body. Everywhere that Thaddeus looked, there were dead Folk. Most looked as if they had been savagely attacked, although every so often, they would encounter a body with no marks on it at all, but still very much dead.

"Like we saw up north," Shireen said, standing up after she had squatted next to a middle-aged woman, who was propped up against the low wall of a garden, her sightless eyes staring at nothing, and a terrible expression of fear frozen on her face. "It's like she sat here and died of fright."

"Or something took her," Thaddeus said, his own voice sounding hollow in his ears.

"What do you mean?" Orlando asked.

"The stories, surely you remember. They're called Soul Gaunts because that's what they do, right? They take your soul. Like hers." He indicated the woman in front of them with a quick nod, then turned away. But no matter where he looked, death waited.

"Why though?" Shireen said. "Why would it take one person's soul, but cut down others? It doesn't make sense."

"It was hungry," Thaddeus said, and was horrified to hear a slight giggle issue from his mouth. "I'm sorry. It's not funny. I just don't...I can't..."

Orlando put a hand on his shoulder. "No one thinks you're taking this lightly. What do you mean it was hungry, though?"

"Isn't it obvious? Why else would one take a soul? It must be feeding on it. Maybe this one was the last victim, so it could take its time with her."

He half turned his head so that he could see the woman, without looking fully at her. "There," he said. "Look at the sides of her head. Her hair."

Orlando squatted down near the body again, and gently touched the hair near her temples. The woman had been blonde, but there, and only there, her hair had turned white. "Ah, I missed that. Good eyes, Thaddeus. But what does it mean?"

"I have no idea," he responded. "But I'm willing to bet you'll find more marks like that if you look for them."

The two scouts looked at each other and then started walking slowly again, spreading out, but staying within sight of each other. Their hands were never far from their sword hilts, and as much as he felt like running from the place, Thaddeus followed along.

"Here's another," Shireen said, after a few moments. "No wounds, but what almost looks like frozen spots on each side of his head."

The continued to search, finding more of the same as they moved deeper into the compound. By the time they were approaching the central tree that held the main domicile of House Rustling Elms, they had found several more.

Thaddeus had found the most recent himself, and was examining the marks on the young boy's head when a thought occurred to him. "Why would one Soul Gaunt need to feed this much? If that were so, then wouldn't we have known about them well before this?"

There was no response from either Shireen or Orlando. He looked up, expecting that they had moved on and hadn't heard his question. Instead, they were standing only a few paces away, their faces blank as they looked at the center of the Rustling Elms compound.

"What is it?" he said, standing and moving next to them.

Then, he followed their gaze, and saw what had stopped them so completely. The tree in front of them was a giant, as were all central trees in Greenweald compounds. It had been lovingly tended to and gently shaped over the course of years, if not centuries. While it didn't have the size and sense of immense age of some of the trees from the older Houses, it still was a magnificent specimen.

Or at least it had been. Now, it was dying, and seemed to get worse as they watched. The bark, normally a gray color, was turning black, and peeling off. Fungus was growing on the trunk and mushrooms sprouted from the ground around it. The leaves were curling, and falling in great drifts that piled against the base.

The doors were firmly shut, and the windows had all been shuttered, so that there was no way to see to the inside. Thaddeus swore that he could see a shiver go through the tree, and his heart broke to see such a wonderful thing be so devastated.

"We need to go in, don't we?" he whispered.

"I'm not sure about that…" Orlando said.

"Come on," Shireen said, but Thaddeus heard the strain in her voice. "We need to know."

The three of them slowly approached the entrance to the gigantic tree. Shireen reached out to the handle of one of the double doors and pushed. The door opened a slight amount and then stuck firmly. Orlando, and then finally Thaddeus, helped to push, and with much exertion, it finally opened enough to allow them to slip through the gap, one after another.

Putting a finger to her lips, mostly for his benefit, Thaddeus was sure, Shireen wiggled into the opening. Orlando quickly followed her, leaving Thaddeus to bring up the rear.

He looked at the dark opening, willing himself forward. Every fiber of his being screamed at him not to go inside. There was only death, pain, and madness there. The massacre out here was better than what waited in there.

But the two scouts from Towering Oaks had gone in. Could he do any less?

He took a deep breath, and forced himself to slip through the opening, into the darkness.

CHAPTER 17

Florian poured another drink and brought it to Jediah. "Well," he said, taking a seat in a chair next to him. "What do you think they're going to find?"

"You know what they're going to find," Jediah growled, and tossed down his drink in one gulp.

Florian frowned and sipped at his own drink. He didn't want to admit that Jediah was probably right. He knew both Shireen and Orlando, by reputation at least. Neither of them were proven to flights of fancy. If they said that something had disturbed them that greatly on their patrol, then something had. And he knew of nothing else that it could be.

"Jediah," he began, but then faltered, and covered it with another sip of his drink. How had it come to this? Jediah was at one time his closest friend. As young men, they had hunted together, drank together, and even occasionally pursued the same woman. Even when they got older, and became the Heads of their Houses, they had remained close, and the bonds between Whispering Pines and Towering Oaks had been firm.

But then…Solomon. Jediah hadn't been exaggerating when he had called Solomon the best of them. The likes of him hadn't been seen in the Greenweald since the days of old, the age of heroes, who had taken a wild, brutal land, and changed it into something more civilized and pleasant. Most said that Solomon was reborn from that age, come again at a time that the Greenweald would need him, although no one knew quite why that was.

Maybe they would now.

But no, Solomon was no great hero after all. He had let Florian's only daughter, the light of his eyes, die. He had disobeyed Jediah's direct order, and continued to see her, and taken her to that accursed pool…

He knew he wasn't being entirely fair. If someone had tried to keep him from Shanta, Celia's mother, he would have moved heaven or hell to be with her. If he was being honest, his objection to them being together wasn't so much that she was the daughter of a Head of House, and Solomon merely a soldier. It was more that for the first time, Celia was looking at someone else the way she had always looked at her father. Like a hero.

Except that in Solomon's case, he really was.

And yet, Celia was gone. And unlike Solomon, no one was here begging him to allow her to come back. They couldn't. That option wasn't available for her, so why should it be for him?

"We need to come together on this," he said, finally. The words felt sticky in his throat and he had to force them out. Why was this so hard? He rose and poured himself another drink, then turned and filled Jediah's cup again as well. He needed to slow down, or the liqueur would go to his head, and that wasn't what was needed right now.

"Do you honestly think that's going to matter?" Jediah said quietly. "It's a Soul Gaunt, Florian. You know what that means."

"Yes, it means we hunt it down and kill it. It's not as if that's never been done before."

"No, that's true. It has. And how many died before we found it and were able to put it down? How many died trying to do just that?"

Florian didn't respond. He remembered it well. All those years ago, the Soul Gaunt that had come into the Greenweald had wreaked havoc. It had stayed hidden by day, only coming out at night, and blending into the darkness. It had oozed into the lesser homes of the Folk, claiming victims at random. Finally, it had been stumbled upon by pure, dumb luck, by a soldier who only had time to scream before he died.

Others had run to the noise, bearing torches and surrounded the thing, but it was fast, and deadly. It wielded a long, cold sword, that sliced through the armor of the Folk as if it were paper. Its touch caused agony, and its breath made strong men quail. Before Jediah himself had delivered the final blow, there was a ring of dead bodies around it.

Most weapons hadn't touched it. Only those that had been blessed, or that had been forged with the assistance of a mage seemed to have any effect on the thing. And then only barely. Scratches. But over time, enough of those scratches had finally done it in.

"I remember," Florian said. "I remember that you finally killed it. We'll do the same thing again now. We know more now. We know how to fight it, hopefully how to find it."

"Tell that to the children who will lose parents. Or worse, the parents who will lose children. You, above all others, know how that feels. Would you have others go through that also? When you don't have to?"

"So I should let the killer of *my* child come back home? On the off chance that he could actually help?"

"Off chance? You don't understand. Solomon is our *only* chance of stopping this thing without losing a lot of people. Do you know how many died when that one came in? But when he went after the next one? One. Just one. Solomon tracked it, knew where it would go, and confronted it, on his own. And he beat it."

Florian grimaced. "I find that hard to believe. I was there when we…"

"I know you were there," Jediah interrupted. "Which is why what he did should mean more to you. Do you think that I lie to you, Florian? Why? You were my…"

He trailed off and took a drink himself. Florian watched him, realizing that his old friend was as uncomfortable reliving the past as he was.

"No. No, I don't think you lie to me." He sank back into his chair. "And you were my closest friend, too. But you ask a lot of me."

"Yes, I do. I don't ask it for me, although I'd be more than happy to see Solomon returned to us. I ask it for all of us."

Florian rubbed his eyes, and set his glass down. His head was starting to ache and the liqueur wasn't helping. Dammit. He didn't want the man to come back. He didn't want the killer of his daughter to live among them again.

But…

But, he knew that wasn't fair either. Solomon didn't kill Celia. Not really. Whatever force was in that pool. That was what had killed her. Solomon was guilty of loving her, and disobeying, and failing her. He saw the man's face when he had come back here, to this compound, not to his own, to tell Florian man to man what had happened. He had taken the blows that Florian had rained on him, and never tried to strike back.

When he had summoned the guards, Solomon had never resisted, and had not even offered up a defense in front of Jamshir, other than saying that he had failed her. For all of his abilities, for all of his greatness, when Florian had looked on him that day, he had seen a broken man.

"Dammit," he said again, quietly, but aloud this time. "It's not fair."

"No," Jediah said, and sat down in his own chair. "It's not. She was too bright a light to go out so early. I never said it, but I was sorry, Florian. I still am."

Florian nodded, not looking at his one-time friend. "If I agree to this, what next?"

"I don't know. I don't know how the spell worked, or how to reverse it to get him back. Do you?"

"No, one of Jamshir's pet wizards did it. But Thaddeus might know something. He was always more attuned to that kind of thing than I was."

"Then, we wait. Shireen and Orlando will return soon with news, I'm sure. We'll hear what they have to say, then go see Jamshir."

"Jamshir? Why? If I've agreed to let Solomon back, and Thaddeus can work the magic, then why involve him?"

"He's still our liege lord," Jediah said. "He needs to know that a Soul Gaunt is loose in the Greenweald, if he doesn't already. I have a feeling that he always knows much more than he lets on. Plus, he should know that we've agreed that we need Solomon."

Florian nodded. "Yes, I guess you have a point. Still, something about it…" He stopped, and took another sip of his drink.

"Yes?" Jediah said. "You were saying?"

"How far can I trust you?"

"You always could have. Even after Solomon, I wouldn't have betrayed you, or your confidence."

Florian hesitated and looked around to make sure that none of the servants were within earshot. "I'm sure it's treasonous to say this, but I don't entirely trust Jamshir."

To his surprise, Jediah smirked. "Go on."

"Didn't you ever have the feeling that he was working for the good of his own House, and for his own gain, more so than worrying about what was good for the Greenweald?"

"I've thought that for years. Jamshir is not the man that his father was."

"No, he isn't. Still…I don't think he's necessarily corrupt. More…selfish, maybe?"

"I think that's a good assessment. And if this was anything other than a Soul Gaunt, I'd say to forget him. We'd handle it and fill him in later. But if this thing gets away from us, he does need to know."

"You're right, of course. I'm letting my own prejudices get in the way of the greater good."

He rose, decided on one more glass of the liqueur and refilled Jediah's as well.

"Here's to old friends and allies reunited again" he said, raising his glass.

"About damn time," Jediah replied and took a more lingering sip this time.

CHAPTER 18

Solomon was much happier to see Daisy than he thought he would be. Despite what he had said to Lacy, he had been worried about her. Yes, Hunting Hounds were tough, fast, and fearless, but a Soul Gaunt was a Soul Gaunt, and plenty of tough, fast, fearless things fell before one of them. Since getting back parts of his memory, he knew that first hand.

But either the Gaunt hadn't returned after he had driven it away with the flare, or Daisy had been faster and smarter and had managed to evade it. Either way, she was here, she was fine, and he was very glad of the fact. He rubbed her down briskly once more, then rose to his feet.

"Weren't worried about her at all, huh?" Lacy's voice came from behind him, her footsteps crunching through the gravel on the driveway.

"Well, maybe a little, I guess," he confessed. "I really did think she'd be okay, but I have to admit, I'm glad that I was right."

Lacy reached down and scratched Daisy between the ears, the dog pushing her head up into the woman's hand. "Yeah, she's fine. Aren't you girl?" Daisy ate up the attention. "So, is there any sense looking in the woods now? In the daylight?" She kept petting Daisy, but this was directed at Solomon.

He turned and looked at the woods. "I don't think so. Unless we want to try to find Luke, but even that's a long shot. If the Soul Gaunt has him, he won't be where we can find him that easy."

Lacy nodded. "Let's go inside then. I'll make some coffee, we can decide what we're going to do, and then take a rest. Get some sleep, if we can."

She led the way into the kitchen and busied herself making coffee while Solomon took a seat at the table and looked around. There was none of the grandeur of the Greenweald here, but the home was comfortable, lived in. It had the look of a place that had been inhabited by the same person for years, with everything in its place, even if some of those things were long forgotten. He liked it, it made him feel that he was somewhere that was loved.

A few minutes later, Lacy set a steaming mug in front of him. "Sugar? Cream?"

"Both, please."

She brought them over and Solomon helped himself to two large spoonsful of sugar, and a healthy pour of cream. Lacy watched him over the rim of her cup and chuckled.

"What?"

"I would have taken you for a black coffee man."

"Nah. I don't like bitter. Even at home, I have a sweet tooth. Horrible habit."

"What's it like? Your home, I mean."

"The Greenweald? It's…well, it's wild. It's like those woods out there, but bigger. Much, much bigger. It covers the largest part of the world as we know it. There's areas outside of it, of course. And we, meaning my people, have some interactions with them, but mostly, we stay by ourselves, in the parts that we've come to live with."

"So, you guys live in the forest, in what, like log cabins and stuff? Do you have electricity, and flush toilets, and TV? Or is it like Little House on the Prairie?"

Solomon laughed. "I'm not sure what that is, but no, probably not. No prairie anyway. My people have learned, well, were forced really, to live with nature, and with the trees. We don't cut them down and saw them up. Instead, we shape them into things that we need, and they let us. We care for them and they take care of us in return."

"Sounds very hippyish."

"I guess it is. But our trees are much bigger than those here. Even your biggest ones. The central tree of my house, Towering Oaks? It's big enough around to fit several of this house inside it, side by side. It raises so far into the sky that it's hard to see where it ends. And that's not even the largest. The largest one I know of is the tree that houses Jamshir. He's our ruler, I guess. His house is Glittering Birch, and that tree is huge, even by Greenweald standards."

"It still sounds weird to me," Lacy said, sipping at her coffee. "Living in trees and all. But the way you talk about it. The look you get in your eyes. It makes me wish I could see it."

102

"You'd love it, I'm sure. And I miss it. Now that I remember it, anyway."

"So speaking of that, any ideas on how to get back there, get your sword and kill that thing out in the woods?"

"None," Solomon said. "I've never been attuned to magic, so I have no idea how the spell that sent me here works." He picked up his mug and took a sip, but then stopped at Lacy's expression. "What?"

"Magic? The spell? Come on. Are you putting me on?"

He set his mug down and sat forward, putting his elbows on the table. "Lacy. Are you telling me that you can believe I'm from another world, and that you've seen the Soul Gaunt, but that you'll balk at magic?"

"Of course, I will! Why wouldn't I? None of this makes sense!"

Solomon could see that Lacy was at the edge of exhaustion. He felt worn out himself, and he knew that if he was, a human, no matter how tough, had to be about finished.

"Hey," he said. "Why don't we talk about it more later, huh? Maybe get some sleep?"

Lacy nodded. "Yeah. I don't think the coffee's going to keep me up."

"Good," Solomon smiled. "I'll take the couch, if that's okay."

"Yeah, that's fine. Daisy can stay in here too. I don't want her out there by herself." She rose and collected the two coffee mugs, bringing them to the sink to rinse them. "Solomon. What's going to happen to Ed?"

Solomon sighed. "I don't know. I don't know what the Soul Gaunt's effects will be on a human, but it hurt him badly. Like I said at the hospital, he may not ever recover. I really don't know."

"But is there anyone in your world that could help him? Since you guys have magic and all?"

Solomon sat back. The thought had never crossed his mind. The only Soul Gaunts that he knew of from personal experience had been the one Jediah had killed years ago, and the one that he himself had fought much later. In both cases there had been no wounded to worry about, just bodies.

"I don't know," he finally said. "Maybe. But that still leaves us with the same problem. We need to find a way for me to get home first."

Lacy nodded, suddenly looking too tired to even stay on her feet. She swayed slightly, and Solomon quickly got up and steadied her. "Come on. Let's get you to bed."

A few minutes later, Lacy was laying under the covers of her bed, fully dressed and snoring gently. Solomon smiled slightly as he looked down on her. She really was impressive. Then he returned to the living room, and stretched out as best as he could on the couch, Daisy curled up on the floor next to him. He stared at the ceiling of the room for a few moments before sleep came for him, too.

But he had only been out for a couple of hours before he found himself wide awake again. He lay on his back, staring at the ceiling. There was too much happening at the moment, and he needed to think his way through it, analyze the problem and come up with a plan of attack.

First, and most important, was the Soul Gaunt. He couldn't allow it to remain here, in this world. Humans were woefully unprepared to deal with it. Their weapons wouldn't hurt it, and they had no way to find it if it didn't wish to be. The flare that he used would have surprised it, blinded it for a few moments, and maybe even scared it, if such a thing was possible. But it wouldn't have lasted. And now the Gaunt knew what it was, and that trick wouldn't work on it again. It would hide, come out to kill, and then hide again. Eventually maybe, someone here would figure out a way to stop it, but how many would die before then?

Then there was Ed. Lacy may have hit on something. If he could get Ed back to the Greenweald, maybe someone there would be able to do something. There was healing in that land, simply by being there, to say nothing of magic. Look at Daisy. He had hurt her leg badly when they first met, but she had apparently gone back and a short time later…

Solomon sat up, looking down at the huge, shaggy dog sleeping next to the couch. She had gone back! Of course. Why hadn't he thought of it before? Daisy, and probably all Hunting Hounds, had the ability to cross from this world to the Greenweald, and back. If he could figure out how to get her to do it, maybe he could tag along, bring Ed with him.

But the how of getting her to do it he wasn't sure of. Plus, even if she did understand, he didn't know if she could also bring him through, let alone Ed, who wasn't even from the Greenweald. Maybe that wasn't the answer…but there was something there, he was sure of it.

And there was Luke. What was the connection there? Why was the Soul Gaunt using a human to lure people to it? And why hadn't it sucked out Luke's soul when it first encountered him. Lacy obviously still loved the man, and wanted him back with her. She was a good person, and if he could, Solomon would make that happen.

But it all hinged on that Soul Gaunt. If he managed to kill it, or even drive it out of this world, then he could concentrate on saving Luke, and maybe healing Ed, and finally getting home himself. Once there, he could petition Florian to let him find another way to atone for what had happened to Celia.

He wished he could remember what he had done with his sword, Justice. His eyes widened at that. For the first time, he remembered the name, although almost nothing else. How he had gotten it, and where he had hidden it remained lost in the fog. But the fact that he remembered the name was promising. His memories were slowly seeping back.

What else could he remember? What else could help him? He remembered Shireen and Orlando, his best friends in the Greenweald. Each capable of so much, and so much more when paired together. They had been through a lot together, the three of them. If he had told anyone what he had done with Justice, it would have been them.

If he only had a way to reach them. Then, an idea occurred to him, and he looked back down at Daisy and smiled.

CHAPTER 19

The darkness inside the tree swallowed them up as they entered, and Shireen couldn't see two feet in front of her face. And it was cold. Colder than it had any right to be this time of year.

"Orlando?" she whispered. "Do you feel that?"

"Yes, like those nights up north. Only more…concentrated? Is that right?"

"Yeah, whatever it was, Soul Gaunt or something else, it's here now."

She moved forward slightly, clearing the doorway so that Orlando, and Thaddeus if he were coming, could enter as well. To her surprise, the next voice she heard was Thaddeus's.

"Hold a moment. I have something on my horse that might help."

The light from the partially opened door dimmed as he ducked back out. Shireen was sure that he wouldn't return, but gave him the benefit of the doubt. A few moments later, he did return. In the dim light near the door, she saw him move past Orlando and approach her.

"Here, if you're going first, take this."

Thaddeus reached out his closed hand to her. She hesitated, then put out her own, palm up. The stone that Thaddeus put there was warm, even in the unnatural cold inside the tree. After a moment, it began to glow with a soft light that grew as she held it.

"What is this?" she asked.

Thaddeus shrugged. "Something I've been working on. A toy, really. But maybe here, it would be better than torches?"

She could see Orlando looking at her in the glow of the stone. "What do you think?"

"I think it's brilliant," Orlando said. "Can we turn if off if we need to?"

"Well, yes, just close your fingers around it." Shireen did so, and the glow disappeared. When she opened them again, the glow slowly grew until they could see an area several feet around them. "But I don't know why we would want to," Thaddeus said, shivering as he looked around.

"Let's go," Shireen said.

"Wait a second," Orlando said. "Are we sure we want to do this? Would it make more sense to go back to Jediah and Florian and tell them what we found here? Let them send in more than just us?"

"Of course, that would make sense," she replied. "But what if someone is still alive in here?"

Orlando took a deep breath. "You're right. I wasn't thinking of that."

She looked at him and saw the fear in his face that she was sure was reflected in her own, but also the resolve. She saw the same thing in Thaddeus, even if the fear was more prevalent. But to be fair, maybe that was what she expected to see, so she did. He wasn't showing any signs of running out on them.

Shireen turned to the darkness that stretched out before them and listened. Despite what she had said, she didn't really expect to find anyone alive in here. Not after what they had seen outside. But she had to know, so she listened for the sound of anyone moaning, or crying. There was nothing but silence.

She walked slowly forward, Orlando and Thaddeus staying close, their swords in their hands, as hers was in her right. The stone glowed softly from her left. As she moved, the globe of light moved with her, and they all stayed as close to the center of it as they could, peering into the darkness, trying to see anything moving at all.

The inside of the Rustling Elms central tree was beautiful, as all of the Folk's houses were. The living tree had been shaped into pleasing contours, chambers that opened up to unexpected rooms filled with comfortable furniture. Art hung from living hooks shaped from the walls themselves, and sculptures had been fashioned from the very floor, rising up in a variety of shapes.

Shireen remembered that House Rustling Elms had been gaining a reputation. It was a minor house involved in trading, that was its main business. But it had given rise to quite a few prominent artists of the last few decades, who had been becoming more popular. Their fortunes had been shifting, from one of mere trade, to a valued asset of the Folk. Although Shireen herself had never been much for art appreciation, the Folk in general reveled in, and true artists were treated like celebrities.

But now, something had perverted that art the same way that the tree had been damaged on the outside. Many of the pieces were abstract, but now they had been broken, pieces of living wood broken off and cast aside. Some were realistic, but the faces in the paintings, or on the sculptures, had been changed. Where once they had smiled, or looked wistful, or longing, now they looked in pain. Mouths gaped open as if they were screaming, eyes protruding from their sockets.

One particular sculpture had been defiled so badly that they needed to step away from it, nauseated by what it had been turned into.

The rest of the tree had fared no better. Mushrooms grew from the walls, and the floor cracked under their feet. Slimy fungus coated surfaces, and they had to be careful where they put their hands. Dense, heavy cobwebs hung from the ceiling and although they didn't see anything move, they had the impression that bloated, black spiders waited in the darkness above.

"This can't be a Soul Gaunt, can it?" Orland whispered. "I thought they were mindless spirits, only existing to take someone's life force?"

"No," Thaddeus answered. "That's not right. They are evil, but intelligent, and cruel. They'll twist whatever they can, hurt what's innocent, and destroy what's left. At least, those were the stories I was told."

"I thought you didn't believe us?" Shireen said.

"I didn't. I do now."

Shireen admired Thaddeus's blunt answer in spite of herself. She was beginning to think there was more to the man than simply being the snake in the grass that she had initially had him pegged as. At the very least, he was braver than she had given him credit for.

They moved further into the tree, coming to a wide set of stairs, leading up into the darkness, cobwebs twining among the balusters that had been shaped from the tree. The steps were coated with slime and spongy underfoot, like the wood beneath was rotting even as they carefully climbed.

The second floor was the same as the first. Room after room of decay, some further along than others. The stairs continued, climbing to a third floor, equally as corrupted as the second. Still, they heard and saw nothing that was alive, nothing that would allow them to save even one person from the massacre.

"This is getting us nowhere," Orlando said. "Stop and think for a minute, Shireen. If there is anyone in here, they could be anywhere. We're only on the third floor and we have no idea if we missed anyone on the first two. How many more are there? I think we need to stop, go back and report what we've seen and let the Heads of our Houses decided what to do."

Shireen grit her teeth, staring into the darkness. Orlando was right, and she knew it. He usually was, and was almost always the more rational one. She knew that what he was saying wasn't out of cowardice, but out of good sense. But still, it rankled her to leave without knowing for certain that there was no one that she was leaving behind here.

"You're right," she said. "Let's head back down and…"

"Wait!" Thaddeus hissed. "Listen. What was that?"

The three froze, and Shireen could hear her heartbeat echoing in her ears. She strained to hear whatever it was that Thaddeus had, but there was nothing but the cold, empty silence of the place.

Then, on the edge of hearing, there was a noise. It was a soft, quiet sound, barely there at all. But she could tell from the others faces that they had heard it too. She stayed perfectly still, willing the noise to come again so that they could try to tell where it was coming from.

When it did, she was sure. It was the sound of someone moaning in pain, or fear, or sadness. Regardless, it was the sound of someone in need.

She looked back to Orlando, who stared back at her with wide eyes and then nodded slowly. Thaddeus did the same.

She raised the hand with the glowing stone in it over head and continued on, walking slowly and as silently as only years as a scout could have trained her for. She listened as hard as she could, trying to keep her eyes focused on what was in front of her while still listening for the noise to repeat.

It did, slightly nearer now. They were closing in on it. The sense of rot and decay around them grew stronger. Moss grew underfoot, but not the soft, springy type that appears unexpectedly in the woods at times, but slimy, with tendrils that grew out and waved as if in a breeze that only they could feel. Huge brackets of hard fungi grew from the walls, pale white at the tips, shading to black near their roots.

The noise came again, and this time there was no mistaking it. It was a moan, from the throat of one of the Folk. There may have been words in it as well, but if so, they were garbled and unintelligible. But it was also full of pain, and close now.

Shireen led them through an arch and into another room, stopping when she saw what was there. The room was very large, and the light from the stone didn't penetrate the darkness at the other end. But what she could see was different from the rest of the tree. There was no rot in here, no fungus growing, or slimy moss. It looked pristine and clean, untouched by the evil that was killing the rest of the tree.

The moan came again from the far end of the room. Shireen hurried that way, followed closely by the other two.

"By all that's holy…" she heard Orlando whisper.

She had no words herself. They had found a survivor, of sorts. He wore the robes of an important member of House Rustling Elms. Perhaps he was even the Head of the House, Shireen didn't know. And it didn't matter any longer.

He had been hung on the wall, in a gross parody of the art in the rest of the tree. Spikes of wood from broken sculptures pierced his hands and arms. His legs had been crossed, so that one large jagged piece of wood nailed both feet to the wall. His face was a ruin, as if he had been beaten severely and one eye was gone, as well as most of his teeth.

But most horribly, he had been split open, his intestines dragged out and allowed to puddle on the floor beneath him. Why he was still alive was beyond Shireen to figure out, but he was. As she watched, he opened his bloody mouth and moaned again, the same sound that they had been following.

"Get him down," Orlando said, pushing past her. "Come on! We've got to help him!" He grabbed the stake holding the man's feet to the wall and pulled, but it refused to move. "Help me, damnit!"

Shireen put her sword away and laid her hand on Orlando's arm. "We can't save him," she said quietly.

"Then what? We walk away? Leave him here like this?"

"We provide mercy," Thaddeus said.

Orlando spun on him. "What do you mean? Mercy? Just say what you mean!"

Shireen pulled him around to her, and gently folded him in her arms. "You know what he means. I'd want the same, and so would you."

Orlando clung to her for a moment, then pushed himself away. "No, you're right. Sorry. It just got to me. I'm fine."

The man on the wall moaned again, only this time, it sounded different. There were definitely words in it, or at least a word. He was trying to say something to them.

"What is it?" Shireen said, nearing the man. "We're here. We're going to take care of you."

She hoped the man heard her and understood that his suffering was going to end. She drew her sword and stepped back, when the man tried to speak again. His tongue came out and licked his lips. His breath rattled in his throat as he tried to speak.

Shireen grimaced, her palms sweaty. Although she had agreed with Thaddeus, and knew it was the right thing to do, she had never killed one of her own people before, and wasn't sure that she could now that it came down to it.

The man on the wall writhed, pulled his head forward as far as he could, and drew in a shallow, painful sounding breath. He held it for a moment, then expelled it in one final word.

"Ruuuuun."

CHAPTER 20

The sun slanting in through the windows woke Lacy. She lay there in her bed and took stock. It was early evening now, so she had slept most of the day. She needed it, and even now felt like she could fall back to sleep without much problem.

But there were things to do. She and Solomon still needed to figure out how they were going to help Ed, how they were going to find Luke, how they were going to kill that Soul Gaunt thing, and how Solomon was going to get home. All of which still boggled her mind. She was accepting these events, these fairy-tales, like they were real life without even questioning it.

Ah. Enough of that. She had already been over it again and again. It was either true, or it wasn't. She had seen the damn Soul Gaunt, been touched by it and felt the effects. She had seen Ed and what had happened to him, and she had seen Solomon carrying him with no apparent effort. There was more going on here than would could be accounted for by everyday life, that was for sure.

She pushed the covers off, swung her legs out of bed, stood and stretched. As she did, she looked out the window at her back yard. It seemed like such a nice summer evening. The type where it would be wonderful to take a dip in the pool, have a glass of wine and throw a burger on the grill. She smiled to herself, remembering several nights when she and Luke had done exactly that. Before the troubles started for him.

They were young when they had met, and it certainly hadn't been love at first sight. Lacy was working at the local supermarket, ringing people's groceries though, and Luke was an occasional customer. When he came through her line, he was always polite and friendly, but she thought nothing more of it. He was one of those people who chose to do their shopping every day, rather than once a week or so. She didn't get it herself. Why spend more time at the grocery store than you had to?

Then, she started to notice that he always came to her lane, no matter how many people were in it, or how long he had to wait. If another lane opened, he smiled and told the person in front of him to go ahead. And soon enough, he would be standing in front of her again, smiling his polite smile.

She was a little creeped out by this at first, but then decided that maybe he was shy. So the next time he came through, she stopped, stuck out her hand and said, "Hi, I'm Lacy. We've never really met, have we?"

His polite smile got even bigger as he took her hand. "Luke. It's nice to meet you." But he laughed at the absurdity of it, and she did too. Then, it was the normal thing that happened, and their eyes dropped, and things got awkward. She rang his groceries up, a lime and a package of pork chops, and he went on his way. But when she looked up, he glanced at her at the same time, and lifted his hand in a little wave. She awkwardly returned it, and then turned back to the smirking older woman waiting her turn.

"What?" Lacy asked her.

"Nothing," the woman replied. "Nothing at all. But…he is cute."

Lacy didn't say anything, but she couldn't keep the smile off her face.

It took Luke four more daily trips to the store to finally work up the courage to ask her out. They went to the movies, which is a terrible first date idea, and then to get pie and coffee at Minnie's, which was better. They talked until Minnie politely but firmly informed them that she was closing up.

Lacy was charmed when Luke walked her to her car, and opened the door for her. He kissed her chastely on the cheek and said that he had had a great time, and would love to see her again. She agreed, and went home with her head in the clouds.

And that had been it. From there on out there had been no one else for Lacy. Luke made her laugh, and made her feel pretty and special. They laughed when they were together, and she missed him when they were apart. When they made love for the first time, it was as if they were meant to be together, and she had never been so comfortable being intimate with anyone before.

They married, bought the house and discussed starting a family. Life was exactly as it should be. Even at times when the money was tight, and there were plenty of those, it didn't seem that important. They had each other, and Lacy was good with that.

Luke wanted to be a writer and he had talent. His words flowed onto the page, and Lacy loved reading his stuff. It was all far out things, fantasy, sci-fi, and some horror thrown in here and there. He sent out story after story to the few remaining magazines, and manuscript after manuscript to agents and publishers alike. But he never got beyond polite but firm rejections. It was disheartening, but Lacy didn't let him give up. She believed in him, and believed that he would get his break.

Sighing, Lacy sat back down on the bed, still staring out at the back yard, but her gaze now more focused on the woods beyond.

"Luke," she whispered. "What are you doing now?"

She heard noise from the living room and knew that Solomon was up and moving as well. Frankly, she would have been surprised if he wasn't.

"Hey," she said, when she opened the bedroom door and came out. "Sorry about earlier. I don't know what came over me. I got so tired all of a sudden."

"I think it's called exhaustion," Solomon said. "Don't worry about it. With everything you've been through, it's understandable."

"Coffee?" Lacy asked, moving to the kitchen. "I'll make some food too, but I thought coffee might help chase some of the cobwebs away first."

"Sounds great, but I already made it. Hope you don't mind."

"Pfft. Fresh coffee when I get up? And I don't have to make it? What's to mind?"

She poured herself a cup and held the pot up. He passed his mug over and she filled that one too. After she had taken a few sips, she set it down on the counter, and went to the refrigerator. "How about a salad? Maybe throw a burger or two on the grill? I'm in the mood for one."

"Sure, sounds great. What can I do?"

"Nothing. Hang out. I like doing it."

A short time later, they sat on Lacy's deck, tucking into burgers and enjoying the warm summer evening. Lacy kept scanning the edge of the woods, hoping, but not really expecting, to see Luke appear.

"You miss him, huh?" Solomon said to her.

"Yeah, I do. He was really the only one ever for me. Despite the last few months."

"What happened?"

"Ah, you don't want to hear about that."

"I told you about Celia."

Lacy was quiet for a moment. Then, "It was good for a while, you know? After we got married. Luke was really struggling though. More than I knew. It wasn't about me, or at least I don't think it was. It was his writing. He always kept a good face about it, but I think now that it was eating away at him. He poured himself into those stories, lived them in his mind. I could always tell when he was in the middle of one, because he wouldn't be with me. Not really. He'd be off in some other world inside his own head."

"Luke was a writer? I didn't know that," Solomon said.

"I guess we hadn't talked about it. It's weird. It's only been a couple of days since you showed up in my hospital room, but it feels like forever. Like you've always been around. But yeah, Luke was a writer, just not a published one."

She stopped and took a sip of her wine. Birds flitted among the trees, but nothing else moved in the woods.

"I knew it bothered him, but I didn't know how much. He started drinking. Well, I guess I should say that he started drinking more. He had always had a taste for it. Hell, he and I used to get halfway lit, laugh the night away and fall into bed together at the end of it."

She stopped again, and glanced at Solomon, feeling a faint burn in her cheeks.

"Sorry, I don't know why I said that. TMI, right?"

Solomon smiled. "I'm aware of what husbands and wives do."

She cleared her throat. "Anyway. He started out having a beer in the afternoon. I mean, we had both done that on occasion, no big deal. But he started doing it every afternoon, while I was still at work. Pretty soon, it was more than one. Then, he started to get lonely, and he'd head into town. There were a couple times that Ed called me to come get him.

"But here's the thing. When we were home here, the two of us? He was fine. He never got drunk, and he was his old, charming, fun self. It was hard to reconcile the two."

"Why would Ed call you? Was he getting violent?" Solomon asked.

"No, nothing like that. He'd head into town, probably have a beer or two driving there, and then go to the bar. Then he'd start putting them away. Once he was good and liquored up, he'd start ranting to people. Telling them the stories that he had written, like they were real things that had happened to him. A couple of times, he left the bar and wandered down the sidewalk, trying to talk to whoever was around. He scared a couple of people pretty good.

"I should have noticed more…I should have done something. But I didn't want to believe that there was anything really wrong, you know? He wasn't writing anymore. I finally went and looked, and it was piles of the same stories he'd had for the last couple of years, done over and over. And the writing was bad in the new versions. Really bad. But that's not the worst part.

"He had written notes to himself on them. They were all the same. About how horrible the story was, how worthless he was as a writer and as a man, how he was going to lose me…on and on. After the first few, I couldn't read anymore."

She stopped again and took a sip of her wine. Solomon sat quietly next to her, listening but not saying anything.

"But you know what?" she continued. "It was the damndest thing, but I started to get angry. At him. At Luke. I got it, that he was having a tough time. But this drunk, self-pitying asshole wasn't the man I knew. He wasn't the man who showed himself to me all the time. So I stormed out of his office and found him, and we had a real old fashioned come-to-Jesus dust up. I told him straight up that he wasn't going to lose me, not for not being a published writer, but if he kept up the crap, he had a good chance of doing it that way.

"It worked! For a while, anyway. He cried, I cried. We hugged and talked, and he stopped the drinking. Got himself turned around too. He cleaned up his office and burned all of the new 'editions' of his stories. The old ones, the good ones, he put in a drawer. Then he turned off his computer and asked me if he could take a couple of days to figure out what he was going to do. Of course, I told him yes, pleased as could be that he was turning over a new leaf.

"But those things never last, do they? For the next few days, things were great. I'd come home and he'd have the house cleaned up, dinner cooking away and music playing. It was like we were dating all over again. We'd have dinner and he'd listen to my mundane stories about my day and I'd listen to his. He was walking a lot, to give him time to think, and work off some of that beer gut he'd gotten."

"And then what happened?" Solomon asked quietly.

"He was gone. I came home from work, and he wasn't here. No music, no dinner cooking, nothing. It was like he hadn't been here all day. He was gone. I waited all night, but he never came back. Not then, not the next day, and not the day after that. I called Ed, of course, and he came out, but there was no sign of a struggle or anything like that.

"I got around to thinking that working things out for Luke meant that he didn't want to be here anymore. And that he had decided to go and the easiest way to do that was to leave. No muss, no fuss."

"I'm sorry, Lacy," Solomon said. "That must have been horribly painful for you."

"Oh, it was. Ed checked on me, Maggie too. But I'm tough, Solomon. In case you hadn't noticed. If Luke didn't want me, then okay. It hurt, but I had lived before him, and I'd live after him. I went on thinking that too, until a few days ago."

"When you saw him."

"Yeah. And now I'm thinking that he didn't leave me. Something grabbed him. That Soul Gaunt thing. And while that makes me feel a little better about myself, I'm terrified of what it means for him."

Her voice broke on that last and Solomon reached over and squeezed her hand. She grabbed hold and squeezed back, glad for the contact. After a moment, she collected herself, patted his hand, and let go.

"Thanks," she said.

"We'll find him, Lacy. I'm not letting this go."

She nodded, then a thought occurred to her and she looked around. "Hey, where's Daisy? I haven't seen her since I got up."

Solomon smiled. "I sent her on an errand," he said, and took another sip of his wine.

CHAPTER 21

"Should we go tell Jamshir now?" Florian asked, setting his glass down.

"Tell him what? That Rustling Elms was attacked? He'd only have me investigate it anyway," Jediah said. "No, let's wait here, see what Shireen and Orlando come back with, and go to him with that."

"You're hoping to use it as leverage for bringing Solomon back, aren't you?"

Jediah looked at him. "Why would I need that? We've both agreed that he needs to be. I, the Head of his House, and you, his accuser. Why would he balk at it?"

"Who knows? He's Jamshir, does he need a reason? He could refuse simply because he feels like it. We both know how he is."

Jediah said nothing, but took another sip of his liqueur. To Florian's eyes, he looked almost nervous, certainly uncomfortable.

"What's going on, Jediah?" he said. "I know you too well. I can tell when you're trying to hide your thoughts."

Jediah sighed, grimaced and looked down at his near empty glass. "Jamshir. It's more than him being selfish and a lesser man than his father. I don't know that I trust him anymore. He's changed…become different than he used to be."

Florian lifted an eyebrow, surprised to find his friend talking so bluntly. In truth, he had been feeling much the same way about the leader of the Folk. But he hadn't been so rash to speak of it so freely, not even to Thaddeus.

"You speak dangerous words, my friend."

"Dangerous or not, they're words that need speaking. I think Jamshir has lost his caring for the Greenweald. I think now that Jamshir cares mostly for Jamshir."

Florian nodded. Spies were not unheard of among the Folk, and he was sure that Jamshir had them in both his and Jediah's households, but not here, in this room. Thaddeus was an accomplished enough magic-user to ensure that this room held no magical listening devices, even if he was not on par with the wizards that House Glittering Birch had.

"I've felt the same, for quite some time now. But I'm curious. Why do you say this?"

"Glittering Birch has almost as strong a martial force as we do, in addition to his sorcerers and whatever else he has hidden. Yet any time that danger, of any sort, rears up, it's up to us to put it to rights. At one time, he would join us, spread the glory, sure, but also spread the danger. Now, he sits, consolidating his strength. For what?"

"In case you decide that he's not fit to rule, I would imagine," Florian said. "Glittering Birch is a strong House, there's no doubt of that. But he'd be hard pressed to come up with soldiers who can match your Shireen, or Orlando, and as for Solomon….well."

"So you think he's afraid?"

"Mmm…I don't know if afraid is exactly the word I would use. Cautious is more like it. And opportunistic. He saw a way to remove Solomon from your house, and in doing so removed what he must surely see as the greatest single threat to his rule."

Jediah was silent for a moment. "Then he won't agree to bring him back, will he?"

"My thought is no, he won't. Which is exactly why we should tell him what's happened."

"I don't follow," Jediah said.

"Think about it. Jamshir needs to be shaken out of his complacency. If you say he's been taking no chances with his men, then he needs to be shown that he can't sit on the sidelines. Not for this. Maybe when he loses a few men, he'll not be so slow to agree to bring Solomon back."

Florian was a little surprised to hear himself speaking like this. Only a short time ago, he had been arguing vehemently against this very act, and now here he was, plotting with Jediah for how they could make it happen. But he had always been a practical man, once he let his reason reign over his emotions. He would never embrace Solomon, and would always blame him for what had happened, but he had come around to believing that it also wasn't intentional. The thing in the pool that had taken Celia, that was the real murderer.

"You could be right," Jediah conceded. "Although I have a feeling that he'll tell me to handle it anyway. As long as the Soul Gaunt isn't killing Glittering Birch soldiers, he won't move."

"No, but what if we told him that we couldn't find it?"

"I can't do that, Florian, and neither can you. If we hold off on it, then how many innocents die from other houses."

Florian settled back. In truth, he hadn't thought of that. "You're right, of course. Still, there must be a way to turn this threat so that we get what we need."

"*We* need? You've come around quickly."

"You've made your point convincingly. I will never love Solomon, but I understand the need for him to be here."

There was a knock at the door.

"Come," Florian called out, and another minor member of his House appeared.

"My lord," he said. "There is someone….well, something…here. That I think you should know about."

"What is it?"

"It's a dog, lord."

"A dog?" Florian laughed. "So now I'm to be bothered by every stray dog that wanders into the compound? Give it some food and let it roam as it wishes. It will go away when it's ready."

"It's not just a dog, lord. It looks like a Hunting Hound."

Florian's blood ran cold. He had forgotten the Hunting Hound that he had had Thaddeus send after Solomon. They were trained to kill their quarry, and then return to the one who had sent them with proof. Usually very grisly, and bloody, proof.

"Oh, no," he whispered.

"What did you do, Florian?" Jediah's voice was very quiet.

Instead of answering, Florian walked quickly out of the door, ignoring how such haste must look to his servants. With Jediah on his heels, demanding answers, he left his home and went down the steps to where the Hound waited.

Yes, it looked like the same Hound that Thaddeus had returned with, but really who was to say? They all looked very much alike to him. It could have been a Hound that had been dispatched to find and eliminate *him*. That thought made him glad that Jediah was nearby.

He slowed as he approached, but the Hound did nothing other than to sit, its tongue lolling out of its mouth, watching him as he neared.

"Easy, now," he said quietly. "That's a good boy. No one's going to hurt you."

He looked at the ground in front of the Hound, but there was nothing there, or anywhere around him. There was no blood on the dog's muzzle, and it didn't look as if it had been in a fight. Hunting Hound or not, if it had tangled with Solomon, there would have been some signs of it.

"I don't understand…" he began.

Jediah pushed past him. "For the gods' sake, Florian. How many Hunting Hounds have you seen with a ribbon tied around their necks?"

Florian could only gape as the Hound allowed Jediah to slip off the ribbon that he now saw had been loosely placed around its neck. Attached to the ribbon was a small piece of paper.

Jediah unfolded and read what was written there. Then he looked up at Florian, his face creasing into a smile.

"It's from Solomon," he said. "He's alive, he's got most of his memories back, and he says he needs our help. You're not going to believe this. He says there's a Soul Gaunt on that earth."

Florian felt like the world was spinning out of control. Old stories pop up again, and a supposed killer beast is made into a messenger? What was going on?

"Then we need to help him," he heard his own voice say. "But how?'"

CHAPTER 22

"Ruuuunnn." With that, the man's head flopped forward, his breath hitching in his throat. It looked like he had used his final strength to issue his warning, and for that Shireen was grateful. But what did he mean…?

Her thoughts were interrupted by another sound. In the darkness, at the side of the large room came a dry hiss, long and drawn out, slowly evolving into what sounded like a chuckle. The temperature in the room began to drop rapidly and the overall feeling of wrongness that pervaded the whole tree intensified. The Soul Gaunt was here.

"We need to go," she said, backing away from the poor man hung on the wall and looking around. "Now."

The three of them turned, but then the voice came out of the darkness. "Ruuunnnn…." It was the same word that the man had used to try to warn them, but twisted. Instead of a warning to flee, it was a challenge. Run if you like, it won't matter.

Before they could take another step, the doors that they had come through on the opposite end of the room suddenly slammed shut.

"Come on," Shireen said again. "It's trying to scare us."

"It's working," Thaddeus muttered.

"Yesssss, yesssss….ruuuuunnnn!" The voice was louder now, coming closer through the darkness. Shireen could feel the fear working at her defenses, trying to get her to lie down and surrender to it. She wouldn't! And she wouldn't let Orlando or Thaddeus do it either.

She moved forward, walking quickly and trying to look all around them at once, her breath steaming in the cold air. Out in the wild, the Soul Gaunt hadn't come near their fire, but she didn't know if that was because of the light or the flames themselves. She was hoping it was the light, and held the stone that Thaddeus gave her higher.

The dry chuckle came from behind them, and made her want to flee from it as fast as she could, but she knew that would be a mistake. They needed to stay calm, stay together and get out of this room, then out of the tree, and back to Jediah. They'd return with plenty of House Towering Oaks soldiers and slice this damned creature into ribbons.

"Stay close," she told the other two.

Then, horribly, there was another sound. This one came from in front of them, from between them and the doors. Another chuckle, sounding like bones rattling in a crypt. Shireen was sure that the Soul Gaunt had moved around them, and was now trying to scare them back, away from the exit. But then the noise came from behind them again, at the same time as the one between them and freedom.

There were two Soul Gaunts in here with them. No one could face that, not even Solomon. What chance did they have? She faltered, her steps slowing and felt the terrible, icy, dread sink into her bones.

"Give me the stone," Thaddeus whispered, reaching for her hand.

No, she thought. The stone is light, it's keeping them away. I can't....

"Shireen," Orlando said, his voice gentle "Give the stone to Thaddeus. We need to get out of here."

She nodded and dropped her hand enough to reach Thaddeus's outstretched one. He took it from her and she felt a moment's panic as the light passed away from her. The fear in the chamber was palpable, and her legs didn't want to move. Her sword quaked as she held it out in front of her.

"Start walking," Thaddeus said quietly. Shireen couldn't. There was a Soul Gaunt there, hidden in the darkness. If she went forward, she would walk right to it, and then it would reach out and...

"Come on," Orlando urged. "We're getting out of here."

Thaddeus was speaking in some weird language now, his voice flowing over and around her. The stone in his hand began to brighten, much more than when she had held it. The glow surrounded them and pushed out further into the darkness. As it washed over her more strongly, she felt her old strength of will beginning to reassert itself. She felt embarrassed by her cowardice, but first thing was first. They needed to get out of here.

As the light pushed outward, something in the darkness pushed against it. The Soul Gaunts set up a noise, like the screeching of small animals in pain. It grated against their nerves and echoed in their ears. Shireen could hear the strain in Thaddeus's voice as he continued to cast his spell over the stone in his hand.

The light pulsed, pushing out, then retreating slightly, before pushing out again, each time gaining a little more area. Thaddeus was doing it, but she could hear how hard it was. His breath was rasping in between each word.

"Help him," she said to Orlando, and they supported the wizard, one on each side as they moved toward the doors.

"Ruuuuunnnn" The voice came again, this time from behind them, and to either side. Was the voice echoing, or were there more? How many Soul Gaunts were in here? They moved as quickly as they could to the doors, and tore them open.

Outside of the room it was no better. The air was still frigid and the dread was increasing more and more. They made their way back through the second floor, ignoring the rot and decay everywhere they looked.

Shireen looked back as they left the room and saw a piece of the darkness move out of it, trailing them. Then another followed it, and another. Three of them. There were three Soul Gaunts toying with them.

"Do we have fire?" she asked Orlando, panting as she tried to run, hold her sword and support an increasingly weaker Thaddeus.

"No, not right here," he replied. "Why?"

"Thaddeus isn't going to make it all the way out. Look at him. He can barely walk now and the light is starting to fade."

Thaddeus's voice was starting to crack and falter and, as it did, the light was beginning to waver. She saw one of the black shapes glide forward and the light retreat a couple of inches, the globe that surrounded them becoming smaller.

"I don't have anything, Shireen. Do you?" Despite his outward calm, Shireen could hear the panic beginning to creep into Orlando's voice.

"No, but maybe..." She turned to the wizard. "Thaddeus. This stone? Can you make it hot too? Hot enough to catch something on fire maybe?"

"Tired," he whispered. "Not strong enough...."

"I didn't think so." She stopped moving and stood up straight. "Okay, Orlando." She tried to keep her voice light, as if she was talking about a matter of no consequence at all. "The snake in the grass is spent. Looks like we leave him and make a run for it. I'll grab the stone. Maybe it will keep glowing enough to get us out of here."

She stared at Orlando as she spoke, willing him to understand what she was doing. He looked back at her, wild-eyed, and then down at

Thaddeus. He sighed, and took the wizard's arm from around his shoulder. "Alright. Kind of a shame, but what can you do?"

"Yessss, leave the mage to ussss." The voice hissed from around them and Shireen peered into the darkness. She had been mistaken. There weren't two, or even three Soul Gaunts. Everywhere she looked, pieces of blacker darkness waited. They were surrounded. If her bluff didn't work, they were all dead. Thaddeus, as exhausted as he was, was their only chance.

"No," he muttered. "No, don't leave me…I can…" His voice faded away and his arm started to sag, the light fading further. Outside the dome of it, the black shapes crowded forward eagerly.

"Sorry, but it's every man for himself at this point," Shireen said and began to gently pry open his hand.

"I said no!" Thaddeus screamed, his arm jerking back.

The light exploded from the stone, illuminating every crack and crevice in the tree. The Soul Gaunts screamed, an unearthly, hollow, undulating sound, and fled.

Shireen and Orlando reached down, grabbed Thaddeus and ran, dragging him between them. As they fled, he railed against them, screaming that they couldn't have the stone, he needed it. His fear and desperation must have leant him an unreal strength, because the light continued to flow from the stone in massive amounts.

They gained the stairs, and flew down them, Thaddeus's feet thudding down the steps. The exit was in front of them now, across a large hallway. A few more seconds, and they'd be out, back into the daylight where they'd have a better chance.

Halfway across the hall, the doors thudded shut, causing them to slow down. Shireen put her sword away, reached out and pulled on them, but they were stuck fast, refusing to open.

"I know what you did," Thaddeus said, a half smile on his face, his eyes closing. "Good trick." And then he fell unconscious, his strength obviously gone, and the light went out.

Shireen almost lost her self-control. She pulled harder on the doors, yanking for all she was worth, but they were still stuck fast. Whatever the Soul Gaunt who had slammed them had done, there was no opening them now.

Suddenly, she felt a tug on Thaddeus, his body jerking away from her. She screamed in defiance and grabbed him. An ice-cold hand closed over her wrist and fire erupted in her arm. It went numb and she was helpless to stop it as the wizard was pulled away. In the darkness she heard Orlando curse, and knew that he had tried to hold on also. But it was no use, with a final pull, Thaddeus slid away from them, pulled into the blackness.

That cold, evil chuckle sounded again. "Ahhh....this one will sustain us for a while. His fear is delicious." The sound faded, becoming fainter and the dread that permeated the air around them began to decrease, and the temperature to rise. There was a brief, suddenly cut off wail from Thaddeus, and then silence.

Behind her, the door clicked and opened slightly. She put her hand on it and pulled, letting the sunlight flood into the hallway. It illuminated the mushrooms and fungus, the spider webs blowing in the breeze, the dirt and decay, and nothing else. Thaddeus was gone.

CHAPTER 23

Solomon sat on Lacy's back deck, legs crossed, back against the house wall. He gazed out to the woods, without really seeing it. For the first time since he had awakened in that alley, he was actively trying to concentrate, the way he had been taught all those years ago. Breath, focus, let his mind empty. Work the problem from different angles and let the answer come to him as it would.

The Soul Gaunt was out there, in the woods, yes, but more importantly, in this world. A world that wasn't designed to handle it. They wouldn't believe it was what it was, and would try to capture it. Eventually, someone would have enough and attempt to kill it, and eventually, someone would succeed. But in the meantime, it would do a terrible amount of damage.

He had to be the one to kill it. It came from his world, and he was the only one of the Folk here. He had killed one before, after a fierce battle, so he knew he could do it.

Except that he didn't have his sword, Justice, that burned with a white flame when it encountered evil. It had burned that day, hot enough to raise blisters on his own arms as he wielded it, but also hot enough to destroy the Soul Gaunt. If he had Justice, he could kill this one.

But Justice was still in the Greenweald, somewhere, hidden away, where his memory was still a blank space. Even if he could go home, which he didn't know how to do, he wouldn't be able to find it again. So his sword was useless to him for now, even if Daisy completed her mission and found Jediah.

There was Luke, Lacy's beloved, trapped by the Soul Gaunt for a purpose that he still didn't understand. If he killed the Gaunt, Luke should be free, but in the meantime, he was sure that the Gaunt would kill Luke first, if it looked like that was going to happen. He needed to keep Luke safe somehow as well.

And finally, there was Ed, and Lacy's arm. Damage that the Soul Gaunt had done, that he knew of no way to reverse. Maybe, if he could somehow get Ed and Lacy to the Greenweald, someone there would know what to do and be able to bring Ed back, fix Lacy's arm.

It all came down to the Soul Gaunt. Before anything else, it had to be killed. Once it was dead, Luke could be returned, and Solomon could work on getting back to the Greenweald somehow.

He could simply walk into the woods, search for Luke, and let the Soul Gaunt come to him. He could take it on hand to hand, maybe use a flare again like he did last time. If he held on to it, and didn't let it flee to remove the flare, maybe he could burn the things robe to cinders, allow him to see what was under it, and where its weak spots might be.

That thought was pure foolishness. Solomon knew his own prowess. He knew there wasn't a single person, male or female, among the Folk who could stand against him in combat. Probably not two combined, or even three, who could. None of that equaled a Soul Gaunt. Long before its robe would be burned, he would have succumbed to the things deadly touch.

No, he needed a way to stop it before it got to him, trap it and...

Light. He was remembering more of the fight now. Yes, the flames from Justice had hurt the thing. But the light had hurt it as well. Soul Gaunts were creatures of darkness. They thrived on it, and grew stronger in it. In the light, one of their most potent weapons, fear, was greatly diminished. It's why they only ever attacked at night, and had grown into boogey-man stories for his people. It was never that a Soul Gaunt would get you if you got lost in the woods, it was that they would get you if you got lost in the woods *at night*.

And this world had an advantage that the Greenweald didn't. A huge one. Wonderful, abundant, electricity. He smiled to himself as a plan started to come together.

"We need to wait until tomorrow night?" Lacy sounded incredulous. She and Solomon were seated in the kitchen, nursing mugs of coffee.

"I know," Solomon said. "I understand why it's so frustrating, but I don't think we have a choice right now."

"What happened to going into the woods after it?"

"I'm still going to, but I'll have a much better chance if we can get some supplies tomorrow. Take the day and get set-up. Then, I think I might be able to beat the thing, and keep you, and Luke, safe at the same time."

128

"And what happens if we go after it tonight?"

"Honestly, I think we all die. Luke almost certainly. If the Gaunt feels that threatened, it will kill him out of sheer cruelty. And if it gets by me, and it probably will, it will come here."

Lacy shuddered and looked out the window, where it was starting to get dark. Solomon could see the conflict in her. She wanted to be out there, hunting for Luke and getting him back, but she had also seen, and been touched by, the Soul Gaunt. Her fear, and in this case, good sense, were overcoming her desire.

"But tomorrow night, we go, right?"

"Yes. If you can help me get some things. We might have to go another town."

"I don't care about that. I just want Luke back and that thing to pay for what it did to Ed."

Solomon nodded, understanding exactly how Lacy felt. If he had the chance to face the thing in the pool and get Celia back, nothing would stop him from trying it.

There was knock on the front door, and Lacy looked at him in surprise. "Expecting anyone?"

"Nope. You?"

"Uh uh."

But when Lacy returned to the kitchen a few moments later, Solomon wasn't surprised. The police had finally come to ask them about what had happened to Ed.

"I can't believe they left," Lacy said. The police had come in and asked them about Ed, how he had gotten hurt, and what their role in it was. Lacy had told them she had heard a scream in the woods, followed the noise and come upon Solomon carrying Ed.

Solomon had filled in the rest, although he left out the part about the Soul Gaunt itself, and didn't mention Luke either. Instead, he told them that he and Ed had agreed to keep a watch around Lacy's place after she had been attacked. He told them about Daisy running into the woods and he and Ed following, but that they had become separated.

He had also heard the scream, and found Ed, as he was now, on the forest floor. His adrenaline pumping, he had picked him up, desperate to get him help, which is when Lacy found them. His only guess was that whatever had attacked Lacy had gotten to Ed too, but he had no idea what it was. His dog was still missing, too.

The police seemed to believe everything he told them, and took him at his word. He had to wonder if that was because he was one of the Folk, here in this world, or if some other force were at play. Regardless, the truth would have only resulted in at least one of the officers getting killed. Solomon had no desire to see that happen.

"I think we should rest tonight," he said to Lacy. "Maybe we can check in on Ed tomorrow."

She nodded, but went to the sliding doors and looked over the now darkened back yard. "Do you think he'll be alright?"

Solomon knew that she was talking about Luke. "I think so. I don't know why the Soul Gaunt is using him, but I don't think it's done with him yet."

Lacy shivered again. "I'm not sure if that's good or bad."

"Me neither. We'll get him back."

It took a long time for Solomon to fall asleep, lying on the couch in Lacy's living room. Every noise sounded like sharp, pale claws trying to get into the house. He was sure that Lacy must be feeling the same way. Finally, he passed into a restless sleep, and dreamed that every plan he tried failed, and the Soul Gaunt stood over all of their bodies.

There was no change in Ed when they visited the hospital the next morning. Maggie was there, looking as if she hadn't slept since the night of the attack. They offered to stay with Ed while she got some sleep, but she told them family was coming, and she would rest then. They left, Solomon feeling that he had let his friend down.

"Whatever this plan of yours is," Lacy said, "I want in on it. I want to help kill this thing."

Solomon nodded approvingly. Although vengeance was frowned on both in this world and the Greenweald, he understood it perfectly.

He laid out his plan to her and they went to a couple of stores to get what they needed. The morning turned to afternoon as they gathered the supplies, and the sun was shining high by the time they got back to Lacy's, where Solomon got to work.

"How do you know how to do this stuff?" Lacy asked him. "From what you've told me, it doesn't sound like your world has electricity."

Solomon stopped. It hadn't occurred to him, but how *did* he know? The Greenweald didn't have electricity. Darkness was kept at bay with torches and candles, heat was provided by fire and cooling by clever vents that took advantage of any breezes. So why did he know about wiring, and generators?

"I don't know. You're right, we don't have it. Then again, we don't have cars, or planes, or TV, and those things seem perfectly normal to me too. It's weird."

"Very. Does it mean that if I went to the Greenweald, a huge forest with people living inside the trees would seem normal to me?"

"Good question. Maybe there's some sort of transfer of knowledge that happens when someone moves from one world to another."

"Maybe I could find out one day."

Solomon looked at her. "Are you saying you'd like to see the Greenweald? Even after all this?"

"I think so," Lacy said. "You know, once Luke is back, and the Soul Gaunt is dead."

"Funny you should say that. I've been thinking that it might be a good idea."

"You have?"

"How's your arm?" he asked her.

She moved it, but the action obviously caused her some discomfort. "The same. It doesn't feel like it's getting any better, but it's not getting any worse either, so there's that."

"Like Ed. That's what I was thinking though. Maybe someone there would know of something that could help both of you. I don't know for sure, but it's worth a try, if we can."

"Soul Gaunt first," Lacy said, her mouth set in a line of determination.

"Oh, yes. I think we're going to solve that problem tonight. Are you ready?"

Lacy smiled grimly. "That thing is going to be sorry it came here."

Solomon grinned back. But inside, he was less sure. The plan was risky, but it had merit. At the least, he imagined that it would take care of the Soul Gaunt. He just wasn't sure if he'd still be around after.

CHAPTER 24

Luke could feel it when the sun started to go down without even having to see it. He had learned over the last several weeks that that was when the fear, and the pain, really started. Both of those things were with him all the time now, but in the beginning, they had started at night.

He hadn't meant to leave Lacy. Not for long anyway. He had taken to walking in the woods, trying to clear his thoughts, stop the words that kept playing over and over. It worked, some. Enough so that he was able to focus on something else, lead a normal life, or at least give the appearance of that.

The words, though. They kept coming, telling him of impossible places and people that had never existed. For a while, they had gotten the better of him, and he had taken to trying to drown them in beer, but they had shouted louder. He tried to talk about them, but people were scared of his incoherent rambling, trying to get the words out all at once before they disappeared. He couldn't blame them. He would have been scared, too.

He tried to write them down, but they didn't come out right on the paper either. The same ideas, the same stories that had at one time seemed so promising became twisted and corrupt, and any skill that he had fooled himself into thinking that he had, evaporated. He couldn't stop his pen from scratching out those messages to himself, telling him to give it up, he was nothing, but yet, he kept trying and trying.

Lacy's ultimatum had been his salvation. Those words had cut right through the ones in his head, and he had heard them loud and clear. And, almost as if they were cowed, the ones in his head quieted, became less insistent, and let him think.

Walking became a balm as well. He loved listening to the birds in the trees, and the soft rustling of squirrels and other small animals in the undergrowth. At times, he would stand still, and let the sounds of the forest wash over and through him, and for a brief moment, the words in his head would fall silent, and he was at peace.

So much so that several nights ago, he had lost track of time and distance, and found himself far from home, with darkness beginning to color the sky. He was a little worried. Walking through the woods at night was a fool's errand, and a good way to end up with a broken leg. No, better to find a place to settle, and wait for morning.

He turned back, determined to get as close to home as he could before he lost the light, but he had come further than he thought, and was still far away when he knew that he should stop. Lacy was going to be worried, and furious. She would think he had fallen back into his old behavior, and that thought almost made him weep. He'd show her in the morning that he hadn't, maybe even take her for a walk out here to show her what he had been doing, and let her feel the peacefulness.

Looking around, he found a likely spot to settle down, next to a recently fallen tree. He gathered up a large amount of dead leaves, intending to cover himself with them. It was a warm summer's night, but the air in the woods would get cool overnight, and the leaves would provide some cover, at least.

But the night air got colder than he thought it would, and much earlier than he expected also. He shivered, his arms wrapped around his torso, trying in vain to stay warm. Then, he started to hear those words again, telling him that this wasn't natural, the temperature couldn't drop like this, not here, not this time of year. Maybe it was something else, something that didn't belong to this world.

"Shut up," he moaned. "Leave me alone."

But the words kept coming. If he had paper and pen he could have written them down, and turned them into the scariest story the world had ever known. If he could only find the right ones to string together, to express this feeling of cold dread that was on him now. But he wouldn't be able to. He didn't have the talent for it.

Instead, he sat and shivered, trying to ignore those words flitting through his mind. Pain, terror, regret, loneliness, agony, fear, *fear*, FEAR.

He scrambled to his feet, the dead leaves flying about him and floating gently back to the earth. There was something out there, in the darkness, watching him. He could feel its eyes on him, measuring him for something, evaluating his...worth? Was that it?

"Who are you?" he whispered it. The words should have been shouted, that would be more dramatic and forceful, but all he could manage was that strangled croak. "Where are you?"

His breath steamed in the air and he swore he was getting frostbite in his fingers. He stuck them under his armpits, and turned rapidly, sure that whatever it was that was watching him had snuck up behind him, ready to pounce, and tear, and feed.

There was nothing there. Nothing that he could see anyway. Maybe behind him now!, He spun again, only to find nothing but the darkness, mocking him. Again, and again. He was too exposed here, too out in the open for something that could see in the dark. He needed to find a place where he could put his back, then it could only attack him from the front.

He ran, and made it two steps before he tripped on a tree root, and sprawled into the dirt, like someone in a bad horror movie. The jolt brought him back to himself, and the words in his head quieted. He was able to think a little more clearly.

What was he doing? Running through the woods at night was a recipe for disaster and nothing more. He was letting his imagination run away with him. There was nothing there now that wasn't there in the day. Even if it was an animal, it was going to be more scared of him than he was of it. He chuckled at that thought, finding it hard to believe.

And something in the dark answered him.

A dry, cold chuckle, like the rolling of bones in a cave, came out of the night. Luke couldn't tell from which direction, but at the sound, all reason, all coherent thought fled. He curled up into a fetal ball, closed his eyes and moaned.

"Not real, not real, not real…"

A hand touched him. Freezing cold, so frigid that it burned, it grabbed his ankle, exposed between his sneakers and his jeans when he had fallen. It felt like his flesh froze instantly. It burned like a rope of fire had been pressed into him, melting his skin. He screamed, loudly.

The voice that had chuckled said a word, a strange word that sounded wrong to his ears, and his voice cut off. The pain still seared his ankle, bad enough that if had an axe he would have brought it down without hesitation. But he couldn't scream. His mouth gaped open, his chest worked, and tears flowed from his eyes, but no sound came from him.

The hand left his ankle, grabbed him by the right arm and hauled him to his feet. Even through his shirt sleeve, he could feel the icy touch. He peered into the inky darkness, trying to see who, or what, it was that had grabbed him, but could only see more blackness. Except for two glowing, green spots, that looked like eyes watching him.

134

A pale, skeletal hand, tipped with sharp nails rose, and struck him across the face. He collapsed in a heap, his face burning from the icy touch and his head ringing from the blow.

"Huuumaaan," the thing growled.

Luke scrambled to his hands and knees. He had no thought of the danger of running through the woods now, only of getting away. He only made it a foot or two before he was grabbed again.

The thing held him in front of it, examining him as he might a particularly colorful bug. The cold sank further and further into him, until it felt like it reached his mind. The words screaming in his brain faded, becoming quieter, but so did everything else. Finally, the pain went away as well, and he sank into unconsciousness.

When he woke, it was daylight, but he was lying on a rocky floor in a cave. It wasn't a deep one, more of a semi-shallow depression in a low rock ledge. Those dotted the area around here and provided homes for lots of different animals. This one was only about ten or fifteen feet deep, he guessed. He could clearly see the forest, awash in warm sunlight, through the opening. All he had to do was stand, or crawl even, and he'd be in it in a moment, and the nights terrors would be gone. He'd be free to go home, back to Lacy and to not ever turn off the lights again.

He started to stand, but the ceiling was too low to allow him to, so instead, he struggled onto all fours. Keeping his eyes on the sunlight ahead of him, he began to crawl toward the cave opening.

After a moment, the touch again. The grasp of the same ankle as before and the same, burning cold pain shot through him. He didn't try to scream this time. Instead, a sob escaped him and he collapsed onto his belly. He was dragged back, away from the sunlight and freedom, deeper into the cave. Deeper than the cave went.

He should have been brought up short by the back wall, but instead he kept going, the entrance getting smaller and further away as he was dragged. He tried to cling to the floor of the cave but his fingernails bent back, causing new agony to burst through him, but he kept trying, leaving steaks of blood on the rock. Then, he was pulled around a corner, the sunlight disappeared, and he was in the dark again.

The thing let go of him then, although he sensed it was near. But it didn't touch him. The fear that it generated was still there, as was the bitter cold. He rubbed his damaged hands together and blew on them.

"What do you want?" he said quietly. "Why are you doing this?"

The thing in the dark chuckled again, and Luke knew that he'd get no answers.

His life was nothing more than fear and pain from then on. During the day, he was kept in the cave, unable to see the light, or to keep warm. If he tried to leave, he was grabbed, struck and cut by sharp nails. Whenever that happened, the thing chuckled and hissed, but it never said another word to him.

When the sun would go down, the presence of fear would leave, and he was able to work himself out and into the woods. But if he tried to go home, again he was taken, and hurt badly. Finally, he stopped trying, and it was then that the black thing led him to the compost pile, allowing him to take scraps to eat, and to look at the house that he had once shared with Lacy, long ago, in another lifetime. Then, it would drag him away again, uttering that strange word to stop him from crying out for help.

Once, he went to leave the compost pile, and the thing made him stay for a moment longer, surrounding him in fear until he was paralyzed with it. He was sure that Lacy had gotten a glimpse of him then, and when he was able to think more clearly, he knew that the thing that held him was playing a cruel game.

"I won't help you get her," he said. The black thing was there, in front of him now. It hadn't said a word, but hung in the air, a menace incarnate.

"You will," it hissed, the first thing it had said to him.

Luke's courage almost faltered, but he held on. "I won't. I don't care what you do to me."

"Foolissssshhh." A bone-white finger came out and curled into Luke's right ear. The pain was immediate and intense. He shook his head, trying to break away, but the ice flowed into his brain and he couldn't move. His mouth opened, but no sound came out, except for a high-pitched whine, and spittle flowed down his chin.

How long the thing held him like that, he didn't know. But when it finally let him go, the night was waning and dawn was beginning to lighten the sky. He noticed it in a type of haze. He seemed to be looking at the world through a fog that wouldn't clear, and he was having a hard time remembering where, or who, he was.

"Obey," the thing said, and flowed away.

136

Luke followed, eyes unfocused, an obedient servant. Later on, he had stood and watched, helpless and almost impassive as the thing had attacked and hurt Lacy. There was an ache in his chest as he dragged her to the road after, the thing following and chuckling as he did, but no tears came, and when he dropped her, he turned back to the forest with barely a second thought.

The next time he tried to break free was the night that Ed and the stranger had entered the woods. His dark master had chuckled as he watched them, at first. But then the tall stranger had come nearer and the thing had stopped, hissed, and flowed from the area.

If Luke hadn't known better, he would have sworn that the thing was scared. That thought, as impossible as it was, lent him a little backbone. He watched Ed, who he admired as a friend, and the stranger. There was something about the tall man, something that made Luke ashamed of what he had become. Made him think that he should have been a better man, someone more worthy of Lacy. He remembered his actions the night that the thing had attacked her and felt more ashamed then he ever had before. No more.

He steeled himself, and ran to Ed, telling him to run. But it was too late. The dark thing took Ed, and it was only the actions of the tall man that saved him at all.

Then he was punished, and punished, and punished some more, until he thought he was going mad.

But he didn't. He was half-blind now, his eye gone, and eaten in front of him. He had been tortured and pushed to the point of madness, until he couldn't think of anything other than the pain.

That included the words. The words that had been there for years, shouting and clamoring for his attention, drowning out the world at times. They were gone. The dark thing had pushed them out of his head, and replaced them with others. With words that would always recall the dark and the fear. Words that would remind him time and time again of the hopelessness of the world, and all in it.

Yes, the sun was going down, and the thing would be back. It had herded him closer to Lacy's house, his one-time home, again. He knew that the thing was planning on using him to lure her out here again, where it could hurt her once more.

But that wasn't going to happen. Not if he could help it. He'd warn her, at least, and let the thing do with him what it would.

CHAPTER 25

"We have to go get him," Shireen said, pulling her sword free and taking a step deeper into the entry hall.

"Shireen, stop." Orlando put his hand around her arm. "We can't. There's too many of them."

From deep inside the tree came the sound of a scream. "Let me go!" Shireen pulled her arm free.

"No!" Orlando grabbed her again. "I won't lose you. Think! Thaddeus is gone. I'm sorry, but it's true. I don't know why they let us go, but they did, and we need to take advantage of that, and tell Jediah and Florian what we found."

Shireen jerked her arm again, but Orlando kept a tight grip. Everything that made her who she was, was telling her to go after Thaddeus, to rescue him. He had given his final strength to get them out of there, how could she abandon him now? Without the Soul Gaunts' fear pushing against her, her own strength of will was back in full effect.

She turned to Orlando. "How can we leave him? You heard him just now. He's still alive."

"They're playing with him. They're cruel, and vicious, and horrible. They're going to use his pain to hurt us as well. I hate them too, but we don't stand a chance. We need to get help. Yes, Thaddeus will probably be dead by the time we can get back here, but at this point, that might be a kindness. Now come on!"

He stepped through the doorway and back into the light of the Rustling Elms compound. Shireen reluctantly let herself be led away, but as she did, another scream came from within the tree. She paused, dropped her head and then stepped away.

Outside felt worse than it had when they first arrived. After the darkness and decay of the tree, it should have felt bright and cheerful, but instead, the bodies still strewn everywhere, and the blood that had pooled in sticky puddles attracting flies, made a mockery of the day. It was a grim reminder that either the Soul Gaunts had attacked at night, or they were in league with something that was able to brave the light.

She kept her sword drawn as they walked to their horses and mounted. Orlando took the reins of Thaddeus's horse and they began to ride away, slowly at first, reluctant to leave the mage behind, but quicker as they drew away from the compound.

An hour later, they arrived back at Whispering Pines where they were shown to the main tree and ushered inside immediately.

"What happened? Where's Thaddeus?" Florian was on his feet, a look of worry on his face as they entered the room. Word must have gone ahead of them as they rode through the compound that although three of them had left, only two returned.

"Gone," Shireen said. She felt numb, exhausted. She had kept her sword out the whole ride back, even through the relative safety of the Whispering Pines compound, but now finally sheathed it. "I am sorry, Lord Florian. He saved us though." Her voice was quiet, and she sank into a nearby chair, looking only at the floor.

"What happened?" he asked again, his voice dangerously low.

"Florian, be patient," Jediah said. "We'll get answers. Orlando?"

It was fitting that Jediah ask him rather than her. He knew his people well, their strengths and their weaknesses. He knew that out of the two of them, Orlando was more level-headed and apt to think things through, whereas she had a harder time controlling her emotions.

"It was Soul Gaunts," she heard her love reply, his voice soft and halting. "Not one, but several. A lot. I don't know how many. They took Rustling Elms. Killed everyone and left the bodies. We went in, not knowing what we would find, but the tree was…it was dying, from the inside. They trapped us. At first, we thought it was one, and started to leave, but then…they were everywhere, and the light was dying. Thaddeus. He saved us. He caused the stone to light up again, stronger this time, but it wasted him, used all of his strength."

He paused. Shireen felt a touch on her shoulder and glanced up. Jediah held a cup out to her, filled with a strong wine. She drained it in one quick swallow, while he did the same for Orlando. Florian stood off to the side, his face a mask of icy calm.

Orlando took a drink and continued. "They wouldn't let us leave. They herded us, like animals, to the door, but it was shut tight. We couldn't

140

get it open, and then Thaddeus. He tried, Lord, he tried with all his strength, but it wasn't enough. The light went out, and they took him. They pulled him away from us, into the darkness."

Shireen was glad that he didn't mention them hearing Thaddeus scream. There was no reason to cause Florian more pain than they had to, and she was sure that his mind was supplying plenty of horrors on its own.

"But you got out?" Florian asked.

"Yes. I don't know why. After they…they took him, the doors opened and we were allowed to leave. Shireen wanted to go back in, to try to rescue Thaddeus, but there were so many of them. We needed to warn you."

"You did the right thing," Jediah said.

"Yes." Florian moved to the side board where he poured himself a cup of wine. "Yet, it seems that every time my house interacts with yours, Jediah, I lose someone dear to me."

Shireen saw the quick grimace of pain that crossed Jediah's face before he turned to Florian.

"Don't cheapen his sacrifice, Florian," he said. "Thaddeus saved them. If they had the ability, they would have done the same for him."

"We still can!" Shireen leapt to her feet. "Gather your houses! Both of you. Bring every warrior, mage and priest that you have and we'll get him. We'll storm Rustling Elms, burn it to the ground if we must and save him."

Florian looked at her over the rim of his cup, and then shifted his eyes to Jediah. Shireen saw the sadness in them.

"It wouldn't work, would it?" he asked quietly.

"No," Jediah answered. "Not if there are that many. All of our forces together wouldn't be enough. This settles it. We need to go see Jamshir."

Florian nodded and set his cup down. "Then let us go. Before other Houses meet the same fate."

CHAPTER 26

The plan terrified Lacy. It was a good one, or at least she hoped it was, but her part in it scared her to death. Solomon would be facing the real danger, of course. She couldn't imagine him having it any other way, but still, she'd be there, and so would...that thing, the Soul Gaunt.

But, if it went well, the thing would be dead, and she'd have Luke back. For better or worse, he'd be back. And even if they didn't work out, even if Luke's demons were too great to be beaten, at least he'd be freed from whatever was holding him to that thing.

"Are you ready?" Solomon came across the yard to the deck. He had been at the edge of the woods, finishing a part of the trap that he had set up. It still amazed Lacy that someone from an entirely different world would have any idea how to do the things he had done, and yet, he had. At least, it looked like he had, tonight would be the true test.

"You know what to do, right?"

Lacy nodded, her eyes already scanning the darkening woods, looking for any sign of Luke, but so far, she had seen nothing.

"Lacy," Solomon's voice was calm, yet serious. "Listen to me. It's imperative that you stick to the plan. Even if you think it's going to hurt me, you can't worry about that. You have to go through with it. If not, I don't think it will work, and both you and Luke will be in terrible danger."

"I know," she replied. "I'll do it, don't worry."

"Good. I know you will. But listen, we haven't talked about what happens if the plan fails."

"It won't." Lacy was glad to hear that her own voice sounded steady and determined to her, rather than wavering and cracking with the fear she actually felt.

"I hope not, but there is always the possibility. If it does, you run, understand? You can't face the Soul Gaunt alone. You run to your car and get out of here, as fast as you can, and you don't come back."

She looked at Solomon and nodded. Honestly, she didn't think he had to tell her to run if the Soul Gaunt got the better of him. She didn't think she'd be able to stop herself.

"I'm going in. You stay here, hand on the switch. You know what to do after that."

He hugged her quickly, and then was gone, running into the gloomy woods as if he was heading out for an evening jog. She shivered as she watched him go, then took her place and settled down to wait, her eyes tracing all the electrical lines that now ran across her backyard.

The sun set, and the moon began to rise. It was close to full tonight and cast enough light for her to see across the yard without too much difficulty. But the woods were still in deep shadow, the leaves on the trees blocking the moonlight every bit as effectively as they blocked sunlight during the day. Anything could be moving in there, especially anything that happened to look like living pieces of darkness itself. The Soul Gaunt could be right there, right on the edge of the woods, watching her, waiting to flow across the yard, seize her and freeze her again. Maybe this time it wouldn't stop with her arm, or when she passed out. This time, it would do to her what it had done to Ed.

"Stop it," she told herself, and drew a deep breath. The night air was warm, almost a little muggy, but in spite of that, she shivered.

She couldn't stop from straining her ears, trying to hear if there was the noise of someone running through the woods, crashing through the undergrowth and snapping twigs underfoot. Or worse, the sound of a scream, or a moan of someone in pain. Or even worse yet, the sound of a cold, dry chuckle. But there were only the normal night noises of insects humming against the outside light near the back door, and the occasional hoot of an owl.

The night passed slowly. Two hours went by, then another. Still there were no noises from the woods, and no patch of darkness detached itself and came across the lawn at her. No matter how she stared, or what she thought she saw at first. It was early morning now, and by all rights, she should be exhausted, but she remained alert. If there was one thing the pain and fear that remained from her encounter with the Soul Gaunt had done, it was to keep her focused.

Then, faintly, she heard noises. Was it?

143

Yes, the sound of footsteps, running in the woods. Heavy, but moving quickly. There was no indication that whoever was coming was trying to be quiet, or to hide in any way.

A moment later, Solomon burst from the forest, running full out toward her. Over his shoulder he carried a motionless body, clothed in dirty rags.

"Luke," she breathed. He had done it. Somehow, Solomon had gone into the woods, found him, and pulled Luke out of there.

He panted to a halt in front of her, and dropped Luke to the ground, none too gently. Lacy looked at Solomon and saw that not only was he breathing heavily from his labors, but his left arm was covered in blood and hung at an odd angle.

"You're hurt!"

"I'm okay. It's a little sore, but I avoided the worst of it. Hold on to him, Lacy, and remember the plan!"

With that, he was gone again, running back across the lawn and into the woods. For a moment, she could hear him crashing through again, but then the noise of his progress disappeared and the night was silent once more.

Only this time, it was really silent, more so than any normal night had any business being. The bugs were no longer bumping into the light, there were no sounds coming from the forest. And it wasn't as muggy, or as warm. Instead, the temperature was starting to drop quickly.

Lacy's breath steamed in the air, and she realized that she was breathing heavily too, as if she had been the one to carry Luke out of the forest. But it wasn't exertion that was causing it, it was the feeling of dread, of helplessness, that was creeping in on her.

She looked around her, found the switch that she was supposed to throw when the Soul Gaunt got close. Her hand moved toward it. If she threw it now, she'd be able to see better, and she and Luke would be safe, or at least safer. They could probably make it to the morning. Solomon could run here too then, right?

Her hand inched closer, but with an effort of will, she dragged it back.

"No, dammit! There's a plan. We stick to it."

"Huuunnnhh....whaaa?" Luke mumbled from the ground at her feet.

"Stay still, Luke," she didn't look down at him. The Soul Gaunt was not going to frighten her into ruining the plan. It would regret coming here and messing with her and hers. Her determination helped her to steady herself, and she stayed attentive, peering into the darkness of the woods.

Then, a small segment of that darkness detached, and moved across her lawn. It came in a steady, flowing motion, as if it were floating slightly above the ground rather than walking upon it. It took its time too, allowing the dread around her to intensify.

She was panting, and Luke was starting to stir more loudly now, his limbs twitching and moans escaping from him. She squatted down, her one hand on top of the switch that Solomon had put on a stake that he had driven into the ground, and the other touching Luke's shoulder. Her gaze never left the patch of blackness that came toward her.

"Come on, you sunofabitch," she whispered, using the epitaph as her own encouragement.

The Soul Gaunt's eyes flared, the sickly green color appearing near the top of the shapeless form. It hissed, and then that dry, cold chuckle issued from it.

"The Folk ran away," it said, and Lacy shivered to hear the things voice. Hearing it made it feel as if spiders were running up and down her spine and into her hair. It was every vile and unclean thing in the world, come to life and approaching her. "He left you. Now you're mine, and I'll have you in front of my slave. Your fear and his anguish will be my fodder."

"Then come and get it," Lacy said, her voice cracking in spite of her best effort to sound strong.

The thing chuckled again and came on in a rush. It moved much faster than she had been expecting, and it almost made it to her. Her hand slid down the face of the switch, flipping it. Solomon had been smart, and installed it upside down, so that by simply slapping it, she was able to activate the lights.

All of them. Solomon had wired lights around the edge of the woods, shining in toward the yard. They were large, ultra-bright security lights and they flooded her yard with a brilliance that made her squint. She lost sight of the Soul Gaunt and everything else for a moment, but was rewarded with a loud hiss that she knew came from the creature.

She shielded her eyes and looked again. The Soul Gaunt was spinning in place, desperately looking for a way to escape the light. It was hissing like a tea kettle about to boil, it's bone white hands thrown up in front of its face, as it moved across the yard, trying one direction and then another to escape the glare.

In the light, Lacy could see that what was formless in the darkness was a dirty, stained, black cloak. It was ragged and hung in tatters at the edges, and yet there seemed to be no end to it. Layer upon layer were draped over the thing, so that no matter how it spun or whirled, all that was revealed was more of the dark material. It had a deep hood that even the security lights couldn't penetrate, and except for those clawed, white hands, there was no sign of any other human-like limb. It did float too, as it appeared to in the darkness, the ragged cloak staying a few inches from the ground with no sign of support.

But the hisses were becoming quieter and the spinning was slowing down. The hands stayed up in front of the hood, but now, in between bouts of hissing and spitting, the chuckle was starting to emerge again.

"Silly," it said, finally coming to rest, facing Lacy and Luke. "Light hurts us, yes, but only an inconvenience. I'll take your eyes, then destroy your cursed lights, and let you languish in my darkness for an eternity."

Now would be a good time for Solomon to show back up, Lacy thought. But there was no sign of him as the Soul Gaunt resumed its advance toward her.

CHAPTER 27

Everything was darkness, fear, and pain. There was nothing else in the world.

At first, the pain had been where they grabbed him, their icy touch freezing the flesh beneath his clothes. He had known what he was doing when he gave the rest of his strength to get his friends to the door, but he had expected the soldiers of Towering Oaks to be able to keep him safe. That's what they did, right?

But they had failed him, and let him be taken. The Soul Gaunts had grabbed him, their touch freezing his skin, and pulled him away. The last time he had seen light had been when the door had opened, and Shireen and Orlando had fled, leaving him to his fate. The scream that escaped from him then had been half at that, and half at a new stab of pain, as yet another Soul Gaunt grabbed him, pulling him deeper into the tree.

Finally, they had pulled him back up the stairs and into the room where the three of them had first encountered the Gaunts. They threw him down on the floor in front of the man crucified on the wall and left him. For a moment, he thought that they were going to leave him be, to allow him to leave as they had the other two, but no. Instead, they were toying with him. If he tried to stand, to leave, one of them would come flowing back out of the darkness, grab his arm and force him back to the ground, its touch burning him anew.

He couldn't see, everything in the room was pitch dark, but he knew where he was none-the-less. They had made sure that his hand brushed against the man on the wall before leaving him. Now, he peered into the darkness, trying in vain to see, or hear, anything, but everything in the darkened tree was still and silent.

He scooted around, moving so that his back was against the wall. He shifted to the side to avoid the dead man's foot and the pile of entrails below. He shuddered, aware that his fate was probably the same as this poor fellow.

But no Soul Gaunts came for him. Instead, he sat for what felt like hours, starting at every little sound. He was sure that they were playing games with him, creeping near and allowing the slightest noise to escape them, just to watch him grow more and more frightened. Well, if that was their game, it was going to backfire. You could only be so scared, then your mind started to fight back. Thaddeus's mind was well trained, too. He was used to thinking in certain ways to get magic to work, or to interpret information coming into House Whispering Pines.

Conserving his strength was the key, so he stopped listening for every little noise, stopped trying to get some advance notice of when they would return. As long as he sat quietly, they seemed content to leave him alone, so that was what he did. Instead of dreading their return, he began to think of ways that he would pay back Shireen and Orlando if he was ever able to get out of here.

The dread that permeated the air inside the tree dropped off some, and the temperature warmed. Not as much as it should have, and the atmosphere was still oppressive, but better than it had been. To Thaddeus, that meant that the Soul Gaunts had pulled away, and were no longer in the room with him. Interesting that one of their most potent weapons could also be used to tell how close they were. That was news that he would pass on to Florian.

He realized that he was now thinking in terms of "when" he would escape, rather than "if". There was no delusion on his part that he was still being watched, but he was beginning to think that this was part of their game. Cause him terror, then allow him to run home and spread it around, soften up his own people for when the Soul Gaunts attacked. They'd find tougher going if they came to Whispering Pines. His was one of the great houses, not a minor one like Rustling Elms had been.

At the moment though, no plan for escape came to him, so he sat and stared into the darkness, wishing for another stone to light the way with, or even a simple lantern. But even if he had a stone, there was no way that he had the strength to cause it to glow again. Even now, it was all he could do, in spite of his dire situation, to keep his eyes open.

He didn't know how long he dozed off for, but he woke shivering. The cold was back, and with it, that almost overwhelming sense of dread. Thaddeus shifted back against the wall, pressing into it, eyes bulging as he looked into the darkness. They were back.

He could feel them, coming close to him and then flitting away. Every now and then, a frigid, sharp finger would touch him and the cold would cut into him. Yes, they were playing with him, but knowing that didn't make it any better, and a quiet sob hitched in his throat.

They laughed at that. The cold, dry chuckle sounding from all over the large room. From the sound of it, there were several Soul Gaunts here. Enough to destroy all of the Greenweald, he was sure.

"What do you want?" he said, his voice cracking. It sounded loud in the darkness.

"What we have," a voice whispered back. "Your fear. Your anguish."

Thaddeus sobbed again, but inside, a fire was starting to rage. He may not have slept for long, but it had been enough to allow him to recover a little of his strength. Not a lot, but some. Maybe enough to hurt one of them, anyway.

"Stay away from me!" he said, purposely sounding more desperate than he felt. His fingers worked the hem of his shirt, trying to find a loose thread. He didn't need much.

"We'll have it all, soon…"

Ah. There. A small tail of thread hanging loose.

"You'll have nothing from me! I'll die first!"

"You will. You will die. When we've had enough of you."

A little more thread came loose. Now, he had a piece about an inch long. Not quite enough, he needed a little more. He tugged harder, but the thread stopped. If he pulled harder, he was sure it would snap, maybe leaving him with much less than what he had now.

"My friends will come back for me!"

They chuckled again at that, and Thaddeus felt sick at saying it. Friends? Friends wouldn't have left him here like this. But it had been something to say. The Soul Gaunts seemed to be enjoying his false bravado. Fine, let them.

His fingers kept working at the thread, and finally, a little more came free, about twice the length that he had had. Enough. He grabbed it at the base and gave a sharp yank, tearing it free. Good! More came out with that final pull. He rolled it between his fingers, mashing it up into a tangled ball.

Now was the hard part. He couldn't start to chant the spell, they would know it for what it was right away. He had to do it silently. It wasn't impossible, but much harder, and he would need to concentrate. If they would only leave him alone for a few minutes.

He put his hands over his face, the little tangle of thread between two fingers and pretended to sob. "Leave me be," he moaned, and collapsed onto his side, hoping that they would have had enough of their game for a few seconds.

In his mind, he visualized the spell. Fire, white hot, burning but not consuming. Too hot and intense for its size. Blazing on the floor between he and the Soul Gaunts, turning the horror of the blackness into bright light, driving them back.

He could see it, and could see the words needed to make it happen. He concentrated on them, saying them over and over in his mind. In between his fingers, the thread started to warm, pleasantly at first, but quickly becoming uncomfortable. Another moment and…

The pain was incredible. He shot up, pressed against the wall again. At first, he thought his spell had happened too quickly, and the thread had flared into magical fire too early. Then the realization hit. It wasn't the thread at all. The heat that was running down his hand wasn't from that, it was from his fingers. Specifically, the two that were now gone.

He screamed, for real this time, and pulled his hand back against his chest, feeling his shirt grow wet from the blood. The whole world was nothing but pain, starting in his hand, radiating down his arm and into his torso. He screamed again, the tears flowing down his cheeks as fast as the blood down his arm.

There was a spitting sound and something hit him in the darkness. Even in his agony, he flinched away, but there was nothing further. He groped down with his uninjured hand, and found two cylindrical items on his lap. His fingers.

They had known, the whole time they had known what he was doing, and let him do it, only to take it away at the last moment.

The Soul Gaunts chuckled all around him, the noise worse than it had ever been before.

"Why?" Thaddeus moaned. "I haven't done anything to you. Why?"

They only chuckled louder, and then started to flow away, the feeling of menace growing less, the air warming. Thaddeus lay slumped against the wall, his damaged hand cradled to his chest. Finally, exhaustion, pain, and blood loss took over, and he passed out.

This time, when he came to, there was still no sign, or feeling of, the Soul Gaunts being around him. If anything, the air was warmer than it had been since they had first come into the tree. His hand throbbed and ached, but had stopped bleeding.

But he still felt dizzy and sick. Pushing himself up, he looked around the room, glancing over quickly to see that the man who had been hung there was still in place.

"Didn't take a walk, huh?" he muttered. "Just going to keep hanging around?"

He was horrified to hear his own voice, being so blatantly disrespectful to the dead. But then, what would he care? The corpse's one remaining eye stared out into the darkness, as useless to him as both of Thaddeus's were.

Wait. Why was it that Thaddeus could see the dead man? More, he could see the room. It was still dark, and he couldn't make out details, but he could see the walls, and the shapes of furniture.

Were his eyes adjusting to the darkness, or was it actually getting lighter?

The door to the room creaked, and through the gloom, Thaddeus could see it swing open, revealing nothing but more gloom, not quite total darkness, beyond it. But there was no sense of evil, and no drop in temperature that accompanied the Soul Gaunts.

As Thaddeus watched, a darker shape appeared in the doorway and started to walk toward him. Not glide, hovering above the floor, but taking firm, deliberate steps.

CHAPTER 28

Glittering Birch made all other compounds look lesser in comparison. Not run down, or neglected, just…less. Less grand, less opulent, less wealthy. There had been a time that it hadn't been so. Florian had visited here several times over the years, starting as a child, when he, Jediah, and others would come to play games with Jamshir, then nothing more than a child himself.

At that time it had been a magnificent sight, as all of the Folk's compounds were, even the lesser houses. But it had stood as the first among equals. There was no doubt that you were in the presence of the ruling house, but it hadn't felt the need to flaunt it so much.

But that was the difference between Jamshir and his father. Roland, the previous ruler, had governed by competence and ability. He had the respect of the other Heads of Houses, and had earned it. When the Hairy Men had attacked, it was Roland in the vanguard who had driven them back. As Jediah got older, and showed remarkable promise as a soldier, it was Roland who had encouraged it, and had helped to turn Towering Oaks into the force it was today. He had always had a kind word for Jamshir's friends, and took what seemed to be an honest interest in their pursuits.

Then, time had passed. Out of the three of them, Florian had become the Head of his House first, at an earlier age than most of the Folk did. The memory of the loss of his parents still stung, all these years later. But Roland had been there to offer advice. Florian made his mistakes, of course, but overall, he acquitted himself well, and Whispering Pines continued to flourish.

It was then, he realized, looking around at the magnificent gardens through which they rode, that things had begun to change. Jamshir had always had a sharp wit, but his jibes began to sting more keenly and seemed to be more directly aimed at Florian. Jediah hadn't noticed, but by then, he was more interested in his training than anything else.

"It's a shame," Florian said, talking quietly, so that only Jediah could hear him without straining. Shireen and Orlando rode behind, as did two members of his own House.

"What's that?"

"What happened. To the three of us, I mean. You and I have managed to mend fences, but the divide with Jamshir happened long before that."

"I suppose it did. I was preoccupied in those days, I'm afraid. I should have been there more when your parents died. And I should have made sure that he was too. I am sorry about that."

"That was long ago. And you did come around, and did check up on me. But we were growing into our roles, I understood that then, and I do now. Maybe it was the same for Jamshir."

"Maybe," Jediah said, "but he's still not the man his father was."

Florian saw Jediah look around him with an expression of distaste. The gardens, the sculptures, the fountains, they all seemed to vie for attention. As if there were no real cohesion to them all, but instead had been picked out simply because they were expensive.

"Beauty is in the eye of the beholder, my friend," Florian said, which earned him a wry chuckle from Jediah.

"Indeed. Let's find out if Jamshir really has gone blind."

"Ah, my friends, returned to Glittering Birch after all this time!" Jamshir stood up from what could only be described as a shaped wooden throne and came down the stairs, his silver robes glinting in the light from the high windows.

"It wasn't that long ago that I was here last, Jamshir," Jediah said, his voice with a quiet edge to it.

"What? When was…oh, that. Well, never mind that unpleasantness. Now you're back, and together! It does my heart good to see my two oldest, dearest friends reunited. Come, come. Sit with me."

He led the way to the side of the large room where a grouping of comfortable chairs was placed. Indicating that they should sit, he took one for himself. Florian's guards, and Shireen and Orlando, had been held at the door to the hall, where they stayed now, standing at attention. Not that it mattered. There had to be at least twenty Glittering Birch soldiers spaced around the room, armored and armed to the teeth.

"So, what brings you both here?" Jamshir asked. He snapped his fingers, and a servant stepped forward with three glasses of cool red wine.

"Soul Gaunts," Jediah said with his usual lack of tact. Florian winced. That wasn't how he would have approached the subject.

"Oh? You came to share children's tales with me?" Jamshir leaned back in his chair, sipped his wine and smiled at them over the rim. "Please, continue. I could use a break from the rigors of governing."

"Not tales, Jam…" Jediah began, but Florian interrupted him. "I know how unbelievable this sounds, my friend. I felt the same way when Jediah came to see me, but trust me, it's true. Soul Gaunts have invaded the Greenweald."

Jamshir tilted his head to the side, his smile fading, but not disappearing. "Surely, you jest. I'll admit that I know the blasted things are real, but one hasn't been seen in…."

"Since Solomon defeated the last one." Jediah took a sip of his own wine. "That's why we're here. We need him back."

Jamshir's eyes widened in disbelief as he looked from Jediah to Florian and back again. Then, he threw his head back and burst out laughing. "Oh! I see. What is the occasion today? Some local holiday involving pranks that I've missed out on?" He downed the rest of his wine in a gulp and signaled for more.

Florian saw Jediah's face darken and placed a warning hand on his friend's arm. "No joke, I'm afraid. Jediah's best soldiers, those standing near your doors, have seen them. I, myself, have lost someone dear to me to them. Don't mock this, Jamshir, I beg of you."

Jamshir stopped laughing and regarded the two in silence. Finally, "Tell me."

Jediah told him what had occurred on the patrol to the north that Shireen and Orlando had been sent on, and what they had witnessed inside the Rustling Elms compound.

"Wait," Jamshir interrupted, holding up his hand. "Are you telling me that a House, minor or not, has been wiped out?"

"Yes," Florian said. "Unfortunately, that is the case."

"Why am I just now hearing about it, then?"

Florian saw Jediah glance at him, his own thoughts reflected in his friend's eyes. Maybe if you spent more time ruling, and less on *playing* at being a ruler, you would have known.

"We thought to gather what information we could first," he said, attempting to placate Jamshir. "That way, you'd be better able to formulate a plan."

"I see," Jamshir said quietly, but Florian could hear the distrust in his voice. "Go on."

"It wasn't one Soul Gaunt," Jediah said, "It was several. We've never seen, or faced, more than one before. Honestly, I don't even know how we'll do it now."

"Isn't that your job?" Jamshir asked, his eyes glinting. "I mean, from the time my father helped you, you've developed your house into a military force, am I not correct? If this type of thing isn't what you were building to, then one has to wonder what exactly you are preparing for."

The implication was clear. Jamshir was sure that Towering Oaks was readying itself to attempt a coup. He shook his head, dismayed at their former friend's delusions.

"I don't think the might of Towering Oaks and Glittering Birch together will be enough," Jediah said. "Not even if Whispering Pines and all the other houses were to back us. By the time we finished the job, so many would be dead that we'd be easy prey for anyone outside of the Greenweald."

"Ah. So, then. What do you suggest?"

"As I said, we need Solomon back."

Jamshir sipped at his wine again and regarded the two of them. He sighed, looked around the room and then back to them. "No."

"No? What the blazes do you mean 'no'?" Jediah surged to his feet, an action that caused the guards around the room to put their hands on their sword hilts. They stopped at a signal from Jamshir.

"I mean no. How can I possibly be more clear?"

"Jamshir," Florian said, "we've worked it out. I was wrong to insist on his exile, I know that. I was hurt and grieving and took it out on the wrong person."

"What makes you think I care one whit about that?" Jamshir snorted.

"Then, I don't understand. Why would you say no?"

"Why would I say yes? Why would I want him back?"

"Because we'll need him to defeat the Soul Gaunts, you idiot," Jediah said.

Jamshir stiffened, his glare turning icy as he looked at Jediah. "I'll forgive that, in memory of good times gone past. But don't overstep yourself, Jediah. You can be removed."

Jediah started to respond, but stopped himself and sank back into his chair.

"Jamshir," Florian said. "Forgive Jediah. He's hot headed, and we've known that since we were kids. But his point is valid. Surely you must realize how valuable Solomon is, and how much use he would be during this time of crises. Even I freely admit, he is the best that the Folk have seen in many a generation."

"Exactly," Jamshir said. "So why then would I want someone like that around where they can be used against me?"

"I have no designs on your position," Jediah said. "I never have. You were my friend at one time, and even if you weren't, I would never disrespect your father's memory that way."

"Ah, yes, my father. Such a wise, noble, ruler, wasn't he? Do you think I don't hear the whispers? Not half the man my father was. That's what they say about me, isn't it? Well, maybe it's true. But still, the Greenweald is mine to rule as I see fit, and mine alone. You've made your request, and I've answered it."

"What about the Soul Gaunts?" Florian asked.

"I'll send some of my people to investigate. If, and I highly doubt it, things are as dire as you say, then I'll send word to the Houses. If I find it necessary. Or you may find that House Glittering Birch has resources that you're not aware of, and I'll deal with the problem myself. Either way, you'll know my decision when I choose to tell you. Now, is there anything else?"

Florian looked over at Jediah, who sat in silence with a stony expression on his face.

"No, Jamshir. I think we're finished here."

CHAPTER 29

Solomon finished tying his shirt around the wound in his arm. It had taken longer than he thought it would, and the Soul Gaunt was moving closer to Lacy as he watched. He actually had no idea how the lights were going to affect it. When he had fought the other one, years ago now, the light from his sword seemed to hurt it as much as the blade itself did. With any luck, these lights, being so much brighter, would do more than cause it pain.

He moved his arm gingerly as he watched the thing spin and hiss in the sudden light, a grim smile on his face. It hurt, but he was still able to use it. The Gaunt had gotten a good shot in when he was pulling Luke away from it. Its claws had gone deep, and the cold had penetrated further than the actual cut had. It felt like his arm was bathed in ice water, and there was a deep muscle ache that made him feel that he had no strength left.

Taking the thing by surprise was all that had allowed him to get Luke and get away. He had seen Luke's face too, and knew that the Gaunt had taken one of his eyes. From what he remembered of the old stories, that was a favorite of theirs. He supposed he should be glad that thing had only taken the one.

He flexed his arm, watched and waited for his moment, enjoying every second of the Soul Gaunts misery. But quicker than he would have wished, it stopped its mad gyrations and turned its attention back to Lacy. It began to move forward again, taking its time. Solomon could see the near panic on her face as she looked desperately around, wondering where he was.

"Hold on," he muttered. "You can do it."

He needed the thing to be fully committed. The lights would weaken it, and deaden its senses somewhat, but the more focused on her it was, the better chance he had of taking it by surprise. He had barely been able to pull his arm away when it had latched on to him before, so he was under no delusions that the thing was horrifically strong.

But, so was he. All of the Folk were strong, much more than the humans of this earth, but out of them all, Solomon had the most natural gifts. Even for his own kind, he was fast, strong, smart and deadly. If anyone had a chance, unarmed and one-on-one, with a Soul Gaunt, it was him.

He kept that thought playing in his mind as he braced himself. The Soul Gaunt moved forward, closer to Lacy, hissing again and chuckling, thinking that its prey was frozen in place with fear. Close enough. It was now or never!

He rose and burst through the undergrowth, moving as fast as he could. He covered the ground between he and the Soul Gaunt in a flash, and had just enough time to see it spin around to face him before he barreled into it.

The filthy robes of the thing enveloped him, blocking out the light and making it impossible to see. They stank and he breathed shallowly, trying to keep the stench from going too deep into his lungs. The cold was unbelievable, and he knew he only had moments to do what needed to be done before it began to sap even his strength.

But the most potent weapon, the fear that a Soul Gaunt wielded…that was gone. He could feel its body, somewhere in there, under the robes. It was bony, and thin. If he could get his hand around one of those bones, he'd be able to snap it like a twig. That thought, that sudden reveal of the underlying weakness of the thing, gave him a courage that negated the things fear like the sun dispelled the darkness of night.

Wrapping his arms around it, he squeezed it to him, and bore it to the ground. It hissed and writhed under him like an enraged cat. And like a cat, it had claws. In spite of his best efforts, the Soul Gaunt managed to turn and hook a claw into his shoulder, digging deep. It was like a spike of cold fire had been driven into him, but he gritted his teeth, and squeezed it to him harder.

The Gaunt worked the finger deeper, its sharp claw driving further into him, threatening to kill his whole arm. He struggled to his feet, ignoring the pain and the blood that he could feel flowing down his chest. Then, he spun and fell forward, driving the thing into the ground, hoping that would shock it. It worked for a moment. The force of the blow caused the thing's claw to come out of his shoulder, although the damage was done.

It was the same arm as the one that the Gaunt had cut before, and now it was definitely losing strength rapidly. Solomon knew that not even he could hope to prevail against it one-handed. This needed to end quickly.

158

He surged to his feet again, and took three steps toward the pool. But his arm weakened further, and the thing was able to start working its way around, bringing its clawed hand up between them. As he started to lift it, it slashed that claw forward and a line of fire suddenly bloomed along his face, starting at his hairline and extending down through his right eye, across his nose, and ending at the corner of his mouth. Now it was his turn and he screamed as the world went dark from that eye.

But he held on, taking another step and another. He lifted it up, marveling at how something that was so light could be so strong, and then plunged it down, over the side of the pool and into the water.

The weight of its own robes were a benefit to Solomon now. They helped weigh the thing down, and aided him in holding it there in the water. It struggled, and cut his forearms to shreds, but he held on, keeping it submerged. Soul Gaunts didn't breathe, but drowning it wasn't the plan.

"Now!" he yelled.

"But you'll get…"

"Lacy! Now!"

Out of the corner of his eye, he saw her approach the pool, the heavy-duty cord in her hand. She hesitated, and he groaned as the Gaunt cut into his arm again.

"Hurry, I can't hold it!"

She tossed the end over the side and into the water, holding her other arm in front of her face. There was a flash, and Solomon felt like he had been stung by a thousand wasps, everywhere, all at once. The Soul Gaunt stiffened, vibrating, its claws locked tightly around Solomon's arms. But his were locked on the Soul Gaunt as well, and when his body went rigid, his arms locked, holding the thing there in the water.

His breath stopped, and his chest hurt badly, like a large animal was sitting on it. In his one good eye, everything started to turn red, with black creeping in around the edges.

Then something hit him and he was falling. His hands were empty and he hit the ground hard. His last thought was hoping that the plan had worked. Most things wouldn't kill a Soul Gaunt, but maybe electricity would.

CHAPTER 30

By the way Orlando kept his horse close to hers, Shireen knew that he was well aware of the seething anger she was barely holding in check. In spite of the newly re-forged friendship and alliance between Jediah and Florian, it wouldn't do to speak openly about the meeting with Jamshir. Not yet.

She was hoping that the two Heads of House would separate now, each going back to their own compound to ponder what should be done next about the Soul Gaunts, but there was no such luck. Instead, Jediah rode along next to Florian, taking the path that led back to Whispering Pines.

Breathe, she told herself. Jediah knows more than you. He's older and more experienced and wiser and...

It was no good. Despite telling herself these things, she didn't understand why he had let Jamshir say the things he did, and why the two of them had let him off the hook that easily about Solomon, to say nothing of what had happened at Rustling Elms!

Her ire rising, she shook the reins to step up her pace. Beside her, Orlando muttered an oath and did the same.

"Jediah! What are we doing now? Surely we're not..."

She got no further before Jediah raised his hand. "Peace, Shireen. I'm well aware of your feelings, and I share them. We go now to discuss what we can do and what we will do. I want you and Orlando there, but if you can't control your emotions, then I'll settle for Orlando only."

Rebuked, Shireen hung her head, feeling the blood flush into her cheeks. "Yes, of course. Forgive me, lord, I..."

"It's forgotten. Now please, give Florian and I space to continue our conversation."

That was about as direct a dismissal as Jediah had ever given her, and it stung. Still, she had to admit that she deserved it. Of course, she had no right to intrude on their conversation. She dropped back, fully aware of Orlando doing the same.

"Come on," he said, in low tones, when they had regained their previous positions. "Did you really think that he was just going to let it go? You know better."

"I know, and I don't need you reminding me of my foolishness!" she hissed.

"I'm not. But we're all too keyed up at the moment. We need to stay calm. Let me help you with that." His hand reached out for hers, but she pulled back. "Shireen. Come on. It's what I'm here for. Why we're so good together, remember?"

She sighed and stretched out her hand to clasp his. They rode like this for a couple of moments, and then released each other. The awkwardness of trying to ride while holding hands brought a small smile to her face. The first in days, she felt.

Her mind wandered as they rode through the trees. Was Thaddeus truly dead? There was a part of her that hoped it was so. If not, then unimaginable tortures could be happening to him at the hands of the Soul Gaunts. One was bad enough, but a horde of them? She could imagine the magic user being passed from one to another, in a cruel contest to see which one could make him cry out the loudest, or endure the worst pain without passing out. While she never felt that she had a particularly vivid imagination, it was enough so that it was painting a picture for her now. A picture full of darkness, and bright, red blood.

Any warmth from the day evaporated for her as she remembered the feeling of being inside that tree, surrounded by the Soul Gaunts. She felt like she would never be warm again, and shivered in spite of herself. Orlando seemed fine, or mostly so. How was it that he was so strong, while she felt like she was falling apart?

If only Jamshir would have agreed to bring Solomon back. He'd know what to do, or at least, he'd come up with a plan. She could see him now, that half smile on his face as he contemplated the best way to deal with the Gaunts, and the look of fierce determination that would replace it when it was time for action.

The world warmed, a little, as she thought of it. Shireen loved Orlando deeply, and wouldn't trade one moment of her time with him. Her feelings for Solomon were different. She loved him also, yes, but it was a different type of love. The love for a close friend, of course, but also, the love for something that was better, that showed the world could be a great place, and that took you along with it.

She shook her head, becoming more aware of where they were. Soul Gaunts had openly attacked and destroyed a House of the Folk, and here she was wool-gathering as they rode! Some expert soldier and scout she was!

Throwing back her shoulders, she kept herself at attention, resolved to stay focused until they had reached their destination.

Later, she and Orlando sat at a small table in one of the gardens of House Whispering Pines, a bottle of amber wine between them. Florian had insisted that they take their rest, to recuperate from their ordeals at Rustling Elms, and Jediah had relieved them of duty until he called for them.

She had to admit, it felt good to simply sit, have a glass of cool wine and not worry about anything. It wouldn't last, it couldn't now, but for a few minutes…

Orlando took a drink and sighed. "Looks like our break is over."

She followed his gaze and saw Jediah and Florian approaching. Climbing to her feet, she came to attention, noting as she did that Orlando simply stood casually.

"Alright, Shireen," Jediah said. "I said everything was forgotten. You're allowed to be upset at times. Let's get back to normal, okay?"

She relaxed her posture slightly. "Okay. It won't happen again."

"Good enough. Now, we have some talking to do. Come with me, both of you."

They didn't go far. Florian must have had a spot prepared in another area of the garden. While she may think he was fluffed up, she had to admit that his hospitality was unparalleled. The four sat at yet another table, servants brought more wine and food, and when they had left, Jediah began.

"Florian and I have been talking. It's only the four of us at the moment because what we're going to propose could possible by seen as treason. Although we don't think so, and we think we'll be vindicated. Still, there is a chance that we won't be. And if that turns out to be the case, you two will also be complicit, should you choose to go along with what we propose."

"We're yours to command, of course," Orlando said.

"Not in this. What we're going to ask is not a command, and not doing it will not affect you, or your standing in my House, in any way. Understood?"

"Understood."

"Good. Florian?"

Florian took a sip of wine and wiped his lips with a cloth napkin. "Well. To put it simply, we're going to ignore what Jamshir said. We're going to get Solomon back on our own."

"What? That's wonderful!" Shireen said.

"Yes, it is," Orlando said, but ever more thoughtful than she herself was, he continued. "But how? Jamshir's sorcerers were the ones who sent him away. We don't even know where on that earth he is."

"No," Florian answered. "But someone does."

Jediah gave a soft whistle, and a huge, shaggy, gray dog came around the corner and sat near him. "This," he said, "is Daisy. And apparently, she knows exactly where Solomon is."

Shireen looked at the dog, knowing it for a Hunting Hound. "And you want us to...?"

"Go with her, of course. She has some way of crossing between here and there. Follow her, hold on to her, and hopefully, she'll take you with her."

She looked at the dog doubtfully. Hunting Hounds had fearsome reputations. It was said that no-one except for the Master of Hounds could truly control them. Yet, here one sat, seemingly perfectly content to remain near Jediah, with no sign of aggression at all.

"And we know this one knows where Solomon is because?"

"Because she was sent after him," Florian said. "I had Thaddeus do it when Solomon was first exiled."

There was a strange noise from her left. It took her a moment to realize that it was Orlando quietly laughing. It seemed as if it had been a long, long time since she had heard it.

"And Solomon, of course, not only didn't get killed by the Hound, but actually made friends with it. Why am I not surprised?"

The others smiled also, and she felt her own face mirror theirs. She picked up her wine and raised her glass. "To Solomon. Who in saving himself, will save us all."

CHAPTER 31

Lacy was knocked aside as a body rushed past her, barging into Solomon and knocking him to the ground. The noise, the sound, and the smell of the Soul Gaunt as it cooked in the pool had driven almost everything else out of her head. The fear and despair that the thing generated had almost paralyzed her, and then the thought of electrocuting Solomon also…

With a start, she came to her senses and rushed forward. Luke had done so first, of course, and it was he that had run into Solomon, knocking him away from the pool. The two men lay in a tangle now, groans escaping Luke, but only silence coming from Solomon.

She glanced over the side wall of the pool, afraid to see the Soul Gaunt coming around and rising, dripping and furious. But it was still there, floating in the water with steam coming off it. She knew enough not to touch the water even now. Solomon had wired the cord directly into her circuit breaker box, with no breaker, so the current would still be flowing.

Time enough for that later, though.

"Luke," she said softly, bending over him. "Come on. Can you get up?"

Her husband lay, filthy and emaciated, face down. At the sound of her voice though, he rolled, and Lacy let out a cry when she saw the gaping hole where his left eye had once been. The Soul Gaunt had taken all of her attention before this.

"Oh, Luke. What happened to you?"

He stirred again, opened his remaining eye, and actually smiled at her. "Hey, Gorgeous. Did you get it?"

"Yeah. Yeah, we got it. Well, Solomon did, anyway. Come on, get off of him so that he can get up, too."

She reached a hand down and helped pull Luke to his feet. He rose slowly, and stood, leaning on her, obviously still weak. "I'm sorry," he said, as he looked into her eyes.

"We'll talk about that later. Right now, I'm just glad it's over."

She put her hand on his cheek and smiled at him. Then, she turned to Solomon.

"Solomon? Hey. Can you hear me?"

There was no movement from the tall man lying in the grass. She bent down again.

"Hey. The Soul Gaunt's dead. Or at least I think it is. It's not moving anyway. Solomon? Can you hear me?"

But there was still no response. Luke came over and squatted down near him, picking up his hand and pressing his fingers into Solomon's wrist. "He's got a pulse. Feels strong to me. Not that I really know a weak one."

He was alive, at least. That was a relief. But they couldn't leave him lying here in the yard. "Come on," she said to Luke. "Help me."

She got her hands under one of Solomon's shoulders and started to lift, straining at the weight of his unresponsive body. Luke did the same on the other side, and between them, they managed to get his arms over their shoulders, where they were able to hold them as they dragged him across the lawn.

But when they reached Lacy's deck, they stopped. Luke was panting heavily, reminding Lacy that he had been through an ordeal himself the last several days. She was winded as well, although she sounded better than Luke did, but she knew that she wouldn't be capable of dragging Solomon up the steps.

"Set him down. Gently."

They lowered Solomon to the ground. It was then that Lacy noticed the terrible damage that the Soul Gaunt had done to him. She drew her breath in sharply as she saw his shredded forearms, the blood soaking his right arm and shoulder, and the terrible wound running down the side of his face. He too, she saw, had lost an eye, but unlike Luke's, this wound was fresh and still oozed blood, black and sluggish.

"Stay with him," she told Luke, fighting the nausea that suddenly grew in her stomach. "I'm going to get some blankets, and some first aid stuff."

"What about 911?" Luke asked.

"Let me get him warmed up first. Then we'll call." She couldn't explain her reluctance to call the EMT's. Solomon obviously needed medical attention, more than she could provide. But something was stopping her from wanting them examining him too closely. If he went to the hospital, what if they found out that he wasn't human? What would happen to him then?

She set her jaw as she rummaged in her house, pulling out bandages and iodine from under the bathroom sink. If he didn't improve, or showed any signs of getting worse, no matter how small, then she would call the authorities, but until then, she would keep Solomon here.

She hoped she was making the right decision. On the surface, it seemed wrong in every possible way, but somewhere inside of her, she knew it was what he would want her to do.

When she came back out, she found that Luke had pulled over an old chaise lounge that had been propped up by the side of the deck for the last two years. It has seen better days, but it would serve to get Solomon up off of the ground. Luke took the blanket from her and spread it over the lounge, and then helped her get Solomon onto it.

Once there, she looked at him more closely. The blood wasn't flowing anymore, but was still sticky. Were the wounds not as serious as she had feared, or was this some aspect of his otherworld physiology? It didn't matter. Start with the most severe first.

She took a soft cloth, dipped it into the bowl of warm water she had brought out, and dabbed gently at his face. Soon, the cloth was soaked through and the water in the bowl was a dark red color.

"Can you refill this, please?" she asked Luke. "The sink is…"

"I know," Luke replied, taking it from her. "I remember."

"Of course. Sorry." It felt like it had been years since Luke had lived there with her.

"It's okay, I understand."

He walked slowly up the steps and disappeared into the house. While he was gone, Lacy pulled Solomon's shirt down, exposing the hole that the Soul Gaunt had made in his shoulder. "Ohhh, that one needs stiches, I think." But that was beyond her. Still, it was no longer bleeding, so if she was able to clean it up, then he could make that decision when he recovered.

Luke returned with two bowls of water and more cloths. He helped her clean Solomon, and wrap clean cloths around his forearms. She was glad to see that very little blood seeped through, staining the material. Solomon breathed deeply and steadily, and Luke said that his pulse felt the same to him. Finally, she had done all that she could, and rose stiffly to her feet.

"I'm going to stay here with him," she said. "You should go in, though. Get some real sleep for once."

"Do you really think I'm going to do that? And leave you here by yourself? Don't be silly." He smiled at her and went back up onto the deck. A minute later he reappeared, carrying two chairs down the stairs. He set them down and motioned her to one of them, and then wearily sank into the other himself.

He had no sooner sat down though when he grunted, climbed back to his feet and approached the pool. "Luke, don't!" Lacy shouted, as he reached out and grabbed the cord. But he simply gave it a yank and pulled it out of the water and onto the ground.

She watched the pool with wide eyes, expecting to see the black, wraith-like shape rear up, attack them again. But there was no sense of dread, no feeling of coldness spreading through the air. The Soul Gaunt was dead.

"It's dead," Luke said, and Lacy wasn't sure if he meant the cord, or the Soul Gaunt. Luke looked into the water, shuddered and returned to his chair.

He only sat for a minute or two, though, before shifting uncomfortably. "Umm, I hate to say this, but I really need to shower. Would you mind?"

She glanced over at him and realized how filthy he was, and what bad shape his clothes were in. His stuff was still here, she hadn't had it in her to get rid of it all yet. "Yeah, of course. Your clothes are in the spare bedroom, pretty much thrown on the bed. Everything else is where is always was. When you come out, bring some scissors and we'll lop off a little of that nasty beard, too."

He grinned at her, glanced at Solomon and went into the house, leaving her alone with the unconscious man and the dead thing floating in the pool. She didn't want to think about that. Instead, she checked on Solomon again, then settled back in her chair and tried to keep her imagination from wandering.

Luke was back within half an hour, with scissors in hand. He sat cross-legged on the ground in front of her, and she cut his beard back, then turned him and trimmed his hair, also. She wasn't a hair-stylist, so it was choppy and a little uneven, but better than it had been. Luke sat silently, calmly, while she worked.

167

She wanted to ask him what had happened, how he ended up like he had, in service to that vile thing, and what had happened to his eye. But she was loath to break the silence. Instead, she sat and listened as the night noises resumed.

But there was one noise that didn't fit in. It was off in the woods, quite far back, but coming closer, she was sure. The sound of something large pushing its way through the undergrowth. For a moment she was afraid it was another Soul Gaunt, but then remembered how silently that thing had floated above the ground. Whatever it was, it wasn't that.

Still, she braced herself, her hand finding Luke's as the noise got louder.

Then, Daisy broke from the cover of the woods and raced toward them. Behind her, strode two, tall, thin, grim figures.

CHAPTER 32

Thaddeus pushed himself against the wall again, already conditioned that to try to run was to invite more pain and fear. He watched as the dark figure came closer, the footsteps ringing in the dark of the room.

"Who are you?" he said, and hated the quaver in his voice.

The figure said nothing, but stopped when it was a few feet away. Its hand went to its breast, then came forward, holding something out. Thaddeus shrank back further, readying himself for whatever horror was being presented to him.

It was bread. A small loaf of crusty bread was being held out to him by a perfectly normal looking hand. The fingers were long and slender, much like his own, and although they were pale, they were nothing like the bone white of the Soul Gaunt's sharp claws.

"What is this?"

"Eat," the figure responded. The voice was deep and rich, so different from the whispers and chuckles of the Soul Gaunts that for a moment, Thaddeus wasn't sure he had really heard it.

"What kind of trick is this?" he finally got out. "Where are the Soul Gaunts?"

"No trick. I sent the Soul Gaunts, as you call them, away for now. They will leave you be unless I tell them not to."

Thaddeus didn't like the sound of that. His hand still throbbed where they had bitten off his fingers, and he felt sick and disoriented. He needed the food, needed to keep his strength up as much as he could, or he'd never have a chance to escape.

Tentatively, he reached up, his good hand trembling. The figure stayed still while he took the bread, much as a man feeding a wild animal might. He grabbed the loaf, and pushed back against the wall, afraid of the blow that he was sure would now fall.

But none came. The figure merely stood and watched him. Or at least he assumed it was. It wore a heavy black cloak, with a deep hood that hid

169

its features. It reminded him of the Master of the Hounds, but not as shabby, and much larger. When nothing happened, he bit into the bread, the flavor flooding his mouth. It was the most heavenly thing he had ever eaten, despite its dryness.

He wolfed a couple of bites down, the crumbs catching in his throat, and causing him to explode in a fit of coughing. The figure reached into his cloak again and brought out a water skin, which he held out to Thaddeus.

This time, the mage grabbed it without question or hesitation and tipped it up to his mouth. Ahhh....cool water. It tasted better than the finest wine. His meal of bread and water felt like a feast for kings.

"Water now, wine when you're stronger."

The figure began to turn.

"Wait! Who are you?"

"Time for questions later as well. Finish your meal."

As the figure moved, the room started to darken again. Thaddeus clutched the water skin and bread to his chest, ignoring the pain in his maimed hand.

"Please, leave the light," he begged. "I can't stand the darkness."

But the figure ignored him and left the room. The slight glow that had allowed him to dimly see went with him, and darkness descended once again. Worse, the air became colder, and a feeling of unease came over him. They were there again. Not in the room, but outside the door, passing by it, or gathered in the doorway, watching him.

He nibbled on the bread, sipped at the water, and stared into the blackness. The simple motion of eating and drinking helped him to stay calm. But soon, the bread was gone, and the water skin was dry. Then he had nothing to do but sit and stare, and try not to notice that the man hanging on the wall next to him was starting to stink.

He jerked awake as a line of pain was drawn down his leg. The air was frigid and froze the spittle in his mouth as he cried out. He could see a vague shape, hunched near his leg. A hand, so white it almost glowed in the darkness, reached out and ran down his thigh again. Another line of fire ignited. The thing was running its claw down him, slicing through his pants and into the flesh beneath.

He screamed again as the icy fire flared up, and the Soul Gaunt chuckled in return.

"Hurts, yes? There is more to come. Much more." The voice was a mere whisper, dripping with malicious glee. It began to reach over to his other leg, when the glow that accompanied his benefactor earlier returned.

The Soul Gaunt hissed and jerked upright, its claw withdrawing into the folds of its robe. It spun around and moved away from Thaddeus, but too slowly.

The figure in the black cloak stood in the doorway again. "What is the meaning of this?" The deep voice came out tinged with anger.

"Master, I…"

"None of your excuse, wretch. I told you all that this one was off limits. He was not to be played with."

Unbelievably to Thaddeus, the Soul Gaunt bobbed, almost as if it were bowing.

"Leave, before I decide to deal with you now," the figure said.

The Soul Gaunt glided away, faster than Thaddeus had ever seen one move. It skirted around the figure and flew out the door. The air in the room began to warm again.

"I am sorry for that," the figure said, advancing to Thaddeus. "They are notoriously hard creatures to control, I'm afraid."

He made no move to bandage any of Thaddeus's wounds, but went instead to the side of the room and pulled a chair forward. Seating himself, he reached into his cloak and pulled out another skin. "Do you feel strong enough for wine? Or would you prefer to stay with water for now?"

"Wine," Thaddeus croaked. He would drink as much as he could, let it cloud his mind and take away the nightmare for a while.

"Good," the figure said. He threw back his hood and took a deep drink from the wine skin, and then handed it over to Thaddeus. "Not too much at once. We have things to discuss."

Thaddeus tilted the skin to his mouth and squeezed out a stream of the dark, red wine, watching the man sitting near him as he did.

He was tall, this man, at least as tall as any of the Folk that Thaddeus knew. And while his hands were slender and almost delicate looking, he was wide through the shoulders. He was bearded, and both that and his hair were white. His eyes were pale blue, so pale as to be almost colorless, and they watched him appraisingly.

Then the gloom resettled and the man's features became more indistinct again. Thaddeus realized that for a moment, it had almost been as if a light had shined on the man.

171

He took another healthy swig of the wine, and passed the skin back into the man's outstretched hand.

"Who are you?" he tried again. "Why are you doing this?"

"Two very different questions, neither of which are easily answerable."

"Try."

In the gloom it was hard to tell, but he swore that the man smiled.

"Who I am won't mean much to you. Suffice it to say that I come from north of here. Far north. Beyond the land of the Hairy Men. Farther than any of your kind has ever gone."

"So you're not one of the Folk. I figured that. Why are you attacking us?"

"Attacking you? No, I'm afraid you misunderstand. I'm doing everything I can to save you. To save this whole place. And to save these poor, unfortunate creatures that you call Soul Gaunts, as well."

Thaddeus looked around him, at the devastation they had made of the Rustling Elms compound. He indicated the man hung on the wall next to him. "Tell that to him. And the rest of the people that your pets butchered."

The man sat quietly, watching Thaddeus. "You don't know what they are, do you? Or why they're here. I wonder..." He trailed off, then climbed to his feet and wandered off a few steps. "If you knew the truth, would you believe it? Or would you shut it out, refuse to hear it?"

Thaddeus opened his mouth, but the man held up his hand to stop him. "It doesn't matter. Not at the moment. Keep the wine skin. If you'll listen to my advice, you'll take it slowly. But still, it's up to you. I'll return later, after I've thought of the best way to go about what needs to be done."

He started to leave and the soft glow that semi-illuminated the room went with him.

"I don't suppose you can leave the light?" Thaddeus called.

The man didn't acknowledge the question, or so much as turn his head. When he was gone, the room descended into darkness again. Thaddeus slowly lifted the wine skin to his lips, and ignoring what the man had advised, drank deeply.

His mind was still fuzzy when the man returned, the dim light coming with him. No Soul Gaunts had brought him back to himself this time. The wine was gone, but he didn't think it was as strong as the man had told him.

172

It did dull him somewhat, but there was never a single moment that he forgot where he was, or that the pain from his wounds went away. Instead, he became more unfocused, his stomach was roiling, and he had a horrible taste in his mouth.

"Ah, Thaddeus. It is Thaddeus, isn't it? It looks like you didn't take my advice. Well, there's no teacher like experience, I'm afraid. The wine made in my homeland is different from what you're used to, I'm sure. But don't worry. The effects will pass just the same."

Something felt off. How had the man known his name? Did he tell him in a previous conversation? He didn't think so, but when he tried to replay them in his mind, they slipped away, like water through cupped hands. The wine was really affecting him after all. His mind was his best, most potent weapon, and his ability to remember conversations, no matter how trivial seeming, was one of the reasons he was so valuable to House Whispering Pines.

"I've come to a decision," the man continued. "One that I think you'll like. It's a deal that I have to offer you."

He waited silently while Thaddeus tried to focus. "What kind of deal?"

"The kind where you get to leave. Go home, back to your compound, and tell the Head of your House what you've seen here."

Freedom? He wasn't to be tortured anymore? Or killed by the Soul Gaunts? "Yes," he said, his voice pleading, no matter how much he tried to make it sound firm. "I'd like that. I'd like to go home."

"Of course, you would. Who wouldn't? But, I need you do something for me."

"Anything. Name it." The thought of walking out of this charnel house had helped to focus his thoughts. He could see the daylight welcoming him, warming him.

"I'll need you to spread my message. Well, *our* message I should say."

"Message? Sure. What message?"

"The message that we come in peace, really. That we want these poor creatures to have the justice that they deserve."

Thaddeus glanced around again, his gaze flitting past the man rotting on the wall. "Peace? How is this…"

"Perhaps you're not quite ready to make a deal? Maybe more time would convince you of our sincerity?"

"No! No. Peace, yes, I can see that. I mean, it wasn't the fault of the Soul Gaunts that they…"

"Exactly. These poor creatures, and they prefer to be called Nightwinds by the way, were merely trying to find a place to escape the harsh sun, when they were set upon by the soldiers of this House. They tried to escape, but to no avail. They had no choice but to defend themselves."

"Of course," Thaddeus mumbled. "That makes sense."

"Since that time, we haven't moved from here. We've hurt no one else. Not even the two from that other house who abandoned you here, left you to what they were certain was a hideous death. And yet, here you are, at the mercy of these supposed terrible creatures, and you're fine."

Thaddeus glanced down at his maimed hand and the slashes in his leg. He remembered the cold fire that had burned through him whenever the Soul Gaunts, or Nightwinds, or whatever they were, had touched him. He looked back up to see the man gazing at him calmly, waiting for his reaction.

"Yes, I'm fine. A couple of scratches, really. Nothing more."

"Exactly. Now, here's what I need you to do."

There was more wine, and more whispering. The man left, and came back several times, and in between, the Soul Gaunts returned, bringing their fear and coldness with them. They never touched him, but they were always there, near him in the darkness, until the man with the light came and chased them away.

Finally, after what felt like years, the man told him that he was free to go, but to remember their bargain. Thaddeus nodded weakly, the man helped him to his feet and guided him to the door. Moments later, he stood outside, blinking in the harsh glare of the sunlight. He held his hand up to shield his eyes, and started to stagger back to Whispering Pines.

CHAPTER 33

The two approaching figures had the same body type as Solomon, Luke saw. They were tall and thin, with slightly angular features. Unlike Solomon however, they weren't dressed in normal clothes. Both of them wore what almost looked like clothes you would see at a renaissance fair, in shades of gray. They also carried swords in scabbards at their belts, which was definitely something that you didn't see every day.

In short, they looked like something that had walked out of one of the stories that he had tried to write. He glanced back at Solomon, still unconscious on the lounge nearby. If he hadn't been through what he had over the last several days, he wouldn't have believed any of this.

The huge dog bounded up, then stopped and sniffed at Solomon, a whine rising in her throat.

"I guess he really did make friends with it," one of the newcomers said. It was the man, and his voice sounded forced, like he was trying to make light of a horrible situation.

The other one, the woman, rushed forward and knelt on the ground next to Solomon. She looked him over, her hands reaching out tentatively to his face. "Oh, Solomon. What did you do?"

"He saved us," Lacy said. She watched the woman carefully, obviously unsure of how to react to the newcomers.

"That's not surprising either," the man said. "It's what he does. My name is Orlando, and I'm a friend of Solomon. This is Shireen."

Luke stood and offered his hand. Orlando considered it for a moment, an amused expression on his face, and then took it in a firm grasp.

"If you're done fooling around," Shireen said, "can you help me here?" Her voice was rough, as if she was holding back tears.

"Of course." Orlando knelt on the other side of the chaise lounge and examined Solomon. "He's cut up pretty badly, obviously. But other than the wound to his face, I don't see anything too serious. Not for him, anyway. Who patched him up?"

175

He looked up, and smiled when Lacy tentatively raised her hand.

"You did well," he said to her. "He may have saved your life, but you probably did the same for him."

Luke watched Lacy with disbelief. She had always been so strong and sure of herself that he was having a tough time reconciling that with the timid seeming woman he saw now. He moved closer to her and took her hand. "Lacy and Solomon did more than that. Look in the pool."

The woman, Shireen, glanced at them, but seemed to dismiss them from her thoughts almost as quickly. Bad cop, good cop, Luke thought to himself. Or too concerned with Solomon to spend much thought on us? He felt his blood begin to heat. Not at being dismissed by her himself, but by having her do that to Lacy. If she knew what this woman had done!

"Shireen," Orlando said.

She sighed, stood, and walked to the pool, glancing into the water, and then giving it more of her attention. "Is that...?"

"A Soul Gaunt, yeah," Luke said, his voice hard and cold. "They killed it. The two of them."

"How? I mean, Solomon didn't have his sword, or any weapon that I can see."

"He used what was available here," Lacy said. "The whole thing, it was his plan. To kill the thing, and to get...well..."

"You can say it," Luke said. "Part of the plan was to get me away from the thing. It was holding me captive."

"Why?"

Luke shrugged. "No idea. It hurt me at times and took a lot of pleasure in doing that. It used me as bait to try to get to Lacy, too. But it never told me what it wanted."

"I've never heard of a Soul Gaunt doing such a thing," Shireen said.

"Up until a day ago, we never believe they existed," Orlando said, "so what do we know?"

"Yes, but if they take captives...then maybe..."

"Thaddeus. You're thinking he could still be alive?"

Luke listened to them, feeling a strange sort of detachment. They had no idea what he had been exposed to over the last few days. The constant fear and the bone chilling cold. The occasional glimpse of freedom, given just long enough to fill him with a slight hope, and then cruelly snatched away. The hopelessness and despair after seeing Ed taken, and being forced to lure Lacy in as well.

He may have been putting a good face on it, but inside, he was barely holding it together. He didn't think he'd ever be over it, but at least he was home with Lacy, for now. He'd hold on to that for as long as he could.

"Maybe." Shireen's voice interrupted his thoughts. "We need to get back. I'll take Solomon." With that, she strode quickly back to the lounge and reached down to pull Solomon up onto her shoulders.

"Wait!" Lacy cried. "You can't move him like that! He's hurt!"

Shireen stopped and looked at her. "We must. He must be brought back to the Greenweald. He's done his duty here, that's obvious, and now he's needed there. And we must hurry. Another's life may depend on it."

As if that settled the conversation, she grabbed Solomon's wrist, who chose to let out a groan at that very moment. Shireen jumped back, and they all stared at him. Luke let go of Lacy's hand as she moved to his side. "Solomon? Can you hear me?"

With another groan, his good eye fluttered open. It cast around the yard, finding Lacy, then Luke himself, and finally settling on Daisy. "You came back." His voice was a husky croak. "Good girl. Took you long enough, though." In spite of his words, he scratched the dog between the ears.

"She came as fast as she could," Orlando said. "We could barely keep up."

For the first time, it seemed that Solomon registered that Shireen and Orlando were there. He broke into a smile that was painful to watch as it twisted the horrible wound on his face. "Took you guys long enough, too," he whispered.

Luke stood back as Shireen bent down and squeezed him.

"We have to get you back," she said, when she finally released him and stood. "We'll get you to the healers. Then, we have other things to deal with."

Solomon made a face. "What about my exile?"

"Florian has rescinded it. He and Jediah are working together. We can tell you about it later. For now, say your goodbyes so that we can go."

Luke already had the impression that Shireen wasn't so much the bad cop, but that she was impatient and anxious for action at all times. Orlando looked more serene and willing to wait for events to unfold before reacting. Sort of like he and Lacy, he mused.

"Goodbyes?" Solomon said. "No. Lacy is coming with us. She's been hurt by that thing too, and needs healing. Luke also."

"We can't take humans into the Greenweald!" Shireen exploded. "It's unheard of!"

"A lot of things that have been unheard of are happening," Orlando said, stepping forward and taking her hand. Again, Luke felt that he was watching his own interactions with Lacy play out in someone else.

But this talk of going to the…what was it?…the Greenweald? What was that? He turned to Lacy and raised an eyebrow, a well know expression between the two of them that meant, "what the hell?"

She put her hand on his chest. "I'll explain more later. Just know for now that it's where that horrible thing came from. But it's also where he comes from." She indicated Solomon with a tilt of her head. "So it can't be all bad, right?"

Luke smiled. He was back, and free of the Soul Gaunt, and with Lacy. There was still a lot to atone for. His drinking, his disappearance, his behavior in general. But she seemed willing to put it behind her for the moment. And for now, that was good enough.

"Okay," he said. "Then let's go see another world."

"I still don't like it," Shireen mumbled.

CHAPTER 34

Jediah had returned to his own compound, and Florian sat in one of his many gardens, uneasy, despite the quiet of the afternoon. He had to admit that it felt good to be working with his friend again. Yes, his grief was very real and legitimate, but he was seeing a little more clearly now. He should have listened to his daughter, and not been so stubborn about who she had fallen in love with.

Florian didn't want to admit to being any sort of elitist, but he supposed that he was. He couldn't bring himself to face that his daughter, one of a noble class, had fallen for a common soldier. The fact that Solomon was hardly common didn't enter into the equation. It had all come down to his birth, and the fact that he had been born to commoners. How foolish of him.

Now, he sat in the sunlight and missed his daughter, and nursed his own guilt. At the alienation that had sprung up between them, at her death, and at the misplaced anger that had caused Solomon to be exiled. If he only had it to do again.

And then there was Thaddeus. Florian was second-guessing his decision to send his cousin to the Rustling Elms compound with Jediah's soldiers. He had been so sure that it was something that was being blown out of proportion and had wanted someone that he trusted there to tell him what was really going on. Because he no longer trusted his oldest friend to do what was needed.

For the first time in his life, he felt old, and tired. It felt like mistake after mistake was piling up, until they were in a huge, teetering stack, about to fall and bury him under. Maybe that wouldn't be such a bad thing. Let someone younger, less prone to emotion, take over the responsibility of running a Great House. His choice of successor would have been Thaddeus, with Celia gone, but now that option was gone as well. There was no one else. His family had never been large, the way some of the others were. But now someone from one of the other noble families that swore allegiance to House Whispering Pines would have to be chosen. Enough. That was a task for another day.

He sighed and took a sip of his wine. These were dark days. Even here, sitting in the sunshine in gardens that were the envy of most other Houses, it felt dark and cold.

The servant approached so quietly that Florian hardly even noticed him at first, but when the man hadn't moved on after a moment, he realized that his attention was needed.

"Yes?" he said, trying to keep the irritation from his voice. "What is it?"

"My lord…" the servant hesitated. "You're needed."

"What's that supposed to mean?" He reached for his wine glass again.

"There is someone here, my lord. For you, I mean."

This uncharacteristic fumbling of words in a servant was unusual. But then again, he had been in such a funk for these last several days that who knew how the staff was viewing him now.

"Bring them here then."

"My lord…. it's Thaddeus. He's returned, and he's injured."

Florian's hand stopped with his wine halfway to his mouth. He stared at the servant, too stunned to move. Then the wine glass fell from his grasp to shatter on the ground, and he was up and moving toward the main house, the servant trailing along behind.

"Thaddeus," Florian said quietly. They had laid him in his bed in his chambers and two healers were there poring over his wounds. The one on his hand looked especially bad, but it wasn't until one of the healers had moved, that he saw that two of Thaddeus's fingers were missing entirely. There was also a large cut on his leg, several smaller scrapes and nicks, and bruising all over. It looked as if his cousin had been savagely attacked, and barely escaped with his life.

Florian was sure that was pretty close to the truth.

"Thaddeus?" he tried again, but there was still no movement.

"Give him time, Florian," one of the healers said. She was most competent healer in all the Greenweald, and as such had earned the right of familiarity.

"Alright," he said, and retreated to a chair across the room to leave them to their work.

180

The healers of the Greenweald were unmatched in their craft. Many were the Folk who had been brought back from the other side of death by them. They served no House exclusively, but had taken oaths to do their best to provide aid to any who needed it, regardless of House affiliation. If anyone could help Thaddeus recover from an ordeal with Soul Gaunts, it was they.

Eventually, they finished their work and stepped aside. The female, Willow, who had spoken to him before, approached.

"He should recover. Given time and rest. Keep him here, and make sure he drinks plenty when he wakes. Water, Florian, no wine. At least not yet. For the first full day, give him water only. Then, if he's hungry, he can have a little food. More as time goes on and his strength returns. The important thing is to keep him rested and calm. Whatever did that to him really did a lot of damage, but we'll stay on top of it."

For a moment, Florian was surprised by the last statement. He had been living with the knowledge of the Soul Gaunt invasion and attack for what felt like forever, but he was one of very few who did know it. He wouldn't reveal more, not even to the Healers, without consulting Jediah first.

"We'll do as you say. Thank you for coming."

"It is our duty," Willow replied. She bowed her head, gathered her equipment and left the room.

Florian sank back into the chair. He would wait right there until his cousin woke up.

He woke with a start when he heard the moan from the bed. Instantly, he was on his feet and across the room. His cousin was moving, his forehead slick with sweat, as his head turned on the pillow. His eyes moved under his lids, and another moan escaped from his lips.

"You're home, Thaddeus. You're safe."

Thaddeus stilled for a moment, but then continued to mumble, moan and writhe on the bed. Florian kept talking to him in a calm, quiet voice, telling him that it was over, he was back home, he wouldn't be hurt anymore.

Finally, after what felt like a very long time, Thaddeus quieted, and slipped back into a deeper sleep.

The next time he stirred, Florian was there already. He had stayed sitting on the edge of the bed, his hand resting gently on his cousin's arm since the first time Thaddeus had moved. His back ached and he felt exhausted, but he was determined that his would be the first face that Thaddeus saw when he came to.

A low moan came from him again, not as tortured sounding this time, but more an exclamation of discomfort. Florian watched as his eyes fluttered open, shut again against the brightness of the room, and then opened a slit.

"So bright..." His voice was a rough whisper.

"I'll draw the curtains," Florian said, starting to rise from the bed.

"No! No, I like it."

Thaddeus eyes opened a little wider. Unbelievably, he looked at Florian and gave a small smile. "I didn't think I'd see you again."

"I didn't think you would either. I'm glad we were both wrong."

"Florian, it's Soul Gaunts. Not just one though. There are many. So many." His eyes widened and his voice took on a tone of panic as he said this.

"I know. I know. Relax. They can't get to you here."

"Hah. They can. And they will, if we let them. You can't know..."

"We do. I was here when Shireen and Orlando came back. They told us everything."

"Everything? Including how they abandoned me?" Thaddeus's voice was bitter and he looked away from Florian.

"They thought you were gone. Even with that, Shireen wanted us to marshal both our houses and ride to your rescue. It was only Jediah that was able to calm her down."

"And you, cousin? Did you want to ride to my rescue as well?"

Florian bent his head. "I did, of course. But...I have greater responsibilities. To the whole House. Jediah is the warrior, and his opinion was that both of our houses together wouldn't have been enough..."

"So you left me."

"We thought you were gone. If we had known, believe me, Thaddeus, there wasn't a force in the Greenweald that would have stopped us."

Thaddeus kept his eyes adverted, but then sighed and turned back to his cousin.

"It doesn't matter anyway. I learned things. A lot of things."

"Such as?"

"They're not here for war. They've been driven from their home and need a place to settle. That's all. They're hungry, and scared."

"The Soul Gaunts? You mean the Soul Gaunts are scared? Thaddeus, that's…"

"Unbelievable, I know. Trust me, I felt the same. But then…well, they let me go, didn't they?"

"Looks like they did a lot of damage to you first."

Thaddeus nodded. "But I did some to them before that. They were acting in self-defense. I know this all sounds crazy, but they want peace."

Florian regarded his cousin. He had been through so much, perhaps, too much. Thaddeus's mind had always been his single most valuable asset. But now, maybe it had been damaged too much.

Still, there was no harm in hearing what he had to say.

He rose to his feet and got a cup of water. He handed it to Thaddeus and sat back down in the chair near the window.

"Tell me," he said.

CHAPTER 35

Shireen felt like she was in turmoil, and didn't know which way to turn. That glance into the human's pool had unnerved her more than she wanted to admit. Not only was the sight of the dirty, black material floating in the pool enough to turn her stomach, but there was Solomon himself.

He had done it again. He was already a living legend in the Greenweald, a fact that had only been reinforced when she discovered that he had fought, and beat, a childhood nightmare. But now, he had done it again, and this time with no weapons but his own wits and the strength of his arms. He was her oldest, dearest, friend, and yet now, she felt like she hardly knew him at all.

He was more than the best of them all. He went beyond that to something supernatural.

But Orlando didn't seem to feel the same. She watched as he helped Solomon climb gingerly to his feet and support his first tottering steps. Solomon smiled through the ruin of his face and joked with Orlando as he made his way over to the pool, followed by the two humans.

She stood back, wanting to join them, and yet not wanting to at the same time. They lined the edge of the pool, looking over the walls at the thing that floated there. The thing that she didn't want to see.

Then Solomon looked around, his gaze moving across the yard until he found her. She felt pinned down, and unable to move. He looked quizzical for a moment, but then stepped away from the pool and came toward her, his one remaining eye focused on her.

To her horror, she felt the tears begin. No sobs shook her shoulders, and she didn't open her mouth and wail, but they ran down her cheeks nevertheless. She could feel her face burning. Why? She didn't even cry at the sight of all those bodies at the Rustling Elms compound, regardless of how maimed they were, or the fact that some of them were children, who had never hurt anyone and should never have been...

Then Solomon was there. He didn't say a word to her. He simply wrapped his arms around her and pulled her close. She lay her head on his shoulder and gave in to the grief, the regret, and the relief that all flooded over her at once.

When the storm had passed, she joined the others at the pool. The remains of the Soul Gaunt floated, its face, if it had one, hidden by the mass of sodden black fabric.

"Well," Solomon said, "I guess we should see what we're really dealing with here."

He reached out and snagged the fabric, pulling it closer. Shireen's breath caught as an emaciated white hand slipped free and floated behind, the arm it was attached to disappearing into the sleeve of the cloak. Solomon grabbed it more firmly when it was near and heaved it out of the pool, dumping it to the ground at their feet.

She didn't want to see this. She really didn't. But, it was better to know the enemy, and maybe find a weakness. And as anxious as she was to return to the Greenweald and have Solomon in front of the healers, she knew that they'd probably never have this chance again.

The five of them squatted near the mess, and for the first time, Shireen truly took notice of the humans. They were beneath her, really, as all humans were beneath those of the Folk. But there was something about these two, especially the woman. She had obviously done something to impress Solomon, and that fact alone was enough to pique her interest.

Solomon pulled the cowl back, exposing a hairless, skull like head. It was white, like the underbelly of a toad, or a grub that was exposed when you turned a fallen log. The eyes were sunk deep into their sockets, and in death were nothing more than black marbles. The nose was two slits in the front of its face.

Its mouth was the most terrifying part. It was too large for the head, and stretched well back along the cheeks, as if it would cause the top part of the things head to tip off if it opened wide. Solomon pried the jaws open, exposing a row of sharp, serrated, triangular teeth, made for only one thing, the ripping and tearing of flesh.

"He's a looker," Solomon mumbled.

Shireen looked up to see what the others were doing. Orlando was studying the features of the thing as if it were a puzzle to be solved. She wasn't surprised at that. Ever the thinker, he would work with Solomon to try to find out what other weaknesses the Soul Gaunts would have.

Solomon was Solomon, fearless and determined. He was the one actually touching it, an act that no one else seemed eager to take over.

The humans were...well, they were surprising. They both watched with looks of dread fascination on their faces. A look that she was sure was reflected in her own. The woman, Lacy was it?, had a hold of the man's hand and was squeezing it tightly.

For his part, the man looked down at the thing with his eyes blazing with anger. There were unshed tears standing in them, and he clung to the woman's hand as hard as she hung on to him. Shireen recalled him saying something about being in thrall to the Soul Gaunt, and marveled that he was here to tell the tale.

There was something strange there, for sure. Something they'd have to get to the bottom of.

"Let see what else," Solomon was saying. He grabbed a hold of the nasty cloak and stood, spilling the Soul Gaunt onto the ground.

It looked much like the head and hands would have led you to believe. White and hairless, it didn't look so deadly sprawled on the ground in the sunlight. The ribs showed plainly through the skin, as did the bones in the arms. The torso ended beneath the hips, where legs would normally be. There was no sign of a wound, or any sort of defect, the body simply ended, leaving a stretch of smooth white skin.

Horribly, she almost found herself giggling like a school girl when she realized that it was sexless as well.

"I guess we know they don't walk now," Orlando said. "But what does that tell us?"

"Not to aim for their knees," Solomon replied. "But here's the real question. Do we take it with us?"

They all stood, but stayed gathered, looking down at it. Daisy pushed her way past Solomon's leg and sniffed at the body. She growled, but then licked her lips as if she had tasted something rotten and backed away. Shireen thought that she had the right idea.

She wanted to say, "No! We're not travelling with that thing!" but knew it was the wrong answer. Jediah should see this. Everyone should. Everyone should know what they were truly up against. "Yes," she said, her own voice sounding far away in her ears. "We have to take it."

She looked up, away from the dead Soul Gaunt to see Solomon nodding. "Yep, I think you're right."

Shireen was looking forward to getting back to the Greenweald, and to having Solomon back where he belonged, but the journey had suddenly become much less pleasant.

CHAPTER 36

The trees were changing as they walked. Slowly and subtly, they were getting larger. Daisy walked at a sedate pace, sniffing as she went in seemingly random wanderings through the forest. Solomon wondered if that was how the Hunting Hounds always moved between the worlds, but doubted it. Normally, the dogs were sent after something, a specific target being their prey. In those cases, he thought they probably moved more purposefully.

But for now, Daisy seemed to be in no hurry, and neither was he. While he ached to be back in the Greenweald, he was also dreading it. He was thrilled to be reunited with Shireen and Orlando, and looked forward to seeing Jediah, but he knew that he had to see Florian as well.

His friends had told him that all was, if not forgiven, at least smoothed over. Florian had seen the need for his return and had admitted that while he would never love Solomon for his role in Celia's death, he also recognized that it was a force beyond his control that truly took her.

Still, Solomon felt that he was responsible. He had allowed his love for her to overrule his good sense, and his duty. He would help the Greenweald in any way that he could during this crisis, but after that, he would again throw himself on the mercy of Florian.

But he would be back in the Greenweald, at least for a while, and that was something. And what was more, he was bringing Lacy with him. Hopefully, the healers would be able to do something about her arm. She never said much, but from the way she held it, and favored the other one, he knew that it still bothered her. And who knew what effects lingered for Luke? The Soul Gaunt had hurt him time and time again, and those wounds, even the ones that couldn't be seen, had to be lingering as well.

He knew first hand now. His arms and shoulder ached where the Soul Gaunt had cut him up when they fought. They had stopped bleeding, and the bandages that Lacy rewrapped around them, under the watchful eye of Shireen, stayed clean, but they still felt like claws were shredding them anew with each step.

To say nothing of the wound on his face. It was strange looking at the world out of one eye. His depth perception was off and it was disturbing to not have peripheral vision on that side. Speaking of which...he turned and glanced at Luke, who was fighting the same thing. Only Luke had been dealing with it longer, and seemed to have made peace with it.

Solomon doubted that even the healers of the Greenweald would be able to do much for either of their eyes, but they should be able to ease the constant pain at least.

"Enough of this," he thought to himself. "You're going home. Be thankful for that."

They were all marching in a bunch, trailing slightly behind Daisy as she made her way through the woods. This was how Shireen and Orlando had crossed into the other world, although he didn't believe it was how he had ended up there. He thought that his own arrival was likely much more abrupt and violent.

Orlando had insisted on carrying the body of the Soul Gaunt, wrapped up in an old sheet that Lacy had, which was tied at the corners into a crude bag. The thing was light, but Orlando wouldn't hear of Solomon carrying it himself, and the other three had backed him up. Solomon had held his hands up in surrender and laughingly indicated that the honor was all his.

Even in death, the horrible thing seemed to exude menace and danger. It was dead, there was no doubt about that, but the wrongness of it was still there, just not as strong as when it was alive. As such, it had the effect of making the party walk quietly, talking little.

Except for Solomon. This was the second one that he had killed, and while he still had a healthy respect for them, any fear that he would have felt in the past was gone. They could be beaten. Not easily, that was certain, but they could be.

"Want me to take a turn?" he asked Orlando.

His friend grimaced at him, and Solomon laughed. "Suit yourself, but I feel fine. I can take a turn."

"You've done enough," Shireen said. "We've got this."

Solomon laughed again. Shireen may have said "we", but she made no move to take the burden from Orlando. She was one of the bravest people Solomon had ever met, but she had reached her limit with the Soul

Gaunt. For now, anyway. He had no doubt that if push came to shove, Shireen would be right there, in the thick of it, guarding his and Orlando's backs.

He dropped back to walk next to Lacy. "Feel anything different?"

"I'm not sure. It seems like the trees are getting bigger or something, and there's a different feel in the air. Like…it's cleaner? Is that it?"

"Could be. Listen."

Lacy cocked her head. "What? I don't hear anything out of the ordinary."

"You sure? Here we are, the middle of the day, and all I hear is birds and rustling in the bushes."

"So?"

"So when's the last time that if you really listened, you didn't hear cars, or planes, or some other noise of civilization? It was one of the first things I noticed when I came to your world. All the noise."

Lacy cocked her head again, a funny expression on her face. "You're right. It's like being in the deep, deep woods. Way up in the mountains or something. But the woods around here aren't that remote."

"Around there, you mean. You're not there anymore. And the trees *are* getting bigger."

She looked around her, shading her eyes with her hand as she followed the trunks up into the sky. "Are we in the Greenweald?"

"Not yet," Solomon said. "But soon."

He smiled at Lacy, and then quickened his pace to leave her to experience the change of worlds for herself. He had never done this either, and knew how she felt.

For the next couple of hours, they continued to walk among an increasing number of trees which grew taller and taller. What sun made its way through the leaves warmed them, and the unease generated by the Soul Gaunt's body faded. Soon, they were all talking quietly as if they were taking a friendly afternoon hike.

Solomon was glad for it. Although his wounds still ached, and the sense of foreboding about facing Florian again never really left him, he was more relaxed than he had been in days. He had liked the little town of Martinsburg, and was glad that he had met Ed, and Lacy, and even Luke. He was only sorry that such sorrow and tragedy had come into their lives, and he was sure that some of it, at least, had to do with him.

He was no fool. What were the chances that for the first time ever, a Soul Gaunt had crossed from his world to theirs, and it just happened to do it in the same small, out of the way place that he found himself? It wasn't likely, which meant it was sent.

Yet, Luke had first encountered, and been taken by, the thing a few weeks ago. Long before Solomon had found Martinsburg, or even been exiled. Before Celia was killed even. If it had been sent there after him, the timeline was all messed up.

"Hey," he said to Orlando, "how long have I been gone?"

Orlando looked thoughtful, then, "About five days or so. Why?"

"Hmm. Yeah, that matches up. I was just curious. The thought had suddenly popped into my head that maybe time didn't match up between the two worlds, but I guess it does."

"Never occurred to me either. What made you think of that?"

Solomon told him what he had been thinking. If there was anyone he was close to who would have the wits to figure this out, it was Orlando.

"Huh. Yeah, I see what you mean," his friend said. "It is an awfully big coincidence that the Gaunt would be here at the same time as you." He lowered his voice. "Are you sure that the human is telling you the truth?"

Solomon kept his voice quiet as well. "Lacy backs up how long he was gone for. And I don't know why he'd lie."

"That doesn't mean he was with the Soul Gaunt for that long, though. Maybe he's saying that to cover something else. Maybe it really was only a few days."

"There's nothing *only* about that, but I get your point. But still, I tend to believe him."

"That's because you don't think that way. I'll keep an eye on him. Let's not say anything to Shireen yet, though. She's already on edge enough."

There was the sudden sound of an indrawn breath behind them, and Solomon turned to see Lacy, her hand over her mouth, staring past him. He turned to see what she was looking at.

There, not far in front of them, was home. He had been so engrossed in his conversation that he hadn't even noticed. But the Towering Oaks compound was there, a short distance away through the trees. The forest opened up, became less crowded in the compound, and the central tree, huge and majestic was plain to see.

His eye misted over as he saw it. He was home. A place that he never thought to see again. A horn sounded, its note rising into the air, announcing their arrival to the world. It sounded like a heavenly choir to him.

He turned back and smiled at Lacy, taking in Luke at the same time. "Welcome to the Greenweald."

CHAPTER 37

It all felt so surreal. The trees were enormous, even bigger than the ones she had seen in California when she went there on vacation with her family as a young girl. Then, the sight of those towering trunks had fired her imagination, and gave her a life-long love of being in the forest, living closer to nature. It was why she and Luke had bought their house in the first place, and one of the things they had found they had in common when they first met.

But now, here, for the first time, Lacy truly understood what it was to be in a primal wilderness, regardless of the orderly layout of the compound in front of her.

The trees around her were truly majestic, rising to heights that she could barely comprehend. And yet, the ground around the trunks was almost neat, with little of the tangled undergrowth and piles of dead wood that were common in almost any other forest she had visited. And while the trees grew close together in some areas, there were clear aisles that wound through them, offering ease of passage.

None of it looked as if it had been done by anyone human, or human like, though. There were no signs of stumps or fallen logs left to rot where they fell. She could hear the sounds of birds singing in the branches, some close at hand, others so far up that they were impossible for her to spot. It was as if the forest had grown in an ideal manner, like something out of a storybook.

The thought made her glance over at Luke, who was gazing around in equal awe, turning his head to see from his one remaining eye, and she wondered how he must be feeling. While she loved nature and the woods, Luke did as well, plus he was so into those fantasy worlds that he read and created. He must feel that he had walked into one of his own stories.

Reaching over, she took his hand and gave it a slight tug. "You okay?"

"Yeah, I'm just...wow. I mean, look at this, Lacy. It can't be real, can it?"

"It has to be. We're here, and I can feel you and hear you. Unless I'm hallucinating badly, this is happening."

They didn't have time for any more discussion as the compound in front of them had erupted into a hive of activity at the sound of the horn. In the near distance was a huge tree, bigger by far than any others around it. There were large double doors set into it, at the top of a broad, shallow set of steps. They opened and a tall man, dressed in armor, appeared, holding his hand up to shield his eyes as he peered at them. It was hard to tell from here, but Lacy thought she saw a smile crease the weathered face.

"Jediah," she heard Solomon say quietly, and then he was moving, his long legs eating the distance between himself and the other man. In moments, they had met and embraced like long lost brothers, suddenly reunited.

"Come on," a voice said at her side. She jumped in surprise. She had been so intent on what was happening with Solomon that she had almost forgotten the other two. Orlando was standing next to her, looking at her kindly. "I imagine this is all a little much. Hold on, both of you. It's going to get a little more. You're the first humans ever here in the Greenweald, that I know of, and definitely the first ones at Towering Oaks. So try to ignore the stares."

He took her arm and gently guided her forward. She pulled Luke with her, and they followed Shireen into the compound. Lacy tried to take it all in, but it was simply too much. The compound was orderly, laid out neatly, with plants that grew in defined beds, in almost perfect rows. The trees grew in straight lines, marching away into the distance, all spaced equally, with doors that opened in the same direction on each. Other trees, slightly larger, dotted the lines at equally spaced intervals, and she wondered what their purpose was.

The people that watched with interest as they came were all tall and thin, and many were wearing armor in various shades of gray. Others wore gray robes, or pants and shirts, always in some tone. Now that she noticed it, so did Shireen and Orlando. She, Luke, and Solomon were the only ones not dressed in the color.

"Alright, stop gawking!" Shireen barked as she strode in front of them. "Haven't you ever seen a human before? Get back to work!"

A few turned away, pretending to go back to whatever task they had been doing, but they kept stopping and watching them as they walked toward where Solomon stood talking to the other man.

194

"Ah!" he said, turning to them as they neared. "Jediah, allow me to introduce my friends from earth. This is Lacy Roberts, and her husband Luke. I owe them both my life."

Jediah regarded them in silence. "Be that as it may," he finally said, "I'm not sure of the wisdom of bringing humans here. Especially now."

"Trust me. They've earned the right to see the Greenweald. Besides, they are both in need of healing. Both were wounded by the Soul Gaunt that made its way there."

"As were you, obviously. You're hurt more than you're letting on. Well. What's done is done. Let's get inside, and we'll call for the Healers. Shireen, Orlando, come with us."

He turned away without once directly acknowledging either Lacy or Luke, or commenting on Orlando's burden.

She could feel the tension in her husband, the anger at being ignored, but she squeezed his hand.

Solomon turned to them with a smile. "Don't be offended. For Jediah, that was an outpouring of emotion."

Lacy had to smile at his simple attempt to soothe their feelings. They moved to the steps, and then up, through the doors and into the interior of the Towering Oaks central tree.

They were led to a comfortable room, with chairs made from single pieces of wood, some freestanding, some that appeared to be grown out of the floor itself.

"Sit," Jediah said. "Rest. I'll summon the Healers. For all of you."

He strode off, back ram-rod straight, and despite what Solomon had said, Lacy breathed a little easier with the forceful presence of Jediah gone. Absently, she rubbed at her arm as she looked about her.

"Still hurt?" Solomon asked.

She shrugged. "Some, I guess. I don't really pay much attention to it, but every now and then it flares up. How about you?"

She still couldn't believe the amount of damage that Solomon had taken in killing the Soul Gaunt. If her arm hurt from the thing simply touching her, then how bad did his wounds have to ache? Especially the one across his face, the one that had taken his eye.

"I'm good," he replied, and smiled at her, his face twisting beneath the slash across it. "If anyone can help, it's the Healers here."

"But how?" Luke said. "If the doctors on earth couldn't find anything wrong with Lacy, with all the modern equipment, then how will these healers?"

His voice sounded harsh suddenly, almost argumentative. He was hurting too, Lacy realized. She hadn't had time to think that much about it, but what had the Soul Gaunt done to him in the time that it had him? There was the obvious injury, the loss of his own eye, although there was no accompanying scar down his face. That was bad enough, of course, but what else?

"Luke," she said, quietly. "Easy. Obviously, we're in a different place. Given what we've seen the last several days...what *you've* seen...is it so hard to believe that maybe there's more to this than we would know?"

Luke dropped his gaze. "You're right. I'm sorry. It's been such a long few weeks, and now...I don't know. I feel safe now, I guess, but it's coming back. The horror. The pain. I was so scared, all the time...and the things I did...I can't...I don't know how to..."

Solomon came over and gently put his hand on Luke's shoulder. "It's okay, Luke. You've been through more than the rest of us. I don't know why, but we're going to try to find out. And the Healers can help with all of your pain. The pain of your flesh, and the pain of your mind. The Greenweald itself can help heal your soul, if you let it."

Lacy reached out for Luke's hand again, as he deflated in on himself. "I hope so," he said quietly. "I really do."

The Healers came a short time later. There were several of them, which Orlando told them was unusual. One, Willow, was in charge, and it was she that went to Solomon first.

"Hello, Willow," he said. "It's nice to see you again."

"And you, Solomon," the woman replied, the whole exchange sounding slightly formal to Lacy. Then, Solomon burst into his characteristic smile once more, and hugged the woman tightly.

"I'm glad you're here," he said, releasing her. "I wanted the best to look at my friend, Luke, and I was hoping it would be you."

"I should by taking care of this," Willow said, lightly tracing the wound in Solomon's face.

"Ahh, one of the others can handle this. Luke, though...well, how much do you know?"

"Not enough," a deep voice said, and Lacy turned to see Jediah enter the room. "We haven't told much of anyone what's been going on. But it's time now. Willow, gather the others and sit. We have things to tell you before you begin."

CHAPTER 38

Luke listened to the others tell their stories with growing unease. He heard Shireen and Orlando talk about their trip to the north of here, and felt disquieted as they described the fear they had felt at night. When they talked of the Rustling Elms compound, and what they had found there, his heart froze in his chest and he labored to continue breathing. It was as if he too were dragged away, into the darkness with this Thaddeus fellow, whoever he was.

"Thaddeus has returned," Willow, the supposed healer said. "He is at Whispering Pines, recovering from his wounds. They were severe, although I suspect more than I had thought, now that I know what caused them."

"What?" Shireen cried, rising to her feet. "He's alive? Thank all the gods!"

"See him in a bit, Shireen," Jediah said quietly. "Right now, we have our own to tend to."

"Of course," she replied. She sat back in her chair, but Luke noticed how her hand sought out Orlando's and squeezed tightly. Neither did he miss the grateful look that passed between the two of them at the news of this Thaddeus's safe return.

He wondered if Lacy had had that same expression when Solomon had carried him, over his shoulder no less, out of the woods and dumped him at her feet. If so, he imagined it was for the tall, handsome warrior. The rescuer was usually the one getting the accolades, not the rescued. But he was being silly. Lacy loved him, that was evident. It was simply the almost overwhelming magnetism of Solomon that was picking at him, nothing more.

Then, Solomon told of his short time on their earth, a concept that still felt so strange to Luke. He was really in another world, a place that didn't exist for anyone else that he knew, other than Lacy. And yet, it really didn't seem all that strange to him. He was sitting at his ease inside of a giant tree, listening to people wearing swords and armor talk, and it felt as natural as anything in his life ever had.

Lacy tugged his hand and he came back to the conversation, only to realize that they were all looking at him.

"I'm sorry, what?" he said, feeling his face flush.

"Tell us your story," Jediah said. "How is it that you came to be in service to a Soul Gaunt?"

"I wasn't in service to it!" He felt his temper flare up again. "It wasn't like I had a choice."

He told them then of what had happened, of leaving home, finding solace in the quiet of the woods. Surely these people, if anyone, would understand that. How he had wandered further than he thought, night had fallen, and it had come for him.

His voice broke at that point, and he stared at the floor, not really seeing it, but reliving the darkness, the cold, and the fear.

"I couldn't get away," he whispered. Then he was suddenly aware of how pathetic he must sound. "Well, could any of you?" He raised his eyes and stared at them, one by one, challenging them to tell him that they could have, so that he could tell them they lied, and that they wouldn't know. "You would have, of course," he said, when he came to Solomon. "But any of the rest of you. No one of you could have."

"No one is blaming you." This from Solomon. He was the last person that Luke wanted to hear from at the moment. It's easy to be magnanimous when you're so on top of things. "We're trying to understand why it took you as it did. Why, and I'm sorry to even say this, it didn't simply kill you."

"I don't know. Don't you get it? It's not like we had conversations. The thing hurt me, and used me to lure Lacy and Ed into its reach. That's all. I don't know why." His eyes burned with unshed tears of shame and frustration. Lacy reached for him, but he stood and drew away, not wanting her, or anyone to touch him.

"Enough," a quiet voice said. The tall woman, the so-called healer, stood and approached him. "There will be time for questions later. For now, you need sleep, and healing, and forgetfulness."

She put her hands to his temples, and he looked up into soft brown eyes. His anger started to ebb away and the room to fade into soft shadows. Not blackness, like when the Soul Gaunt had him, but a gently, light gray fog. He sat back down, Willow following him, keeping her hands placed gently on each side of his head. He wondered what Lacy thought of him now, but that thought too flowed out of his mind, and for a little while, he knew nothing more.

When he came to, he was lying in a large bed, his head pillowed by soft cushions. He watched the sunlight play on the wall of the room, the curtain blowing in the breeze causing the shadows to jump. He sighed, remembering his outburst and the shameful thoughts that had started to consume him.

Strangely, he no longer felt the shame. Not even at that outburst. It had happened, and quite frankly, he had had reason for it. But now, he was here, and he was safe, and so was Lacy.

Speaking of…he looked around, but his wife was nowhere to be found. No one else was in the room either, and for that he was grateful. He would lie still for another minute or two, and then get up and go find her and the others. Perhaps, with their help, he would remember more, and be able to help find a way to stop those terrible things from doing more damage.

That would be nice.

He was still thinking that when he slipped away into sleep again.

This time when he awoke, it was dark. But someone had left a couple of candles burning in the room. While they weren't bright enough to wake him, or to do something like read by, they were enough to allow him to see the room, into all the corners, and be assured that nothing else was there.

There was movement, and he realized that Lacy was lying in the bed next to him. He didn't know when she had joined him, but he was glad that they had let her. He rolled onto his side and put his arm over her.

He wasn't particularly tired anymore. Maybe that was the effect of being active at night for the last several weeks now. But lying here, holding Lacy and feeling her breathe, felt nice, and he was in no hurry to rise.

He must have made a noise, or else she felt his embrace, because Lacy turned to him, staying under his arm as she did.

"Hey. Feeling better?" she asked.

"Yeah. Sorry about that."

"Don't apologize. You've been through hell. We all know that."

"Thanks. Is everyone asleep? I guess I'm ready to talk about it again. Or at least try?"

"No, they're around. But there's no huge hurry. Nothing will be decided right now. We can stay here for a few."

He suddenly remembered that he wasn't the only one who was wounded. "How's your arm?"

"A little better, I think. The Healer said it would still be awhile, but they think they got a lot of the damage undone."

"Good. And Solomon?"

"He was insisting that Willow, the one who helped you, stay with you. But she overruled him. I think she's the only person ever to do that. She said that you were fine for now, and that she had plenty of time to see to him. She took him off into another room, and we haven't seen them since."

I bet, Luke thought to himself, but shoved the thought down inside as being unworthy of both Solomon and the Healer. He was feeling better, but apparently, Willow hadn't done enough to his mind to keep such petty thoughts at bay. But there were still some things he could do for himself. And the sleep that she had helped him get gave him a good platform to start from.

He smiled at Lacy, almost feeling it for real, and pulled her closer to him.

A short time later, they returned to the room where they had told the Healers of what had happened to each of them. Orlando and Shireen were still there, sitting apart and talking quietly with one another, a clear, yellow drink set on the table before each. Orlando glanced up and declined his head in acknowledgment of their presence. Shireen simply looked up, and then turned her attention back to Orlando.

Sure, we're beneath her notice, Luke thought. The mighty warrior, who couldn't even look at the dead Soul Gaunt until she was shamed into it. I wonder how she would have fared, being held by the thing for so long.

Again, he pushed the thoughts down as fast as they rose in his mind. What was wrong with him? When the Soul Gaunt had him, all he could think about was how grateful he would be to get away from it, how much he missed Lacy, and how badly he wanted to make amends. Now, he was here, in another world, and every other thought was some snarky comment about someone who had done him no wrong.

Well, that wasn't exactly true though, was it? While Shireen had done him no physical harm, she certainly hadn't been friendly either, not even when it was revealed that her precious Solomon would be a smoking ruin without his help. That was fine. He didn't need her approval, or anyone else's, except maybe Lacy's. But the fact that Shireen treated Lacy that way as well…that was what was really intolerable.

Not that he could do anything about it.

The door on the far side of the room opened, and Willow entered, followed by Solomon. The change in the man was drastic. While his eye was still gone, the gash in his face had been healed, the wound closed, leaving only a white scar that ran from his right temple, down across the bridge of his nose, and into the left corner of his mouth. It left him with a slight upturn to his lips there, but on Solomon, it only served to add more character to his face.

He also moved more easily now, showing no sign of pain in his shoulder, or in his arms which were now crisscrossed with white scar lines.

Luke could feel a darkness in his mind, like a cloud waiting to obscure the sun. It was there, pushing at him, fueling the derision he was feeling for everyone around him. If the healer could help Solomon, why couldn't she help him?

Maybe she doesn't want to, he thought. Then, maybe I should ask her.

But he didn't really want to. He didn't want her touching him again. He put a smile on his face that he didn't feel, and called out to Solomon. "Look at you! A couple of hours with a Healer and you're almost like new."

Solomon smiled at him. "Willow can work miracles. How are you feeling?"

"Better. Much better. You're right about the miracle working. I'm ready to finish up telling you all what happened with me, if you are."

"Are you sure?" Lacy asked him, her face a mask of concern.

"Yeah, I'm positive. Don't worry. Like I said, she worked a miracle for me too."

They were returning to their seats when the door opened and an obvious servant entered. For such an "enlightened" place, there sure were a lot of second-class citizens around, Luke thought.

The man spoke to Jediah, listened to his murmured reply, and left.

"A moment before you begin," the Head of House said. "We have two others joining us."

Two tall men, dressed in shades of green entered, and Shireen and Orlando jumped to their feet. "Thaddeus!" Shireen said, and rushed forward.

She embraced the man, while Orlando clasped his hand warmly.

Luke watched as Thaddeus's eyes scanned the room over Shireen's shoulder, finally coming to rest on his own. It was like an electric wire had been planted in his brain. He jerked back, tearing his gaze free.

"Luke?" Lacy said, "are you okay?"

"Yeah. No, I'm fine. Just a sudden stab of headache. It passed."

But when he looked back, Thaddeus was still staring at him, and the pain in his head was every bit as strong.

CHAPTER 39

The ride from the Whispering Pines compound to Towering Oaks had been strange for Florian. He and Thaddeus hardly spoke, and their escort trailed a respectful distance behind, so it was mostly made in silence. Which gave him plenty of time to try to sort out the maelstrom in his head.

He didn't believe a word that his cousin had told him. Not about the true nature of the Soul Gaunts and not about the intentions of the mysterious man that controlled them. What he was really afraid of though, was whether or not Thaddeus did. If he did, it meant that he had been fooled, taken in, and his mind broken by what had happened to him. Florian could see that, considering the dark, the pain and the constant fear that the things generated.

But if he didn't truly believe what he had told Florian, then that meant that Thaddeus, for all intents and purposes, was now working with the enemy. That was a thought that he didn't even want to entertain. It was unthinkable. Wasn't it?

He glanced over at his cousin, who rode along with a hood cast over his face, despite the warmth of the day. Almost as if he were hiding from the Greenweald itself.

"Take your hood off," Florian said, breaking the silence. "You look ridiculous."

Thaddeus reached up and pulled it from his head, so that it hung down his back again. He blinked as he looked around, and then dropped his gaze to the ground in front of his horse. Not once did he look over at Florian.

"It's bright out here," he said. "A little too bright, I think. I don't know what they did to me in there, but the sunlight hurts my eyes."

Florian grunted. That was almost an admission that harm had indeed been done to him. "Keep trying. I'm sure you'll get used to it."

Thaddeus didn't reply, and they continued to ride along side by side, not saying anything.

Then, "What will you do, cousin?"

Florian looked at him. "What do you mean?"

"Solomon. What will you do when you see him?"

"I don't know. Nothing, I suppose. I've spoken with Jediah and come to terms with what happened."

"Huh. Strange."

"What is?"

Now Thaddeus did look at him. "That you've come to terms with the man who was responsible for your daughter's death. And it wasn't even that long ago."

Florian swallowed hard, his mouth suddenly dry. "Why would you say that?"

"I mean no harm. I just find it strange."

"Do you think I'm doing the wrong thing? That I should demand his head on a pike again?"

"Far be it from me to make a decision like that," Thaddeus said. "I made an observation, that's all."

Florian felt his temper begin to rise. "Well, keep it to yourself. If I want to hear your 'observations', I'll ask for them." He spurred his horse into a quicker trot, pulling ahead.

"Yes, cousin,' he heard Thaddeus say from behind him.

In truth, Thaddeus's words had cut deeply into Florian. There was a part, a huge part, that felt like he was betraying his daughter's memory, by agreeing to forgive, and even work with, the man responsible for her death. And yet, he wasn't truly responsible, right? He was there, but he wasn't the one who had drowned her...

He had been through all of this. Over and over in his mind. He had spoken of it with Jediah, who, yes, had a vested interest in getting Solomon back, but was also his oldest friend. He had acted out in the grip of a father's grief, and Jediah himself didn't blame him for it. So how then could he blame Solomon for what had happened?

Because he had refused to obey the orders of both his Head of House and of his love's father, that's how.

Damn Thaddeus! As if he didn't have enough to occupy his mind already.

They arrived at the Towering Oaks compound shortly after, and were shown to a large room where the others were gathered. This time, Florian didn't ask, but simply reached over and tugged Thaddeus's hood down, from where it had found its way onto his head again. His cousin didn't so much as move, and Florian noticed that his eyes were fixed on a human male that was seated in the room.

But he wasn't able to stare for long. Shireen bounded to her feet as they entered, and hugged Thaddeus tightly. The other one, Orlando, came over and patted him on the shoulder, both of them telling his cousin how glad they were to see him. It didn't escape Florian's notice that while Thaddeus didn't pull away, he also didn't return the embrace or the warm welcome. Instead, he continued to stare at the one-eyed human.

There was another human in the room as well, a female. She said something to the male, who looked at her, then returned his gaze back to Thaddeus. Was it possible that they knew each other? Thaddeus had been to that earth once before, but it seemed unlikely that he would run into someone that he knew here, in the Greenweald. Which begged the question, why *were* there humans in the Greenweald?

He'd get the answer for that later. But for now, he needed to focus, prepare himself for when he saw…

Solomon.

He was there, sitting rigidly in a chair, waiting for Florian to see him, his hand placed on top of the Hounds head. He had been wounded. There was a scar running across his face, and like the human, he too was missing an eye. If he had beaten the Soul Gaunt that made its way to that earth, it had cost him.

Florian waited for the anger to rise, to feel his blood begin to boil, but it never came. Instead, he simply felt sad. His daughter had had so much potential, so much life. It had all been snuffed out, because she fell for a man who everyone said, and Florian had to agree with, had been the best of them all. The strongest, the fastest, the most capable. Everyone loved Solomon, who took it all with a humbleness that never once rang false.

And now, this great man, this shining hope of them all, sat before him, scarred and wounded, with what would be called an expression of fear on anyone else. No, that's what it was on Solomon as well, as unbelievable as that seemed.

He took a deep breath, drew his shoulders back, and strode across the room, until he stood in front of Solomon. He looked down into his one remaining eye, and didn't see his daughter's killer anymore, just a man in almost as much pain as he himself was.

"I'm glad you're back," he said, his voice quiet. "Later, we should talk."

"Lord Florian, I…" Solomon began.

"Later," he interrupted. "The two of us, alone. We'll talk, and we'll remember her. Maybe we can help each other heal."

Solomon nodded and dropped his gaze, but not before Florian saw the tears that were standing unshed in his eye. Brushing away his own, he turned back to the room, only to find everyone staring at them.

"What are you all looking at?" he said. "Am I wrong, or do we have a lot to talk about?"

CHAPTER 40

Thaddeus disengaged himself from Shireen and stepped back away from Orlando's hand.

"It's good to see you both as well," he said, the lie sliding smoothly off his tongue. "but please forgive me. I'm still not recovered fully and need to sit."

"Of course," Orlando said. "Can I get you anything?"

"No, truly. I'm fine. I just need to rest for a moment." He smiled and moved away from the two, taking a seat at the side of the room, where he could keep an eye on everyone present. He knew them all, including Willow and the other healers. Or almost all. He did not know the two humans.

The male across the room from him had the mark of the Soul Gaunts on him, as surely as Thaddeus did himself. It wasn't something that one could see, but he could sense it nevertheless. It shined like a bright light in the darkness, something that Thaddeus was too familiar with these days. But who was this human, and how had he come to be here?

He was insanely curious, but also extremely apprehensive about approaching him. What if the man could recognize the same mark on him, and shouted it out for everyone to hear? There was no protection that Florian could give, even if he would want to, should it be revealed that Thaddeus was really working with their enemies now.

Although, that wasn't really it. It wasn't so much that he was working with them as it was that he wanted to live, and didn't want to be hurt anymore. He saw the numbers of Soul Gaunts that were at the Rustling Elms compound, and he knew the stories. Florian himself had told him of the time that one had come into the Greenweald, and how much damage it had done before it was destroyed. And it had been destroyed by Jediah, no less. A man whose prowess was only slightly behind Solomon's if you believed the stories. So how did any of them stand a chance against the might that was gathered there now? They didn't.

The Greenweald would be destroyed, and its people either killed or enslaved. The man in charge had told him that much. They were tired of being pushed to the end of the world, far to the north, beyond the realm of the Hairy Men. There, they eked out life by feeding on what they could find, but game was sparse in those frozen wastes, and the Soul Gaunts were dying off. Now, they would take the Greenweald, and all its bounty. Never again would they starve and waste away to nothing.

Which all sounded very reasonable, but Thaddeus knew it for what it was. Lies. Pure and simple. They were here because they were evil, and they fed on fear and misery. They enjoyed causing pain. They may grow fat on the wealth of this land and its people, but that was merely a side-effect. In truth, they were here to kill because they could, and they liked it.

If the Greenweald was doomed, then why shouldn't he look out for himself? He was promised a position of authority and privilege. The Soul Gaunts would need someone to help keep the new slaves in line and make sure that they bred, to keep the food supply strong. There was no reason that shouldn't be Thaddeus. He had paid the price after all.

It had taken all his considerable self-control to hold his tongue as Shireen and Orlando had come to him with their false platitudes. They were oh-so-happy to see him alive, were they? Then why had they run, and left him there in the darkness? Orlando would be one of the first to go, if he had his way. Perhaps he'd ask that Shireen be spared, and given to him when all was said and done. She was attractive enough, and when he tired of her, he could always give her back to them then.

The thought made him smile, and he noticed that the human was watching him, although he appeared to be trying not to. He looked at Thaddeus, winced, turned away, and then repeated the whole thing a few moments later. Thaddeus fought to keep an even bigger smile off his face at that. It seemed that the human could see the mark on him as well, but was made of far weaker material. Good.

Ah, and there was the man himself, scratching the head of that worthless Hound. Solomon the great! Solomon the magnificent! Solomon the hero! Pfft. Let others worship him. Thaddeus knew he was dangerous, but no one ever claimed he was all that smart. He'd talk, and let the details of whatever plan he had out, and then Thaddeus would use that to his advantage.

While he would love to see Solomon humiliated, if for no other reason than to show the rest of the fools what misplaced trust in heroes brings, he also recognized that the man was simply too dangerous. No, he would have to be killed first, and the man controlling the Soul Gaunts had a plan for that, he was sure.

He watched as his cousin walked to Solomon and spoke in low tones, then wiped tears from his eyes. How touching. It appeared that the two had reconciled their differences. That was unfortunate. If he had convinced Florian that Solomon was still his enemy, and sowed discord here, he was sure that his reward would have been greater.

"What are you all looking at? Am I wrong, or do we have a lot to talk about?"

Florian made it sound like a joke, but Thaddeus could hear the pain in his voice. Forgiveness or not, seeing Solomon had had an effect on him.

For a moment, Thaddeus's mind went back to better times. Times before he was held in the tree and abandoned by those he considered friends. Back before Solomon had been exiled and been the talk of the Greenweald. Back even before Celia, young and foolish, had fallen for the soldier.

It was brighter then, and he had enjoyed working for his cousin, to the betterment of their House. He had enjoyed gathering information on the other houses, and viewed it as a challenge. One that he was quite good at. And practicing his magic. The minor spells that provided light in darkness, or heat in cold, or helped struggling plants to grow.

But then it had all ended. Celia had died and his cousin had grown remote, angry and vengeful. Thaddeus had played his part in Solomon's exile, and heard the whispers from the other houses about how it was unfair, that Solomon should never have been punished for what wasn't his fault.

And then the darkness, and the fear, and the pain. He only had to look down at his mangled hand to remember fully. No, there was no beating what was coming. Better to be on the winning side.

Finally, he stood and walked to the two humans.

"I don't believe we've met," he said. "I'm Thaddeus, of House Whispering Pines."

"Oh," the woman said. "I'm Lacy. From earth, I guess. We came with Solomon."

"Luke," the man said, not meeting his gaze.

"I'm interested to hear how two humans come to be in our land," Thaddeus said. "But first, may I get you anything? I've been to your world, and I know what a shock this must be to you."

"No, thank you. I'm fine. Luke? What about you?"

"I'm fine too," the man said, and still didn't so much as glance up.

"Well. I wanted to make sure that you were both doing well here in our world. Please, if you need anything at all, don't hesitate to ask. Those of us who linger at the fringes of the great have to stick together."

The woman, Lacy, was it, smiled back at him, but again, the man stayed silent, his gaze averted. Thaddeus nodded and walked back to his seat, acknowledging Willow's lifted hand with a nod of his own.

His quick visit told him that what he had suspected was certainly true. The human male did sense the mark of the Soul Gaunts on him. He would find a way to use that. Anything that would stop him being dragged back into the darkness again.

CHAPTER 41

Jediah called them all to the table, and Shireen took a seat. With her was Orlando, of course, as well as Florian, Thaddeus, and Willow. She was sure the healer was included so that she could prepare the rest of her team for what was coming and ensure that they were fully stocked with needed supplies. *Her* presence she understood, but what she didn't understand was why the two humans were included.

"Excuse me," she said, before Jediah could speak. "But I have reservations about letting a couple of people here in on our plans."

Solomon looked over at her. "Me?"

She laughed briefly. "Of course, not, and you know it." She turned her attention to the humans. "I'm sorry, but I don't understand why you two are here. What can you possibly bring to the conversation?"

Lacy still looked awe-struck at being in the Greenweald and merely looked back at Shireen in surprise, as if she had no answer. Luke, on the other hand, looked angry and resentful at his presence being questioned.

"Gee, I don't know," he said. "Maybe you could actually listen to someone who spent weeks with one of those damn things, instead of being so high-and-mighty about it."

"There is truth to that, Shireen," Jediah said. "This human may have insights into the behavior of the Soul Gaunts that even Thaddeus wouldn't. Out of all of us, he's spent the most time near one."

"Exactly my point," she argued. "Who really knows what damage might have been done that we can't see."

She could almost feel the rage coming from Luke, but ignored it. It was her duty to bring up things that she thought could jeopardize them, and too bad if he didn't realize that.

"Willow?" Jediah asked. "Is there anything you can say that would reassure our scout?"

The healer looked for a moment at Luke, her brow furrowed slightly, before turning back to the group. "There is still trauma there, but that's to be expected. I believe Luke is very angry, and very hurt still. He has the right to be, with what he's been through. However, if you're asking me if I think he would betray us to some hidden agenda to help the Soul Gaunts, then I'd have to say no, I don't believe he would."

"There you have it, then," Solomon said. "Shireen, I'll vouch for him, and for Lacy. If it weren't for both of them, I wouldn't be here and you know that. I understand your caution, but in this case, I think it's misplaced."

Shireen bowed her head in acknowledgment. "I needed to raise the question." She turned back to Luke. "I meant no offense. It's my job to raise the possibilities."

For a moment Luke glared back at her, but then he dropped his eyes and mumbled, "It's fine. No problem."

"Then let us go on," Jediah said. "First order of business is Thaddeus. While the human has had more time with one of these things, that one is now dead. Thaddeus has the most recent contact with them here in the Greenweald. So, what can you tell us?"

Shireen watched her friend carefully. While she had raised the objection of the humans, she had misgivings about Thaddeus also. His whole demeanor felt different since he had entered the room a little while ago. Of course, this could also be an effect of his captivity, and the torture that he had endured. One only needed to look at his hand to realize the extent of what had happened to him. She hoped she was jumping at shadows, and that Thaddeus was the same loyal servant to Florian that he always had been. Ironic, since that was the very thing that had caused her to call him a snake not so long ago.

His first words made her feel that perhaps her fears were right after all.

"To begin with, I think we're misreading their intentions."

"What?" the exclamation burst out of her before she could stop it.

"I understand your reaction," Thaddeus said, "and I would have shared it only a few days ago. But then, I was left behind. Not that I blame you, obviously. I know you tried your best to get to me, but you couldn't."

That stung. She had tried to go after him, but Orlando had dragged her back, as he should have. She had begged for them to gather their forces and return, but everyone, herself included had assumed he was dead by that point. It may have been in her imagination, but there almost felt like an undercurrent of glee in what Thaddeus was saying, as if he was twisting the knife, and enjoying it.

"But that may have turned out to be a blessing for all of us," he was continuing. "Yes, I was scared, terrified even. But until I tried to ignite a fire spell, I wasn't actually hurt. And even then, the Nightwind, as they call themselves, was startled by the flash, and reacted instinctively, like an animal would. That's really all they are, you see, animals. Predators that have lived in a harsh environment that they're now being forced to flee from."

There was silence around the table. Florian sat with his head down, hiding his expression from anyone. Orlando looked thoughtful as always. Jediah stern, and Solomon openly incredulous. Willow's face was carefully neutral, even as she gazed steadily at Thaddeus.

"That's complete B.S!" This from Lacy. "One of those things attacked me for no reason at all! And what was it doing on my earth in the first place?"

"Ah. I've been thinking about that, ever since I first came in and saw the two of you. I think that one was a rogue, like what you call a 'mad dog', I believe. I think it lost its pack somehow and ended up alone and I don't believe they do well when they're separated from their own kind."

"Then how did it even get to our earth?" she asked. Shireen was impressed. This Lacy didn't let up when she wanted something. Maybe there was slightly more to her than she had thought.

"Who knows?" Thaddeus shrugged. "How do the Hunting Hounds do it? You followed one back here, didn't you? Do you know how it worked?"

"No, but I'm not from here."

"True. Then allow me to ask one further question. Do you know how everything on your earth works? If I were to ask you how you make moving pictures appear on a box on your wall, could you tell me?"

"Well, no…" Lacy began.

"Then it's unfair to ask me the how of everything also. I'm not trying to downplay this, please. But I simply don't know how it got there."

He paused, but no one else said anything. Shireen got the impression that they were all waiting for whatever else Thaddeus had to say. After a moment, he went on.

"The Nightwinds have an advocate with them. Someone who has lived among them for years, studying them and earning their trust. During that time, he never showed any aggression to them, and took care to guard

214

himself from the cold that they naturally generate. Because he took the time to take such precautions, the Nightwinds sensed no threat from him, and he slowly began to communicate with them."

"The one that held me communicated plenty," Luke cut in. "Always horrible things, about what it would do to me, or to Lacy. I have a hard time believing any of this."

"As would I, if I had had your experience. But as I said, I believe that one, and the two that came down here on their own several years ago, were outliers. Criminally insane, I believe you would say. A mass-murderer on your world hardly speaks for your whole species, does it? The same can be applied here."

Again, Thaddeus fell silent, and waited. This time, Jediah spoke. "What do they want then, Thaddeus? What does this 'advocate' say?"

"They simply want a new place to live, one that's warmer, more bountiful, and safe. They have no interest in attacking the Folk, or anyone else. Yes, they're hunters and they will take game, but there are comparatively few of them, so it wouldn't stress our resources. Most of the time we wouldn't even know they were here since they avoid the daylight whenever they can. It hurts them, much as their cold hurts us."

"And this man, what does he gain?" Florian asked.

"He wishes to be allowed to live among us, although he doesn't want to align with a House, even if that were allowed. He will live apart, in his own place, much like the Master of Hounds, and continue to study the Nightwinds. I guess you could call him a type of naturalist."

"I still think this is nonsense," Shireen said. "Thaddeus, I know you've been through hell, but I can't believe that you're actually buying this."

"But you weren't there, were you? You didn't feel the terror of being dragged off, or the relief from realizing that you weren't to be killed. You didn't talk to their advocate and see what he saw. That the Nightwinds are no more than a primitive type people, less advanced than the Hairy Men even. It's easy to cast judgment from here, Shireen, but quite different if you've been through it."

"I've been through it, and I think you're full of it, too," Luke said.

Thaddeus sighed. "Again, I can only say that you're judging an entire race on the actions of one deranged individual."

Shireen snorted. "I agree with the human. It's crap. I say we gather our forces, move on them in the broad daylight, and end them all."

"I don't know that I agree." The soft voice was from Orlando. Shireen turned to him in surprise.

"What? How can you say that?"

"It sounds unbelievable to me, too. But. What if it's not? What if Thaddeus is right, and we could resolve this without conflict? We know what they can do. We may win in a war against them, especially now, but several people will die, and we know that. If there is any chance, at all, of avoiding it, don't we have to take itIf there is any chance, at all, of avoiding it, don't we have to take it? Besides, we know how hard they are to kill. An enchanted or blessed weapon, right?"

"Actually, no," Willow said. "I've had a chance to look at the one that you brought back here with you. I think the legend of needing a magic weapon has grown out of how hard they are to hit. But there is nothing about their physical presence that would make that so. Instead, their cloaks create much more area than their bodies, and according to Solomon, they are very fast. Combine those two, add in the panic that those facing them feel, and most blows simply miss. But they can be hurt by an ordinary weapon, even if they are tough. Their skin and muscle is like old wood, hard and resilient, but able to be cut. That doesn't make them easy targets, by any means, but they can be defeated. That does not take into account how many will die in doing so, however."

To Shireen's horror, Jediah and Florian both looked thoughtful. They were actually taking Thaddeus's words seriously and considering applying for peace with those things!

"You must be joking," she said. "Jediah, surely..."

"We're not going to be stupid about this, Shireen," Jediah said. "But Orlando is right. If we have a chance, however slim, of avoiding the bloodshed, we have to take it."

Solomon spoke up for the first time. "I agree," he said. "But they have a saying on that other earth. Hope for the best, but plan for the worst. And that's exactly what we're going to do."

CHAPTER 42

All eyes turned to him after he made his statement. Solomon could feel his face twist as he grinned.

"Here's what I propose," he said. "Florian and Jediah should go speak with this advocate to feel him out and see what they think. They're the oldest of all of us here, and have the most experience but they can't go alone, obviously. Shireen, Orlando, and whoever else they deem necessary should also go."

"Why not you?" Shireen asked. "What are you going to be doing?"

"You going to Rustling Elms is hoping for the best. I'll be doing the planning for the worst part."

"Which means what, exactly?" Florian asked.

"I need to find Justice, or at least see if I can remember what I did with it."

In truth there was a lot that Solomon didn't remember still. His life before waking up on that other earth was full of holes and missing parts. He didn't remember much of his childhood, and had only vague recollections of his mother and father, although he knew that they had died when he was very young. He had been raised here in Towering Oaks, as a sort of ward of the House, but had no memories of any friends, beyond Orlando, and even with him he only remembered some of their adventures.

There were no memories of his early days as a scout, or much of his days as a foot-soldier in service to Jediah. Bits and pieces floated to the surface, and it felt like more came all the time, but overall, he still felt like there were huge gaps.

"I still can't remember where I put it, and I don't know exactly why I hid it in the first place. I also don't know where I got it, or from who, or why. And beyond flashes of that one fight I had with a Soul Gaunt, I don't remember ever using it."

"Then how do you expect to find out where it is?" Shireen asked.

"Because I'm hoping that Thaddeus here can reverse the spell that he cast when they exiled me."

He looked at the mage sitting across the table from him.

"I can't," Thaddeus said. "I would if I could, I'm sure you know that, but the spell I cast can't be reversed. Your memory loss isn't magical, it's an effect of the spell that made it happen. It erased all those memories for good, so they're not blocked, they're actually gone. Frankly, I'm shocked that you've recovered any of them."

"That seems like an awfully powerful spell," Willow said. "I wasn't aware that you were that accomplished a mage."

Thaddeus bowed his head to her. "I'm not, but thank you. That spell was at the absolute limit of what I've ever been able to do and I wasn't even sure that it worked. And seeing that it wasn't permanent, I don't think I did get it quite right. Which I'm grateful for, of course."

"I guess I need another way of trying to recover that memory then," Solomon said.

"I don't get it," Luke said. "What's the big deal about one sword? I mean, even if it's magic or something, so what? According to Thaddeus, there are a ton of Soul Gaunts, and I saw how hard it was for Solomon to beat one. Shouldn't you all be arming everyone to the teeth now, and worry about this one sword later?"

"I don't think I can really answer that," Solomon said. "I feel that having Justice back is our best chance, but I don't really remember why."

"I do," Jediah cut in. "Justice is a legendary weapon, although it hasn't always been called that. It's had many names in its long history. Where it came from, no one is really sure of anymore. Some say it was forged in the heart of a star at the beginning of time, while others say it's a mighty warrior, cursed into that form forever more. Yet others say that it was blessed by the creator himself, but the truth is that no-one knows, and the stories about it go back for centuries.

"They always have the same theme. An exceptional warrior is chosen to wield it, either by the one who held it before or by the sword itself, depending on who you believe. It's to be used in times when the Greenweald has faced great peril, or to protect a loved one, or to vanquish a terrible evil. The chosen champion always prevails in these tales, and the foe is conquered.

"But then, a change comes over the champion. Some of them become slaves to their own fame and rest on their laurels, content to let others confront danger, but never giving the sword to anyone else. Others become consumed with rooting out wrongs, no matter how small, and dealing with them harshly and permanently. Whichever way it goes, the end is never good. The champion always comes to a cursed end, and the sword passes out of knowledge until it appears again with a new champion, and the cycle repeats.

"To say I was concerned when Solomon showed up with it is an understatement. But, I held my peace and hoped that the stories were exaggerated. When he came back from a patrol without it, and told me of using it to defeat a Soul Gaunt, he was the first of the Folk I had ever heard of to avoid the curse."

"But why?" Solomon asked. "What did I say when I came back?"

Jediah shrugged. "You wouldn't say why. You simply said that the sword was too dangerous for any one man to wield, and that you had hid it in a spot that you could get to if needed. A place where it would be safe and that it could stay unless the Greenweald was in dire need."

"I'd say we're there now," Florian said.

"There may be a way for you to regain more memories," Willow said. "From what I've been told, you first got some of them back when the Soul Gaunt touched you. A traumatic event, to be sure, and since then they've slowly been coming back to you. It's possible that given time, you will get them all back."

"Which is exactly what we don't have," Solomon said.

"No," Willow agreed, "we don't. But perhaps another trauma or shock would shake more memories loose. It's risky, and certainly not something I would recommend in most circumstances, but these are hardly normal times."

"What are you saying? That Solomon should go get himself attacked by one those things again?" Lacy asked.

"No, I'm most definitely not saying that. I don't know what sort of shock it would have to be, but it would have to be significant to work. At least, that's my hope, and my fear."

Solomon's mind went to the one thing that he was fairly certain would work. He was reluctant to say it out-loud, in front of everyone, but it was worth the risk. He looked up, and locked eyes with Florian as he spoke.

"I'll go back to the pool where Celia was lost."

"That's crazy!" Shireen said. "What are you going to do? Go there and get drowned yourself? How will that help any of us?"

"I won't drown. Whatever it was could have then, and it didn't. Plus, I wasn't ready for it then. Now, I will be."

"How? How are you going to be ready for something that you don't even know what it is?"

Solomon shrugged. "I just will be. It took me by surprise last time. This time, it won't."

Shireen snorted and turned away, obviously not believing in him, not this time at least. He wanted to smile at that. It was good to know that after everything, Shireen at least still thought of him as fallible.

"Let us go with you, then" Orlando said. "We can at least stand by, ready to help if need be."

"No, you need to go with Jediah and Florian."

"I have other guards and scouts," Jediah said. "As does Florian. We can spare them to help you in your quest."

"I know, but it's more than that. I need to do this alone. Totally alone." He looked over at Daisy, who was laying on the floor nearby. "Lacy, can you watch out for Daisy for me while I'm gone?"

"Of course," she replied. "But do you even remember where that pool is?"

"It's one of the things I do remember."

"And you really think you can have revenge on the thing that killed my daughter?" Florian asked.

Solomon shrugged. "Maybe, but I need to do something. And even if I can't but it helps me remember, then what have we lost? In the meantime, maybe Thaddeus will be proven right, you'll be successful, and we won't even need the sword."

"Hope for the best, plan for the worst," Orlando said. "Although, I'm not entirely sure that I like this plan. But I have to admit, I don't have anything better. Does anyone?"

Solomon looked up and down the table, but no one spoke. "Then it looks like we know what to do."

"Wait," a quiet voice said. Solomon looked around and realized that Lacy had spoken, her eyes fixed on the table in front of her.

"Go ahead, Lacy."

"I...we...don't belong here, mixed up in this. I mean, the Greenweald is wonderful, at least the little I've seen of it. And simply breathing the air makes you feel more alive and…I don't know…connected to everything else? But, I can't help with what's going on. I can't pick up a sword and go fight those things, like you or Shireen or Orlando can. I can't cast some sort of magic spell like Thaddeus, or heal people like Willow. I can't do anything, except be in the way. Luke too. I'd love to see more of the Greenweald, but maybe now isn't the time for us to do it."

"I agree," Jediah said.

"I do too, in theory," Solomon said. "But the thing is, I didn't bring you here to help *us*. I brought you here so that you could *be* helped and healed. Neither of you asked for what happened and both of you need time to recover. There's no better place that I know of to get well than the Greenweald."

"But we're only in the way. Even right now. We shouldn't be here. We have nothing to contribute to the conversation."

"Not true," Solomon said. "You've survived an attack by a Soul Gaunt. Something that many of the Folk wouldn't be able to say. And Luke has survived, with his mind intact no less, an ordeal that the rest of can't even imagine. Maybe right now things feel overwhelming, but what if as we move forward either of you have an insight that could help us? You may not have strength of arms, or magical ability, but you have knowledge, and we may need that."

Lacy looked up at him. "So then what? We tag along and try to stay out of the way?"

"No," Florian said. "I have a better option, I think. Come with me to Whispering Pines. My House is of a different nature than this one. It's less military, and more suited to rest and healing of the spirit. I have several cottages, and can give you one for your use. You can stay, reap the benefits of the Greenweald and heal, yet still be available should we need you."

Lacy looked at Luke, who glanced back at her and shrugged his shoulders.

"That sounds good, thank you. And Daisy can stay with us, too."

"Good, then it's settled," Solomon said. "I'm glad you're staying. This crisis will pass, and then we'll have more time to be good hosts and show you a proper thank-you for what you've done."

"There is one more thing," Lacy said. "What about Ed?"

"Oh, I haven't forgotten Ed. When this is said and done, Willow and I will go see him, and bring him here if necessary. Which it very well may be. I don't want everyone in your world to know about us, but Ed is a good man and I'll do whatever I can to help him too."

"Who's this Ed?" Shireen asked.

Solomon smiled again. "Someone you'd like. He's a law man on that other earth. Nice guy, good heart, but pretty no-nonsense."

"So, a male version of her," Orlando quipped.

"Something like that," Solomon agreed. "And someone who will need our help too. I haven't forgotten, Lacy. But for now, I think we have a plan? Yes?"

This time, no one spoke up.

"Alright, let's get to it then."

CHAPTER 43

In all the stories that Luke had written, he had never had a character that couldn't be redeemed. Unless it was the true villain of the piece, who deserved their come-uppance. But for everyone else, their flaws were overcome, their baser natures were outdone by their noble ones and they all came through in the end. It was no wonder that he never got published. That wasn't even close to real, not even in some made-up fantasy world.

He was proof of that, if any was needed. He had made it, to another world, a whole other reality, and look at the place! Trees the size of office buildings, and a forest that any fairy-tale creature would be at home in. Tall, thin, beautiful people who were better than the normal human, yet helpful and wise. Air that made you feel clean and pure by the simple act of breathing it in.

And Luke couldn't care less about any of it. He could feel the Greenweald, sure, trying to work its own kind of magic in him. Trying to heal his mind and his soul. But that was up against the whispering that was always in his ears. Telling him that the world, whether this one or his own, was dark and cold. People, human or Folk, would leave you, betray you, and hurt you. All of them. Any of them.

He looked ahead, at Lacy walking along with Florian, Daisy on her other side. She wasn't a tall woman compared to anyone, but walking between the overly tall lord and the huge dog made her seem even tinier. She had been strangely subdued ever since the two scouts had arrived in their yard, but looked like she was coming out of it. She asked Florian questions about her surroundings, listening as he answered and pointed out more sights for her to see. If Luke had wanted he could have concentrated and joined in on the conversation, but he had no interest in it.

Instead, he looked at the trees that would soon be nothing more than decaying, broken stumps. The plants that would be trampled beneath hard boots as the people who supposedly loved them moved to the attack. He took a breath of the warm, clean air, that would soon be cold, and tasting of nothing but death.

If they were lucky they'd be gone from here by then, back home, where they could wait for the same thing to happen there. But at least they'd be home and together. Lacy was the one person who he still felt a fondness for…no, more than that. He loved her still. If he could save her from what was coming he would, but since he couldn't, he would at least be with her until the end.

"You seem distracted," a quiet voice said.

Thaddeus was accompanying them back to his home compound as well, saying that he still needed time to recover from his ordeal and could do so the best in his own chambers. Luke understood, but thought the man melodramatic. He had been held for a few days. He should try a few weeks.

"Tired," Luke said, avoiding the other man's gaze. "It's been a long couple of days."

"More than that. It's been a lifetime for you. I hope you find the peace that you're seeking. House Whispering Pines is a good place for that."

"Thanks," Luke mumbled. Thaddeus gave a slight bow and dropped back to walk behind the small group once again.

The "cottage" was something else that should have come straight out of a story. It, like every building he had seen in the Greenweald, was a tree. It wasn't huge for this world, but the door opened to a round room, a good twenty feet in diameter, with comfortable furnishings. Windows let in plenty of light, filtered through the leaves of the forest giants that surrounded them, and there was a spiral staircase off to the left side.

"It's not much, I know," Florian was saying. "But I think you'll be comfortable here. There is a bed on the second floor, along with a small balcony, where you can get a better view of some of the birds if you wish."

"This is gorgeous, Lord Florian. How can we thank you?" Lacy said.

"No thanks are needed. I feel that your part in this is not yet over, but even if it is, you've done a great deal already. Besides, I think my daughter would have liked you…and I think I would like to be more like her."

Lacy took the tall man's hand and squeezed it. He looked surprised for a moment, and then returned the gesture. "Touching," Luke thought to himself, and for a moment, wasn't sure if he meant it or not.

"My servants will provide your meals and anything else that you may want," Florian said.

He showed them how to contact the servants when they were needed and other features of the "cottage". Luke hoped that Lacy was paying attention, because he really wasn't. He was tired and wanted the two others to leave, maybe take the dog with them, so that he could sleep and for a short while get rid of the horrible thoughts running through his mind.

Finally, the tour was over and the goodbyes were said. Florian and Thaddeus took their leave, with promises to check in on them as they could and wishes for their speedy recoveries.

"Wow," Lacy said, when they were alone. "This is something, huh?"

"Yeah, I guess," Luke replied.

"You guess? Come on, really? Look at where we are, Luke! This is like one of your stories! I mean, I'm all excited, now that I'm over my shock and not wandering around like a moon-struck cow. I can't even imagine how you feel."

Luke shrugged.

"You're doing that a lot lately," Lacy said. "Maybe I can make you a little more definite about something…"

She moved closer to him, and slid her arms around his waist, her face turned up to his, lips slightly parted.

"I'm tired," he said, and pulled away from her embrace. "I think I'll go lay down."

When he woke, the room was in shadow, and for a moment, he felt the panic start to set in. But then the flickering light of a candle caught his attention, and the cave that he was sure he was in faded away to become the comfortable bedroom again. He lay there staring at the flame, remembering times when he would have given anything for the mere sight of one.

There was no more sleep coming for him this night. The habit of being up all night, even if it meant more pain and fear, was a hard one for him to break. It seemed to be getting worse, if anything. He felt more of an affinity with the darkness than he did the light, as if that was where he really belonged now. A creature of the night, for however many more of them he had left.

Lacy was lying in the bed, her back toward him. He listened to the soft sound of her breathing for a moment. His hand came up, lifted toward her back as if he would stroke it, but then dropped back gently to the bed. He sighed, sat up, and swung his legs over the edge.

She didn't stir when he left the bedroom and started down the stairs. Luke wasn't surprised. With everything that had happened, he was sure she was as exhausted as he was. Let her sleep, she needed it.

Downstairs, he found Thaddeus, sitting quietly in the corner, his dark eyes glinting as they watched Luke.

"What the…? What are you doing here?" Luke hissed.

"I came to talk to you," Thaddeus said, his voice loud in the silence of the cottage.

"Shh! You'll wake Lacy." Luke glanced back up the stairs, sure that he would hear her rising from the bed. For some reason that he couldn't define, he didn't want her to get up and see Thaddeus here.

"No, she'll sleep until I say otherwise, as will the Hound," Thaddeus said.

For the first time, Luke noticed Daisy, curled up on the floor near the stairs. She hadn't made a sound when Thaddeus must have entered, and showed no sign that she knew either of them were there now.

"What did you do?" Luke asked.

"A simple spell. Nothing harmful, I assure you. But we needed to talk, and we needed to do it undisturbed."

"Damn it! You can't come in here and do something to Lacy like that!" Luke could feel his anger rising at the thought. How dare he? He and Lacy were people, to be respected and treated as such! Not lab rats here for the amusement of some immoral…

"Peace," Thaddeus said. "I swear to you that no harm will come to her. I simply thought it would be less cruel this way."

"What do you mean? What would be less cruel?"

"Than for her to hear what we will talk about, of course. You have the mark on you, Luke Roberts. I can see it, as surely as you can see it on me."

"I don't know what you're talking about," Luke replied, but of course, he did. He had felt it when he had first seen Thaddeus, that feeling like there was a wire in his brain, humming and sparking with electricity. It had faded somewhat, but he could still feel it whenever he looked at Thaddeus.

"You do. You know exactly what I'm talking about."

"What if I do? It doesn't mean anything."

226

"Of course, it does. It means you know as well as I do what is coming. I've seen the dozens, maybe more, that are arrayed against us. You have intimate knowledge of just one of them. Can you imagine the might when that many are gathered together? Do you honestly believe that any of us, including Solomon, would have a chance to survive an attack like that?"

"No," Luke said, vehemence in his voice, glad to finally say it out-loud. "No, alright? There is no chance. Not for you, or your lord, or Solomon, or this whole place. Lacy and I are going home."

"And do you think they won't come there when they're finished here? Why do you think one was there in the first place? It was no rabid animal separated from its pack. It was sent there, as a scout. Solomon may have killed it, but too late. They know they can go there now, and that they have a whole other world to take as their own."

Luke sank down into a chair, burying his head in his hands. "Then we are done for. I've felt that ever since the thing came, but I thought…I hoped…that it was just my mind playing tricks again."

"It's the truth. But, perhaps your hope is not misplaced."

Luke's head came up. "What hope? You said there was none."

"There isn't, for most. But for you and me, it could be different. I already know that they'll use me to manage things among the Folk for them. To ensure that they have what they need for years to come. In return I'll be rewarded, and more importantly, I'll be allowed to live and to stay free. They'll need the same thing on your world and it could be you. I believe it's why you weren't killed."

"And be some kind of Judas? No. I won't do that. I'm not a coward."

"Saving yourself, and those you love," Thaddeus glanced up the stairs as he spoke, "is no betrayal. If anything, it has a certain nobility to it."

"Justify it all you want, it's still what it is."

Thaddeus sighed. "I was hoping to talk sense into you. But if you won't see the inevitable for what it is, then I can't help you. You, and she, will end with the rest of them. I hope for her sake that the Nightwinds kill her quickly. They have ways of drawing these things out…as I'm sure you know." He rose to leave. "Goodbye then, Luke Roberts. I hope the end comes for you both quickly."

Luke watched him stride across the floor to the door, but his mind was already far from there. Into the near future, watching as the Soul Gaunts overflowed everything, and pulled Lacy from his grasp. He could hear her cries as he was held helpless to do anything about them.

"Wait," he said quietly. Thaddeus stopped, his hand on the door handle. "What do I have to do?"

"Come with me and talk to the man who has shown me what is coming. Let him take the measure of you, and perhaps you can be of use, and saved as well."

"And if I don't, there is no hope for us."

"Worse. I believe that if we who have been marked do not do this, we will suffer worst of all."

"Why me?"

Thaddeus shrugged. "Because you were there? A target of opportunity, perhaps. Why was I chosen? It doesn't matter. What matters now is what we do."

Luke stood and looked up the stairs again. Daisy still made no movement at all. "You swear she's going to be alright?"

"From my spell? Yes. As soon as we leave here, I will reverse it. Well, once we get a little further away, so that the Hound won't sense us. More than that, I can only say what I have."

Luke glared at Thaddeus for a moment, then glanced at the stairs again. Up to where Lacy lay sleeping, unaware of the terrible choice that was being forced upon him. He could betray everyone he knew and save her. Or he could stay faithful to his own kind, and watch as she was tortured and killed in front of him. He had already been shown a small piece of what that would be like.

In the end, it was really no contest. He nodded, and followed Thaddeus out the door.

CHAPTER 44

"I don't like this," Shireen said. "Not one bit."

"Neither do I, but what are we going to do about it?" Orlando spoke quietly, pitching his voice so that Shireen could hear him, but not Jediah and Florian who rode ahead of them.

Two guards from House Whispering Pines had the lead, a position that Shireen would normally have fought for, but now she wanted to ride behind, where she could see what was happening. She knew the two guards well enough to know that they were competent. Not up to Towering Oaks standards, but able to handle any ordinary threats that may appear and since it was daylight she didn't think they had to worry about Soul Gaunts. At least, not until they had arrived at House Rustling Elms.

"We should have waited for Solomon to come back," she murmured.

"That's the point though. If Solomon brings back his sword, Jediah and Florian are going to be less inclined to try to talk to this 'advocate' guy, whoever he is. They both know it, so they're hoping that maybe Thaddeus is right and they can get it settled before he gets back."

"That's another thing. You felt it too, right? Thaddeus was off. Something happened to him in there that changed him."

"Of course, it did," Orlando said. "How could it not have?"

"I'm just worried..." she trailed off, not wanting to say it out loud.

"That he's been compromised and is working with the enemy? You're not the only one to think that. I'm pretty sure that Jediah, and even Florian, are thinking the same thing."

"Then why are we even doing this?"

"On the off chance that they can save lives. Let's say that we're all wrong, and Thaddeus isn't turned. Isn't it worth a discussion? Before we send soldiers into a battle that's going to kill a bunch of them?"

Shireen sighed. "Of course. But I still don't like it."

"As I said, neither do I. But what do we know? We're just grunts."

He smiled at her, but Shireen found it hard to return. Her entire inner being was shouting at her that this was wrong, that it was a set-up. She had learned to trust her instincts over her years as a scout. At times when the trail had grown cold, she had been able to follow it anyway, trusting to subtle clues that her subconscious picked up without her even being aware. It was one of the reasons she was trusted by Jediah so much. And when you combined that with Orlando's ability to reason through any situation, and to stay methodical and rational...there wasn't much that they couldn't do.

It grated on her nerves that Jediah hadn't even consulted her before making this decision. But then again, this was a bigger deal, a much bigger deal, then anything that she had ever encountered in his service before. Maybe now was the time that the Head of House needed to step forward and make a decision based on *his* gut feeling, and *his* experience.

Yeah, that was it. For all that Shireen trusted and believed in her own abilities, she respected Jediah's above all others except perhaps for Solomon's. And he too had thought that this parlay was worth trying.

It was time to be a good soldier and do what was expected of her. Follow orders, protect both her Head of House and Lord Florian, and trust in the better judgement of her leader.

She was still working this out in her mind when the horses ahead of her pulled up sharply. They had arrived, but the Rustling Elms compound was nothing that she had expected.

The bodies that had littered the ground were gone, leaving no sign that the area had once looked like a slaughter-yard. But more than that, there was also no trace of blood or gore anywhere. Shireen looked around wildly. How was this possible? Some of the pools of blood had been thick and soaked into the dirt. The stones that lined some of the paths had been splattered with it, not to mention the plants that had leaves that looked as if they had been dipped in red paint.

Where had it all gone?

"What the...?" Orlando was looking around him with the same confusion on his face that she was sure was on her own.

"This is quite different from what you described," Jediah said.

"I don't understand it," Orlando said, still looking around in disbelief. "This whole area...the bodies..."

"It appears that our presence was anticipated," Florian said. "I'm not sure if I should be comforted or not by the fact that they cleaned up."

230

"It's more than that," Shireen said. "*How* did they clean up? The bodies, sure, that I can understand. But how did they get rid of all the blood?"

"There's more here than the Soul Gaunts," Jediah said. "That much must be true. Now the question is, what is it? And what does it mean for us?"

"Only one way to find out," Florian said. "We do what we came to." He took a deep breath and sat up straighter in the saddle as he looked at the shut doors in the main tree of the compound.

Shireen suppressed a shudder as she followed his gaze. The last time she had gone up those steps had led to horror and loss. She wasn't eager to revisit, and still had no faith at all that anything other than that waited there. But she remembered her promise to herself, to let those in charge make the decisions; no matter how stupid she thought those decisions were.

"How do we play this?" she asked.

"We go knock on the door," Florian said, "and see who opens it."

"And if we don't like who answers?" Orlando asked.

"We run," Jediah said, startling Shireen who never thought she would hear those words come from him. "Don't look so shaken, Shireen. We're here to talk, not to fight. I'm not vain enough to imagine that the six of us can defeat dozens of those things. We're here to find out if there is any truth to Thaddeus's words. If there are, fine, we'll talk and try to keep open minds. But if that door opens to Soul Gaunts, we get out of here, and come back when Solomon has found his sword."

"Agreed," Florian said. "Be ready for anything, all of you."

The short climb up the steps to the door of the tree was the hardest that Shireen had ever taken. Her chest was tight, and the bright day seemed to be overcast, although there were no clouds visible through the leaves of the trees around them. There were only three steps, but it took what felt like hours to climb them, and yet in an instant, they were there.

Jediah stepped forward without hesitation and banged his fist on the door. There was no response from inside. The doors didn't open, and there was no sound of anyone approaching. He knocked again, to the same lack of response. Then, putting one hand on the hilt of his sword, he tried the handle. The doors were firmly locked, and only shook slightly in their frames as Jediah tried to open them.

"Hm. Maybe they don't want to talk after all."

They waited another moment and then moved off, down the steps and back to where their horses waited. The beasts shifted nervously, telling Shireen that there was danger here still. Sometimes, animals had better sense than Folk did.

"Now what?" Shireen asked.

"We have two choices," Florian said. "We either leave here and wait for Solomon to come back, or we stay here and try again."

"I'm not a big fan of the waiting here option," Orlando said. "If we linger too much longer, the sun will begin setting, and I'm not keen on being near a bunch of Soul Gaunts in the dark."

"None of us are," Jediah said, "besides which, we didn't come here to be kept waiting like beggars on the doorstep. We're the Heads of our Houses! If this 'advocate' can't be bothered to answer the door, then so be it."

Shireen was glad to hear it, not only because she also didn't want to hang around until dark, but because of the fire in Jediah's voice. *That* was her leader, the Head of House that she knew and was honored to serve.

They began to mount their horses when there was a noise from the tree. Shireen paused with one foot in the stirrup and looked around. With a creak that made it sound as if were hundreds of years old, the door opened. They watched as a tall, thin man, dressed in black robes with a hood thrown over his face came out.

"I am sorry for the delay in getting out here," he called, his voice deep and cultured. "I was resting when one of the Nightwinds came and told me there were guests at the door. I thought it better to open it myself and avoid any misunderstandings."

He reached up and pushed the hood back, revealing a tanned face, with long white hair. From his features and build he could have easily passed as one of the Folk, but Shireen had never seen him before.

"Please," he continued, "won't you come in?"

Shireen almost laughed at that, in spite of the fury that the comment caused to rise up in her. Who did he think he was? He stood there and invited them into a house that he had taken over, ruined, and massacred the people of.

"I think not," Florian said, "but we would like to speak with you. Out here, in the sunlight, if you would."

232

"Of course," the man said, walking down the steps. "I can understand your hesitation. Earned or not, the Nightwinds do have a…shall we say, dangerous…reputation."

"I would say it's earned," Jediah said. His voice sounded rough next to the smooth voice of this man, and the practiced dignity of Florian's.

"That may be so," the man conceded. "They are horribly efficient predators, after all. Only a fool wouldn't be careful around such animals."

"Ah," Florian said. "Animals. And yet Thaddeus told us that you claimed they are simply a misunderstood race of people."

The man smiled. "And how is my friend Thaddeus? I do hope he is recovering from his ordeal."

Jediah started to speak, but Florian motioned him to silence and took the lead himself. Shireen was glad. Jediah was a fearsome warrior, and a great leader, but Florian was much more the diplomat, more suited to bandying words. If action was called for, then Jediah would step into the more prominent role.

"Thaddeus is recovering well, thank you. But I find it strange that you would admit to his having undergone any sort of ordeal."

"Why is that? He did. Before I knew he was here, some of the more wild Nightwinds had gotten at him. It was regrettable, but Thaddeus came to understand it as the acts of a scared and hungry predator. Nothing more."

"Yes, so he told us. He also told us that you wish to live here. To settle and let the Soul Gaunts roam the Greenweald as they would. Is that true?"

"In a sense, yes. But that makes it sound so dangerous. And really, it isn't. I have a rapport with them. And I will contain them, stop them from going near any compounds, or any individual houses. I'll make sure that they only take game, and that at a sustainable rate."

"See, that is where I admit to some confusion. I'm sure we all do." Florian stopped to look around at Shireen and the others, silently asking for their agreement. "In one sentence, you talk about them as if they were animals, then in the next, as if you can speak to them. We're not sure which it is."

"Oh!" the man seemed surprised at Florian's statement. "Now I understand! You must forgive me. I've spent so much time with them that I forget that not everyone knows them as I do. Yes, I can definitely see why you're confused."

He stopped and chuckled. Florian raised an eyebrow, and Jediah glowered at the man. Shireen herself felt her hackles rise at the sound of the laughter. There was something wrong here. More than the whole situation, there was a bigger threat. She looked around the compound, but saw nothing out of place.

"Well," the man said when he stopped laughing. "Perhaps you'd care to see for yourself."

"No," Florian said, "thanks all the same. As I've said, I think we're more comfortable out here at the moment."

"You misunderstand. I insist!"

He raised his hand and the doors to the main tree flew open, and darkness flowed out of it. The temperature surrounding Shireen dropped immediately to a numbing cold, and the air grew dimmer as if storm clouds had obscured the sun. The man was chanting in a harsh language, filled with crashing consonants, and the sky blackened further.

Shireen tore her sword from its sheath and put her back to Orlando's, aware of Jediah and the two Whispering Pines soldiers surrounding Florian.

The horses screamed, reared onto their hind legs and tore off without their riders. Even the best trained horse couldn't stand in the face of the fear that gnawed at them. Shireen could feel it eating at her resolve already.

They would take them, take her, and drag her into that tree. Back to where it was pitch black, with unclean things growing and death and rot and sickness all around. They'd kill Orlando and make her watch, laughing at his suffering and then do the same things to her, but even more slowly.

Her sword trembled in her hand, and she could feel Orlando's own shivers against her back.

A Soul Gaunt flowed up in front of her, and she swung wildly, slashing where it had been for an instant, but hitting nothing. There was a chuckle from nearby, a vile sound that made it feel like worms were crawling through her flesh.

Orlando let out a sudden cry, and she spun in time to see a Soul Gaunt rake its claws across his chest as it flew past. The sharp nails made a skittering noise as they slide off the chain link of his armor, but the force of the blow was enough to drive him to the side and send him stumbling. Shireen lunged toward him, but then let out her own cry as sharp claws clutched the back of her thigh, puncturing through and causing her to stumble forward.

She fell to one knee, but scrambled up, turning and thrusting with her sword. The point entered the black cloak floating before her, but met no resistance. Remembering the sight of the one laying on the ground on that other earth, she drove her sword up, keeping the blade vertical and felt it make solid contact. The thing before her screeched, pulled back and was gone, leaving no sign of damage behind it.

By the time she got to Orlando, he had recovered and was fighting a Soul Gaunt of his own, his sword weaving patterns in the air as he tried to hit it. The Soul Gaunt evaded, its green eyes glowing in the depths of its cloak as it looked for its own opening.

Shireen took it in the side, swinging her sword like a woodsman's axe and catching it solidly below the arm. It too let out a horrible screech, and dropped to the ground, but before either Shireen or Orlando could attack again, it sped away, leaving them panting.

Shireen could feel blood running down the back of her leg, and Orlando was holding his left arm oddly. She saw that when the Soul Gaunt had raked its claws across his chest, they had caught in the muscle of his bicep and ripped it badly. His face was pale, and he was breathing heavily, but his eyes scanned the deepening gloom for any more enemies.

"Where are they?" he said.

"We just drove two of them away."

"Yeah, but how many came out? It looked like a lot. So where are they?"

For the first time Shireen realized that the fury of battle had driven them away from Florian and Jediah. She peered into the dark, trying to see them, but couldn't. There was the noise of fighting though, and she ran that way, trusting that Orlando would follow.

She tripped on something and went sprawling. Looking back, it was the body of one of the Whispering Pines soldiers, his throat torn out, staring lifelessly up at the darkened trees.

Shireen scrambled to her feet, running after Orlando who had now taken the lead. The sounds of the struggle receded in front of her, and she could hear the still chanting voice of the Advocate growing in volume.

Suddenly, everything went pitch black, as if she was in a cave deep under the earth with no source of light. There was the cry of a man's voice and the air turned so cold that she could hardly breath. But strangely, the sense of dread began to fade away.

A moment later, and the light began to slowly return. Orlando stood a few yards from her, frozen in place as she was by the dark and the cold. Ahead, the doors to House Rustling Elms stood open, and the Soul Gaunts were flowing back into it. Shireen looked around wildly, but there was no sign of Jediah or Florian.

The Advocate still stood at the bottom of the steps, coming more clearly into view with the gradual lightening of the sky. He stared at her, then his face split into a wide grin. He turned, climbed the three steps and entered the darkness within the tree. The doors slammed, leaving her, Orlando, and one of Florian's guards behind.

CHAPTER 45

It was every bit as dark and suffocating with fear that it had been the last time Thaddeus had been in the Rustling Elms tree. The Soul Gaunts were all around, but kept their distance, seeming content to stay hidden in the shadows, chuckling as he strode through, trying to keep his back straight and his head high. In spite of the cold, sweat stood out on his brow, and his fingers itched to grab the stone in his pocket, say the words and have it blaze with light. But he knew that could well be fatal, regardless of what the Advocate said.

The human trailed behind him, showing none of the dignity and resolve that Thaddeus was trying to project. He walked along, hunched over, his arms hugging his sides, muttering to himself. If this was the best that the Soul Gaunts could find to serve them on that earth, then he pitied the place. But that was none of his affair. He had done as requested, brought the Advocates message to the Head of his House, and found out the plans for his response. Additionally, he had taken the initiative and brought Luke here. He was sure he would be rewarded extra for that.

It was early morning when they had arrived at the compound, and the doors to the main tree were shut fast. Luke had moaned at the sight of the bodies scattered around, but Thaddeus had told him to shut his eyes, and led him up the steps to the entrance. Although he found the man to be rather pathetic in general, he couldn't blame him in this particular case. The view was far from pleasant.

He had no idea where to find the Advocate, and when he had asked the question to the dark shapes watching them, his only answer had been dry, cold laughter. They wanted him to walk through them, feel the dread that they caused and feed on his fear. Thaddeus hoped they choked on it, and resolved to give them as little as he could.

While he had no doubts that the Soul Gaunts would triumph and had decided to serve the winning side, he also had no illusion about what they were. Regardless of what the Advocate told him, or what he himself had told the rest, they were evil. A bunch of wild animals or a race of lesser developed people, it didn't matter. They existed to cause fear, pain and misery, simply because they could, and they enjoyed it.

Thaddeus wasn't entirely sure what that made him for agreeing to serve them, but he did know that at the very least it made him a survivor, and that was all that mattered.

He kept walking though the darkness, feeling his way as he needed to, his hands finding slimy lichens and soft fungi. He led Luke up the stairs and into the room where he had been held the last time. There was no more light in there than there was anywhere else in the tree, but he could tell by the stench that the poor man that had been hung on the wall was still there. Why wouldn't he be? To take him down would be to show a modicum of compassion. Plus, it added menace to the room, not that it needed it.

"Ah, Thaddeus." The voice of the Advocate came out of the darkness. "And you've brought a friend. How lovely. Please, be seated."

Thaddeus stood unmoving, refusing to be baited.

"Oh, of course. My apologies." The voice started to whisper a chant, but cut off abruptly. "You know, on second thought, why don't *you* make the light? That way, you can moderate it how it seems best to you."

"And keep me weaker," Thaddeus thought to himself. But pulled the stone from his pocket and cast the spell that caused it to faintly glow. It did little to illuminate the room, which was fine with him, but it did spread enough light for him to see the Advocate seated comfortably in a chair, with another positioned so that it was facing him.

Thaddeus took that one, carefully setting the stone down on the arm of it.

"You also," the Advocate said, looking at Luke. "Sit, please."

Luke looked around, but there were no other chairs visible in the small circle of light. He glanced into the darkness and shivered, and then sat on the floor at the side of the chair that Thaddeus had taken.

"Perhaps that's fitting," the Advocate said, smiling down at the human, and then shifting his gaze away as if Luke no longer mattered. "What do you have to tell me?"

Thaddeus hesitated. Now that the matter was at hand, he found himself unsure. The thought of truly betraying Florian, his cousin and Head of House, was bothering him more than he thought it would. He had reconciled himself to the reality that not only Florian, but all of House Whispering Pines, and the other Houses, would be destroyed. He knew that

238

they would never bow to the Soul Gaunts, and even if they did, many, most really, would end up as food. But still…

"Thaddeus," the Advocate said, his voice growing colder, "we had a deal. I would hate to think that I wasn't able to trust you."

He leaned back in his chair as he said this, and suddenly, the light from the stone began to dim. Thaddeus fought back, chanting under his breath, the sweat now running down his face, but it did no good. The light flickered, and against all of his will, went out.

They moved in. Luke whimpered beside his chair, and Thaddeus could feel the dread pushing from every side. He couldn't see a single inch in front of his face, but could feel them there. If he reached out, he would touch one, perhaps in the torso, or worse, in the face. Where the jaws could open, and let his fingers pass through to snap shut on them.

"No," he half screamed. "I wasn't hesitating! I was only trying to figure out which to tell you first!"

"Oh, well that's different then," the Advocate said, and slowly the light welled from the stone again. There was no sign of a Soul Gaunt anywhere near him; only Luke, bent over at the waist, his face hidden between his hands. Feeling an uncharacteristic bout of pity, he reached down and put his hand on the human's shoulder. Luke stiffened for a moment, then started to tremble as sobs racked his body.

"Now," the Advocate said, ignoring Luke and sounding for all the world as if he were simply asking the time of day, "what can you tell me?"

"They're coming to talk to you. Today."

"Really? How convenient. And by they, who do you mean, exactly?"

"Florian and Jediah, as well as the two who were with me when I…when you…before. The two scouts from Towering Oaks, Shireen and Orlando. Maybe more, I'm not sure."

"Both Lords Florian and Jediah. How interesting. And they are coming here for what purpose?"

"I did as you instructed me to," Thaddeus began, but the Advocate interrupted him.

"Thaddeus, my dear friend, I *instructed* you to do nothing. I merely *asked* for a favor."

"Of course, my mistake."

"Try to be more careful. Precision in language is so important with these things. It can really make a huge difference." He smiled sincerely at Thaddeus, who struggled to return it.

"Yes, you're right, of course. As I say, my mistake. I did as you asked me, then. I told them about how the Soul...excuse me, Nightwinds, are predators, forced to flee from their home and looking for a new place to live in peace."

"And how did they respond?"

"As you predicted, with skepticism. For Shireen, with outright derision. She doesn't believe it at all, and had no problem saying so. To be honest, I don't think any of them actually believe it."

"Then again I ask, why are they coming here?"

Thaddeus shrugged. "On the chance that they can avoid bloodshed."

"They're concerned about spilling the blood of the Nightwinds?"

"No, their own peoples," Thaddeus answered, before he realized that the Advocate was being sarcastic. "You know that, of course."

The Advocate smiled again. "They are afraid. And rightly so. And you, Thaddeus? Are you afraid?"

"Terrified," Thaddeus admitted.

"There is no need to be. You are safe here, with us. But now, I have another question. One has come back, one who the Nightwinds know and speak of in whispers among themselves. One who scares even them, if you can believe that."

"Solomon."

"Yes, Solomon. What of him?"

"He won't be with them when they come. He's gone off to find his missing sword."

The Advocate frowned. "What sword is this?" His voice had gone deathly quiet.

"His sword Justice. A legendary weapon according to Jediah. It's had other names though. I'm not sure of..."

"Nightslayer!" hissed the Advocate. "He was the one who had it! We wondered..."

Thaddeus had a moment to wonder about the "we" before the Advocate was speaking again, urgency in his voice. "Where is it? Where is he going to retrieve it?"

"The pool where Florian's daughter was killed. I'm not sure exactly where..."

"I know, fool!" the Advocate snapped, springing to his feet. He turned to the darkness covering the deeper parts of the room.

240

"You! Take five others! Find him and kill him before he gets that sword! Track him down and show no mercy! Don't play with him, do you hear me? He's too dangerous! Kill him, take the sword and bring it to me!"

There were hissings and chitterings from the dark, noises that grated on Thaddeus's nerves and caused Luke to whimper and curl into himself again. This was the Soul Gaunts' own language, alien and cruel to both Folk and human.

But the Advocate didn't seem to mind it at all. "The rest will stay here. I have other plans for you." He turned back to Thaddeus. "Take the human and find a place to settle. I don't care where, this place is full of rooms. Stay there until I summon you."

Thaddeus knew better than to argue. He stood and gently coaxed Luke to his feet, grabbed the stone and stumbled from the room.

"Why did you bring me here?" Luke asked from where he now sat, curled into a corner of what was once an opulent bedroom. Now, the bed was rotting in on itself and the air smelled of decay. But it was one of the better rooms that Thaddeus had found, although he hadn't looked for long. Soul Gaunts were everywhere in the tree, and even though they kept their distance, they had obviously been given no orders that they had to make him feel comfortable. The innate fear and cold that they generated was everywhere, and there was no getting used to it.

In this room though, he and Luke were left alone. No Soul Gaunts came into it or tried to interfere when Thaddeus had shut the door. They had been there for hours now, Luke curled into the corner, Thaddeus seated in a chair that wasn't quite rotted yet, trying to get his thoughts in order. Luke's sudden question startled him.

"To save you," he answered automatically, but then was surprised to find that he spoke the truth. Yes, he had initially done it thinking that the Advocate would reward him for his forethought, but it was more than that. The man had been through a lot, as Thaddeus himself had been. That bound them together more than a mark made on the spirit by being in thrall to these vile things.

"You have to find your strength," Thaddeus told him, rising from his chair and moving to squat down near him. "If they think you're useless, why would they not simply kill you? Stop cowering and show that you can face them enough to do the things they need you to."

Luke shook his head. "This was a mistake. I can't go through with it."

"You must! They won't let you walk out of here now. They'll take you again, and you know what they'll do. When the end comes, when they've taken everyone, they'll have Lacy too. And they won't be kind to her. If you serve them, perhaps the Advocate will let you save her as well."

"Perhaps? You told me that they would!"

Thaddeus turned his head away. "I thought they would. Now…I don't know. But still, it's the best opportunity. Otherwise, there is no chance at all. You know this."

Luke bowed his head again, but his tears had stopped. He sat silently for a moment and then took a deep breath. "What do I need to do?"

"Nothing at the moment." Thaddeus looked around. "In truth, there's nothing to do at the moment. For either of us. We sit here, in this festering room, until we're called on."

"No," Luke said. "That's not right." He climbed to his feet. "We should go, move around the place."

Thaddeus sat back in surprise. "Really? Suddenly you're eager to go sight-seeing? There are still Soul Gaunts out there, you know."

"When the one had me on my earth, it didn't care what I did during the day, or even at night, as long as I didn't try to get away or disobey when it gave me instructions. When I did do something like that, it hurt me. A lot. But if I was good, it left me alone."

"And you think that same thing applies here? Even with all of them around?"

"I don't think they really think much of us at all. We're off limits right now, thanks to your arrangement with that other guy. They'll like scaring and mocking us, but otherwise, I don't think they'll touch us."

"That's an awfully big assumption," Thaddeus said. "I don't think I care to put it to the test."

Luke shrugged. "Suit yourself. I'm tired of sitting here."

He started toward the door while Thaddeus watched him with amusement. "And what about light? How will you see?"

Luke stopped and looked back at him. "I guess I won't." He turned and continued to the door, opened it, and stepped out.

Thaddeus waited for a scream, or for him to come running back through the door, but neither of those things happened. After a minute or two had passed, he frowned and rose to his feet, his curiosity getting the better of him.

Taking his stone, he exited the room and looked around. There was Luke, a short distance down the hallway, keeping his hand in contact with the wall and visibly shuddering when his fingers encountered unpleasantness. But he was moving ahead, in spite of the dread and the cold, he was ignoring everything around him and simply walking.

Thaddeus shook his head and strode forward, catching up to him and slowing his pace to walk beside him. "Are all humans as obstinate as you?"

Luke glanced at him. "This is nothing. You should try dealing with Lacy when she's made up her mind."

He had to smile at the normalcy of such a comment, one that just as easily could have been made by any long-married man of the Folk. For a single moment in time, Thaddeus almost forgot where he was.

Then he noticed that there were no Soul Gaunts nearby. They had the hallway to themselves, and the lack of the ever-present fear is what had allowed Luke to make his comment and for Thaddeus to respond to it in kind. He looked around, risking making the light from the stone brighter. But there were no protesting screeches, or sharp claws coming to snatch it away.

"Where have they all gone?" he said, mostly to himself, but Luke answered.

"They were around when I first came out. I don't know where they went, though. Maybe it's some kind of test, to see what we'll do."

"Maybe. But I don't think...."

He was interrupted by the noise of the large main doors of the tree creaking open. He looked at Luke and without a word turned and ran to the staircase leading to the entry hall, the human on his heels.

When he arrived, he slid to a halt and watched as the Advocate walked out the door. The Soul Gaunts were all gathered around, staying back from the sunlight that spilled through. They heard the Advocate talking, and the sound of Florian answering him.

For a moment, Thaddeus fought the urge to run forward, holding his stone aloft and letting it blaze like the sun. But that wouldn't do anything but guarantee that he'd be killed along with the rest. He dropped his eyes, and turned away from the stairs.

"Where are you going?" Luke hissed.

"Away from here. I don't want to see this. I don't think you do either."

He didn't wait to hear a response, but returned to the room they had claimed as their own and shut the door. A few minutes later, it opened and Luke found his way inside.

"You could have waited for me with the light," he muttered, but Thaddeus didn't answer him. He sat, his head down, staring at the floor in front of him, fighting down nausea.

The scream when it came confirmed it. He was truly a traitor to his own kind.

CHAPTER 46

For a moment, Lacy couldn't remember where she was. She rolled over enjoying the sunshine on her face and the feel of the soft bedclothes beneath her. The birds were singing outside and it felt like a beautiful day. Perfect for going out, working in the garden and then taking a dip in the pool. She smiled as she turned over to see if Luke was awake.

Then, the room came clearly into focus, and she remembered that she was in the Greenweald, an entirely different world, and that it was currently in peril from those vile creatures. Suddenly, the perfect summer day didn't seem as glorious. There was no garden of her own here, no pool, and as she felt around, no Luke.

She sat up. "Luke. Luke! Where are you?"

There was no answer and no sound of anyone moving around the cottage. The place was pretty small so she was sure that if he were there, he would have heard her and answered. Then, there was movement from below and she breathed out a sigh of relief. But the noise became the click of nails and Daisy appeared, coming up the stairs and shaking her head. The dog looked like something was bothering her, like she had something in her ear or throat that she couldn't dislodge.

"What's wrong, girl?" Lacy said, and climbed out of bed to tend to her.

Daisy sat and allowed herself to be examined, but Lacy couldn't find anything wrong with her. Although, now that she was up and moving, she had to admit that she felt a little off also. She had a strange disconnected feeling, like she was still dreaming, or of déjà vu. It was weird and no wonder she couldn't remember where she was for the first few minutes when she woke.

"I don't see anything, girl," she said, roughing Daisy's fur. "But where's Luke gone off to?"

She rose and walked down the stairs, followed by Daisy, but as she suspected, there was no sign of Luke down there either. She went to the door, opened it and stood looking out over the Whispering Pines compound. There were a few of the Folk at work in the gardens and walking along the paths, but no sign of her husband.

"Huh, maybe he went to find breakfast? No, that'd be silly. Florian showed us how to call the servants when we needed something. Besides, where would he go?"

Daisy didn't answer her, but she did stand by her side, her nose lifted in the air and sniffing. After a moment, she whined softly and went back inside, still sniffing. Lacy watched as she made her way to a chair in the corner of the room, stuck her nose on the seat and let out a soft woofing noise. She ran back up the stairs, came down them again, nose to the ground and back to another chair. Finally, she raised her head and looked toward Lacy.

Lacy watched her do this. It was behavior that she had never seen a dog do, not even Daisy. But she didn't understand what she was doing. Then, Daisy walked over to her, turned, and repeated the entire sequence of actions.

"What are you trying to tell me?" Lacy mused.

On the third pass, she started to get it.

"Wait. Someone came in and sat in that chair? Then, someone, Luke, I guess, came down the stairs and sat in the other one. Then, they left. Is that what you're trying to tell me?"

Daisy barked once, then sat on her haunches, tongue lolling out of her mouth and looked at Lacy.

"Wow, can't believe I figured that one out," she muttered to herself.
"
o Luke met someone here and they left. But why didn't I hear them? And why didn't you?"

She thought of the fuzziness she had felt on waking, and about Daisy's behavior when she first came up the stairs. Maybe that had something to do with it. Maybe they had been drugged, or...well, something.

While she was thinking about this there was a soft knock on the door. She opened it to find the healer, Willow.

"Oh, hi," Lacy said, surprised by the early morning visit.

"Hello," Willow said. "I hope it's not too early. I wanted to check on you and Luke. Is it alright to come in?"

"Of course!" Lacy stepped aside, letting the tall, graceful woman enter. As she passed, Lacy grimaced. She had never been tall, but the people here were making her feel like she was only half-grown.

"How are you feeling?" Willow asked her.

"Me? I'm pretty good actually. My arm is feeling quite a bit better, thanks to you. Not all the way there, but it doesn't hurt so much to use it now. The constant ache is less, too."

"Excellent. I have to be honest, I wasn't sure if what we did would work. We have very little experience in treating injuries from a Soul Gaunt. I'm sad to say, but most of the time…well, there isn't the need."

Lacy shuddered. "I can understand that. Believe me, I know how lucky I was that Solomon came along. Speaking of, have you seen him?"

"No," Willow smiled. "I believe he has gone on his quest already. He's not one to waste time once he's put his mind to something. I am glad though that you're doing so well. And Luke?"

"Actually, I'm not sure." Lacy tried to keep her voice light and not show the worry that was coiling in her stomach. "When I woke up, he was gone."

Willow frowned. "Really? And he said nothing to you of where he was going?"

"No. I'm not even sure when he left. Although…I kind of think he went with someone."

"Why would you think that?"

Lacy told her what Daisy had done right before she got there.

"Hmm. I think you may be right. Hunting Hounds are known for being quite intelligent, and I think that Daisy, as small as she is for one, may be even more so."

"Daisy is small?"

"For a Hunting Hound, yes. Some of them are much larger than her. The Master of Hounds is known to have no love for Florian, or any other Head of House, so I suspect that he passed off a runt. Such a thing would amuse him, vile creature that he is."

"Runt?" Lacy bent over and scratched Daisy between the ears. "Is that you? I don't think so. And even if you are, who cares?"

Daisy pressed against her hand, and Lacy smiled in spite of her worry about Luke. When she looked up, Willow was watching them with amusement.

"May I wait here? I really would like to check on Luke. While your arm was serious enough, I'm much more concerned with the damage that may have been done to Luke that we can't see."

"But in the meeting yesterday you said that you thought he was okay."

"I said that I thought he was not working with the Soul Gaunts. I still think that. That doesn't mean that he's whole in mind and spirit though. That's what I would like to check."

"Of course, you can stay," Lacy said. "I mean, that's not even a question. But I wish I knew where he went. Why don't we sit down while we wait? I can get some coffee, or...do you have coffee here?"

"Yes," Willow laughed. "I think you'll find most of our foods similar to your own."

"Great. Hold on then."

While Willow took a seat, Lacy rang the small hand bell that Florian had shown her. It made a delicate tinkling sound, and that was all. She had no idea how a servant would hear it, but a few minutes later, there was a discrete knock on the door. Lacy answered it to find a servant patiently waiting. She asked for coffee and if there were any sort of fruit pastry type things that they could get.

When the servant had left, she lowered herself into a chair near Willow with a sigh.

"Are you sure your arm is better?" the Healer asked her.

"Oh yeah, my arm is fine. Why?"

"When you sat down you sounded as if it was still bothering you more than you're saying."

"No, my arm is fine. I just feel...I don't know...off, I guess. Ever since I got up. I've had this weird fuzzy feeling in my head, you know? Like I can't quite wake up all the way. Daisy was acting funny too, at first. It's silly I know, but right before you came, I was wondering if we got drugged or something."

She laughed softly, but when she looked at Willow she saw that the other woman was looking at her with a deadly serious expression.

"Describe the feeling to me. Especially when you first woke up."

"Oh, come on. I'm being silly. It's waking up in a new place, you know how that is. Plus, finding that Luke's out somewhere, and..."

"Lacy," Willow interrupted, "this is important."

"I'm sure it's nothing."

248

But when she was done talking, Willow rose to her feet. "Thaddeus," she said.

"Thaddeus what?"

"He was here. He and Luke…I should have realized. Oh, how could I have been so blind?"

"What are you talking about?" Lacy asked.

"I was wrong. Luke's mind isn't healing, and neither is Thaddeus's. The Soul Gaunts have them more firmly than I would have thought."

"Wait," Lacy said. "That's a pretty big jump isn't it?"

"Who else? What you're feeling is the aftereffects of a spell that made you sleep. The Hound too, that's the only reason she didn't stir when he came here. Hardly anyone knows you're here, and out of them, he's the only one other than me capable of doing such a thing. For whatever reason, he came here, and Luke left with him."

"Where?"

"You know where, Lacy. We have to go. It's not safe here."

"I can't leave! Luke won't know where to find me!"

"Exactly. For now, we have no choice but to consider him, and Thaddeus, dangerous. I'm sorry."

Lacy couldn't believe her ears. There was no way that Luke would work with those things, or that he would have left her…But then she remembered that night in the woods. The night that she was attacked. Luke had lured her out into the woods, taken her to the thing. And then had left her by the side of the road, where who knew if help would come.

"Oh, Luke," she breathed. Instead of being angry, she found herself incredibly sad for him. In spite of everything, she knew that he loved her. If he was doing this, then it was against his will, or he was being coerced somehow, or something. There was some rational explanation.

"Come," Willow was saying. "We need to go. I'll take you back to Towering Oaks. It's not as nice, or comfortable, but there's nowhere that's safer."

Lacy nodded and calling Daisy to her, followed the Healer out the door, into the bright daylight.

The path to Towering Oaks wound through the forest, passing huge trees with barks of gray, brown and silver. Ferns grew in abundance, and birds flitted through the branches overhead. As beautiful and peaceful as it was, Lacy had no time for it. She hurried along, trying to keep pace with the long-legged woman who led her, Daisy always walking by her side.

"How much farther is it?" she panted. When she had come this way yesterday with Florian, she had been distracted by the Greenweald itself and the things he told her. It had made the trip seem short, but really, she had no idea how long it had taken.

"A good distance yet," Willow said, "but we can rest if you need...wait...what was that?"

Lacy stopped and cocked her head, listening for whatever noise the healer had heard.

"I don't hear anything..." she started to say, but then a hissing noise came from the woods on her right side. Her head snapped around, in time to see a black shape hide behind a tree.

"What was that?" she said, trying to keep her voice steady.

"I'm not sure," Willow replied. "Let's keep moving."

But before they could go, another noise, this time the cold chuckle that Lacy had heard before sounded. And not only from the side, but from all around. She spun and saw them. Approaching through the trees, out in the broad daylight, were Soul Gaunts. At least six of them, coming from every direction.

Daisy let out a bark, and tried to surge forward, but Willow grabbed her. She bent down and whispered to the dog. Daisy glanced back at the two of them and then took off, running between the trees in a flash and disappearing. The Soul Gaunts ignored her.

"How?" she said, her voice quavering. "How are they here? It's daylight! They can't be here!"

"Apparently, they can," Willow said.

The Soul Gaunts surrounded them, but made no move to touch them. Even from here, Lacy could feel the cold that emanated from them. It sank into her bones and made her feel even more helpless.

One of them stretched out an arm and pointed back down the path the way they had come. Glancing back, Lacy saw the ones behind them part, so that they could pass between them. She didn't want to, but the one in front of them moved closer. Anything was better than being touched by it, so she went, Willow walking proudly by her side.

She admired the Healer. While Lacy felt like she was about to fall apart from the terror of what was happening, Willow walked like a queen.

"Stay strong, Lacy," she muttered, and took Lacy's hand.

Immediately, a warmth spread through her. One that helped to counter the mind-numbing cold from the Soul Gaunts. It didn't remove it, but it did let her think more clearly, and find that anger that always welled up in her when she was scared.

"Where are you taking us?" she demanded.

There was no answer from the Soul Gaunts, other than another point, and another chuckle.

"That's really getting on my nerves," she muttered, and Willow squeezed her hand.

The Soul Gaunts moved them along the path, making them turn off and pass the way to Whispering Pines.

"Ah," Willow said quietly. "I should have guessed."

"What?" Lacy said. "Should have guessed what?"

"Where they are taking us. We are going to Rustling Elms."

"Isn't that where…"

"Yes," Willow said. "They're taking us to their master."

CHAPTER 47

A soft mist rose from the surface of the water, coiling above it in the warm, night air. Solomon stood on the bank, his mind going back to the last time he was there. It was right where he was standing that he had dragged himself from the water. He dove from there, and from over there also, looking for a hidden passage or an underwater tunnel that led deeper, but had found nothing. It was nothing more than a simple forest pool, formed from a stream that tumbled down the rocks, eroding the bottom and giving the water a place to gather before it overflowed the far side and continued its journey.

It was a beautiful place, really, with moss on the rocks, and ferns growing from the sides. The water was clear during the day, allowing one to see all the way down to the sandy bottom. Easy to see any threats, or so you would think.

He shook himself out of his memories, stripped down to his underclothes and dove into the pool. Going all the way to the bottom he looked around, but couldn't see much in the darkness. His hands dug into the sand and he swam along, repeating what he had done the last time, only calmer, more methodically now.

Still he found nothing. He took his time and covered the whole pool, but there was no sign of a hidden cave, no sudden abyss below him and nothing grabbed at him, pulling him under. He surfaced, and with a sigh, pulled himself up onto a stone to think.

When he was here with Celia it had been daylight. They had taken a swim to find relief from a hot, summer afternoon. Perhaps whatever it was only came out during the day, an opposite of the Soul Gaunts, although just as evil. As much as the thought of wasting the time galled him, he didn't see any other option. If this didn't work he didn't know what would possibly jar loose his memories.

He redressed and was pulling on his boots when he shivered. His clothes were damp now from being put on over his wet body, and he thought that was the cause. But then he noticed that his breath was starting to steam slightly, and realized that the air temperature itself was dropping. He stood up quickly and stared around.

There. Was that a shadow, moving slowly against the darker backdrop of the forest? And it was silent, like in the woods around Lacy's house. Not a bird call or insect whir disturbed the night. They were here.

He was moving when the first strike came. The bone white claw shot out of the darkness, but Solomon avoided it, slipping beneath it, and spinning to avoid the next one. He reached out and grabbed the things cloak, continuing his movement and throwing it away from him. His momentum and strength launched the Soul Gaunt out over the water.

There was a hiss that turned into a screech as the water in the pool started to boil up. A few splatters got on the Soul Gaunt's cloak and it started to smoke where it touched. The Soul Gaunt screeched again and tried to flow back to the land, but it was as if it was being held there. More water soaked the bottom of the cloak and the thing began to sink closer to the surface. The closer it got, the more water touched it, and the faster it sank. Soon, it was in the water, and its screeches had turned to a high-pitched wail. Moments later, it was completely submerged, the water stilled and there was no sign of the Soul Gaunt.

But it was still frigidly cold and the sense of menace hung in the air. Solomon looked around and saw them approaching. More than he could fight.

He turned and leapt into the water, bracing himself for whatever would come. But the water remained calm and did nothing other than soak him through. It was much harder to tread water with his boots and sword-belt, so he kicked off his footwear and was unbuckling his belt when he thought better of it. He would hold onto the sword for now, until daylight came and the Soul Gaunts were driven away. It might make it more difficult through the night, but he would deal with that.

The Soul Gaunts surrounded the pool, but wouldn't come near the water. Instead, they hovered back away from the edge, hissing and spitting.

"Come out," they called to him, their voices dry and cold. "Come out, or we'll freeze the water around you."

Solomon laughed. "Go ahead," he said. "If you could have, you would have done it already." He splashed at the nearest one. The water hit its cloak, but had no effect on it. "Guess they actually have to come into it," he thought. "Too bad."

He ignored the taunting of the things and tried to concentrate on his situation. If he could outlast them, he'd have to find another way to remember where his sword was, or come up with a plan that didn't depend on it. There were other things in the Greenweald that were deadly to them; this pool was proof enough of that. Unfortunately, he didn't think there was going to be much time to do research...

There was a cold squeeze of his ankle and he was yanked beneath the water, not even having time to draw a breath. He kicked, hard, and was able to free himself and get to the surface, where he sucked in a huge lungful of air before he was grabbed again. This time, he let it drag him under.

Looking down, he saw a hand, blue and slim, firmly grasping his leg. A slender arm led to a beautiful face, large eyes staring back at him. Solomon flipped, forcefully bringing his legs up, while his arms went down. He reached out blindly and caught the thing on each side of its torso. He could feel a fragile rib cage between his hands, and he pulled it to him.

The thing fought, twisting and squirming in his grasp, but he hugged it to him, ignoring its flailings. He kicked for the surface and dragged the thing up and into the air. As soon as he broke water, the thing started gasping, its eyes growing larger. It stopped fighting and its hands went to its neck, trying to dribble water into the gill slits located there.

Around the edge of the pool, the Soul Gaunts had gone silent, but they were still there, watching. Solomon took a risk, and dragged the rapidly fading creature to the shallower end, so that he could get his feet under him. The Soul Gaunts nearest slid away, not leaving the area, but far enough back to be out of range of any water thrown from the creature.

He held on to the thing, and its trashing and gasping slowed, and then finally stopped. He kept it raised out of the water for another moment to make sure, and then lowered it back in, submerging it, but holding it firmly by the arms.

At first, the creature simply floated in his grasp, but then the eyes popped open, and it began to thrash around once more.

"Enough," Solomon said loudly. "If you don't stop I'll pull you out again."

The thing glared at him, and tried once more to pull away, but Solomon acted as if he would yank it up into the air again and it went quiet.

"Better," he said. "Do you understand what I'm saying?"

The thing nodded its head.

"Good. Is there some way that you can talk to me?"

Again, it nodded, and gently tugged one arm in Solomon's grip.

"Alright, I'll let one arm go. But know that I can yank you out of there with the other one. So don't try anything."

The thing nodded for a third time. Solomon let its arm go. It pointed at him, then at the water and beckoned him to come under.

"Do you think I'm crazy?" he said. "Why would I do that? So you can drown me like you did her?"

The thing got a confused expression on its face and then motioned for him again.

"What the hell," Solomon said with a sigh. He moved deeper into the water, still holding the thing and ducked under.

It came closer to him and moved its free arm around in a circle over both their heads. The pressure of the water became less, and he drew a hesitant breath, and found that he was able to.

"There," it said, "now we can talk." Its voice was light and almost musical, and clearly feminine. As she spoke, she looked at Solomon out of huge eyes that were the same green-blue as the water of her pool.

"Why did you do it?" Solomon asked. His voice echoed back to him, as if he were speaking into a hollow tube, but he had no problem talking underwater.

"You were not invited to swim in my pool," the thing answered, as if that were all the reason she needed.

"Why didn't you just say so? You kicked me out. Why did you have to kill her?" Solomon wasn't sure if he was crying or not.

He had thought that when he caught the thing that had killed Celia, he would have been furious and destroyed it without a second thought. But now that he was here, he was just sad, and tired. He was tired of killing and of fighting. Yes, he was good at it, but he didn't want to do it anymore. Not even now. He wanted answers.

"I kicked you out because…" the water spirit started to say, but then dropped her eyes from his face.

"Why? Why not take us both?"

"Because you were too beautiful. Even now, your light shines in my pool like a beacon. It drew me to you then, as it does now."

"That's ridiculous. And it doesn't tell me why you killed Celia! You didn't have to."

To his disgust, the water creature laughed and then, "And who says that I killed her?"

Solomon opened his mouth to reply, but no sound came out. There was a sudden ache in his stomach, like he had been kicked. Even in this underwater bubble that the spirit had put them in, there was no air, and he couldn't draw in a breath.

He struggled, his mouth opening and closing and finally managed to croak out, "No...that's...it's not possible. You took her and drowned her..."

"No, that is what you thought. I took her yes, but I merely put her somewhere else. Somewhere far from you."

Solomon roared, seeing everything around him through a haze of red. He pulled the creature to him and wrapped his other hand around her throat, squeezing. The water spirits eyes bugged out even more and she thrashed in his grasp. She tried to raise her hand, to circle it around them and end the spell that was allowing him to breath, but he shook her violently, and she dropped it.

He pushed off from the bottom and dragged the spirit into the shallows again, standing and pulling her out of the water. She went limp and stared at him in terror. Solomon didn't care. This thing, this vile, nasty creature had made him think...

He stopped, realizing what he was about to do in his fury. If he killed her, he would never know where Celia was, or how to get to her. He plunged her under the water again, and waded deeper.

Ducking under, he allowed her to recast her spell.

"Where is she?" he said, fighting to maintain his calm.

"In another realm. I can take you there, but it's far."

"How far?"

"For me, a mere moment. I can cross as I would, wherever the water takes me. But for you, it will be days to get there, days to find her and days to come back."

"But you can change that, can't you?" He squeezed her arm a little, emphasizing the implied threat if she didn't.

She stared at him and then dropped her eyes again. "No, Solomon. I cannot. It is not my doing, but the nature of the magic. I am sorry. I am sorry for all of it. I didn't know now much you loved her and only thought..."

Again, she stopped. Solomon found that he didn't care what she had thought. Celia was alive and he needed to find her, even if it took days. He would let Jediah know...but he couldn't. He couldn't leave for days right now. His friends needed him and were counting on him. He looked up through the water to see that the sky was still dark. It was still nighttime and he was sure that the Soul Gaunts were still there, waiting for him to leave the safety of the pool.

Fine, he would go recover Justice, end the threat to the Greenweald and get back here. If he needed to use Justice to boil this whole pool away to force the water spirit to take him to Celia, he would do it. First thing though was to get past the Guardian and...

He remembered! He remembered where his sword was, who he had left it with and why. He had had a very good reason for letting it go, but that didn't matter now. What mattered was that the Greenweald was in danger, and he had the means to protect it.

First his duty, then he would tell Florian that his daughter was alive and then he would go recover her. After that, he would tell Jediah that he was done with all things warlike and beg Florian to allow him to marry Celia, and settle down to raise a family together. He thought that now, there was a good chance that her father would agree.

But first, he needed to get out of here.

"The cave of the Guardian," he said to the spirit, "do you know it?"

"I do," she replied. "But I avoid the area. It is his realm, not mine."

"I don't care about that. Can you get me there?"

"Why? The Guardian will surely destroy you."

"That's my problem. Yours is getting me there. Can you or not?"

The spirit grimaced. "I can. If I must."

"You must," Solomon said. "And then I'm going to come back here, when all this is over. And you're going to take me to Celia."

"You are wasted on her, when you could be so much more."

"Enough. Do we have a deal, or should I pull you out of the water and throw you to the Soul Gaunts?"

The spirit regarded him for a moment. "I believe you would, too. Fine then. I swear."

"You swear what?" Solomon said. "I'm not so foolish as to let you off with being vague."

"I swear to deliver you safely to the water nearest the cave of the Guardian. I swear that when you return and call for me, I will come and safely lead you to the realm where Celia now is. More than that, I cannot do."

"That will be enough," Solomon let her arm go. "Now, take me there."

CHAPTER 48

He thought of Cassandra, and the pain was eased. It wasn't gone, but it didn't seem to matter as much. Soon, he'd be with her again, and with Celia, and none of this would matter.

The claw came out of the darkness and cut into him again, the hissing chuckle following. Florian drew his breath in sharply, the line of cold fire that erupted across his stomach taking him out of his memories for a moment, but then he focused on her face, and the agony sank into the background again.

She was so beautiful, so gracious and kind, warm and loving. It amazed Florian that she had fallen for him, when they were both so young, before he was the Head of House. Two young lovers, walking through the Greenweald, admiring the trees, exchanging kisses and sighs as they gazed at each other.

He smiled through bloody lips as he recalled the looks that they got. Some with the type of amusement that comes with age, watching back through time and remembering their own moon-struck moments. Others with open disdain, disgusted by the displays of public affection. For someone who would become such a model of decorum and poise, he certainly didn't care about those looks then.

His quiet laugh became a cry, as a bony finger found its way into the slash on his stomach, spearing deeper, cutting through the layers beneath and opening him further.

"This can all stop, you know," the voice of the Advocate came out of the darkness. "There would be nothing easier. All you need do is say the things I've told you. Your friend already has."

At that, Florian truly laughed, despite the pain from his many wounds.

"Now I know you're a liar. As if I needed any more proof of that. If I haven't agreed to your ludicrous demands, I know he hasn't."

"You are wrong, Lord Florian. You have no idea the amount of pain that we can cause. But you're right, of course. Jediah is much more resilient than you are. We simply doubled our efforts with him. Shall we do the same with you?"

Florian didn't answer. He knew it didn't matter. All of this was an excuse. They didn't need him to go back to Whispering Pines and tell his people to stand down, to bow to their new masters. They would take what they wanted anyway. The Advocate wanted to hear him break.

It wouldn't happen. Not while she was watching him. Cassandra had been watching over him since she died, the illness taking her so quickly that even the Healers didn't know what it was. One moment, she was full of life and lighting up their tree like the sun itself had come inside, and the next, she was on the floor, shaking and crying. By the end of the day she was gone, and all Florian had been able to do was hold on to Celia, and promise that he would always be there for her.

But Cassandra hadn't gone far, not really. He could feel her, watching as he raised their daughter. As time had passed, she had retreated a bit further, to give them time to be alive and whole themselves, but she was always there. Florian had never forgotten that.

Now, she was closer than she had been at any time since he had last held her in his arms. She was there…right there with him. And every time they hurt him, she planted a soft, warm kiss on the corner of his damaged mouth, and eased the dread and warmed the air a little.

"Don't be a fool, Florian," the Advocate said, dropping any pretense of calling him "Lord". "We can make you scream and scream."

He ignored that as well, but not because he didn't believe them. On the contrary he knew very well that they could, and had. He had cried out when they first took him, and yelled defiance when they tore Jediah and him apart, taking them each their own way in the darkness. And then he had truly screamed when they had strapped him to this table and gone to work on him.

But then she was there. Whispering to him and telling him that it was going to be okay. A little longer and she'd be with him again. Strange that she hadn't said anything about Celia. He was anxious to see her again, too.

This time, they did drag a scream from him when they pulled him from his memories. The agony from his hand was too great to ignore. He couldn't lift his head to see what they had done, but the cold laughter around him told him that whatever it was, it was something the Soul Gaunts had enjoyed. It wasn't stopping either. It felt like his hand was on fire, or the skin was being peeled from it, or…

No, one of them flowed up next to him, and in the pale light that came from somewhere in the room, showed him something red and wet, before it opened its mouth and ate it.

"Hope you choke on it…" Florian muttered. And then, mercifully, he passed out.

It could have been hours, or only seconds, before the new pain shocked him awake. It came from his groin. The Advocate hadn't been exaggerating, they were very inventive in causing pain. He felt no shame in screaming this time either.

"Shhh, beloved. All will be well. It will be over soon. Stay with me, my love, and soon, we will have all time to be together as one."

Even through his tears, Florian smiled, and wished he could reach out for her.

"Cousin," a new voice said, "why do you resist? Give them what they want. Please!"

"Thaddeus?" Florian's voice came out in a croak. How long had it been since he had had water?

"Yes, Florian, it's me. Give them what they want."

"Poor Thaddeus. I want you to know…I don't blame you. You had to save yourself. It's in your nature."

"It's in all of our natures," his cousin said, coming closer. "What else is there if not your own life?"

"My life is my House. That's what it means, you know."

"Don't insult me with clichés."

"Heh. That's why I was Head of House. It's not a cliché when it's the truth." He turned his head, one of the only movements allowed him, so that he couldn't see Thaddeus any longer.

"Cousin, please," he heard Thaddeus say, "I would save you if I could."

Florian ignored him, and waited for Cassandra to come again, to appear in the dark like a small piece of heaven, sent here only for him. After a moment, he was vaguely aware of his cousin moving away.

"Fool," the Advocate's voice said, but somehow, it didn't sound displeased.

The end, when it finally came, was anticlimactic. They hurt him more. They made him scream, and cry. But they could never drive Cassandra away, and finally, when they went too far, he smiled, sat up free of his bonds, and went to her.

CHAPTER 49

They were both exhausted by the time they stumbled back to the Towering Oaks compound. Shireen had sent the Whispering Pines soldier back to his own House, to tell his superiors of what had happened, and to rally them to Towering Oaks.

Orlando was moving weakly, the wound in his arm bothering him and Shireen was walking gingerly herself. The Soul Gaunts' attacks left gashes that didn't want to heal and continued to seep blood. Shireen had bandaged Orlando's arm the best she could as they moved, but now, the scrap of cloth she had taken from the uniform of the dead Whispering Pines soldier was soaked through with blood.

At the gate to the compound, she collapsed against the nearest tree and waved to the sentry. It was hard to even lift her arm, and was getting even harder to think. Looking down, she saw that her leg was covered in blood. Who knew how much she had lost on her way here? But at least Willow and the other Healers would still be here, and now they were safe. They could be worked on while she told Lawrence what had happened.

Orlando was slumped at her feet, his back against the tree trunk and his face ashen.

"Hey," Shireen said. "Are you alright?"

Orlando didn't respond. His eyes were closed and his breathing was shallow. As she watched, his breath hitched in his throat and he gasped.

"Hey! Orlando!" She squatted down at his side, ignoring the flare of pain from her leg. "Come on! We made it."

There was still no response, and Shireen felt ice form in her veins. He really didn't look good at all, and the thought of losing Orlando, even as it flickered through her mind and was forcefully rejected, was scarier than anything the Soul Gaunts could generate.

She stood and looked wildly around. To her relief, several soldiers were running toward them. Within moments they were there and had lifted Orlando gently, bearing him away toward the scouts' barracks. Two of the them stayed with her, and despite her well-known pride, insisted that she lean on them as they followed more slowly.

She felt a little of the fear flow out of her as she saw two Healers running to the barracks. Neither of them was Willow, which was a little disappointing, but any Healers who travelled with her were well-versed in all manner of wound care. Orlando was in good hands. She actually smiled as she felt her leg give way and barely remembered the other soldiers lifting her.

When she opened her eyes, it was to find her commander, Lawrence, standing nearby. She was lying face down on a table, a pillow under her cheek.

"How long was I…?"

"Not long," Lawrence replied. "I asked the Healers to bring you around as quickly as they could. I'm sorry for that, since they should be looking at your leg, but I need to know what happened."

"You did the right thing." She winced as a Healer began cutting the leg of her pants. "I can deal with the leg, but you need to get everyone assembled, the whole House. Whispering Pines should be coming too."

"First I need to know what happened. Where is Jediah?"

Shireen realized that Lawrence didn't know about the Soul Gaunts. In order to avoid any unnecessary panic, Jediah and Florian had kept the news of the invasion to very few people. But the time for secrecy was gone.

"It's a long story, but I can tell you the gist of it now. When we have more time, I'll fill you in on everything."

"I don't like being kept in the dark by one of my subordinates, Shireen." Lawrence's voice was dangerously low.

"Blame Jediah," she answered. "He made the decision on who should be told. There's two things you need to know right now, though. First is that Jediah is gone. I can't imagine that he's still alive." She stopped, drew in a breath and tried to keep her calm. "It's Soul Gaunts. More than you can believe. They took over Rustling Elms, killed everyone, and took both Jediah and Florian."

She paused, not to give Lawrence a chance to question her, but to gather her thoughts. Her commander seemed to sense this and stood by, brows furrowed as he waited for her to continue.

"The Soul Gaunts are with a man, he looks like one of us, but I don't know who he is. He cast a spell that made the sky darken, and they came out…Orlando and I, and two from Whispering Pines, fought as hard as we could. I don't think they wanted us dead though. I think they wanted us to get away, to tell everyone…" She stopped, the words choking her.

Lawrence's eyes went to the Healer who was still working on her leg. "How is it?"

"Bad," a voice from behind her said. "There is some foulness at work here. The wound doesn't want to close, but I'm getting it. Don't worry."

"What about Orlando?" Shireen asked, avoiding Lawrence's eyes in case it was the worst news.

"They're working on him. He's stable, but in bad shape. Tell me the rest. Why was Jediah with Florian?"

"That's not important right now. We need to gather all our forces and go back to Rustling Elms. It will be horrible, but the two Houses together can…"

"Can get killed," Lawrence interrupted. "That's why Jediah and Florian went there as they did, right? Because they knew that even the combined forces of the two Houses wouldn't be enough. But why didn't they go to Jamshir?"

"They did. He denied them any help, told Jediah that it was his role to protect the Greenweald."

"I still don't understand how Jediah and Florian are together. Why did Florian allow…"

"Because by bringing Solomon back we have a chance. He's gone to get Justice."

Lawrence was quiet, his face thoughtful. "So the whole exile was for nothing."

"Maybe not. Solomon did good on that earth. He killed a Soul Gaunt there. But now he's needed here. Florian agreed to it, but Jamshir didn't. So, they did it on their own, Jediah sent me and Orlando after him. Now, he's off somewhere, looking for his sword. That's the other reason they went to Rustling Elms like they did. They were trying to buy time."

Lawrence stepped away, turning his back to Shireen. She could see the tension in his shoulders. Finally, he sighed and turned back to her.

"There is much that I obviously don't know. You will fill me in on all of it, omitting nothing. If Jediah is truly gone, then his orders no longer matter and we must do what's best for our House. At the moment, I will assume command, until a new Head can be chosen. From this moment on, I am to be filled in on everything. Clear?"

"Clear," Shireen said.

"Good. Now, rest while the Healers work on you. You can see Orlando when they say. Then, find me. We have work to do."

He stalked away, leaving Shireen to lay her head down again and try to ignore the throbbing pain in her leg.

The Healer was working on her for more than two hours. Well past the time that it should have taken. "It's a strange wound," he said. "How did you get it?"

"Weren't you listening?" she responded.

The man laughed softly. "People always think that. But when we're working on a wound, or trying to cure a sickness, we're concentrating on that. I know you and Lawrence were talking, but that's all I know."

"It was a Soul Gaunt," Shireen said, keeping her voice as neutral as she could, trying to keep her impatience under control.

"Oh." The Healer's voice sank to a whisper. "Oh, dear. Willow must be told. We have to prepare."

"Where is Willow anyway?"

"No idea. This morning, she went to check on those humans who came home with you. We haven't seen her since."

A cold dread, almost as if a Soul Gaunt itself was in the room with them, settled over Shireen. "Are you almost done?"

"Just about." The Healer hummed to himself as he continued to tend to the wound, then, "There. That's about the best I can do. You have to be careful on it, though. It's a bad wound, and could reopen."

Shireen rolled over and gingerly climbed off the table. Her leg was stiff, and was sore when she tried to walk, but she could manage. "Where's Orlando?" she asked.

The Healer, an elderly man of the Folk, she could now see, indicated the next room. "He's in there...but..."

"But nothing. I'm going to see him." Without another word she hobbled toward the doorway. Her leg was definitely stiff, but she gritted her teeth and kept moving.

Inside the other room, Orlando lay on a table, face up. One Healer was standing near his head, hands placed on each side of his temples. Another stood at his side, massaging his chest, her voice muttering a soft chant. Yet a third tended to his arm, that one bent over, sweat dripping from his brow as he concentrated, a pile of bloody rags at his feet.

Shireen stood and stared for a moment, feeling her chest tighten. She knew his injury was worse than her own, but she had had no idea that it was that bad. And as always, he hadn't complained as they returned to the compound.

"Is he going to be okay?" Her voice came out thin and watery. None of the Healers paid any attention to her, and she found herself grateful for that. It was far better that they concentrate on Orlando, and besides, she was terrified of what the answer could be.

As she stood watching, the horns sounded from the guards, playing the distinctive series of notes that meant an army was approaching. It was a signal that hadn't been heard in the Greenweald in many a year, but that every soldier of Towering Oaks was trained to recognize. Whispering Pines had obviously come. She was surprised that they had mobilized so quickly.

With one last look at Orlando, she hobbled away, toward the gate where she could be with Lawrence as they greeted their allies.

It took longer than it should have for her to get there. When she did, she found not only Lawrence, but several other Towering Oaks soldiers, all standing in readiness, hands close to sword hilts or bows.

"What's going on?" she muttered to herself, making her way forward. If it was Whispering Pines, then why the tension? She had told Lawrence to expect them. If it wasn't them, who else? The Soul Gaunts would have simply attacked.

She moved as fast as she could, and climbed onto the viewing platform that Lawrence stood on.

There, filling the woods before the Towering Oaks compound, stretching back as far as she could see, stood rank upon rank of soldiers. All wearing the silver colors of House Glittering Birch. Jamshir himself sat astride a magnificent horse, and the Whispering Pines soldier that Shireen had sent off lay bound and unconscious on the ground in front of it.

"House Towering Oaks!" Jamshir called out. "Lay down your arms. Send out Jediah. He has been found guilty of treason and sedition, and his House is forfeit."

CHAPTER 50

It was like being in the cave all over again. The constant dark and the ever-present fear, both the natural kind from being in peril, and the dread that emanated from the Soul Gaunts. There, there had been only one, and the fear and threat of harm had been enough to keep Luke in line, make him obey whatever the thing had asked of him.

Now, he was surrounded. Soul Gaunts haunted the whole tree, and ever since coming back in with their prizes, they had taken to entering the room that Thaddeus and he had claimed. They didn't harm him, but they seemed to take great glee in flowing up to him, out of the darkness and pressing near, their black cloaks around him, sometimes touching him. Although they never used their claws, they laughed every time he flinched away. No matter how much it happened, he never got used to it.

Finally, they came to the room and forced him away from Thaddeus, flowing between the two and hissing at him.

"Out," one said, pointing at the door, through which there was nothing but inky black.

"Thaddeus," he said, trying to peer around the thing in front of him, "can you give me the stone?"

Before the mage could answer, the Soul Gaunt in front of Luke reached out and raked its claws across the front of his chest. The searing cold bit into him, and he screamed and reeled back. Blood seeped into his shirt from the shallow cuts it had left.

"Out," it repeated, and Luke fled from the room.

In the hall others came. They surrounded him and pushed him down the hall, their cold claws clutching at him whenever he would stumble, their voices hissing and chuckling. He didn't know where they were taking him, but tried to run straight, banging into furniture that sometimes decayed when he hit it, and sometimes stayed solid but covered in slimy fungi. He ran into walls, causing the Soul Gaunts to laugh all the more, but when he fell, they reached down, sharp nails biting into him and pulled him to his feet.

He ran for what felt like hours, sure that he was going mad. No matter how long he was here, his eyes couldn't seem to adjust to the dark. They should have, but he was sure it was some effect of the nightmare creatures around him. So he ran, stumbling and gasping for breath, doing his best not to fall to the ground, not to be touched by them any more than he had to be.

Finally, they herded him into a room. One of them grabbed the back of his head, sending waves of pain though him and bright sparks of light dancing in his vision. He dropped to his knees with a cry and it let go, allowing him to collapse forward.

"Oh, come now," the smooth, deep voice of the Advocate said. "Don't be so melodramatic."

Luke didn't, and wasn't sure that he could, say anything. He simply stayed on the ground, hunched over, not looking at the tall man.

"Nothing to say," the Advocate mused. "Typical for your kind. I've found much the same thing when I've visited your earth. Oh, you all talk a lot, endlessly running on, but with no real substance."

Luke looked up in surprise. There was the soft light in the room that often accompanied visits from the Advocate. He was there, seated in apparent comfort, in a chair that showed no sign of rot or decay. The Soul Gaunts had all left the room, although the feeling of dread was still near.

"What? You didn't think we went to your world? Think again. We have been many places, and seen many things."

"We?" Luke managed to croak out.

"Yes," the Advocate smiled. "But that's not for one such as you to know. I only called you here to thank you for your service, and to let you know that it has come to an end."

"Then you'll kill me now?" Luke was relieved. At last it would all be over. The pain, the fear, and the shame would all soon be gone. Not just from the time when he was taken to now, but from before, when he let the voices overcome him and had caused such misery in Lacy's life. The end was fine with him.

"Not as such, no," the Advocate answered, smiling again when he saw the disappointment that Luke knew he hadn't been able to hide. "Nothing that easy. You see, I promised my friends that they could have you, in return for the life of one of their own on your wretched earth."

269

While the thought of death didn't scare him, the thought of being turned over to the Soul Gaunts to play with did. He tried to think, to come up with something that would keep him from that fate, prove that he was still valuable.

"Thaddeus mentioned that you were going to go to earth after you were done here. You'll need someone. Someone to pave the way and help you. I can do that." He hated hearing himself whine and plead, but anything, no matter how shameful, was better than being cast to those creatures.

"And why would I need that?"

"To do the things there that Thaddeus will do for you here. Anything. Tell me what you need, and I'll help."

The Advocate laughed, a sound of pure delight. "Oh, you humans. You really are something. Thaddeus has abilities that we may find useful. That is why we allow him to live and to continue to serve us. You, on the other hand, have nothing we need anymore. You've shown us how easy it is to bend you, to break you. We don't expect any more resistance on your earth than what we've seen from you."

"That's where you're wrong." Luke felt his temper unexpectedly flare up. Ever since he had come to this horrible place, and even before, he had been treated as less than, as something to be pushed around and used. And maybe he was, fine. He was never the bravest or most daring of people, but there were others. "You're wrong," he said again. "There are others much stronger than me. And with weapons. You have no idea."

"On the contrary, we have every idea. Perhaps a demonstration would be in order. To give you something to think about while my friends amuse themselves with you."

He motioned to the door, and the light grew slightly brighter. Luke watched in horror as two Soul Gaunts floated into the room, and parted to reveal Lacy.

No! What was she doing here? He had left her at the Whispering Pines compound, safe! Why was she here?

The Soul Gaunts herded her further into the room, until she finally saw him there, crouched on the floor. He was suddenly even more ashamed than he had been, hating that she would see him like this. With an effort, never taking his eyes from her, he rose to his feet.

"Luke?" Lacy cried. "What are you…" She made to move to him as she spoke, but a Soul Gaunt moved between them, it's claws raised in a warning. Lacy stopped and looked around it. "What…" she began.

"Enough," the Advocate interrupted in a bored tone. "I really don't need to see the histrionics. I've had her brought here simply as an object lesson. For both of you. Now, crawl to me. Kiss my feet."

He leaned back in his chair and extended a black boot from under the long, black robes that he wore. Luke looked at it, then looked back at Lacy, watching him.

Enough was enough. They were going to hurt him anyway, and eventually kill him. They were going to go to earth, and start killing and destroying there as well. They'd have a fight, and maybe they'd even be defeated eventually, but they would do horrible things in the meantime. But for Luke, he had had enough.

"No," he said quietly. "I'm done. Take me where you want, do what you want. Lacy is tough, she can bear watching it happen if that's what you're thinking."

"Luke, no!" Lacy cried, but he ignored her and turned to the Advocate.

"I'm through," he said.

"Is that so?" The Advocate seemed greatly amused. "I must say, you are showing a remarkable amount of backbone. I like it, and didn't see it coming. Well done, sir." He pulled his foot back under his robe and sat forward in his chair. "However, you misunderstand."

Luke saw the man's eyes flicker to the Soul Gaunts and heard Lacy's scream. He spun around to see one grabbing her wrist, it's claws sinking into her arm and pulling her toward it. Its other claw came up, one bony, sharp finger extended and inching toward her eye.

"What do you say?" the Advocate asked him. "Should we make the two of you a matched pair, or…?" He slid his foot forward again.

This time, there was no hesitation. Luke dropped to the ground, and started forward on his hands and knees. "Lower," the Advocate purred. He dropped to his belly and wormed along, until he reached the Advocate. Without stopping, he pressed his lips to the man's boot.

The Advocate laughed, then kicked Luke, smashing his lips against his teeth. He rolled, clutching at his bloody mouth, but looking back. The Soul Gaunt had let Lacy go. The Advocate laughed softly, motioned, and she was herded from the room.

She was safe, for the moment anyway, and that was all that mattered. The rest, Solomon, the Greenweald, earth itself, could all burn. They had all done this anyway.

"Enjoy yourself," the Advocate sneered, and walked from the room, leaving Luke in the dark once again.

CHAPTER 51

Lacy was forced back to the room that she and Willow had been held in when they were first brought to the tree. It was a small chamber, at one time a sitting room of some sort, perhaps. All the furniture, the sturdy chairs, the delicate side tables and even the carpets were decaying badly, and the place stank like a dead raccoon that had been laying on the roadside during the hot summer.

At first, they were left there alone, in the near-dark. The Soul Gaunts had hurried them along the forest paths, and almost seemed relieved when they were able to reenter the darkness of the Rustling Elms tree. She remembered what the one on her earth had said; the light hurt them, but it didn't kill them. But something must have driven them out to come after Willow, because she couldn't imagine why they wanted her. She was no threat to them, she was just in the wrong place at the wrong time.

There was a dim light in the room that came from a small stone, set in a dish on one of the tables. Lacy remembered Shireen's story about being here and Thaddeus's stone, and thought that the two must be similar. It was a small kindness that she had never expected to find.

The Soul Gaunts who had driven them here flowed away when they entered the tree, but others quickly took their place. At first, they surrounded them, making that horrible, annoying sound. But Willow stood tall and faced them down with no sign of fear. After a moment, the chuckling stopped and changed to hisses and spits. They motioned for them to move deeper into the tree, ordering it in their cold voices, but they didn't approach too closely.

For some reason, they seemed to be afraid of Willow. More so even than the one on earth had been afraid of Solomon. They threatened, and rushed forward, but always veered away before they came within her reach.

Willow had put it to the test at first, refusing to move and even taking a step back toward the doors, but they had cut her off and refused to move.

As she approached, they stood firm, and although they didn't actually touch her, they raised their claws and hissed.

"Even if they won't touch me, for whatever reason," she had muttered to Lacy, "I'm afraid of what they'll do to you."

So they had moved on, the Soul Gaunts taking them deeper and deeper into the tree until they had come to the room they were now in. Then, and only then, they were left alone and the Soul Gaunts disappeared.

They stayed there for hours, jumping when they suddenly heard screams coming from elsewhere in the tree. For Lacy, it was hard to stay put, and not to run to see if she could help, but she knew that it was agony to do so for the Healer. The screams lasted for a long time, but were finally cut short. Lacy hoped that whoever it was, they were at peace now.

It was shortly after that when they came for her.

Two Soul Gaunts entered the room, pointing at her. "You will come with us," one hissed.

"She will not!" Willow said, pulling Lacy closer to her.

"Your time will come, Healer," one of them spat, but Willow simply stared defiance at it.

Lacy couldn't take her eyes off the Soul Gaunts, so she almost missed the dark figure slipping into the room behind them. A moment later, he stepped forward and she recognized Thaddeus.

"Hey! Where's Luke?" Lacy felt the old familiar anger resurface when she saw him.

He glanced at her, then ignored her and approached Willow.

"Willow," he said, glancing side-long at the Soul Gaunts as he passed them. "Please, you must help me. It's Florian, he's been hurt and…"

But when he neared, he suddenly lashed out, connecting a solid blow to the Healer's chin. Willow went over like a felled sapling, Thaddeus standing over her, nursing his hand.

"What are you doing?" Lacy screamed.

The mage didn't look at her. "Go with them," he said quietly. "It's for the best."

Lacy wanted to run at him, pummel him into the ground and force him to tell her where Luke was. But when she took a step, the Soul Gaunts neared. They reached for her, and she shrank away.

"No!" Thaddeus said. "She's not to be touched. Go with them, Lacy."

She stopped, glared at him for a moment and then turned her back. "Traitor."

They had taken her to a room where she found Luke, and watched as he tried to be brave and defy the Advocate. But she knew that no matter what, if they hurt her, he would do whatever they asked. When the claws dug in and the cold seeped into her arm again, she couldn't help but scream, even though the wound itself wasn't bad. Her heart nearly broke as she watched Luke crawl without hesitation, knowing he was doing it for her. Then she had been taken away, leaving him there to be tortured and die, and there was nothing she could do about it.

Even if the tree had been fully lit, she wouldn't have been able to see from the tears in her eyes. The tears that caused a great deal of joy in the Soul Gaunts around her. They flowed next to her, whispering of the things they would do to Luke.

When she was forced back into their room, she sank to her knees, head in her hands and sobbed. Willow was still laying on the floor unconscious, and there was no sign of Thaddeus. She tried to stifle her sobs so that she could listen, trying in vain to hear if they had started on Luke yet. But so far, there was only silence. She wasn't sure if that was a good sign or a bad one.

After a few more minutes, Willow groaned and stirred. Pushing her own grief down inside of her, Lacy rose and ran to the woman, helping her to sit up.

"I'm sorry," Lacy said. "I should have helped you right away…what can I do?"

Willow shook her head gently, her eyes opening wide for a moment in the soft glow of the room. "There's nothing. I'm alright. Thaddeus must have put a small spell on me after he hit me. He isn't that tough."

Lacy felt giggles starting in her stomach. It was entirely inappropriate and there was nothing funny about anything, but Willow's statement had caught her by surprise. She snorted as she tried to contain them, earning her a confused glance from the Healer. Another followed, and then she couldn't contain them. They burst forth, until she was holding her stomach and rocking.

"Are you alright?" Willow asked, which only made her laugh harder.

After a few seconds, Willow's mouth twitched, and she giggled herself. Soon, the two of them were laughing together, holding on to one another.

Lacy wasn't sure when the laughter turned back into tears, but she was glad the Healer was there to hold onto. When they pulled apart, she saw the wet tracks running down Willow's cheeks that matched her own.

"I'm sorry," Lacy said again, "but it's so much. And it was such a weird thing to say about Thaddeus. And Luke is…"

"It's okay. We will survive this. But now, let me look at that arm."

"It's fine, really. They didn't hurt me very much."

"Not on the surface, maybe. But Soul Gaunt wounds can be deeper than they seem."

She bent over Lacy's arm, her fingers light on her skin. A warmth spread out, countering the chill that she now realized had been there since the Soul Gaunt had grabbed her. It helped ease the pain in her arm and in her heart, although it was still heavy with grief and fear about Luke.

"They're going to kill Luke," she whispered. "I don't know what to do."

"We'll fight," Willow murmured. "We're not done yet."

"What a nice sentiment," a deep voice said. They turned, and there in the doorway stood the Advocate. "And such laughter. It's been long since this place has heard any. Not since my friends got bored and broke their toys, anyway. But now they have a new one, and that will keep them occupied for a while."

"Why are you doing this?" Lacy said, reaching over to take Willow's hand. "We didn't do anything to you."

"No, you didn't. Not that it matters. But I have a reason for holding on to you. Both of you, really. And I'm sure that reason will come storming in here, doing his best to free you both. Although, I have taken steps to see that that won't happen. Still, I have to admit that he is resourceful, and if he does overcome what I've sent his way, why then, you'll be my little insurance policy, as I believe they say in your wretched world."

He smiled at them both and turned to leave the room.

"Wait!" Willow called. "Why kill Luke though? You don't have to. And who was that screaming before?"

The Advocate turned back. "Of course, I don't *have* to kill Luke. Being able to is simply a bonus, and one that will tie my friends even closer to me. As for the poor soul you heard before…well, let us say that Lord

276

Florian had much more to him than I would have thought. He lasted much longer than expected. But by the end, dear Healer, he was beyond even your skills."

Florian. If it was possible, Lacy's heart fell even further. He had been kind to them, seen that they were out of place and offered a part of his own home for their use. There was a certain grace and charm to him. And it was now gone. She bowed her head and felt Willow's hand tighten on hers. She squeezed back, wanting to rant and rail, but knowing it would only amuse the Advocate. Instead, she silently willed herself to stay calm.

"You'll pay for that," Willow said through clenched teeth.

The Advocate laughed out loud. "Oh, very good! I was so hoping someone would tell me that. Now I feel like a proper villain."

Still laughing, he strode from the room, and the light in the stone slowly dimmed to nothing.

CHAPTER 52

Solomon stepped from the waterfall and into the cave, shaking the water from his hair. Through the falling curtain he could see the forest, stretching away into the evening. He recognized both the view and the cave itself. The water spirit had done as she promised and delivered him to the cave of the Guardian.

Solomon turned back to the waterfall where she appeared, a wistful expression on her face. "I'll be back. When all this is over, I'll return to your pool. And you will take me to Celia, no matter how far or difficult the journey."

The spirit nodded and lifted her hand in a tentative farewell. Solomon grimaced but returned the gesture, and then turned away and walked deeper into the cave.

Now, the trick was to summon the Guardian, and then to convince him to let him pass. No easy feat, which is why he had left the sword here in the first place. It was easy enough to get him to appear if you were leaving something with him, but much more difficult if you came to take something away, even if it did belong to you. The Guardian was jealous of the things he had.

Might as well try the easy way first he thought. "Guardian! Come out and show yourself! It's Solomon, and I have need of something that I left in your care!"

There was no answer and no one appeared. He hadn't thought it would be that simple, so with a sigh, he headed deeper into the cave. It soon took a turn, plunging the passageway into total darkness. For most, that would be enough to cause them to pause, but Solomon knew that to be a mistake. Without hesitation he strode forward, into the darkness, keeping his hands to his sides so that he wouldn't be tempted to put them out in front of him to feel the way.

He took three, four, and then five steps, making sure each was measured and confident, showing no sign of being afraid of the dark or any unseen obstacles. After taking the fifth step, the walls began to glow a pleasant yellow color.

Step one, Solomon thought to himself. That was the easy part.

He continued on, coming to a chasm that crossed the floor of the cavern.

"This is new," Solomon said aloud, and inched to the edge to look over. The floor dropped away, sheer rock walls disappearing into the gloom with no sign of the bottom in sight. Still, it wasn't very wide and he could easily leap across. He took a few backwards steps, but as he started forward, flames shot up from the crack, reaching to the ceiling of the tunnel and blistering the air with their heat.

Solomon skidded to a halt, arm thrown up in front of his face.

"Hmmm." He studied the flames for a moment, then smiled and walked calmly forward.

The heat was intense and he could feel his skin turning red and smell his hair burning. The pain only increased as he moved forward, but he gritted his teeth in a rictus grin and kept going.

When he reached the edge of the chasm where the flames rose highest, he simply continued walking, taking a step that would carry him over the edge and into the heart of the fire. Instantly, the flames disappeared, and there was no sign of the abyss that had been there moments before.

"How did you know?" The voice came out of what seemed to be thin air.

Solomon took a breath, almost afraid to look at his skin. But when he did, he was perfectly whole and unburnt. The pain he had felt had vanished with the flames.

"I know you too well, Guardian," he said. "Plus, come on. A chasm *and* flames? Overdoing it a little, aren't you?"

"I was afraid of that," the voice said. "but I liked the visual of the whole thing."

"It was very dramatic, I'll give you that. Now, any more tests? Or are you going to come out and talk to me?"

"I'll come out, but you can't have it, you know."

"We'll see. Come on."

There was a grinding noise from in front of him, and a section of the tunnel wall slid back to reveal a well-lit chamber beyond. A huge figure blocked out the light as it came to the doorway and entered the cavern.

It was nearly ten feet tall at the shoulder, and covered in what was either a thick, coarse coat of black hair, or wearing a pelt of some unidentified animal. Its arms were long, hanging down to almost touch the cavern floor, while its legs were short, and slightly bowed. A broad, powerful chest led to a thick neck, supporting a large head, with a sloping brow and two huge fangs projecting from its lower jaw.

But for all that, the eyes spoke of great intelligence and cunning. They were a bright green and took in Solomon as if the Guardian knew all his secrets.

"It's good to see you in the Greenweald again, Solomon," it said, and bowed to him.

Solomon returned the formal greeting. "It's good to see you too, Guardian, and to be home again."

"Be that as it may, I'm afraid I have to stand by my statement. You can't have it back."

"And I'm afraid that I must insist. The Greenweald is in great danger. Soul Gaunts have invaded, an army of them, and Justice is the only thing that can drive them away again."

For most, the mention of Soul Gaunts brought a terrified look, shudders, and a quick glance around to make sure that none were nearby. The Guardian simply shrugged, as if the news were no more bothersome than saying there would be a spot of rain today.

"That doesn't really concern me. They won't find me here, and even if they did, I have precautions to prevent them from entering."

"But the rest of the Greenweald isn't so lucky," Solomon said. "There will be death, terror and pain for everyone else."

"I am sorry about that. But my answer remains the same. Do you remember why you gave it to me?"

"I didn't give it to you, Guardian. I left it in your keeping."

"Semantics. You knew what you were doing. But do you remember why?"

"I do."

"Then you know that out of all the things left here, that is the one that I can't allow to leave. Especially with you."

"Isn't there an easier way of doing this?" Solomon asked.

"I'm afraid not."

"Then I am sorry too." Solomon sprang forward, moving as quickly as he could to get past the huge being in front of him. But no matter how fast he was, the Guardian was quicker.

His long arms caught Solomon by the back of his shirt, and with an almost casual toss, hurled him back down the tunnel in the direction that he had come. He crashed to the floor in a heap, lay there for a moment, and then climbed to his feet with a groan.

He turned and grinned at the Guardian. "Didn't think that would work, but had to give it a shot."

This time, he strode forward more purposefully, hands up and balled into fists. He stayed on his toes, ready to move. The Guardian watched him come, his head tilted to the side.

"Do you mean to fight me, Solomon? As great as you are, surely you know you have no chance."

"Maybe. But I need that sword, so I'll do what I have to."

The Guardian made no move to defend himself, but let Solomon come within striking range. He took advantage of it and unleashed a haymaker, aimed for the Guardian's chin, with all his considerable strength behind it. It landed with a sound like a piece of meat being slapped onto a table.

His hand felt like he had smashed it into solid rock, and he jumped back, shaking it furiously. The Guardian looked at him, then slowly rubbed his chin. "I felt that," he said, and then punched Solomon in the chest.

This time, he flew even further back down the tunnel, feeling as if his chest had caved in. Sparks danced in his vision as he tried to draw breath into lungs that felt like they would never inflate again.

"By the way," the Guardian said. "While I'm sure it's vexing to you, the one-eyed look is a good one for you. Very rugged."

"Thanks," Solomon wheezed, picking himself up and bending over, hands on his knees. "Have you had enough?"

"I think I can take a little more."

"Great."

This time, when he stood, he had his dagger in his hand, glinting in the yellow light of the cave walls.

"Oh, Solomon," the Guardian said, sounding incredibly sad and disappointed. "A weapon? But you know the rules. Hand to hand is fine. But a weapon means that now our fight is real. You know this."

"I do. That should show you how serious I am."

"It does. But it changes nothing." The Guardian sighed, his huge shoulders rising and falling. "Very well, then. Come ahead. And know in advance that the Greenweald will be a much sorrier place without you."

Solomon came in low, trying to make as small of a target of himself as he could. The Guardian was too fast, too strong, and too tough for him to take on directly. He hated what he had planned, but desperate times called for desperate measures. He hoped that it wouldn't back-fire on him.

The Guardian reached down, trying to grab hold of him again. Only this time, Solomon knew he wouldn't be tossed back down the tunnel. No, him taking out the dagger had changed that. Now the Guardian would pull him into his embrace, and squeeze until Solomon passed out, and only then, if he was lucky, would he let him go.

But he was ready for it, so when the enormous hands came near, he dropped even lower, down onto his knees and slashed with the blade, catching the Guardian squarely across his left palm. The giant drew his breath in sharply and pulled his hand back, drops of green blood flecking the cavern floor.

"Ouch! Why you nasty, little…" His voice had become rougher, more bestial, and his eyes glowed with an inner light. This time, when he moved closer to Solomon, it was with a growl from deep in his chest.

Solomon had leapt back to his feet when the Guardian pulled his hand back. He waited, still crouched low, knife at the ready. This time, the Guardian lashed out with a fist, intending to catch Solomon full in the face, but he twisted to the side, feeling the disturbance in the air on his cheek as the massive fist went past. Again, the dagger flicked out, this time scoring a hit across the back of the Guardian's hand.

"Blast and damnation!" the Guardian roared, and spun on Solomon, who had taken the brief opportunity to slip past him.

Now was the most dangerous time. The Guardian glowered at him, sucking at the back of his hand, his eyes aflame. Suddenly, he sprang forward, that same hand coming around in a vicious back-hand slap, almost too fast to follow. It caught Solomon full on the shoulder, and with a grunt he hit the floor hard.

"Hah!" The Guardian leapt forward, foot raised high, ready to bring it down on Solomon's chest, crushing his heart and lungs.

But as his foot descended, Solomon rolled, holding the dagger point up, hilt braced against the cavern floor.

The Guardian's own great strength did what Solomon couldn't. The dagger pierced his foot, driven clean through. The howl from the Guardian was loud enough to shake rubble loose from the ceiling, which rained down on them both.

"Ohhh! My foot! Nasty little man! How dare you?"

Solomon looked up from where he had been shielding his head against the falling debris. The Guardian was sitting on the floor, holding his foot in both hands, with huge tears rolling down his hairy cheeks.

"I need the sword," Solomon said. "I'm sorry it had to come to this."

"You're a nasty little man," the Guardian repeated.

"Maybe so, but I have to get moving. Are we through?"

The Guardian nodded, sniffed loudly and pointed at the door he had come out of. "In there," he said, then returned to examining his foot and moaning loudly.

Solomon took a quick look at the giant's foot before he walked away. It was bloody, but the flow was stopping already. In minutes, at most, the Guardian would be able to pull the dagger free, and would be up and walking like normal in no time. He healed even more quickly than one of the Folk.

With the Guardian defeated, Solomon entered the inner chamber.

There were weapons and treasure everywhere. It hung from or leaned against the walls and was stacked in heaps on the floor and shelves. Gold, silver, armor, swords, axes, shields, cups, plates and all manner of things. It was like a fabled dragon's horde.

But there, set off by itself, almost glowing in the dim light of the cavern was a lone sword. It was about a yard long, slim, and made of beautiful burnished steel. The hilt was unadorned, merely wrapped in leather to provide a good grip. The edges gleamed, giving a hint of its sharpness. Next to it was a simple belt and sheath, made of serviceable, but non-ornate, leather.

"Justice," he breathed, and crossed the room. He reached for the sword, but stopped, hesitating. The last time he had used it had almost been his downfall. Would now be any different? Now, when he would have to use it so much more?

But what choice did he have? None. Not if he wanted to save his friends and the Greenweald. He had no doubt that this man who lived with the Soul Gaunts was up to no good. Jediah's and Florian's mission would do no more than stall the inevitable, then it would come down to him.

Grimacing, his heart racing in his chest, he grasped the hilt, not lifting the sword, only holding on to it. The feeling that surged through him was not unexpected, but it still took him a moment to fight down the urge to run from the cave, cutting down the Guardian if he stood in his way, and take the fight to the Soul Gaunts immediately. Plans be damned. With this, the only plan he needed was to have them in his sight. No one could touch him.

His arm trembled as he released it, blowing out a sigh as he proved to himself that he could. He let it stay where it was while he donned the sword belt, and adjusted the sheath so that it rode at his side comfortably. Only then did he pick up the sword.

Sweat broke out on his brow as he raised it before him. He told himself to put it away, slide it safely into the leather sheath, but instead he stared at it. Tiny tongues of white fire curled along the length of the blade, fascinating in their patterns and power. With an effort of will that was almost too much for him, he lowered it, and then slid it home at his belt.

The feeling of invincibility was still there, but muted now. More like an inflated sense of confidence. There was no foe too great for him to defeat, no enemy that could stand against him.

"Solomon," the Guardian's voice said from behind him. "What will you do?"

"I'll kill them all if I have to."

"You know you're not really invincible, right? It's the sword that makes you feel that way."

"Hmph. And how would *you* know that, Guardian?"

"It's my job, and my nature. And you know I'm right."

Solomon fought down the arrogance that he knew he was exhibiting. "I'm sorry. Of course, it is. I'm trying to get a handle on this feeling again."

The Guardian regarded him for a long, slow moment. "If anyone can, it would be you. When this over, will you return it here?"

"If I'm able. I need it now, but you're right. It doesn't belong in the world."

"Then I wish you luck, and will be here to receive it when you're done."

"Thank you, Guardian," Solomon said, bowing. He straightened and walked to the door of the chamber.

"One more thing," the Guardian said, stopping him.

Solomon turned back.

"Are there really a lot of them? I've never heard of such a thing before."

"There are. Far too many. Even with Justice…" He let the statement trail off, unfinished.

The Guardian sighed, and held up a finger for him to wait. He rummaged around on a shelf, until he turned with another object in his hand.

It was an ancient lantern, the type that you opened and placed a flame inside of, then closed and focused the light through the cloudy glass on the front.

"Take this too, then." The Guardian held it out to Solomon.

"What is it?"

"What's it look like? It's a lamp. It lights things up."

Solomon took it, but felt nothing special about it. "I don't understand."

"Perhaps you will," the Guardian said. "Oh, and take this as well."

He handed Solomon the dagger that had been lodged in his foot. He took it with a small smile. "Sorry about that."

"It's over. And not a trick you'll be able to use again with me."

"I sincerely hope that I'll never again have need of any tricks with you."

"Good luck, Solomon. I hope to see you again."

With that, the Guardian turned and walked away, no sign of a limp hindering him in the least. Solomon stuck the dagger through the belt opposite of Justice, glanced at the lantern in his hand, and walked from the cavern.

CHAPTER 53

Shireen couldn't believe her eyes. What was house Glittering Birch doing here? And why had they stopped the Whispering Pines soldier from getting to his own House? Sedition? Treason? It was all so ridiculous that for a moment, she doubted her own ears.

"Lord Jamshir," Lawrence called out. "I'm afraid you've taken us unawares. Lord Jediah isn't here at the moment, but even if he was, he has never been anything but loyal to you and your house. I don't understand."

Jamshir sat astride his horse, looking around as if he were bored by what Lawrence was saying and merely waiting for him to finish.

"If Jediah does not come out of the gates within the next five minutes, my House will be forced to come in. Is that really what you want?"

"Of course not, Lord Jamshir, but again, Jediah is not here. He and Lord Florian went off together."

Jamshir snorted. "You expect me to believe that? The two hate each other. Why would they be together now?"

"You know they've put aside their differences," Shireen shouted, forgetting herself in her outrage. "They visited you together! To warn you about the Soul Gaunts!"

Lawrence grabbed her arm and spun her toward him, his eyes blazing with anger. She felt herself blush, but it was too late. The murmuring had already started on their side of the barricades. She could hear the whispers of "Soul Gaunts?", "What is she talking about?", "What does she mean, Soul Gaunts?"

"You forget yourself," Lawrence growled. "Remain calm!"

"Is this what House Towering Oaks has descended into?" Jamshir called out, amusement plain in his voice. "A common soldier speaks over her commander, out of turn?"

"A momentary lapse, Lord Jamshir, I assure you," Lawrence replied. "However, her point is valid. I believe that Lords Jediah and Florian did

286

visit you together, not so long ago. That fact may have slipped your mind, but it does speak to the truth of what I say. Lord Jediah is not here."

"I see," Jamshir said. "Well, fine. Let's say that I believe you." He made no concession that the visit had taken place. "In that case, it seems to me to that the best course of action would be to occupy this compound, so that I can deal with his crimes immediately on his return."

"This is ridiculous," Shireen said, her voice coming out in a sharp whisper. "We can't let him in!"

"I don't know that we have a choice," Lawrence mumbled, keeping his eyes on the soldiers arrayed before them. "That's Glittering Birch out there."

"*We're* Towering Oaks. *We* are the strongest House when it comes to fighting. It's what we do! We can hold them until Jediah returns."

"Are you suggesting we openly disobey Jamshir? That would be treason."

"Then let it be. I'm telling you, if we let him in, Jediah, Solomon, you, me and everyone we hold dear will die."

Lawrence looked into her eyes and must have seen the resolve in them. He was well aware that she had seen and been through things recently that he hadn't, that she had been in Jediah's confidence. Her esteem for her commander rose even higher when she saw that he took all that into account, ignored any personal feelings that he may have had about it, and trusted her, as he always had.

"Lord Jamshir!" He turned back to the ruler of the Greenweald. "I am sorry, but I can't allow you to enter the compound. Not without express orders from Lord Jediah. If I could simply ask you to be patient, he'll be back shortly, I'm sure."

The look of shock on Jamshir's face faded to one of contempt. "You believe that, don't you? You know, I was always somewhat unnerved by Jediah. I don't mind admitting it. Not only because of his personal prowess, and the way in which he turned his House into the...well whatever it is, that he has. But because I always thought he was smart enough to surround himself with competent aides. I see now that I was jumping at shadows."

"I'm sorry? I'm afraid I don't understand."

"Jediah will not be returning. Surely you realize that? If not, ask the scout next to you. She knows where he went. Although, by the look on her face, she's surprised that I do."

Again, the murmurings started from the soldiers around them. Lawrence gestured for silence.

Shireen was proud of the discipline that the Towering Oaks soldiers were showing. They had just heard of Soul Gaunts being in the Greenweald, learned that Jediah and Florian were once again allies and had gone on a mysterious mission together, and been informed that the ruling House of the Greenweald was here to take them over. But they still obeyed their acting commander, gave him the same respect they would a true Head of House and stayed ready.

Then, she looked back out over the soldiers of Glittering Birch and her blood cooled. They too were showing remarkable discipline. They stood, row upon row, silent and expressionless. None of what they heard was causing any of them to whisper, or to even glance at the one beside him. They acted as if they had heard it all already, and were here to do an ordinary job, like it was any other day.

"Ah," Jamshir said with a smile on his face. "Yes, you get it now, do you? My House is prepared for this. We have had time, and my commanders have been readying their troops. They know where the traitors lie, and that we have no choice but to root them out."

"You know we're not traitors, Lord Jamshir," Lawrence said. "And neither is House Whispering Pines. Please, is there any way that we can discuss this calmly?"

Jamshir seemed to consider. "I'll tell you what," he said after a moment. "I'm feeling generous. Let's say it's for past services rendered. I'll have a pavilion set up, right here, and I'll draw my troops back. Since you seem to be the current mouth-piece, I'll meet with you and one other. That one next to you will do fine. I'll bring one of mine.

"One hour. You'll have a few minutes to convince me of why I shouldn't raze your House to the ground, or for me to show you the wisdom of simply surrendering. If not, an hour's delay before I begin won't matter. Agreed?"

"Agreed. And thank you for your courtesy."

Jamshir bowed his head slightly in acknowledgement, wheeled his horse around and rode slowly away. There were calls from commanders and the army turned and retreated, showing their backs to the soldiers of Towering Oaks without a care. Minutes later, several servants came forward bearing a roll of canvas. They began to set up a pavilion within easy bow shot of the Towering Oaks barricades. Jamshir was showing that he had no fear of their House.

Soldiers crowded around them as Lawrence and Shireen climbed down from the platform. They stayed quiet but Shireen could see the questions in their eyes.

"Company commanders to the war room," Lawrence said. "We don't have much time."

Although she wasn't a commander, Shireen accompanied Lawrence to the briefing. She had more knowledge than he did about what was going on, and had been there when Jediah and Florian met with Jamshir, and had been rebuffed.

At first, the other Towering Oaks commanders didn't want to believe her. Not about Jamshir, not about the Soul Gaunts, and certainly not about Jediah being taken into the Rustling Elms tree. But they all knew her, and knew her to be steady and reliable, if hot-headed at times. Before long, even the most incredulous of them had come around.

"So what now?" was the most prevalent question.

"There is one more piece of news that Shireen didn't give you," Lawrence said. "And it's the one that I think will end up dictating our actions now. You know that Solomon has returned. But what you don't know, is that he's gone to retrieve his sword. With that, we may have a chance."

Shireen sat back, waiting for the commotion to die down. All of them here knew Solomon's worth, and knew that with him on their side, a situation that seemed hopeless suddenly seemed less dire.

"We need to buy him time," she said, when the room had calmed down. "I don't know when he'll be back, but it can't be long. I think that when Jamshir sees him, he'll be a lot less eager to attack. Even if he wins, he knows that having Solomon here tips the odds in our favor."

"It won't stop him, though," Lawrence said. "Solomon is Solomon, but he's still only one man. Jamshir won't be deterred."

"No, but it's our best hope right now. That and trying to get word to Whispering Pines."

"Then we meet with Jamshir and try to keep him talking. In the meantime, we send out a scout. Someone who can maybe slip through and get to Whispering Pines. The more time we buy, the better."

There were nods around the table, but Shireen saw a lot of doubtful expressions as the commanders went to round up their troops, and ready them for a coming battle. She hoped that they were able to put braver faces on then, and wished she had time to go see Orlando before she walked into a possible lion's den.

"Let's go," Lawrence said to her. "I don't want to be late and give him any excuses."

They were the first to arrive in the pavilion, a white open-sided tent, exposed to the views of both armies. A small table had been set up with two chairs on each side. Servants of House Glittering Birch stood to the side, bringing Lawrence and Shireen cups of cool wine when they entered. Lawrence looked down at his and then set it on the table. Shireen followed suit.

"You don't think he'd…"

"After what you've told me, I put nothing past him."

They didn't have the chance to get any further before Jamshir entered, followed by one of his generals, a truly huge man, tall as the Folk always were, but broad of shoulder also. He glared at the two Towering Oaks soldiers while he pulled a chair out for Jamshir. Shireen couldn't imagine Jediah expecting, or even allowing such a thing, and struggled to conceal the disdain she felt from showing on her face.

Once Jamshir was seated, the general took his own, as did Lawrence and Shireen. The servants brought cups of wine for the new arrivals and then withdrew. Jamshir laughed as he noticed their cups still untouched on the table, and then took a long drink himself. "If I wanted you dead," he said, "I'd simply have Bragnold here sound the attack."

"I don't think that would go as easy as you're implying," Lawrence replied. "What's more, I don't believe you really think that either."

"Ah, Jediah," Jamshir mused, swirling the wine in his cup. "He cultivated an environment of bluntness, didn't he? But I'll be the bigger man and ignore the rudeness so we can get on with this."

Shireen was watching the ruler of the Greenweald with unease. This was wrong. He had to know that they would try to get someone to Whispering Pines, and even if he was confident that his men would find and stop them, why take the chance and spend this time? Why not simply attack?

Lawrence inclined his head, indicating that Jamshir should speak first.

290

"Thank you," the ruler said, mocking the politeness. "I suppose it is only right that I air my grievances first, as the injured party." He took a sip of his wine. "Now, as I stated earlier, Jediah is guilty of treason and sedition, and as such his House is forfeit. I'm sure we can both agree on that as a starting point."

"I'll agree that you said it, not that there's any truth to it."

"Hmm," Jamshir pursed his lips. "That is too bad. You might have been my choice to replace him, but I can see that you're still misguided and loyal to him. How about you?" This last was directed at Shireen.

He gazed at her with apparent laziness, as if the answer didn't really matter to him. But she saw the gleam in his eyes as he stared at her, and she realized what his motivation here was. If he could get even one of them to turn his revenge on Jediah for any imagined slight would be so much sweeter. It wouldn't be her.

"I respectfully decline," she said between gritted teeth.

Jamshir threw his head back and laughed, while his general smirked. "Of course not. Very noble of you both. And really, I expected nothing less. Here's the thing, though. You're already doomed, you just don't know it. You all are. First this House, then Whispering Pines, then any others that dare to put themselves above my own House."

Lawrence had a look of absolute horror on his face. For him, it was the first time he had heard Jamshir be so openly derisive of their House, or any other. For her, she had been expecting it since he first came to the gates.

"But…that's…you're our ruler, Jamshir! And House Towering Oaks has never been anything but loyal. To you and your father."

"Don't talk to me about my father!" Jamshir screamed, spittle flying from his lips. But as quickly as the outburst came, it ended. "Yes, Towering Oaks was loyal to my father, there was no doubt of that. Loyal to the point that he began viewing Jediah, and even that fop Florian, as his real sons. Worthier than I to rule the Greenweald, certainly. Well, we'll put those thoughts to rest soon enough."

"You're insane," Shireen whispered, which earned her a sharp look from Lawrence. Jamshir on the other hand seemed not to have heard her, while General Bragnold ignored the comment.

"Jediah has been plotting with Florian for weeks now to take my place. Oh, he turned his house into a mighty force, there's no doubt of that. Almost as mighty as my own. Almost. But he never realized that there were other forms of power. Forms that even Florian and his whisperers and spies knew nothing about."

"The Soul Gaunts," Lawrence said, the disbelief evident in his voice. "You brought them here."

"Of course, I did. Not me personally, but others in my service, another resource at my disposal. They were the ones who made the contact and now control the vile things. And they'll continue to do so, until I've removed my enemies within the Greenweald. Then, I'll be free to concentrate on those outside our borders. To keep us safe from those who would do us harm."

"The Hairy Men," Shireen said. "That was you, too?"

"Beasts, little better than animals. They're no great loss and don't pretend otherwise. But they served a purpose. They allowed my servants to learn how to best control the Soul Gaunts, perfect their methods, if you will."

Through all of this, Shireen still felt that something was wrong, beyond the obvious paranoia and madness of Jamshir. Beyond the fact that he had an entire army that still followed his command. Beyond even the fact that he had allied himself with one of the worst enemies any of the Folk had ever faced.

She gasped audibly as she realized what it was. She leapt out of her chair, and ran to the edge of the pavilion, looking up, her heart thudding in her chest. The sky was beginning to darken. Soon it would be night time, and then…

No one else had moved when she did. When she turned back, Jamshir was smiling at her. "Yes, it's getting late. They'll be on their way soon. And then, we won't even have to lose any of our own good people. Isn't that right, General?"

Bragnold nodded sharply once, but continued to stare straight ahead.

"How can you do this?" Shireen said to the General. "How can you follow a madman who would unleash our worst enemies?"

"Don't bother," Jamshir yawned. "Bragnold here was always loyal. To my father, and to me, but mostly to the Greenweald. He's so rigid that I'm surprised he can bend to sit, but his men will follow him anywhere. It really wasn't so hard for my servants in the hidden House to turn him into a more…. shall we say, compliant?...soldier."

"The hidden House?" Lawrence said.

"Ah, that's right. You wouldn't know. Yes, House Subtle Hemlock has served me well. A small House, but powerful in ways that quite frankly disturb even me. They do well from the shadows, where their methods and magics don't offend those who don't understand. Like Jediah, for instance."

"And you trust them? After giving them control of the Soul Gaunts. You're a bigger fool than I thought," Shireen said.

Jamshir looked at her coldly, his face stiffening. "Perhaps I'll ask them to make sure you survive what's coming. Then you can really see who the fool is. I'll let you watch as they kill everyone you care about, and then go through to that other world." He relaxed and smiled at her once more. "That was the promise, you see. They serve me, and they can have that world without interference."

He paused to drain his wine cup.

"But enough of this. My generous offer of peace has been rebuked, and most rudely. The General will attest to that. We have no choice, regrettably, but to take House Towering Oaks over. I imagine you'll want to put up a fight. Pity. Now, you may return to your hovel, and pass the remaining time as you would. But you have my solemn oath, if any of you try to leave before darkness falls, you'll be taken, and what the Soul Gaunts would do to you will look like a kindness compared to what I will do."

He stood and dashed his cup to the ground, General Bragnold doing the same a moment later.

"There, now it looks as if you've said something rude to me." Jamshir smiled. "Thus do I serve those who would take what's mine. Be assured however, you're only the first."

He strode from the tent, leaving Lawrence in stunned silence.

"Come on," Shireen said, shaking his shoulder. "Snap out of it. We need to make a plan. The Soul Gaunts will be here soon."

Lawrence looked at her. "How? What plan?"

"I don't know, but we need to come up with something. Jamshir was delaying us, waiting for nightfall. Fine. It worked in our favor too, though. Every minute we hold off, is another minute for Solomon to get here."

CHAPTER 54

His hand hurt, but that was good. It gave him something to concentrate on. Something other than the screams that his cousin had made. Or, what they were going to do to the human, Luke, even after he had told him that coming here was his best chance for survival. It did remind him of what he had done to Willow, but he was trying not to think about that. Instead, he was concentrating on the immediate. His hand hurt.

He had the run of the tree at this point, and the Soul Gaunts stayed away from him. The stone that he carried gave adequate light for him to see, although there wasn't much that he wanted to look at. You've seen one rotting piece of furniture, you've seen them all. The thought brought a slight giggle from him, that threatened to turn into something else, so he shut it down and turned his attention back to his hand. It hurt.

If truth be told, he was wandering the tree, looking for any sign of Jediah. The Head of House Towering Oaks had been taken along with Florian, but Thaddeus hadn't heard any screams from him. Jediah was tough as steel, there was no doubt about that, but even he would break eventually. Maybe they were saving him for something else, but that was something he didn't want to think about either.

Without conscious thought, he wandered back to the room that he had been held in when he first came here. The Rustling Elms house member was still hung on the wall, his condition markedly worse than the last time Thaddeus had seen him. Either the smell was gone or he was getting used to it. Either way he wasn't sure what it said about him, that he could stand here in front of such horror and feel nothing. Nothing but the throbbing pain in his hand.

"There you are." The voice of the Advocate came from behind him. "What are you doing?"

Thaddeus shrugged. "Visiting old friends, I guess." He didn't turn around.

294

The Advocate laughed briefly. "Old friends? I like it. But enough of that. Come with me."

"Where?"

"Wherever I say." Now the voice had changed, grown colder and less patient. Thaddeus knew when to push his luck and when not to.

They climbed the stairs to the upper levels of the tree. Soul Gaunts flitted around, passing them in the darkness, lurking in passageways. But when they had gone up a few more levels, the tree changed.

It was no longer rotting and the windows let the sunlight in. It was as if the realm of the Soul Gaunts ended at the level below, but up here, the normal opulence of the main tree had been allowed to remain.

"Ahhh," the Advocate sighed, and pushed his hood back onto his shoulders. "That's better. I get tired of all the dark and disgust. Don't you?"

Thaddeus had a hard time finding his voice. He looked everywhere as they walked along a hallway and entered into a fine sitting room, with clean, comfortable furniture. There was even a bowl of fruit, ripe and wholesome, waiting on a table. The Advocate reached out and grabbed a piece as he walked by, before flopping down into a chair.

"Help yourself," he said. "And stop looking around like a fish out of water. What did you expect? That I lived with those things? Of course, I don't. Could you?"

Thaddeus made his way to a chair and sank into it. The change in the Advocate was profound, and not a little disturbing. Where before he had appeared cold, pitiless and in control, here he appeared almost…normal.

"I don't understand…"

"No, I imagine you don't. But you will. You're smart. Which is why we're having this talk. Are you sure you don't want a piece of fruit? Wine, perhaps?"

"Wine. Yes. Wine would be good." He knew that it might not be the smartest thing, to drink alcohol in his current mental state, but at the moment he was finding it hard to care.

The Advocate grunted, got to his feet and went to the sideboard where he poured two glasses of a deep, red vintage. He handed one to Thaddeus and retook his seat.

"Now, where should I start? I don't suppose you have any idea of who I am? What House I belong to?"

"You said you didn't have a House. That you were a lone scholar, studying the Nightwinds."

The Advocated laughed. "Nightwinds. Did you like that? I came up with that on the fly. Pretty good, I thought. They're Soul Gaunts. Always have been and always will be. And you were all right. They are nothing but evil, distilled down into a moving, living form."

"Then why?"

"Why? Why is the wrong question, at least for the moment. We'll get to that. I take it from your lack of response that you don't know about my House. Have you ever even heard of House Subtle Hemlock?"

Thaddeus shook his head, sipping at his wine in an attempt to hide his confusion. He knew all the Houses, all their strengths and weaknesses. He had been in them all at one time or another, ferreting out secrets in case his cousin needed them. He'd even been inside Glittering Birch, albeit briefly. There was no Subtle Hemlock. He would have known if there was.

"I'm both pleased and disappointed that you haven't heard of us. Pleased because that's how we like it. Disappointed because as someone who's going to become one of us, I had hoped you were onto us already. That's alright though, very few ever are."

"Become one of you? I can't, I'm Whispering Pines…" He was still reeling from the revelation of the uninjured parts of Rustling Elms, the change in the Advocate and the news of a hidden House.

"True, but we're not like the other Houses. You're not born into Subtle Hemlock, you're brought into it. Usually by one of us who has some interaction with you, but occasionally by simply being outstanding in some way."

Thaddeus didn't ask which he was. "I still don't understand. Who do you serve? I mean, why are you doing this with the Soul Gaunts?"

"As for who we serve, we serve ourselves. Although at the moment, Jamshir thinks we're serving him. It fits our purpose to let him think that. He's planning on using our control of the Soul Gaunts to remove those he thinks are enemies. In return, he'll help us move into the other earth. Again, or so he thinks." He stopped and sipped his wine. "Care to guess what's really going on?"

"You're not working for him?" Thaddeus said weakly.

"No, we are, but only because it suits our purposes. We'll send the Soul Gaunts out and wipe out House Towering Oaks tonight. Your old house will go soon after. Then, we'll help Jamshir eliminate anyone else he feels needs it. But the whole time we'll be consolidating our power, of course. We've already got control of his top general, which Jamshir thinks

296

is for his benefit, when really, we can turn him to our side whenever we want."

"For what purpose though? To rule the Greenweald yourselves? Who is your Head of House that would take Jamshir's place?"

The Advocate laughed again. "We don't have one. We have a council that makes decisions and gives us direction. As for the purpose, it's all about knowledge and power. We know now that we can control the Soul Gaunts, and there are other equally horrible things out there. Can we control them as well? Who knows? But we're off to a good start.

And the knowledge in that other earth! They don't have the magic of the Greenweald, no, but other things? Weapons that kill from a distance, that turn the very air poisonous, or sicken their foes in mass quantities. We can do all that too, of course, but for every move we make, there is someone like Willow that can counter it. But. If we take over that other earth, there will be no stopping us."

"So it is all about conquest, after all." Thaddeus said.

"Mm. In a way, I guess. For me though, it's more an exercise of the mind. *Can* we do it? If so, how? You must be curious yourself."

In spite of his misgivings, Thaddeus found that he was. "But isn't it answered already? You have your claws into House Glittering Birch, you have the Soul Gaunts. What could possibly stop you?"

"There is one, and I think you know who it is."

"Solomon? Come on, he's only one man."

"Yes, but he's a remarkable man, who's after an even more remarkable weapon. He is the fault in our plans. The one thing we can't account for. We thought we had gotten rid of him, that he would be executed for his 'failure', but he was left alive. We sent the Soul Gaunt to that earth to finish him, but he proved too resourceful there as well. Every way we turn, Solomon is there, blocking us. We need him gone."

"You were responsible for the death of Celia?" Thaddeus felt a hot flush beginning at the base of his neck. She was his family, and a bright light. To think that she had been casually disposed of to further some stupid political end...

"No, actually we didn't. There are still things in the world that are beyond our control or forethought. We didn't see that coming, although we were looking at her relationship with Solomon to see how we could exploit it. Celia was killed by a jealous water spirit. We had nothing to do with it, and neither did he. We simply used it."

Thaddeus nodded, still not pleased. "I see. While I applaud your efforts to get rid of Solomon, you can't imagine that I would be happy about this."

"Fine with us. You can be angry, or you can be part of it. It's your choice. We hope you see fit to join us, but if not, House Subtle Hemlock will go on as we always have."

"And Solomon? If he's such a bane to your plans, how will you take account for him?"

"Even Solomon can't stand against this many Soul Gaunts, not even with that sword. We'll use them to overwhelm him with sheer numbers. Several of the Soul Gaunts will be destroyed, I'm sure, but really, that's what they're there for."

"You took Lacy and Willow to lure him here."

The Advocate nodded. "Indeed. We know him well enough to know that he will come to rescue them, if he finds out they're here. If he goes to the battle at Towering Oaks first, so be it, he'll be killed there. But if he somehow comes through it…well, he'll be weakened, we'll still have them, and we'll keep some Soul Gaunts here in reserve."

"There are flaws in your plan."

"I would imagine so. The question is, do you know how to fix them?"

Thaddeus hesitated. He did. But to implement it meant that he would have truly, irrevocably turned his back on his former House.

"If you need to time consider," the Advocate said, "I'm happy to let you have it. However, I am afraid it will have to be downstairs…"

"Is that really how you want my cooperation? By threatening me? How loyal would I be to Subtle Hemlock then?"

"You really are very good," the Advocate laughed. "Very well then, what would you suggest?"

"Solomon needs to see a friendly face when he comes here; one that he has no reason to not trust. I'll meet him, tell him that I know where Lacy is being held. He'll follow me, and I'll lead him into an ambush. Somewhere tight, where he can't use the sword easily. After that, it shouldn't be a problem."

"Don't underestimate him! Nothing about defeating him will be easy."

"Maybe you haven't done the right thing," Thaddeus said.

The Advocate lifted his glass in a salute. "Perhaps you're right. Welcome to House Subtle Hemlock."

CHAPTER 55

"Bastard," Lacy whispered after the Advocate left the room and they had been plunged into darkness again.

She felt Willow squeeze her hand before pulling away. "Where are you going?" She hated the quaver in her voice, but after everything that had happened, she had no more left to give. She was done, and ready to lie down and sleep. Forget everything and wake up back in her own house, ready to enjoy a nice summer's day.

"Not far," Willow said quietly.

Lacy could hear her hesitantly moving around the room, bumping into things. Then, there was a quiet, "aha", and the light glowed softly once more. Willow had the stone from the dish in her hand, and it was glowing again. Not as brightly as it did. The light wavered, pulsing irregularly, fading away to almost nothing, then recovering enough to shine on the Healer's face, but not much else.

"How?" Lacy asked.

Willow smiled at her. "I have some small amount of magic outside of healing myself. It's not much, not even close to what someone like Thaddeus controls. But enough for this."

She motioned to Lacy to scoot over and the two sat with their back against the wall. It was slimy and cold, but better than trying to sit in one of the ruined chairs. The light, meager though it was, made Lacy feel better.

She sighed as she looked at the stone. "I haven't heard anything from Luke," she said. "No screams, I mean. Not like with….before. Maybe they haven't done anything to him. Maybe that man was lying."

"Maybe," Willow replied, but Lacy could hear the doubt in her voice.

"It could be true," she insisted. "He could have been trying to torture me, the same way he got Luke to do what he wanted."

"It is possible. But even if they haven't yet, I don't think they'll hold off for long."

"Then why haven't we heard him?"

The Healer shrugged, but Lacy knew what she was thinking. Maybe Luke couldn't scream, maybe he was too hurt, or they had done something…or maybe they had killed him already. The light blurred as her eyes filled with tears again.

"I have to go," she said. "I have to see what they've done."

She was expecting Willow to protest, to tell her that it was hopeless and that they'd never make it to the other room. Instead, she was silent. When Lacy glanced at her, she saw the Healer was staring at the stone in her hand, her mouth moving in a silent whisper.

After a moment she finished, and then looked at Lacy. "There," she said. "That will help stabilize it. Maybe long enough." She rose to her feet. "Let's try."

The hallway was strangely abandoned. There was no sign of the Soul Gaunts anywhere around. Not in the hall itself, or in any of the rooms that they passed. It was as if they had all left or were gathered elsewhere. Lacy swallowed hard, trying not to imagine that they were all around Luke.

She led the way, staying within the radius of the dim light that Willow carried. Moments later, she came to the room that she had been taken to a short time ago. They stopped in the hall, and then slowly peeked around the corner of the doorway to see if anything waited for them inside.

Luke was curled up on the floor, his head buried in his hands. There was no sign of a Soul Gaunt anywhere near. Lacy rushed to him, followed closely by Willow.

"Luke!" she hissed, but he didn't stir.

She reached out and pulled his hand away from his face, but even that elicited no response. Luke's eyes were open, but they stared straight ahead, unseeing.

"Luke? Come on. We're getting out of here."

Still nothing.

Lacy looked him over but didn't see any more marks or wounds on him than those she had seen the last time. Cuts and punctures covered his arms where the Soul Gaunts had grabbed him, but nothing more. "Willow," she said, "what's wrong with him?"

The Healer knelt next to Luke and placed her hand on his temple. She closed her eyes and the light in the stone dimmed to a mere flicker. "He's gone deep inside himself," she muttered. "He's afraid. Afraid of what is coming for him. And for you."

"Can you help him?"

"I can try," Willow said. She handed the stone to Lacy, who expected it to be warm, but found that it was still the normal coolness of any other round pebble. Then, Willow worked her other hand under Luke's head, so that she touched his other temple. Her eyes stayed closed, but she went silent, her body rigid.

They stayed like that, Lacy holding the dimly glowing stone, Willow, her hands on Luke's head, bolt upright, and Luke, staring blindly at the wall. But after a moment, a low moan came from Luke. He blinked, and Willow sagged, her own eyes opening.

"Luke?" Lacy said, bending so that he would be able to see her.

For a moment, he didn't seem to register that she was there, but then she saw the recognition bloom in his eyes.

"Lacy," he croaked. "What are you doing here?"

"We came for you, you dope. Can you move? We're getting out of here."

"I think so," he said, and pushed himself gingerly up into a sitting position. He glanced over and found Willow as he did. "I heard you," he said to her. "Thank you."

She nodded tiredly, and smiled at him. "I'm glad you heard me."

"What happened, Luke?" Lacy asked. She knew they had to get out of there, but Luke didn't look like he was in any condition to move quite yet. They had to give him a moment or two to recover and get at least a little bit of strength back.

"I'm not sure." His voice trembled. "After they took you, the rest left too, but then one or two of them came back. They were trying to scare me. You know, rush up, claws out, hissing, but then not doing anything. After I stopped flinching, they must have gotten bored with that, so then they'd touch me. Not hard, not enough to cut. They'd run their finger along my face, or my arm, wherever they could. The cold! It was like being cut but not."

He stopped and shivered. Lacy moved closer and put her arm around him. "I shouldn't have asked. I'm sorry."

"It's not your fault. They kept at it, laughing with that annoying sound like they do. Then, I don't know…one was in here, touching me and making me squirm to get away. It stopped suddenly, like it heard something and then it was gone, and I was alone."

"You never screamed," Lacy said.

"No, I wasn't going to give them the satisfaction. Besides…I knew you'd hear it. I wasn't going to do that to you. Then, I started thinking about what could be happening to you…they kept saying things when they were in here. About the things that…horrible things. I thought they were doing them, but I couldn't do anything. I couldn't…I wanted to go…but. Then, I went away. I tried to go somewhere that I wouldn't have to hear them anymore. I'm sorry."

He fell silent and hung his head, but Lacy knew what he meant. He wanted to come find her, but he was too afraid. He felt like a coward and a failure. Lacy didn't feel that way, though. He had been through so much, and just put himself through more to try to protect her.

"Shhh," she whispered, tightening her arms around him. "It's all good. I'm here, and we're going to get out of this place."

She held him for a minute, feeling his body shiver against hers. Finally, he calmed enough to talk.

"Lacy," he said, and his voice sounded steadier, more like the Luke she knew. "I'm sorry. For all of it."

"I know. We can talk more about it when we get home."

"Home would be good," he said.

"It will be. But first, let's get out of this stinking tree." She stood, helping him to his feet, and then reached out a hand to Willow, who had sat quietly by while they talked.

The Soul Gaunts were all gathered around the main entry to the tree. Lacy and the others watched them, hidden in the shadows at the top of the stairs, the stone's light doused. The Advocate stood in front of the double doors.

"Soon," he was saying. "In a few minutes the sun will be down enough that we can go. Follow me, and when we get there…kill them all!"

Lacy was almost sick at the apparent glee the Advocate was taking in giving the order. The Soul Gaunts hissed, chuckled and flitted through the air, obviously eager to be gone. She was eager for them to leave as well. She wasn't sure where they would go, but at least it would be away from there.

There was no sign of Thaddeus anywhere either, but wherever he was, he had made his bed, so he could lie in it. It was enough that she would get Luke and Willow out.

The Advocate cracked open the doors and looked out. He stepped back, and with a dramatic flourish, flung them open all the way. Dim

302

evening light flooded the entry hall, and the three of them shrank back so that they wouldn't be exposed. Lacy kept her head up enough to be able to see.

The Soul Gaunts raised an unholy wail, all of them making the same eerie, undulating sound. Lacy gasped, and ducked back under cover, her hands clapped over her ears. The noise went on and on, rising and falling, piercing into her brain. Willow was doing the same as her, while Luke was curled up again, his hands also tightly pressed against his head.

It was a war-cry, she realized, made to frighten their enemies before they took the field. She didn't know if there were any Folk within range of the sound, but she hoped not. How anyone could hear such a noise and still have the will to fight was beyond her.

Finally, the wailing started to fade, and she carefully peeked back down the stairs. The Advocate was gone, and the Soul Gaunts were flowing out the doors, into the darkening forest and away. The noise they were making went with them, and she wondered if they would keep it going all the way to wherever they were headed.

The last one flew out of the door, and silence fell over the tree once more. The doors stood wide open, only a few feet away. Down the stairs, across the floor and out! From there, they could hide in the woods, let Willow guide them back to Whispering Pines, where they could figure out a way to get home.

"Come on," she whispered. The Soul Gaunts were gone, but speaking in a loud voice still seemed imprudent somehow. As if the sound of her voice could summon them back.

She pulled Luke to his feet, and Willow joined her in helping him to get down the stairs. They moved slowly, keeping their eyes peeled, looking for any sign of a Soul Gaunt, the Advocate, or Thaddeus.

"I think we're going to make it," she said, and smiled at the Healer. Willow smiled back, but her expression became more solemn when she looked at Luke.

"We'll make it," Lacy said more firmly.

Luke still didn't look good. In the dim light coming in the doors, she could see how pale he was, and how shallow his breathing. They may not have damaged him much physically this time, but the mental wounds were obviously severe. She hoped that when they were out and safe, Willow would be able to do something. Beyond that, maybe getting home to their own house and resting for a while would help. She didn't like to think that this whole episode would make Luke's prior problems that much worse.

They made the bottom of the stairs without any problem and started across the floor, their eyes locked on the view of the outside.

"Almost there," Lacy muttered, and the doors swung shut with a boom.

They stopped, their vision totally gone in the sudden darkness. Out of the gloom in front of them came that horrible noise, the one they had all grown too familiar with. Willow chanted loudly and the stone in her hand began to glow feebly. It wasn't much, but enough that they could see the four darker shapes in front of them. The hisses that accompanied them told them everything they needed to know. The Soul Gaunts had let them come this far, but were not going to let them go.

Luke sobbed, and sagged against Lacy, who struggled to hold him up.

"Come on," she said, and started to back away.

Behind them, came another cold chuckle. The stairs were blocked off and they had nowhere to go.

"What do you want?" she screamed at them, her voice echoing in the hall. "We're going back! Leave us alone!"

"That one." A lone Soul Gaunt came near, close enough to be seen in the light of the stone, but still not within touching distance of Willow. It raised its bone white claw and pointed at Luke. "Leave it. It belongs to us."

"No." Willow spoke calmly, but she stepped in front of Luke. "You can't have him."

"We will take him. And her, too. Step away, Healer. Your time will come."

"You keep saying that, but I think you're afraid of me. Are you afraid that I can heal you? That I can take away whatever pain it is that keeps you as you are?"

The Soul Gaunt laughed, a dry hissing sound. "You know less than nothing. Move aside, or we'll take you too."

It raised its claws and came on, and Lacy could see the vague shapes of the others coming closer also. Willow's bluff had failed. They may have been frightened of her, but not enough. The nearest one reached out, and raked his claws in the air, barely missing the Healer. Willow flinched back, her eyes suddenly less certain.

Then, she regained her confidence. Stepping forward quickly, she grabbed the things arm and began whispering. The effect was astounding.

The Soul Gaunt screamed, sounding more human than Lacy had ever heard, and writhed in Willow's grip, trying to pull free. She smiled, glad that the tables were finally turned.

But the others rushed forward and the one behind her grabbed Luke, tearing him from her grasp.

"No!" she screamed and lunged for him. She screamed again as an icy hand closed around her shoulder. It was on the same arm that had been injured at home, and all that pain seemed to flare to life again. It was intense enough to drive her to her knees, her vision blurring.

In what almost felt like a dream, she watched as Luke was dragged away, his body limp and unresisting. She saw Willow struggle to hold on to the one she had grabbed, but then fall to the ground as another reared up next to her, and grabbed her head with both of its sharp claws.

"It's over," she mumbled, as the Soul Gaunt squeezed her shoulder and she felt bones grind together.

The world was becoming even darker as she pitched forward.

But then there was a loud noise, like the crack of doom, and a brilliant white light lit up the room. The Soul Gaunts screamed, loudly and horribly, and Lacy smiled again.

CHAPTER 56

Solomon stepped through the waterfall, back into the Greenweald. Justice rode in the scabbard at his side, and the lantern the Guardian had given him was hung opposite. His hand was placed on the sword hilt, ready to draw it should there be any sign of a Soul Gaunt anywhere near. But the woods were quiet and peaceful, the normal sounds of the Greenweald the only thing disturbing the silence.

It was early afternoon, and he needed to make haste if he was going to get back to the Towering Oaks compound before dark. There was no particular reason to think that the Soul Gaunts would attack on this night, but better safe than sorry. If they didn't, all the better, and maybe Jediah's mission would prove to be a success. If not, then he would be there, Justice in hand, ready to do what was needed.

He walked at a brisk pace through the giant trees, thinking back to his first fight with a Soul Gaunt. The fight that revealed the true nature of Justice to him, and spurred him to leave it with the Guardian. It was hard to put the sword away after that fight, harder than anything he had ever done. At first, when he had come upon the Gaunt, everything seemed normal, or at least as much as it could be when confronting an evil that most thought was only a story.

His sword against the things claws, cold, and fear. They had almost danced back and forth, weaving among the trees, each looking for an opening. Then, Solomon had scored a hit, and the things robe had split open. A tiny lick of flame appeared along Justice's edges and Solomon had felt an unexpected glee flow through him.

Soul Gaunts! What were they? Nothing compared to him!

Solomon had always been confident and sure of his abilities. But he had never been arrogant, never thought that he was unbeatable, or better than anyone else. The gifts he had were just that. Gifts. They would fade with time if not used, and there was always someone or something out there with more of them.

306

But after he had hit the Soul Gaunt, there wasn't a doubt in his mind that he would come out of this fight victorious. He stepped in and slashed the thing again, this time a powerful hit, starting at its shoulder and running down in a diagonal slash across its torso. It screamed, and Solomon laughed. He expected it to flee, and was preparing to chase it, but it did no such thing. Instead, it came on stronger, hissing and whirling almost too fast for him to follow.

But the end was a foregone conclusion. Solomon stood his ground and brilliant, white flames shot up from Justice, the heat intense. He lunged forward, the sword point catching the Gaunt solidly in the middle of the blackness beneath its hood, and it erupted into flame.

The Soul Gaunt screamed, cursed, and flailed but to no avail. The white fire ate at it, devouring the robe and then the white corpse-like being beneath. Solomon watched it in fascination, a smile on his face. Let it burn! That's what happened to those who would challenge him.

When the flames finally died down, there was no sign of the Soul Gaunt, and no burnt spot on the forest floor showing where it had died. Solomon felt a great weariness come over him, but the heat and exhilaration of the battle still roared through his veins. He looked around to see if there was another nearby. Another victim for his rage.

There wasn't, so he lifted the sword to return it to its scabbard. But he felt reluctant to do so. He wanted to keep it out, admire the way the flames danced along its edges, even though he was so tired that he could barely hold it up. Maybe he could keep it out, return to the Towering Oaks compound with it, and if anyone commented on it, he would show them what the sword could do. Strike them down, let everyone know who was in charge.

Solomon was horrified by his thoughts. He looked down at Justice and knew the sword was influencing his emotions. Jediah had warned him that it came with its own hazards, and now Solomon knew what those were.

He concentrated, ignored the feelings of invincibility and arrogance. The sword weighed a hundred pounds, maybe two. But he got the point into the scabbard, and with a grunt, drove it home, the flames flickering out as he did. He panted, swayed and then sat down heavily against a tree. He stayed there for a long time before heading back to Towering Oaks. When he did, he had already made the decision to give the sword into the Guardian's keeping.

He was so lost in the memory of that day that he almost didn't hear the barking.

"Daisy?"

The Hound came bursting through the trees, running full bore toward Solomon, barking for all she was worth.

"Daisy!" He dropped to one knee and hugged the massive dog's head. She licked his face and pushed into him for a moment, but then wriggled free, stepped back and barked at him again.

"Okay, okay, I'm glad to see you too. Where's Lacy and Luke? They must be with you." He looked in the direction that Daisy had come from, but there was no sign of the two humans, or anyone else for that matter. He frowned as he looked back at the dog.

"Where are Lacy and Luke? Are they with you?" But even as he asked, he knew the answer. "Damn." If Daisy wasn't with them, something must have happened. She wouldn't have left them otherwise. And if something had happened to them, there was a good chance that other things were happening, and Towering Oaks could be in grave danger.

He hesitated, unsure of what to do. To go to Towering Oaks meant that he was abandoning the two humans that he had brought here. But to go to them meant that he was letting his own House face a grave danger without him. Unless they were at Towering Oaks, but he didn't believe that. So, was it go help his people or go try to rescue Lacy and Luke? Really, there was no choice.

"Go ahead," he said to Daisy, "I'm right behind you."

By the time the Hound had led him to Rustling Elms the sun was beginning to go down. Long before they reached the ruined compound though, Solomon knew where they were going. He had spent the last couple of hours of their journey trying to tamp down the fear that he would be too late. That they were already dead, or had already been horribly tortured.

He arrived in time to see the doors to the main tree flung open and a tall man step out, looking very much like one of the Folk in a black robe. Solomon ducked behind a trunk as a horrible sound began to come from the tree. It was an eerie, disturbing sound. He shook his head and grimaced, and Daisy whined and pressed her head against his legs.

The black-robed man walked away, looking for all the world like someone out enjoying an afternoon stroll. But Soul Gaunts followed him. They poured from the wounded tree, spreading out and flowing along the ground, that horrible sound coming from within their hoods. There were scores of them, and they all moved with a single-minded purpose.

Solomon felt the sword at his side pushing at his thoughts. You could end it all right here, right now, it seemed to be saying. He could see himself, freeing Justice and striding forth, striking down any Soul Gaunt who dared to come within its reach. Hunting down those cowardly enough to flee. It was so strong that he had to stop his hand from grasping the hilt.

But he held on, ignoring the urges and watched as they all disappeared into the forest, their evil song slowly fading.

Telling Daisy to stay, he left his hiding place and crept toward the Rustling Elms tree, watchful for any Soul Gaunts that had been left behind as guards. There was no movement, no sounds, until the doors suddenly swung shut with a crash. He froze, waiting for something else to happen, but nothing did.

Not until he heard the scream from inside. One that sounded very much like it might have come from Lacy.

He charged up the stairs, any attempt at stealth forgotten. Drawing Justice, he gave himself over to the feelings that the sword inspired. Nothing would stand in his way. One blow from the sword was all that was needed to burst the doors open, slamming them into the walls behind with a deafening boom.

The light from Justice flared into the entry hall, showing five Soul Gaunts, two around Willow, who was prone on the floor, two dragging an unresisting Luke away, and one, its claw squeezing Lacy's shoulder as she pitched forward.

He saw it all in an instant as he stalked into the hall. The Soul Gaunts screamed when the light from Justice fell on them, a sound of terror and dismay. It made Solomon smile, even as he tried to guard against the unnatural confidence he was feeling.

The ones around Willow were the first to die. The first swing of the sword caught the one nearest to Solomon in the back. The force of the blow flung it away from the Healer and he followed it, the next swing taking the things head off. White fire flew from Justice as he swung it, igniting the Soul Gaunt's cloak.

He felt a brief tug at his belt, but didn't have time to look as he turned to the next one. It was hunched over Willow, its claws at her neck, hissing at him.

Solomon moved faster than he ever thought he was capable of. He lunged and his swords point went through the Soul Gaunt's hood, as it had in that other fight all those years ago. This one didn't even have time to scream before its hood burst into flames. He kicked it away from Willow as he felt that same tug.

This time, he saw what it was. When Justice ignited the things robe, a small tongue of fire curled back, reaching to the lantern hung at his side. He put his hand down near it, but it showed no sign of being affected by the flame.

There was no time to think about it though. He turned to Lacy. The Soul Gaunt that had been grasping her shoulder was speeding toward him, trying to take him by surprise. It failed miserably.

He swatted it aside almost casually with a back-hand blow. It screamed as it crashed into the wall, the flames beginning to devour its cloak and adding to the illumination in the entry hall. He could see the two still dragging Luke up the stairs, blood running down his arms from their claws. The sight filled him with a red rage.

He ran, cursing them as he neared. They dropped Luke, letting him tumble down the steps. Solomon leapt over him, increasing his speed. He caught them before they made it to the second floor, and cut them down from behind with two swings of the sword. Two more tugs from the lantern.

The whole battle had taken only seconds. Solomon turned, scanning the area below him for another enemy. Someone else to feel the fire of Justice. There was no one. But there could be in the rest of tree. He would hunt them down, ferret them out of hiding and slay them without mercy.

His friends were lying in the entry hall like so many broken dolls. Luke was crumpled at the foot of the stairs where he had fallen. Both Lacy and Willow were sprawled on the floor, unconscious. Those responsible would pay. He'd find all of them…

He concentrated, keeping them all in his vision, refusing to look away to anything else. They needed help. He needed to stop what he was doing and go to them.

But there could be others here. Others who needed to pay.

Stop! He commanded himself with every bit of his considerable willpower. He slammed Justice home into its sheath and collapsed on the stairs, his legs and arms suddenly feeling like lead.

With a groan he got to his feet and slowly made his way down the stairs. He made sure that Luke was still breathing, and moved him from the awkward pose that he was in to one that would be more comfortable. The man moaned as he did, his eyes fluttering, but he stayed unconscious.

He checked Lacy next, but she was already starting to come around when he got to her, her hand moving to rub her shoulder. Willow stirred also as he squatted near them.

"Jediah," Willow whispered.

"What?" Solomon leaned closer to her. "I couldn't hear you."

"Jediah," she repeated. "He's here, somewhere. I don't know where."

Solomon helped her sit up, his eyes scanning the stairway ascending into the darkness.

"Go," Willow said. "Find him. I'm alright, and I'll stay with them."

Solomon wasn't so sure. He saw the bruises at her temples, but she seemed to be fine. Still, he had seen what that could do when Ed had been grabbed like that.

"Solomon," she was looking at him, her eyes still a little fuzzy, but clearing. "I'm fine. They didn't have as much power over me. Go find Jediah."

He stood, wondering if his Head of House was still even alive. When he hesitated, Willow made an annoyed shooing gesture with her hand and moved over to Lacy. With a last look, he ran to the stairs and up into the darkness.

Pausing halfway, he removed the lantern and held it in front of him. There was no sign of the fire that had flowed from his sword to it. No spark or glow came from behind the glass lens, and now that he looked at it more carefully, he didn't even see a way to open the thing. He had no idea what good it was, but the Guardian didn't give out things randomly. He would have to figure it out later on.

He was loath to take Justice out of its sheath again, but he needed light. Plus, he was incredibly tired, and even though he would pay for it later, the sword would help him keep going. The white flames that flickered along the blade lit up the hallway that he walked along, revealing all the damage and decay that the Soul Gaunts had done.

This was once a noble House. Not one of the great ones, no, but they had been honorable men and women, who had been simply living their lives. They didn't deserve what had happened to them, but the Soul Gaunts and the man who led them, would get their comeuppance.

Room after room opened to the same things. Rotted furniture, ruined walls and floors and the occasional cadaver.

Finally, he found Florian, or what was left of him. He bowed his head, his sorrow penetrating even the fury being fed by the sword, and said a prayer over the fallen Lord. He was even sorrier that Florian had died not knowing that Celia still lived.

His limbs felt heavy as he moved from that room to the next, where he finally found Jediah.

His Head of House was still alive, but looked to be barely so. He was covered in blood, his breathing shallow and erratic.

"Jediah," Solomon said, kneeling next to him. "Jediah, can you hear me? It's over."

Jediah stirred, one swollen eye opening. "I heard what they did to Florian," he whispered. "I hope you killed them all."

"I killed a few. The rest have gone away. Can you walk?"

Jediah didn't bother with an answer. Slowly he put his hands beneath him and pushed himself up, first to all fours and then to a kneeling position. He stopped there, breathing heavily. Solomon put out a hand to help steady him.

When he was ready, Solomon helped him to his feet. The two of them slowly made their way from the room, Jediah's arm around Solomon's neck. For his part, Solomon supported his Lord with one arm, while the other held Justice to light the way.

It took considerably longer to find their way back to the entry hall. They stopped a few times for both of them to rest. Despite the sword's power, Solomon was spent, and was supporting Jediah from sheer willpower alone.

The stairs were the worst part. He put Justice away, feeling little resistance this time, as if the sword sensed that his energy reserves were at an end, and navigated the steps in the dark by touch. The doors still stood open, but night had fallen and they opened only to a slightly brighter patch of darkness. He couldn't see any sign of Willow, Luke or Lacy, but assumed they had left the tree to wait outside.

Finally, they made it down, and shuffled across the entry hall, and out the doors, breathing in the clean night air. Solomon let Jediah sink down and slumped next to him, still on the steps leading from the ground to the doorway in the tree.

His eyes closed, and he could feel sleep coming, whether he wanted it to or not.

"He's got Willow!" The voice seemed to come from far away. Like it was at the end of a tunnel.

Someone shook him, hard. His eyes opened, and through blurred vision he saw Lacy, shaking him by the shoulders.

"Solomon! Wake up! He's got Willow!"

"Who?" he muttered, trying to understand what Lacy was saying.

"Thaddeus! He came out of nowhere and threw some spell or something on her. She fell asleep and he took her. I had Luke and couldn't get to her in time."

Solomon smiled at that. What good would that have done? Lacy was no match for a mage like Thaddeus. She wouldn't have been able to rescue the Healer.

"Solomon!" There was a sharp, stinging slap on his cheek and his eyes snapped open.

What Lacy had been saying suddenly registered and he climbed to his feet. He had to stop for a moment to shake off the dizziness that the sudden move caused, but he was beginning to be able to focus.

"Where?"

"Inside. He took her through a door behind the stairs."

"Stay here," he said. "Look after Jediah."

His hand on Justice's hilt, Solomon strode back into the Rustling Elms tree.

CHAPTER 57

It was unbelievable. Soul Gaunts should not, could not, be destroyed by a simple swipe of a sword, magic or not. Thaddeus wasn't the most accomplished mage in the Greenweald, but he knew enough. Soul Gaunts were much stronger than that. He knew it intimately, you only had to look as his maimed hand to recognize that.

But Solomon waded through the five that were playing with his friends like they were nothing more than bothersome insects. That sword was unstoppable, to say nothing of the lantern that he carried as well. Solomon obviously didn't have any idea what it was, but its power radiated to Thaddeus like the sun itself had come into the tree. And every time Solomon casually killed a Soul Gaunt, it got stronger.

Not that he knew exactly what it was or did either, but at least he knew it was something to be feared. As was Solomon himself. When the last Soul Gaunt had been killed, Thaddeus had watched from his hidden vantage point on the second floor as the man had wrestled with himself, had seen the monumental effort he had made to put the sword away. And it hadn't escaped his notice that Solomon had succeeded. The man was truly amazing, and now Thaddeus fully understood why the Advocate had been so afraid of him.

He had been left here to watch Willow and the humans, to make sure that not only did they not escape, but to ensure that the Soul Gaunts didn't harm them too badly. At least the two women, Luke they could have. He was still not sure of his new role, or of his authority over the Gaunts, but they did listen when he had told them to leave Lacy alone earlier.

But now all that was gone, and he had failed in his first assignment for his new House. He didn't know much about them, but he imagined that failure was not well-tolerated. Now, all he could do was watch, and wait for an opening that might allow him to scavenge something from this disaster.

Solomon looked bone tired, about to fall asleep on his feet, but he still went back down the stairs to tend to his friends. Thaddeus listened as

Willow told him that Jediah was still there somewhere, and slid back into the deeper shadows as Solomon came up the stairs and moved past him to begin his search. Thaddeus knew where Jediah was, so he knew it would take a while to find him. Time enough to do a little damage control of his own.

As he snuck down the stairs, Willow moved to Lacy and got her to her feet. He could feel the magic flow from the Healer as she tended to Lacy's injured shoulder. Together, they got Luke on his feet and half helped, half dragged him to the doors. It crossed his mind to cause the doors to slam shut again, if for no other reason than to hear them scream, but he resisted the urge. Better not to give Willow any sort of warning.

He followed them at a distance, walking as silently as only someone who was adept at getting in and out of places unseen could. They made it to the steps outside, carefully descending with Luke still between them. At the bottom, they rested for a moment.

Then, the dog, that damned Hunting Hound, showed up. It had obviously been left out there by Solomon, and now it was capering around the three others, looking for attention. Willow took a moment to pat it on the head, and then they all continued away from the tree.

Thaddeus concentrated, whispering words as he rolled a small piece of wood plucked from a rotting table between his fingers. Then, he cast the spell, and below him, Daisy's ears pricked up at the sudden noise in the forest. Willow looked that way as well, then said something to Lacy, who moved off, supporting Luke on her own.

Daisy continued to stare into the forest, at whatever it was that had caught her attention. Thaddeus had no idea what that would be. The spell simply made Daisy think there was *something* there, something that posed a threat to them all. Knowing the Hunting Hounds, even one as unusual as Daisy should go after it. The beauty of the spell is that it would keep her thinking that whatever it was, it was always in front of her, never quite able to be caught.

Thaddeus's true strength lay in magics of the mind. The light spell he had used on the stone was fine, and he had a few others like that, but really, he found playing with perceptions to be forever fascinating. Maybe that was why Subtle Hemlock had some use for him.

A moment later and the compulsion became too much. Daisy growled deep in her throat and took off like an arrow from a bow. Willow called out, but the dog paid no attention to her, and was out of sight in seconds.

Now was the time.

Not caring if he was seen, Thaddeus ran down the steps, the spell already forming. He shouted it out, the time for subtlety past. He needed to hit Willow with it like a hammer, put her down before she could shore up any defenses that she might have.

The Healer turned in surprise at the sound of his voice, her mouth open in an "oh". But before she could say another word, the spell hit her, and she dropped like a stone. Thaddeus was there, pulling her limp body up into his arms before the other woman could react.

"Hey!" he heard Lacy shout, but ignored her. He took Willow under the arms and dragged her back to the tree. Now time was of the essence. Solomon could be returning at any moment, and the thought of what he would do if he saw Thaddeus dragging an unconscious Willow toward the tree lent strength to his limbs. He half ran, half stumbled, up the steps, and back into the darkness of the Rustling Elms tree.

He heard Lacy coming and knew that he only had moments. While he was sure that he could dispose of the human if he had to, it would cost him valuable time. Time that he might not have. He made it to the door behind the main stairs as Lacy rushed into the entry hall.

"Stop!" she shouted, but he still ignored her.

Thaddeus opened the door, stepped through, dumped Willow to the ground and slammed it home. It shuddered as Lacy hit the other side of it, but he was safe for the moment. He slid the bolt across, locking it, and took a minute to catch his breath and take his bearings.

The chamber he was in was nothing more than a broom closet. All houses had them, tucked away in a place like this, where the servants could access what was needed, but the nobility didn't have to see them.

But what everyone *didn't* know…Thaddeus ran his hands along the wall, looking for something that….ah, there it was. A small divot in the wood, not very deep at all. A gentle push in, turning slightly at the same time and….the wall slid aside, revealing a staircase leading up.

Years ago, when wars between the Houses were more common, the trees were equipped with secret passages that would allow one to escape, or to come out behind an enemy. Over the years, that need had faded, but the old passages were remembered and even occasionally used, usually by a young person seeking to leave the compound without being seen.

316

But now, this one would serve his purpose. It went straight to the third floor, so he could wait until he was sure Solomon was on his way down and pass by him, without him ever even knowing. From there, up again to the unruined levels, where he hoped he would find something that would help him get out there, or to contact House Subtle Hemlock for further instructions.

He looked at the staircase climbing into the darkness and sighed. There was no way to both carry Willow and have a stone light the way at the same time. But what must be done, must be, so he picked up the Healer under the arms again, and started dragging her up the stairs.

It wasn't until he was almost at the top that he heard the door below him burst open. Far down, he could see a white glow, and knew that Solomon was coming and had the sword out again.

He swallowed hard and hurried faster, his arms and legs burning. Willow moaned and started to move. He cursed and tried to whisper the spell to keep her asleep, but he was breathing too hard and the light rapidly rising up the stairs made it too difficult to concentrate.

He gained the door and pushed it open, coming out into a darkened hallway, not far from the stairs leading to the clean area. He was almost there. The irony of him trying to make it the last few yards mirroring what Willow and Lacy had been doing was not lost on him, but he failed to find the amusement in it.

He could hear Solomon coming but he was going to make it. Willow said something and pulled against him, but he locked one arm around her throat and squeezed. She made a choking noise, but stopped struggling when he pressed harder.

"Good," he said, his voice pitched low. "You keep still, I don't cut off your air. Got it?"

Willow must have recovered more from his spell than he would have expected. She nodded, her chin digging into his arm. He squeezed her again. "Don't try anything. Please. I don't want to hurt you."

And really, he didn't. He liked Willow, he always had, but he needed her in order to get away. There was no place for him at Whispering Pines anymore. Solomon would surely kill him if he stayed here, and Subtle Hemlock would require more proof of his abilities than what he had shown so far. He had no choice but to take her.

He kept his eyes focused on the door he had just come through, while shuffling backward, feeling for the bottom stair leading to the fourth floor. His heel hit the step as Solomon burst into the hallway.

"Stop!" he shouted, as Solomon turned toward him. "If you come any closer, I'll kill her. I'll snap her neck and you know I can do it!"

In truth, he didn't know if he could or not. He had never tried to kill anyone like that before. But if he had to, he would try, and even if he only injured her, it might be enough of a distraction that he could get away.

Solomon didn't say a word while he continued to walk forward, his eyes blazing in the light of the white flames curling along the sword. For a brief moment, Thaddeus wondered if some of that flame would curl into the lantern if Solomon cut him with it. Or was that only for the Soul Gaunts?

"I mean it! Stop!" In his panic, he tightened his grip on Willow's throat. She began to gasp and choke. "See! I'll do it!"

"I believe you," Solomon said, but he kept coming.

Thaddeus's arm began to ache, the muscles cramping up. He thought it was from the tension he was keeping on it, but the pain started to get worse, feeling like the bone itself was breaking. He looked down, taking his eyes off Solomon, to see Willow's hands on his arm. He heard the crack when the bone actually broke.

He shoved her toward Solomon with a scream, but was stunned as Solomon stepped aside and let her drop to the ground, making no attempt to catch her. Instead, he kept walking toward Thaddeus, his sword pointed at him.

Thaddeus cradled his arm to his chest. "Look. I'm sorry. I didn't want to do it, but I had no choice. They were going to do so much more to me. And they're going to win, so I had to. You can see that right?'

He backed up, aware that he was babbling but unable to help himself. Solomon showed no sign of hearing him and didn't answer. Willow staggered to her feet and turned to him as well. His magic had abandoned him, and he couldn't remember a spell to save his life, even if he had ever known one that would.

"Don't…" he begged, as Solomon neared and raised the sword.

Out of the corner of his eye, Thaddeus saw a tall man in all black, very much like the Advocate, step out of the shadows near the wall. A thin hand grabbed hold of him and yanked. He stumbled, there was a sudden flash of multicolored light and everything went dark.

318

CHAPTER 58

House Glittering Birch had moved up again, their soldiers still several yards back, but within easy striking distance of the Towering Oaks compound. Jamshir was showing his disdain for them. The Greenweald compounds weren't designed to be defensible against a larger army. They never had to be. The "wars" between houses that took place with much more frequency in the past were really skirmishes, brought on by some imagined insult or slight, and over as quickly. One House proved their worth over another at the cost of relatively few causalities and they moved on, the defeated House usually paying some sort of tribute to the winner.

But for the last several centuries, even that had become much more infrequent. Now, disputes were settled between Houses by talking, and diplomacy. Given that, and the Folks love of the Greenweald, there were no true walls around Towering Oaks to block the views, or around any other compound. There was a low barricade, more like a fence to keep wandering animals out, with viewing platforms fashioned from massive stumps every so often. That fence would slow Glittering Birch some, but not enough to matter.

The only reason that Shireen could see why Glittering Birch wasn't attacking already was because of the reputation of House Towering Oaks. While attacks within the Greenweald were rare, other lands outside of it were less genteel. The Hairy Men were just one. There were always border skirmishes, or invasions to repel, and her House took the forefront in those. Thus, their soldiers were the most experienced and well trained, their reputations well-earned.

That, and the fact that all Glittering Birch had to do was wait for nightfall. Then the Soul Gaunts would come, and neither the fence nor the reputation would slow them down at all.

She looked out from the viewing platform at the ranks of soldiers arrayed before them.

"We need to attack," she told Lawrence.

"If we do, we give up any advantage that we have," he protested.

"What advantage? The fence? What's that going to do? Let's take the fight to them, now, before the Soul Gaunts come."

Lawrence didn't answer, but continued to look out over the opposing army. He turned and regarded their own, assembled in the compound. There were many fewer than Glittering Birch had, but these were Towering Oaks. Shireen had no doubt they'd acquit themselves well, and even if the day was lost, they'd take a lot of the others with them.

"You're right," Lawrence finally said. "Proceed."

Shireen gave a grim smile and turned back to her House. She raised her hand, let it drop and House Towering Oaks began to move.

First the bowmen moved forward, crossing the compound until they stood close to the fence. They raised their bows, arrows nocked, and waited for a signal.

On the other side of the fence, Shireen saw the first signs of cracks in the discipline she had noticed before. Now some of the Glittering Birch soldiers did react, glancing at the person beside them and whispering. Several had looks of incredulity on their faces, as if they couldn't believe another House would actually defy them.

For her own part, Shireen hesitated. If she gave the signal the arrows would fly and the battle would be joined. There would be no going back from this. Then she looked further and saw Jamshir astride his horse, General Bragnold at his side. She remembered the madness in him, and his admission that it was he who had brought the Soul Gaunts here and eradicated House Rustling Elms.

She gave the signal and death flew through the air.

She had to give the Glittering Birch soldiers credit. They didn't flee. Shields were raised overhead, even while they rushed forward, trying to get ahead of where the arrows would fall. Some succeeded, while others paid the price.

The arrows rained down, piercing armor and the flesh underneath. The air was filled with the sudden screams of the wounded and the noise of soldiers falling, never to rise again. She signaled again, and another round of arrows flew, causing even more damage. But now, Glittering Birch was running forward and there was no time for a third.

The archers had done their work well, and corpses littered the ground in front of the compound, but Glittering Birch had their own archers, and now they loosed, firing over the heads of their own attacking troops. While they weren't as effective as the Towering Oaks marksmen, they still took a heavy toll.

Lawrence jumped down from the viewing platform and yelled for his horse. He vaulted into the saddle and led the counter-charge of Towering Oaks soldiers. The horses poured from the gate and leapt the fence, closing the distance between the armies in a flash. Shireen held back and watched as he lay about him with his sword, cutting a swath through the enemy.

The two armies came together with a crash. At first, House Towering Oaks was vastly outnumbered. But as more of them made it through the gate and over the fence, the numbers started to even. Only because all of Glittering Birch had not engaged. She looked over the battlefield, ignoring the cries and screams and saw that Bragnold had held fully a half of his army in reserve.

Even if Towering Oaks was victorious here, they'd have another fight equally as big in front of them, and that was to say nothing of the Soul Gaunts.

"Where are you?" she muttered, trying in vain to see Solomon arriving.

With a curse, she left the viewing platform and marched toward the fence.

"Not going without me, are you?"

She turned to find Orlando, his arm heavily bandaged, but holding his sword steady.

"What are you doing? Get back to the Healers!"

He laughed. "Not a chance. If you're going out there, so am I. Besides, they'll have more important things to do soon enough."

Shireen glared at him, but then stepped forward and kissed him hard. After a moment, she drew back.

"Come on," she said. "What's the worst that can happen?"

Orlando smiled, that same expression that always made her heart lighter, and together they headed into the battle.

She had never killed so many before. Not when fighting the Hairy Men, or any other enemies of the Greenweald. It was as if she was stabbed in the heart every time she struck down one of her own race, or heard one of her own soldiers cry out. Her arm rose and fell, hacking into the meat of bodies that were trying to do the same to her. She took wounds herself, but hardly felt them.

Orlando fought at her side, protecting her back. When she had a moment to glance at him, she saw the same stricken look on his face that she knew was on her own.

It went on and on, seeming to never end. More soldiers coming for her, more that needed to be killed. The smell of blood in the air was nauseating and she had to watch her footing in ground that was slick with it.

Then, there was an open space around her. Anyone she could see still ready to fight was in the colors of Towering Oaks, and the silver and purple of Glittering Birch was running away. She let her sword point sag and watched them go, panting and covered in gore.

A cheer went up from those around her, but most of them didn't know what she did. That was only the beginning. She looked up at the sky and was surprised to find that not much time had passed at all. Maybe a half-hour at the most. They had held off the first wave, and did it in enough time that they were still safe from the Soul Gaunts.

She hurried back to the viewing platform, Orlando right there with her. She didn't see Lawrence anywhere, and hoped that he had made it through the battle. Jamshir and Bragnold were riding forward through the remaining ranks of their army. They didn't so much as glance down at the dead, and rode over them, both Glittering Birch and Towering Oaks alike.

When they were near enough, Jamshir stopped and called out. "Bravely done! My congratulations to House Towering Oaks on a stunning victory!" Then he laughed. "Or at least, for the moment. Still, you brought great honor to your House. I have a proposition. Who will hear it?"

Shireen looked around, waiting for Lawrence to respond, but there was only silence. Either he was unconscious or dead. Heads turned to look up at her, and she realized that they were expecting her to answer.

Behind her, Orlando muttered, "Go ahead. We're with you."

While she was grateful for his support, it did little to ease her uncertainty. She was a scout, nothing more. She had no right to speak for the whole House. And yet, everyone seemed to expect it.

"What do you want, Jamshir?"

"Ah. It's you. Very good. I was expecting that other one…Laurent? Something like that anyway. But you seem sensible enough."

"Get on with it," she growled.

Jamshir laughed again. He didn't seem to be concerned or bothered about the dead bodies around him at all. Shireen wanted to signal the archers, tell them to kill him now, but she wasn't sure that he didn't have a way to still stop the Soul Gaunts. If he could be taken alive...

She started to raise her hand, intending to signal the attack again.

"Ah, ah." Jamshir saw the gesture. "If you do, you'll never know where Jediah is, or how to get him back."

"You lie."

"Maybe, but can you take the chance?"

She had never wanted to kill anyone, or anything, as much as she wanted to kill Jamshir. The damnable part of it was that he was right. She couldn't take the chance.

"What do you want then?"

"Call off your forces. Stand down and allow my men to come in without resistance."

"Why would I do that?"

"Well, for starters, how about this? I swear not to enter your compound myself. General Bragnold will do it. And I won't demand the forfeit of the entire House. Instead, he'll negotiate a truce with you, and we'll come to a suitable arrangement for Towering Oaks to pay for Jediah's indiscretions."

"You honestly think we would agree to that? Or that he would?" Shireen asked.

"That hardly matters. While I won't demand the complete turn-over of the House, I must insist that Jediah is removed as Head of House."

"Never."

"Don't be so quick to refuse. I have in mind to replace him with you."

Shireen laughed. "You really don't know us at all, Jamshir. I would never betray Jediah, and I'm not interested in being the Head of any House."

"Too bad. Well, you can't say that I didn't try." He looked around at the dead littering the ground. "My, there are a lot of silver and purple uniforms out here. Of course, there are even more of them over there, waiting. And...I could be mistaken, but I see quite a few in gray too. How many more do you have in there?"

He smiled and turned his horse around.

"Oh, and I won't make the same mistake again. You are fierce fighters, indeed! I'll keep my forces back, out of bowshot, but close enough to keep you here. You can choose to charge, of course. We'll see how well that works when my archers have time." He paused, and glanced up at the sky, and at the sun that was starting to dip below the trees. "Time. I wonder how much more you have?"

Shireen climbed down from the viewing platform and gathered the company commanders to her. Soldiers went out of the gate, unarmed and under the flag of truce to drag the bodies of their fallen comrades back into the compound. Glittering Birch soldiers did the same with their own, and for all of his madness, Jamshir actually respected the time-honored tradition.

"We have to attack," Shireen said to the gathered commanders. "We have no choice."

"We can't," one of them told her. "The distance is too great. His bowmen will cut us to shreds before we can even reach his lines, and then there won't be enough of us to matter."

"The Soul Gaunts will come," she said. "As soon as it's dark enough, which will be soon. Then Jamshir won't even have to send his own troops in."

"How many could there be?" another protested. "I know they're terrible, but we can surround them, pull them down and destroy them that way."

"Even if that works, Jamshir will come in right behind and mop up what's left of us. We have no choice but to attack now!"

"There is one other option," Orlando said quietly. "We could leave. We don't have to stay here. We could leave by the back of the compound, let Jamshir have the place until we get help."

"And who will help us? Once they know that Towering Oaks has been defeated, who will dare to stand up to him? No one. We need to attack, and take Jamshir alive. We can force him to stop the Soul Gaunts."

She watched the commanders look at one another, slowly coming to the realization that she was right. They were in an untenable position, and the only possible way out was to capture Jamshir.

"Line them up," Shireen said, trying to ignore the roiling in her stomach.

The charge to the Glittering Birch lines was as bad as they feared. Arrows rained down, but the Towering Oaks soldiers kept going, running even as their friends collapsed to the ground. Shireen ran in the front, her

324

sword in hand and Orlando at her side. Miraculously, neither of them were struck.

This was the final battle. At the end of this, House Towering Oaks would be devastated, maybe too much so to ever recover. But if they could get Jamshir, they may save the rest of the Greenweald from his insanity.

The Glittering Birch soldiers held on, fighting back fiercely, but the Towering Oaks soldiers that remained were relentless. They had been attacked for no reason, and knew that Jamshir was responsible for awakening an evil that most of them thought only legends and folktales. They fought with a fury that was unmatched.

"We're going to do it," Shireen thought, as she dispatched another Glittering Birch soldier. "We're going to get to him."

She could see Jamshir, still on his horse, still with General Bragnold by his side. He sat at his ease, watching the battle come closer to him with amusement.

"I'll wipe that smirk off his face," she muttered, but she must have spoken louder than she thought, because Orlando laughed.

"And I'll help you," he panted. "But first we need to get to him."

The Glittering Birch soldiers were beginning to fail. Even though they out-numbered their adversaries, the Towering Oaks fighters were too well-trained, and defending their home. Slowly, Glittering Birch fell back. In moments, it would be a rout.

Over the din of the battle, Shireen heard a noise from deeper in the forest. A horrible, undulating wail. It was quiet, but growing stronger.

"What is that?" Orlando asked.

Shireen pushed the man she was fighting away and glanced up. The sun had dropped much further, and there was spreading darkness under the trees. The noise increased, the air grew colder, and soldiers stopped fighting on both sides, looking around with fearful expressions.

Even over the dreadful sound, Shireen swore she could hear Jamshir laughing.

CHAPTER 59

They made a sorry parade as they trekked through the Greenweald. Luke was being supported by Lacy, and Jediah was being tended to by Willow, even as they walked. His injuries were extensive, and although Willow was healing them, the work was taking a toll on her as well. Out of them all, only Lacy and Daisy, who had returned as Solomon came out of the tree, seemed mostly whole.

For his part, Solomon was exhausted. His legs were weights that had to be lifted with an effort for every step he took. His arms hung from his shoulders like two slabs of dead meat, and he was having trouble focusing.

But there was no stopping. The Soul Gaunts were headed for Towering Oaks. While it was possible that they would go to Whispering Pines, he didn't think so. They would try to take out the stronger House first. After that, who knew? Maybe Glittering Birch, itself.

He had been infuriated when Thaddeus had gotten away, with the aid of yet another mysterious figure in a black cloak. The rage he felt had been so strong, so intense, that it took all his will-power to not lash out at anything nearby. But that would have only depleted his strength even further, so he had forced himself to re-sheath Justice, and he and Willow felt their way back to the stairs, down and out of the tree.

"I need to go," he said, when they were all gathered together. "The Soul Gaunts have a good lead, so I need to catch them. I'll leave Daisy here with you and…"

"No," Jediah interrupted. "We'll all go."

"You're in no shape to move, certainly not quickly."

"Don't argue with me, Solomon. I'm still your Head of House. Besides, you're not looking that great yourself."

It was true, he was swaying on his feet, trying to stay alert. The thought of the Soul Gaunts attacking his House was keeping him somewhat focused, but he could feel the weariness pressing in on him.

"Besides," Willow said. "I can help Jediah as we go. Maybe I can even do something for you."

Solomon knew when he was being outvoted, plus Jediah was right, he was the Head of House, and as such, he made the final decisions. So it was that they all left together, staggering through the forest, trying their best to keep moving.

"You were right about the sword," Solomon said as he walked along next to Jediah.

"How so?"

"Its side effects, and what you said happened to those who held it in the past. When I use it, I get this feeling of invincibility, like I can't lose, or even be harmed. And it's so much easier to lose my temper, or to feel that I'm better than anyone else. It's like in return for its power, it's amplifying my baser nature."

"That fits with what we know. If your baser nature was worse, I'd be worried."

"Don't joke," Solomon said. He lowered his voice. "I'm not sure I can control it."

"Then stop using it."

"I will, as soon as this is over. But you saw what it can do. It destroys those things with one blow, one touch really. Otherwise, every battle with even a single Soul Gaunt is huge. How many of our people can I save with it?"

"At what cost, though?"

"Any," Solomon said.

They walked on in silence, the evening drawing down around them. It was already getting dark enough under the trees that the Soul Gaunts could be hidden by it. He only hoped that in the slightly more open area around the compound, they'd be less inclined to attack, and would wait a little longer.

"What is that lantern?" Jediah asked him.

Solomon looked down at it. "I don't know. Something the Guardian gave me. He said it might help, but I have no idea how."

"Hmpf. So that's where you left the sword. Clever. You'll have to tell me how you got it back later. But the Guardian doesn't give things out randomly. If he said that lantern could help, then it can."

"I agree. I just don't know how."

"Maybe if we…" But then Jediah stopped. There was a noise coming through the forest from the direction they were headed.

"It's them," Lacy said. "That's the same noise they were making when they left. We caught up with them."

"Maybe," Solomon said.

They continued on, hurrying along as quickly as they could. Luke seemed barely conscious, and Willow had done all she could for him. Jediah was walking more steadily now, but was still weak. Willow herself was pale and drawn, but still walked with her head held high.

As they drew near, the noise started to change. The undulating wail echoing among the trees stopped. For a moment, there was silence. Then, a horrible screech erupted from the Soul Gaunts, sounding as if it was coming from all of them at once. It was followed by the screams of the Folk.

Solomon ran forward, loosening Justice in its sheath, but not drawing it yet.

In front of him was a battle, but unlike any he had seen before. Glittering Birch itself was in disarray in front of the Towering Oaks compound. Soldiers from both houses lay dead on the ground, but there, off in the rear, sat Jamshir, watching it all with a look of glee on his face.

"What's going on?" Solomon whispered to himself.

Jediah stumbled to a halt next to him, his face a mask of horror. "He wouldn't have," he said. "Oh, Jamshir. You utter fool."

"You're all staying here," Solomon said, turning to them. "No, you too," he told Jediah, forestalling his objections. "You're in no condition to fight and I can't watch over you."

He looked back, in time to see a Soul Gaunt swoop in on a Towering Oaks soldier, its claws raking the man's face, taking him to the ground. The soldier's screams were pitiful as the Soul Gaunt covered him, and blood began to seep out onto the ground. All around the compound, the same was happening.

Soldiers fought back to back, doing their best to hold them at bay, but they were being swamped by two, three, or more Soul Gaunts. Some of them broke under the ever-present fear that the Gaunts generated and dropped their weapons, pleading for mercy, only to find that there was none.

The temperature had dropped enough that the breath from both man and horse was visible in the night air. The Soul Gaunts reveled in it, swooping down on either one, claws extended, hissing and screeching.

"Daisy, stay with them!" Solomon said. He pulled the lantern from his belt and tossed it to Jediah. "See if you can figure anything out with this!"

Then he was running, pulling Justice from his belt. At first, it was all he could do to start moving, but then the sword gave him strength again, and he sped into the battle.

The first Soul Gaunt he hit never saw it coming. Solomon slashed across its back while it was attacking a soldier and its cloak burst into flame. He moved on, not taking the time to check on the man he had saved.

All the soldiers being attacked wore the colors of House Towering Oaks. Any others, those from Glittering Birch, fled the battlefield, and the Soul Gaunts let them go. Solomon noted this, and his rage increased. There was treachery here. Against his House and against him! How dare they! How dare Jamshir!

When he finished with the Soul Gaunts, Jamshir would be next. He paused, looking across the field to see the ruler of House Glittering Birch staring back at him. The expression on his face was unreadable, but he didn't look happy. Solomon smiled, pointed Justice at him, and then ran to his next target.

Soul Gaunts burst into flames every time he hit one, small pieces of white fire flying off into the night. With every kill he made, it seemed to get easier. But the Soul Gaunts started to avoid him. Rather than come near the flaming sword, they veered away, moving on to another attack, to claim another victim.

The thought infuriated him. Cowards!

Even in his rage, Solomon could hear the screaming of the dying, and the screech of the Soul Gaunts. He could smell the blood in the air, and feel the coldness seeping into his bones. The sword protected him from some of it, but he was starting to wear down. His movements were becoming slower, his swings not quite as powerful.

"Too slow," he thought. "I can't get them all."

He stopped, and stood panting and swaying. He looked around him, watching as the Soul Gaunts continued with the slaughter. Jamshir sat, safely to the rear of what was left of his army, now reformed in front of him. This time, he laughed when he saw Solomon looking.

The rage was beginning to fade, and with it went a lot of his strength. Justice was becoming heavier, and the flames along its edge were beginning to flicker.

There was a sharp pain across his back. He spun to find that a Soul Gaunt had managed to get in close while he was distracted. The thought that he had actually been hit by one again, that it had dared, made his vision turn red. With a savage slash, he cut the thing almost in half, and the flames roared to life again, one small piece of it flying off into the night.

He was slammed into from his blind side, and turned, lashing out with the sword. He barely managed to pull his swing, stopping the blade inches from cutting into Shireen.

"Solomon!" she cried. "About time!"

He couldn't answer her. His breath was coming in gasps, and the momentary flare up was starting to die down.

"Solomon? Hey! What are you doing? Come on! We need you!"

Shireen's voice sounded far away, like Lacy's had back at the tree. He needed to answer her. "I'm here," he muttered, and lifted Justice again.

It was all he could do to follow her, slashing at any Soul Gaunt who came too close, but they avoided him easily now. The flames on the sword were down to tiny tongues that crawled along it.

"It's not enough," he muttered, as the Soul Gaunts kept killing and killing.

CHAPTER 60

Lacy could only watch as Solomon ran to the battle. She had never witnessed anything like this before and never wanted to again. Even from here, it felt surreal, a nightmare that had come to be a reality. The screams of the dying and the horrible noises of the monsters flying through the air. The sounds of horses being killed in agony. She wasn't even sure when the tears began to flow, but they ran down her cheeks unchecked.

A hand found hers and squeezed gently. It was Luke, recovered enough to see what was going on.

"It's not going to be enough," he said quietly.

"What isn't?"

"Solomon. Look. They're staying away from him. They're avoiding him and killing others. He can't reach them all, there's too many of them."

"No, he has to," Lacy said. "That's what he does, right? Everyone says so."

"I don't think everyone realized how many of them there were."

It was true. The number of Soul Gaunts was astounding. They flew around the battle in great clouds of darkness, rising into the air, or flowing along the ground like a black mist. Soldiers died from being surrounded, or from being attacked from behind, or simply from being outfought, face to face.

Solomon killed any that he was able to reach, and every time he did, a small piece of white fire flew from his sword, flashing across the sky and descending to enter the lantern that he had left with Jediah. Despite that, the lantern sat on the ground, cold and dark, showing no sign that it was affected by the fire at all.

Jediah was studying it, his face thoughtful.

"Can't you do anything?" Lacy asked him. The Head of House Towering Oaks looked up at her, a slightly puzzled look on his face.

"I'm not sure," he said. "I might know…" And then he turned back to studying the lantern again.

Almost against her will, Lacy went back to watching the battle, seeing Solomon pause in the midst of it and stand swaying. "He's exhausted," she thought. "It's too much. The sword is drawing too much energy from him."

There was a strange sound behind her, like the noise it made when you put a steak on a hot grill, and a sharp intake of breath. She and Luke both spun around, only to see Jediah, rising with the lantern held by its handle. Smoke was rising from his hand and his face was contorted with pain.

"I know what this is," he gasped. "I remember reading about it..."

He smiled at them, a truly ghastly sight, and then turned to Willow. "He'll need you when this is done. Find him quickly."

Ignoring the Healers protests, he turned and staggered away, toward the battle, staying hidden as much as possible among the trees as he went. A Soul Gaunt saw him and swept in, but Willow ran next to him and it veered away with a shriek. Jediah looked at her in gratitude and kept going.

From where Lacy was, it looked like Jediah almost started to glow as he reached the edge of the battle. He stood among the dead, and held the lantern up as high as he could. A white light flared around him, making him look like the negative of a photograph, and Lacy realized that some of the light was glowing from inside him, and that wisps of smoke were rising from his body.

There was a loud rushing noise, like a cyclone was tearing through the forest.

Out on the battlefield, Solomon suddenly stopped and held Justice straight up into the air. It erupted with fire much greater than any she had seen so far. It shot out from the sword, up into the sky, illuminating everything in a brilliant column of white light.

The Soul Gaunts screamed, a horrible ear-piercing shriek that almost drowned out the roar from the fire.

The flame twisted in the air above Solomon, growing larger. With a roar, it slashed across the sky and down into Jediah. His body stiffened as the fire flowed into him, the lantern still held high. The flames crawled across him, up his arm and into the lantern. It looked like he was being held up by the fire alone. Lacy saw Jediah reach up with a trembling hand and turn the lens.

The white fire streaked out from the lantern, forking into a hundred tongues, each one lashing out and finding a Soul Gaunt. They shrieked, and jerked like fish on the ends of lines as their robes caught fire. Even as they burned they were drawn up into the sky, their struggles becoming weaker.

With a boom, the Soul Gaunts exploded, showering the ground below with sparks. Nearby, the fire snapped back into the lantern, while out on the field Justice stopped spewing it into the sky. Lacy's head turned back and forth, trying to watch everything as both Jediah and Solomon collapsed into heaps.

She couldn't see Solomon from here, but Jediah's body was smoking, and she knew he needed help, if he was even still alive. She took off running, Willow by her side. She was vaguely aware of Luke cursing, and then running off as well, as best as he could.

Only while she ran toward the Head of House Towering Oaks, Luke ran straight for the battlefield.

CHAPTER 61

The battle seemed hopeless. The Soul Gaunts simply stayed away from Solomon, but everywhere else that Shireen looked she saw them killing her friends and comrades. Every now and then, someone would score a hit on one of the creatures, but they shrugged it off and continued the attack, overwhelming their opponents.

She and Orlando stayed near Solomon, trying to protect him, but there was no need. If a Soul Gaunt did get near, he dispatched it with no apparent effort. But the majority of them stayed out of reach, which meant they were out of her reach also. She moved off, Orlando with her, seeking adversaries who would stand their ground.

There wasn't much time left. The Towering Oaks forces were starting to wear down, with more and more of them dropping their weapons and succumbing to despair. If the innate fear generated by the Soul Gaunts didn't do it, the sight of so many of their own dying horrible deaths did. Soon, there wouldn't be enough left to make a difference.

"Hold!" she yelled, trying to rally support. "Keep fighting! Give Solomon time!"

But it was no use. The Soul Gaunts were too smart, and not only avoided the white flames of Solomon's sword, but began killing in the most horrible ways imaginable, letting their victims stay alive to scream and plead for death. The din was horrible.

She ran at a Soul Gaunt who was busy torturing a soldier that it had down on the ground and caught it a ferocious blow across the back of its head. It screeched and pitched forward and she plunged the point of her sword into its back, pinning it to the ground. Orlando rushed up and hacked at it, swinging like a lumberjack cutting into a log with an axe, until it stopped moving entirely.

But it was only one. The Soul Gaunts were all over the place, and for every one they killed, it seemed like another simply took its place.

She looked at Orlando, his face pale and chest heaving. "I love you," she said, and he smiled back at her. If today was to be her last day, at least she was here with him.

She pulled her sword free of the Soul Gaunt's body and was turning to find another target, when there was a sound like the rush of a powerful wind, but there was no sign of the treetops moving. Then, a loud roar answered it, and she spun around to see what it was.

Solomon stood, his face contorted into a mask of pain as he held Justice straight up into the air. White fire exploded from the sword, pouring into the sky, forming a raging column of flame that lit up the battlefield like it was high noon. Soul Gaunts screamed, abandoned the things they had been doing to their victims and tried to flee.

But the flame began to twist and spin in the air, bending through the sky until it touched down on the far side of the battle. Shireen couldn't see where it hit, but suddenly, there was an answer. The fire bounced back, split into a myriad of smaller ropes that each reached out and snagged a fleeing Soul Gaunt.

They were all lifted into the air, fighting and screeching the whole way. The horrible chuckling noise that they made was gone, as was the sense of dread. Instead, they screamed for their lives and Shireen laughed out loud at the sound of it.

They exploded, almost as one, the sound a deafening boom that rang through the Greenweald and sparks showered the air. By the time they had descended to the ground they had cooled and dissipated, the Soul Gaunts utterly gone, leaving behind only death and devastation.

The column of fire sprang back straight into the air and with a rush disappeared back into Justice. Solomon's body convulsed as it did, his eye closed, and he collapsed to the ground.

"Solomon!" she shouted, her voice the only sound ringing out in the suddenly silent night.

There was no movement. Time stopped as she looked at Orlando, relieved that he was still alive and mostly unharmed. She turned back to Solomon, took a step forward, but then froze as the horns rang out behind her, shattering the illusion of peace.

She wasn't sure which way to turn. Solomon needed help, but the attack from Glittering Birch was coming, and she needed to be with her troops. She wasn't exactly sure when she had started thinking of them as "her" troops, but the fact was that she did.

She hesitated for another moment, and then the human, Luke, ran by her, shouting something as he headed for Solomon. Her instinct was to rush over with him and protect her friend, but she had a greater duty now. She would have to trust the human, whether she liked it or not.

"Come on," she said to Orlando, and started toward the Glittering Birch lines, where they were still waiting.

Just because his main weapon had been destroyed didn't mean that Jamshir had given up the attack. All around Shireen lay bodies, most in the gray uniforms of House Towering Oaks. What Glittering Birch hadn't been able to accomplish, the Soul Gaunts had. Towering Oaks had been cut to ribbons, and now Jamshir was coming to mop up the pieces.

CHAPTER 62

Luke didn't have much time to reach Solomon before the battle began once more. When the Soul Gaunts had been destroyed, he had turned his attention to Jamshir and saw the rage on his face. Luke had seen the number of soldiers, some perfectly fine, some wounded, lined up in a neat formation, waiting. There was no doubt what the intention was. Let the Soul Gaunts do the dirty work, and move in after.

Now, it was after. Now, they would come. Luke wasn't a soldier, or a fighter, but there were others who could handle that, and take the fight to Glittering Birch. Lacy and Willow were headed for Jediah, who was close by, although to Luke, it looked like he was already gone.

But the battle was about to be joined again, and Solomon lay unconscious on the ground, his sword beneath him. While almost everyone else was staring open-mouthed into the sky, unable to believe that the Soul Gaunts were truly gone, Luke was on his way, unsure of why he was doing it, but feeling like he was repaying a debt, or at least a small part of it.

He passed Shireen as the horns blew from the Glittering Birch lines.

"I've got him," he yelled as he sped by, not taking the time to see if she heard him.

A moment later he was at Solomon's side. Solomon lay face down, but Luke rolled him over, put his own face near the unconscious man's, and felt a faint breeze on his cheek. Solomon was still alive. Luke heard Shireen shouting for the Towering Oaks soldiers to stand ready, to pick up their swords. His heart pounded in his chest as he tried to think of what the best thing to do would be.

Already, near where Glittering Birch had waited, the sounds of fighting resumed. The screams of the wounded and the clash of weapons ringing out. All around him, soldiers were running toward the battle.

Luke picked up Justice, intending to slide it into the sheath at Solomon's side, but paused. He could feel the strength of the sword flowing into him. Maybe not as much as Solomon, but then again, who would? No

one could compare with the mighty savior of the Folk, right? Although....
maybe Luke could.

He could see himself, striding across the battlefield, striking down
any soldier in purple and silver who dared to come against him. He'd wade
through them like a farmer cutting grain, until he reached Jamshir himself.
Without hesitation, he'd cut him down, ending this whole stupid little war.

Wouldn't that be something? For him to be the hero, rather than
Solomon. To have Lacy look at him with something other than sadness and
pity, as he had seen in her eyes far too often these last several weeks. She'd
gaze at him in adoration and love.

All he needed to do was take the sword and walk away.

Then, he saw a little further. He saw Solomon, left there helpless, to
possibly be trampled or even die from the wounds he had suffered. The
wounds that had started on that other earth, on Luke's earth, when
Solomon had done all he could to help save a man he didn't even know.
He looked down at the unconscious man and his hand come up, almost
without him even realizing it, and touched the skin around his empty eye-
socket, remembering how badly it had hurt when the Soul Gaunt had taken
his eye.

The same thing had happened to Solomon, when he was fighting for
Luke's life and freedom, and Solomon had never said a word to him about
it.

Suddenly, the vision of him striding through the battle, cutting into
others, changed. It wasn't a glorious thing, it was nauseating. The sound the
sword would make as it cleaved into someone, the pain it would cause, the
sight and smell of the blood. It was all Luke could do to hold down his
gorge.

He reached down, grabbed the scabbard at Solomon's side and slide
Justice home.

Standing, he took a deep breath, and shook his head.

He felt like he had been standing there, imagining his triumph and
then studying Solomon, forever, but he saw that it was mere moments.
Most Towering Oaks soldiers were still running toward the battle, while a
few others were still shaking off the effects of the Soul Gaunts attack.

But the noise of the fight was coming closer. Glittering Birch was
pushing forward, cutting their way through the Towering Oaks forces. He
saw Shireen, Orlando at her side as always, rallying her comrades and
pushing back against Jamshir's army, and for a brief moment felt an

338

unexpected pang of gratitude that she had trusted him to take care of Solomon, after all.

He grabbed Solomon under the arms and lifted, grunting with the effort. How could someone so thin be so heavy? Panting and cursing, he dragged Solomon away, not stopping no matter how his arms burned or his breath labored. Not until he was out of the battle, behind a tree that would shelter them from the worst of it.

He lay Solomon back down gently and collapsed next to him. It had taken everything he had to get him here, and he needed a moment to recover. But there was no time, really. The noise of the battle was growing, which meant it was coming this way still.

He peeked around the tree and confirmed his fear. The Glittering Birch soldiers were having the best of it, pushing the Towering Oaks forces back toward their own compound. Although Luke was no soldier, even he could see that it wouldn't be long now. He needed to get up and get moving again, take Solomon somewhere safer until he could recover.

More horns sounded. This was it then.

But then, Luke noticed some of the Glittering Birch soldiers start to turn, looks of surprise on those faces that he could see. They began to run, heading back in the direction they had come from. A horse charged into view, a soldier dressed in dark green on it, hacking down with a sword at the Glittering Birch soldiers.

Dark green? Who had worn dark green?

Thaddeus. And Florian. And all the rest of the Folk he had seen at the Whispering Pines compound. They had come at last.

The battle turned, and Towering Oaks pushed forward, aided by the new arrivals. As Luke watched, more and more Glittering Birch soldiers took to their heels, fleeing into the shadows of the Greenweald trees.

He smiled and sat back. It was over. He would wait here until the last bits of fighting were finished, and then find Shireen, or Willow. Whoever could take care of Solomon, and then he could find Lacy and go home.

"I suppose I should thank you before I kill you," a cold voice said.

Luke's head whipped around. The Advocate was standing on the other side of Solomon. "I don't know how you managed to survive before, but I am glad you did. At least you pulled this fool out of the way. For that, I'll make it quick. But first..."

The Advocate bent down, his hand reaching for Justice's hilt.

"No!" Luke shouted, and without thinking about it, tackled him.

It felt like he hit a brick wall, but he did stagger the Advocate, causing him to let the sword go and stumble backward. Luke held on, his arms wrapped around the man's waist.

"You dare?" the Advocate snarled.

There was a flare of pain on the back of Luke's neck and the smell of something burning. He screamed, let go and fell to the ground, rolling onto his back. Above him, the Advocate sneered down, his hands glowing with a red light.

"I take it back. You can suffer."

He bent forward, the glow and heat that was coming from his hands increasing. He reached for Luke's face, and Luke knew what was coming. He had been here before, when the Soul Gaunt had reached down and taken his eye. He squeezed his remaining eye closed, unwilling to see the glowing fingers coming closer.

But then there was a growling noise, a thud and an outraged expletive from the Advocate. The heat was gone. Luke opened his eye to find that the Advocate was no longer standing over him. He turned his head and saw the man climbing to his feet, the arms of his black robe shredded.

In front of him, growling, hair raised all along her back, was Daisy.

CHAPTER 63

Solomon stirred, feeling like he had been run over by a truck on that other earth. Everything hurt, and he wasn't sure where he was. The sound of the column of fire had almost deafened him, and he couldn't make out what he was hearing now.

It sounded like a battle was still going on, somewhere in the distance, but the Soul Gaunts were all dead, weren't they? And there was something else. Something growled. He didn't know what that was.

He wasn't at all sure that he could move. The last time he had was before Justice had pinned him to the ground, frozen his muscles in place so that he was merely a fuel source for its fire. When it was done, and the flames had disappeared back into the sword, it had let him go, and that was the last he knew.

He tried to move now, a finger at first. If he could do that, maybe his hand, and then his arm. But it was nice to lay there, eyes closed, enjoying the night air. Yes, there was a battle going on still, but let someone else worry about that.

His finger twitched. Good. That was step one. Now...his hand moved. It really wasn't even that hard. He could open his eyes if wanted, although he'd only be able to see out of the one, of course. It was almost funny, really, now that it didn't hurt anymore.

Open your eyes...eye. Open your eye. There was nothing above him but the leaves of a tree, dimly seen and rustling slightly in the dark. Night was a horrible time to fight a battle, wasn't it?

That growl sounded again, and Solomon sighed. What was it?

He moved his head, another great achievement and saw a large dog confronting a tall man dressed in a black robe. Luke, (that was his name, right?), stood nearby, a heavy branch held awkwardly in his hand and an angry red burn blistering the back of his neck. Solomon smiled at that. Luke wasn't a fighter, so it was a good thing that Daisy was there.

Wait. What was going on? He pushed himself up on his elbows. As he watched, Daisy darted in, her jaws snapping, and the Advocate, (that's who it was!), lashed out, his hands glowing red. Daisy yelped as she was hit, a sizzle and smell of burnt hair and skin rising into the air. Luke stepped forward and brought the branch down on the Advocate's arm. The Advocate cursed and tried to reach for him, but Daisy rushed in at his legs, causing him to jump back.

The sound of Daisy's second whine brought Solomon out of his malaise. He scrambled to his feet, ignoring the pounding in his head. Beyond the dog, the Advocate's eyes widened in shock.

"Luke, Daisy," Solomon said quietly. "Move away. I'll take it."

He was exhausted, and felt that he could hardly move. But there was one more thing to take care of right now. He drew Justice, and found that it wasn't affecting his mood at all. It also wasn't giving him any added strength or vitality. The sword felt every bit as heavy as it would to any other exhausted man.

"Look at you," the Advocate said. "You can barely stand up."

The point of his sword was drooping toward the ground and it trembled in his grasp, but Solomon kept moving forward, not bothering to reply. Luke and Daisy stood back, but remained nearby.

"What do you want?" the Advocate asked, backing away and changing tactics. "Tell me, and my House will provide it."

Solomon ignored that also and moved closer, Justice coming up to point at the man.

"So be it," the Advocate said. He sprang forward, his hands glowing and steaming.

Solomon's first cut removed the Advocate's hands as they reached for him, dropping them both to the ground. The Advocate's mouth opened, but the scream never came. Solomon stepped forward and his next swing took off the Advocate's head.

He watched as the black robed body fell to the ground, and felt nothing. No shame, no sadness, no vengeance, nothing.

"We should go find Lacy," he mumbled, his voice sounding thick in his own ears.

Luke stepped near, took Solomon by the arm, and the two slowly walked around the tree and back toward where they had left the others, Daisy keeping pace behind- them.

"Wait," Solomon said, and they paused while he looked out at the battle, still in its final stages.

The dead were everywhere. Many were in the silver and purple of House Glittering Birch. A few were in the dark green of Whispering Pines, but most were the gray of his own House. Towering Oaks had borne the greatest cost of Jamshir's wrath. He didn't know if they would ever recover.

Glittering Birch was in full retreat. There was no sign of Jamshir, or of the large man who had sat beside him. Solomon didn't know exactly what had happened here, why Jamshir had attacked when the Soul Gaunts had as well, but he had his suspicions, and rather than angry, they made him sad. He was sure the anger would come later.

"Let's go," he said, and he and Luke helped each other move forward.

Solomon tried to avoid looking too closely at the faces of the fallen. There would be time for that later. Right now, he needed the living.

They found Lacy and Willow, kneeling next to Jediah's body. One look at Willow's face was enough to tell him all he needed to know. He sank down next to the Head of his House and his friend.

No one spoke. Willow touched Solomon's shoulder softly, while Luke embraced Lacy.

Solomon watched the end of the battle unfold. He could see Shireen and Orlando, fighting on until the end. Let them handle it, he thought, looking back at Jediah. He had done enough.

CHAPTER 64

The last Glittering Birch soldier had fled, and the day, or night as it were, was theirs. Thanks to their allies in Whispering Pines, and thanks to Solomon for destroying the Soul Gaunts, House Towering Oaks would survive another day.

But as she looked around, Shireen realized the extent of the damage. Fully half, if not three quarters, of the soldiers who had taken the field against Jamshir lay dead. Many more were wounded, some stoically staying silent, while others moaned and writhed on the ground. The Healers would be busy for the next several days, saving who they could and providing a gentle release for those they couldn't.

She sighed and leaned against Orlando, using his support for a moment. He put his arm around her and she leaned into him, glad that he, at least, had come through the battle relatively unscathed. They both had a myriad of cuts and small wounds, but neither of them had taken any serious ones.

"Solomon?" Orlando asked. "Have you seen him?"

"Not since the human pulled him away." Shireen sighed, and stood up straight. "Let's go find him."

It wasn't hard. Soldiers that were still able to walk had begun to gather in a group, although they stayed silent, heads bowed. Shireen felt her heart rise into her throat as she walked toward them. There wasn't much that would cause such a reaction, but Solomon's death would be one of them.

"Move aside," she said softly, and her soldiers obeyed. That wouldn't last for long, once Jediah was back and…she stopped when she saw the tableau in front of her.

Solomon sat on the ground, Justice in the sheath at his side running out behind him. Next to him knelt Willow, with the two humans behind her. The female, Lacy, had her hand on Willow's shoulder, and the male, Luke had his arm around her.

But in front of them all, laying with his hands crossed on his chest and his eyes closed, was Jediah, his body blackened and burnt. Shireen didn't need to bend down and test for breath. It was obvious that he was gone. House Towering Oaks was without its Head.

The rest of the night went by in a blur of exhaustion and half-remembered orders. The first priority was to get Jediah off of the battlefield and into the Towering Oaks compound where he could be laid in state. And the wounded needed to be cared for. Those that could be moved were brought into the compound, while those that couldn't were treated where they lay, if they could be.

The dead needed to be removed to a place where they could be prepared for an honorable funeral. Shireen even made sure that the Glittering Birch dead were treated with respect, and their wounded were tended to as well. House Whispering Pines helped, their commanders taking their cues from her.

The details were never ending. It was all Shireen could do to stay calm and not lash out at those who asked questions. Orlando stayed with her through it all, taking the burden where he could, and supporting her at every turn.

As the light began to filter through the leaves of the trees, they came upon Lawrence. The Soul Gaunts had done terrible things to him, but he had died with his sword in his hand. Shireen closed his eyes, and called for him to be carried into the compound and placed near Jediah.

The light was growing stronger before she was able to step away. Things were as arranged as she could get them, and the work was proceeding as she had directed. It was time to go into the compound herself.

Besides, she didn't want to see the site of the battle in full daylight. Not yet.

She and Orlando left the battlefield and entered the Towering Oaks compound. Her vision was blurred and her thoughts fuzzy. She needed to talk to Solomon, but first she needed sleep. When she stumbled, Orlando was there to catch her, as he always was. It was so nice to have him with her. She smiled as that thought followed her down into sleep.

"Of course, you're going to be the Head of House now," she said to Solomon.

Shireen had awakened after sleeping for only a few hours. While she still felt disoriented, she was far better than she had been, and even the short nap had done her good. She could sleep more later, right now there were things that needed to be done.

"There's no 'of course' about it," Solomon protested. "Jediah didn't name a successor."

"He didn't have any family, so who else would it be?"

"You," Solomon said.

"Me? You're out of your mind. I'm not Head of House. I'm a scout. Besides, Jamshir made me the same offer and I turned him down, too."

Solomon grimaced. "What makes you think I want it?"

"Do you honestly think you have a choice?" Shireen laughed. "They're going to vote on it. That's how it works now, and no one else is even being discussed. You're it."

Solomon sighed and looked away, his hand finding Daisy and scratching behind her ears.

"I have things I need to do first," he said.

"What things?"

"Luke and Lacy for one. They want to go home, and who can blame them?"

"That will take a whole day. Nice try. What else?"

Solomon shrugged. "I have to go somewhere, soon. I can't say where."

"That's crap. You'll either have to, or abdicate and leave the House without a Head again."

"We'll see," Solomon said, and smiled. Shireen didn't like the way he was looking at her at all.

"Damn him!" She tried to ignore Orlando's quiet laugh from the bed. The Greenweald looked beautiful from their bedroom window at night At least it did when there weren't horrible monsters and an invading army at the gates.

"Come on back to bed," Orlando said. "What's done is done. Besides, you'll do a great job."

She climbed back into bed and put her head on his chest. "Well, it better not be for long."

Orlando squeezed her to him. "It's Solomon," he said. "How long could something like that take him?"

Shireen didn't answer. There were still an awful lot of questions to be answered. What would happen with Jamshir now that all the Houses knew what he had done? And what was going on with that other house, the secret one?

Solomon had smiled when she brought those matters up and said that they'd get worked out.

She hated him. She hated him almost as much as she loved him for who and what he was.

Never mind, she decided. I'll deal with him tomorrow. For tonight…she turned her face up to Orlando's.

CHAPTER 65

Solomon took a deep breath. The air here still smelled different. Not bad, or worse than the Greenweald, just different. If there was anything, other than the size of the trees that told him he was back in that other earth, the air would have done it.

Lacy looked happy, and almost ran ahead of them, bursting out of the trees and onto her lawn. It made Solomon glad to see it, but the feeling was tempered some by Luke. He had been quiet as they walked through the woods, and Solomon guessed that he was reliving his experiences there.

"You okay?" he asked quietly.

Luke glanced at him. "Yeah. I guess, but this was bad. What happened here. And…" He faltered and looked down at the ground.

"They're gone," Solomon said. "But it's normal to be unsure. With all you've been through…I don't think you realize how strong you are."

Luke snorted. "Yeah, right. I'm a strong bait, that's about it."

Solomon reached out and touched the back of Luke's neck, the skin there still shiny, but no longer painful thanks to Willow's careful ministrations. "If not for you, the Advocate would have Justice right now, and who knows what would be happening."

"Thanks," Luke mumbled.

They both paused to watch Lacy. She had almost run across the yard to her garden, where she was already pulling weeds and "tsking" over the state of her tomatoes. Daisy had her nose buried in the grass, sniffing as she moved about the yard.

"She's happy to be home," Solomon said, indicating Lacy with a nod. "And even more so because you're here with her. You know that, right?"

Luke shrugged.

"You have to know it," Solomon continued. "While you've done amazing things, so has she. And she did a lot of them for you. Don't throw that aside so easily. Both of you, you did it for each other. You're both pretty remarkable, and I'm glad to call both of you my friends."

He stuck his hand out and after a moment, Luke took it. Solomon pulled him into an embrace before turning away and striking out across the lawn himself.

"Looks a little worse for wear," he said.

Lacy stood up from her weeding and looked around. "Yeah, I guess. But nothing we can't fix. Have to change the water in the pool, obviously. A few other things."

Solomon smiled. Lacy's optimism was refreshing. There were electrical cables run all over the yard, including the thick one that they had dropped into the pool. He shuddered looking at it, remembering the feeling of the current passing through him. Another time that Luke had risen to the occasion when needed, although Solomon wasn't sure if he would even think of that.

He hadn't been kidding. Both Luke and Lacy were made of tougher stuff than they thought they were. They might not have the physical abilities that some of the Folk did, or the magic, but they had their own gifts. They had steel inside of them. If all humans were like that, then Solomon almost pitied anyone who tried to take them on.

"Give me a few and I'll get some stuff together for supper," Lacy called, already heading for the house.

The light was growing dim outside by the time they finished eating.

"Excellent meal, Lacy! Thank you." Solomon stifled a burp.

"Glad you liked it. Now, should I fix up the couch?"

"No, I need to get back. I still have a lot to do."

"So we've heard. Shireen wasn't happy."

Solomon laughed. "No, but she'll do great. And I will take the job back as soon as I can, but I do need to do a couple of things first."

"Do you really think you can find her?" Luke asked. Solomon had told them both what he had learned about Celia during their journey back.

He took a deep breath. "I hope so. I have to try."

"You will," Lacy said. "I have no doubt about it."

Solomon rose, bent to kiss Lacy on the cheek and put his hand on Luke's shoulder.

"You two take care. I'll check in every so often. You won't get rid of me that easy." He smiled at them and walked toward the door.

"C'mon, Daisy," he said.

Daisy didn't move. She sat where she was, looked at him and then back at Lacy and whined.

"Really? You're staying here?" He laughed again. "Well, you have to ask them."

Daisy rose and walked over to Luke, laying her massive head on his lap and staring up at him. He seemed surprised, but then reached down and roughed her up.

"Of course. I mean, if it's okay with Lacy too."

Lacy laughed. "We'd love to have Daisy stay with us. She's part of the family now."

Solomon smiled, returned to hug the Hound, waved one final time and left the house.

As he walked back into the woods, he thought about what the future held. Yes, Shireen could hold down the House for now. But there were things that needed to be taken care of. Jamshir would have to pay for his crimes, and Solomon would expose that secret House, and find Thaddeus in the bargain.

There was a lot to do. But he would deal with it all when he was able to. He still had a couple of other things to take care of first.

EPILOGUE

The yard was cleared and the garden was back in order. Luke had drained and refilled the pool, and they were almost to the point that they could actually imagine using it again. The fact that the end of the summer was proving to be so hot was certainly driving them toward it. But the memory of that vile thing's body floating there was still strong.

Luke still had nightmares at times, but that seemed to be the bulk of his troubles. He didn't hear the voices anymore and had even started dabbling with writing again. The few things that he had shown Lacy had a new, much lighter, upbeat air to them. She liked them a lot.

It was weird getting used to having him home again, but she was enjoying it. They didn't talk much about the Greenweald, or Solomon, although Daisy's presence assured that the thoughts were never too far from their minds.

And it was Daisy that signaled them when Solomon came back a few days later. She started barking and running toward the forest while Luke and Lacy were working in the yard. A few moments later and she ran back out of the woods, followed shortly by Solomon and another tall figure. It took Lacy only a second to realize who it was.

"Willow!" she cried, and ran forward to hug the tall Healer. "What are you doing here?"

"I came to check on you both."

"We're great! But I'm glad you came. Come on, sit down."

They climbed the steps to the deck and sat at the table there, but after a moment Willow rose. She moved behind Luke and examined his neck.

"Good," she said, after looking for a few moments. "I wasn't sure if there would be other damage that I couldn't see at first. But there isn't."

Luke rubbed the back of his neck. "Feels fine," he said. "You did a good job."

"So how is Shireen doing?" Lacy asked.

"Shireen is fine," Solomon laughed. "And she's holding up well under the pressure. Better than she thought she would, I believe. Although Orlando keeps telling me to get my business settled. They both send their regards."

"Say hi back," Lacy smiled. "And why are you really here? It's nice that you thought of us, but it's only been a couple of days."

Solomon looked from her to Luke. "We have something we need to do, and it would be easier if you were with us. Plus, I'd like you to come back to the Greenweald."

Luke's face stiffened and he sat up straight. "I don't think…"

Solomon held up his hand. "Not for long. A day or two. We are going to lay Jediah and Florian to rest, and we'd like you both to be there."

"Oh," Luke said, looking down at the table. "Yeah, I mean, of course, then. That is if…"

"Of course, we'll go," Lacy said. "When do we leave?"

"Today, as soon as you're ready. But we have another stop to make first."

Maggie Caufield was tired. Ed hadn't gotten any worse, but he hadn't shown any signs of improvement either. After a few days, the hospital had sent him home with her, promising care that never seemed to be quite enough. Maggie did everything that needed doing, and although she wouldn't have had it any other way, the emotional strain of the past couple of weeks was taking a toll on her.

"What now?" she muttered, when she heard the barking outside. "If it's the Sullivan's mutt again, I'll…"

But it wasn't. When she looked out the widow, she saw a huge, shaggy, gray dog bounding up the driveway. She recognized Daisy immediately, and behind her came Solomon, tall as ever, but in strangely fashioned clothes. With him was a tall, stately woman, dressed in a gold gown, more suitable to a costume ball than broad daylight. And behind them, of all people, were Luke and Lacy Roberts.

"What on earth are you doing here?" she asked as she opened the door.

"Hello, Maggie," Solomon said. "I'd like you to meet Willow. She's a friend of mine, and she's going to help Ed."

352

"What?" Maggie's eyes filled with tears. No one had been able to help Ed, or tell her what had happened to him in the first place. But when Solomon said it, she believed it could be true.

"Well, I will try," the woman said. She touched Maggie's arm and she felt a warmth flow through her, and a calmness that she hadn't experienced since Ed had been hurt.

"He's in here," she whispered, and led the way to the bedroom.

Once there, Solomon, Lacy, and Luke stood quietly near the doorway, while Willow sat on the edge of the bed. She motioned Maggie to the other side and took Ed's head between her hands. Maggie watched as she closed her eyes and began to softly chant in a strange language.

Ed's eyes moved under his lids and his lips parted. Maggie took his hand, trying not to hope for too much. Willow's chant grew softer, until it was barely a whisper.

A few moments later, she stopped entirely, released Ed's head and stood. She swayed slightly and Solomon moved to support her.

"Maggie?" The voice was a whisper, but it was more than Ed had said in days. Ever since that horrible night.

"Ed?!" She could barely keep her voice under control.

Ed didn't move much, but his mouth opened and he whispered something too quietly to hear. Maggie bent to him, then collapsed on his chest, sobs pouring out of her.

"I love you too, you big dope," she finally managed to squeak. Ed's hand came up and found her back.

"Thank you," Maggie finally said, when the worst of her sobs had passed. She sat up and glanced at Willow but kept her gaze mostly on Ed's face.

"This is just the beginning, Maggie," Solomon said. "I'm sure Willow can bring him back all the way. But you have to come with us."

"Where?"

"Well." Solomon ran his hand through his hair, "That's kind of a long story."

End

AFTERWORD

Writing Solomon's Exile was a much different experience than the other books that I've done. The first thing that stands out to me is the fact that it's not nearly as humorous, nor is it meant to be. Although I did still try to give Solomon, and some of the others, a sense of humor, the overall tone of the book is much darker than my previous works.

It was also different writing one continuous story, not broken into sections. I enjoyed it, although I have to admit, it did take some extra planning to keep the threads straight. In the end, they came together nicely, I think, and I hope you agree and enjoyed the read.

I'd like to thank my early readers; Joyce Maxstadt, Marty Roberts and Tom Siler, all who provided valuable insight and made the book better. And of course, my wife Barb, who has to listen as I read the chapters to her as I finish them, then correct them, and put up with me pouting when she tells me something doesn't work, even though she's always right.

Thanks also to you, for picking up the book and reading it. If you'd be so kind, a review on Amazon would be wonderful, since authors like me depend on those greatly.

I sincerely hope you enjoyed the book. Solomon will be back, I'm sure. After all, he does have to go find Celia.

Please, if you enjoyed this story, leave a review on Amazon. It's a HUGE help to independent authors like me. Thanks, and Happy Reading!

Solomon returns in Solomon's Journey! Turn the page to check out a sneak preview.

PROLOGUE

The ruler of the Greenweald sat in his darkened room, staring at the walls. He hated the dark and the things it hid. The vile Soul Gaunts and those from the secret House. The ones that betrayed him and tried to usurp his throne.

But the light outside was too bright. If he drew the curtains wide it would flood the room, exposing all the hidden corners, especially those in his mind. The ones that hid his father, staring at him disapprovingly. The way he had always looked at Jamshir, from the time he was a boy and Jediah first knocked him sprawling when they played.

"No tears," Roland had said.

Lord Roland. Let's not forget that. He was always Lord Roland. Never Daddy, or Dad, or even Father. Always always always Lord Roland.

"No, Lord Roland," Jamshir had muttered, climbing to his feet and casting a grateful glance at Jediah, who helped him up with a kind smile and words of encouragement.

Words that reached Lord Roland's ears, of course, as Jediah had known they would.

"There," the ruler of the Greenweald smiled, "that's how a gracious victor should act. Remember that, Jamshir."

And he tousled Jediah's hair before walking away, off to the important business of ruling. Jamshir couldn't remember the last time his father had touched him at all.

"Enough," he whispered to himself, his voice cutting into the silence of the room. No one was there to hear, other than him and his memories. No one else, neither his father, nor his dead friend, in the corner of the room. He should get up, throw back the curtains, and let all the sunlight in.

But he didn't. He stayed seated in his chair, staring at the wall, muttering to himself.

#

Hours passed. Servants came with food, which went mostly untouched, and wine, which was finished quickly. They said nothing to him, and none of them attempted to open the drapes, or commented on the smell in the room.

Even he was beginning to notice that. A sharp, rank smell. It came from him and his refusal to leave the room for days now. The bucket in the corner that he used when the occasion called for it was near to overflowing. Servants had attempted to remove it, but he screamed at them to leave it.

Who knew what those in the hidden House could do with his precious fluids?

#

The room grew darker as night fell over the Greenweald, and still he sat. His back ached, and his legs throbbed. He itched all over, and his eyes felt gummy and hard to keep open.

"Enough of this," he thought. "It's night now. It's okay to open the drapes and look out on my realm. The moonlight through the trees isn't enough to bother me."

He sat for a moment more, and then, slowly, trying not to groan loud enough for the guards posted at his door to hear, he stood. The back of the chair supplied much needed support as he let his legs stabilize under him. He slowly shuffled to the window and opened the curtain.

The moon was full, a thought that hadn't occurred to him, and lit up the gardens below far better than he expected. Members of his House strolled the paths, enjoying the warm summer air. Lovers held hands, friends laughed with one another and servants hurried on their way.

Life, in other words, continued as always for Glittering Birch. It wouldn't last. It couldn't. When word of his allegiance with the Soul Gaunts got out….

He shuddered and turned from the window. The light of the moon illuminated his bedchambers, showing the mess he created over the last several days. Clothes thrown in heaps, bedcovers soiled and in disarray. Books were scattered across the floor, some ripped in half, their pages spilling out of them like fallen leaves.

And there, in the corner, was a man cloaked all in black. A man who stepped forward and bowed as Jamshir stared at him and tried not to scream.

"Greetings, Lord Jamshir," the man said.

He was tall, as all the Folk were, but the rest of his body was concealed by the long, black robe. The hood was deep enough to keep the face within hidden in shadow. Jamshir didn't know this man. The only member of House Subtle Hemlock he had met was the one who called himself the Advocate. A ridiculous name or title, whichever it was supposed to be.

But that one had been killed, cut down by Solomon at the end of the debacle that was supposed to have been his triumph.

Well, served him right. That was the price for failing to please your ruler, secret House or not.

"What do you want?" he demanded, or at least tried to. His voice, which he hoped would be strong and commanding, instead came out with a squeak and a slight waver. He cleared his throat and reached for his wine to cover his embarrassment.

"I come on behalf of my House to offer our congratulations," the man from the corner said.

"What congratulations? What are you talking about?"

"On your victory, of course."

Jamshir could only stare at the man, absentmindedly wiping a bit of drool from his chin. Was there something he wasn't remembering?

"I … there was no victory … Solomon came…."

"Oh, yes, we know that, of course. Solomon, the hero, returned just in time to pull Towering Oaks from the fire. Or did he?"

"Did he? Of course, he did, you dolt! I watched him with my own eyes! He destroyed the Soul Gaunts with his blasted magic sword!"

He was panting now, a little dizzy from his outburst. He sank into a chair and gulped down the rest of his wine.

The other man moved forward smoothly and poured Jamshir another cup.

"You misunderstand me. Please calm yourself, Lord Jamshir. What I meant was that yes, he did return, but did he really do it in time?"

"What are you talking about?"

"How many died? Before he got there. How many Towering Oaks soldiers were laid beneath the trees?"

"A lot," Jamshir replied. His voice grew quiet, almost petulant. He didn't care. Let this man think what he wanted. When word got out….

"Yes. A lot. Including Jediah, who always had designs on your throne, as he did your father. He is gone, and yet, here *you* are."

At the mention of his father, Jamshir scowled into his wine. Why were people always bringing him up? Comparing them. Letting Jamshir know by signs subtle and not that they didn't think he was half the ruler, or man, that Roland was.

Lord Roland. Jamshir chuckled and took a drink. *Lord* Roland. Mustn't forget that.

"Lord Jamshir," the man in black continued, "again, allow me to convey the well-wishes of House Subtle Hemlock, and congratulations on a job performed masterfully."

"I did win," Jamshir whispered.

"Now," the man went on, as if Jamshir hadn't said a word. "There is more to be done."

"More?"

"Oh, yes. More. You must strike now, while the time is ripe, before Towering Oaks can recover their full strength."

"I don't know. There are still many of them left, to say nothing of Whispering Pines. Perhaps I'd be better off going in another direction."

"Such as?" A hint of suspicion entered the other man's voice, and Jamshir grinned. If he wasn't mistaken, a hint of fear was there, as well.

He affected an air of nonchalance and shrugged. "Perhaps the other Houses would like to know of the existence of House Subtle Hemlock, and how they corrupted their beloved ruler."

He laughed, but the other man stayed silent.

"That would be a very bad idea, Jamshir," he said after a moment.

Jamshir surged to his feet. "*Lord* Jamshir!" he screamed. "It's *Lord* Jamshir!"

The man in the black robe bowed slightly again. "Of course, Lord Jamshir," he muttered. "My apologies."

Jamshir allowed himself to sink back into his chair.

"Remember who you work for," he said, raising his cup to his lips again.

"We never forget," the other man said softly.

Chapter 1

"No!" Shireen jumped to her feet, which didn't surprise Solomon in the least. He had figured on that being her reaction.

It was a couple of weeks after the burials of Florian and Jediah. Luke, Lacy and Daisy stayed on as guests for a few days, saw more of the Greenweald, and then returned home. He smiled thinking of them. They were doing well, and Daisy was adjusting to being just a dog, not a Hunting Hound any longer.

The paperwork and details that came with cleaning up after Jamshir and the Soul Gaunt attack was more than Solomon had been anticipating, and before he knew it, days had gone by. Enough to have sent Shireen and Orlando out on a scouting mission, to make sure that all was at peace in the Greenweald once again.

It was, with no sign of any errant Soul Gaunts or other dangers. The two even went to Whispering Pines, where they were given a polite, though slightly chilly welcome. Whispering Pines had not chosen a new Head of House to replace Florian yet, and was being overseen by a council of elders.

But now, the bulk of the details were taken care of and House Towering Oaks was operating again. They still had a long recovery, but they were moving in the right direction.

Solomon accepted the position of Head of House, although reluctantly. Not that he had much choice, he reflected.

But he only accepted under one condition; that he would take the time to find Celia first. He would bring her home, and if she still wished, he'd stay by her side for the rest of his life.

And now was that time.

"You agreed," Solomon said, his voice light as he sat back in the chair behind Jediah's desk. His desk now, he thought, fighting back the wave of sadness that threatened to drag him under when he remembered his lost friend.

"Yes, but." Shireen stopped, her mouth working as she tried to come up with a reason to push this day back further. She sat back down, glaring at him.

"But?" Solomon prompted.

"But…it's not time yet. Whispering Pines doesn't even have a Head of House."

"And?" He was trying not to smile.

"And, well, maybe they'll want your input."

She was reaching. Now Solomon did smile. "They haven't asked me yet," he said. "What else do you have?"

He really wasn't playing games with her. Shireen didn't have any desire to be Head of House, even for a short time. She told him that she didn't have the temperament for it, although recently, she had shown how capable she really was. Solomon wanted to honestly answer any objections she had before putting this burden on her.

Shireen continued to glare at him. "What about the Advocate and whatever House he belonged to?"

"Oh, I haven't forgotten them. For now, let them skulk in the shadows. They got their heads handed to them, so I think they'll stay out of sight, licking their wounds. But when I get back, they're the first priority."

"And Jamshir?"

Solomon shrugged. "He is who he is. We'll deal with him too, through cooperation with the other Houses. He won't be the first ruler of the Greenweald to lose his throne."

Shireen sat back, her face softening, and Solomon could see that she was coming around to acceptance. "When?" she asked quietly.

"Right away. Tomorrow morning."

"That soon? Fine. How long will you be?"

Solomon shrugged again. "I've no idea. I don't even know where she is, but I'll find her. Then I'll come back as quickly as I can."

To his surprise, Shireen's eyes were bright with unshed tears. "Don't be long," she said, looking directly at him. "You just came back."

Solomon smiled, trying to dispel her worries. "Yeah," he said, "but this time, I remember everything."

James Maxstadt lives in Burlington, NC with his beautiful wife Barbara and their old dog, Manny. When not writing, he's usually found reading, watching mindless TV, or performing a home renovation project. (Thanks, Dad!) But rather than read about James, he would much rather have you read the adventures of Duke Grandfather and his friends, or visit his website at www.jamesmaxstadt.com!

Made in the USA
Monee, IL
16 February 2021